Kandy She ... ... s a
magazine ed ... ... ves
on a small f ... ey,
Australia, wi ... ... rie
of animal friends. Kandy believes in love at first sight
and real-life romance – they worked for her! Kandy
loves to hear from her readers. Visit her website at:
www.kandyshepherd.com

New Zealander **Alison Roberts** has written more than
eighty romance novels for Mills and Boon. She has
also worked as a primary school teacher, a cardiology
research technician and a paramedic. Currently, she is
living her dream of living – and writing – in a gorgeous
village in the south of France.

Award-winning romance author **Kerri Carpenter**
writes contemporary romances that are sweet, sexy, and
sparkly. When she's not writing, Kerri enjoys reading,
cooking, watching movies, taking Zumba classes,
rooting for Pittsburgh sports teams, and anything
sparkly. Kerri lives in Northern Virginia with her
adorable (and mischievous) rescued poodle mix, Harry.
Kerri loves chatting with readers. Visit her at
kerricarpenter.com or on Facebook, Twitter or Instagram
to connect today.

Wedding Belles

June 2021
Summer Weddings

September 2021
The Billion Dollar Bride

July 2021
The Wedding Date

October 2021
Falling for Mr Right

August 2021
The Wedding Planner

November 2021
**Dreaming of a White
Wedding**

Wedding Belles: The Wedding Planner

KANDY SHEPHERD

ALISON ROBERTS

KERRI CARPENTER

MILLS & BOON

All rights reserved including the right of reproduction in whole or in part in any form. This edition is published by arrangement with Harlequin Books S.A.

This is a work of fiction. Names, characters, places, locations and incidents are purely fictional and bear no relationship to any real life individuals, living or dead, or to any actual places, business establishments, locations, events or incidents. Any resemblance is entirely coincidental.

This book is sold subject to the condition that it shall not, by way of trade or otherwise, be lent, resold, hired out or otherwise circulated without the prior consent of the publisher in any form of binding or cover other than that in which it is published and without a similar condition including this condition being imposed on the subsequent purchaser.

® and TM are trademarks owned and used by the trademark owner and/or its licensee. Trademarks marked with ® are registered with the United Kingdom Patent Office and/or the Office for Harmonisation in the Internal Market and in other countries.

First Published in Great Britain 2021
By Mills & Boon, an imprint of HarperCollins*Publishers,* Ltd
1 London Bridge Street, London, SE1 9GF

www.harpercollins.co.uk

HarperCollins*Publishers*
1st Floor, Watermarque Building,
Ringsend Road, Dublin 4, Ireland

WEDDING BELLES: THE WEDDING PLANNER © 2021 Harlequin Books S.A.

The Tycoon and the Wedding Planner © 2014 Kandy Shepherd
The Wedding Planner and the CEO © 2015 Alison Roberts
The Wedding Truce © 2019 Kerri Carpenter

ISBN: 978-0-263-30248-6

MIX
Paper from
responsible sources
FSC™ C007454

This book is produced from independently certified FSC™ paper to ensure responsible forest management.

For more information visit: www.harpercollins.co.uk/green

Printed and bound in Spain
by CPI, Barcelona

THE TYCOON AND THE WEDDING PLANNER

KANDY SHEPHERD

To my wonderful husband and daughter for your
love and inspiration—thank you!

CHAPTER ONE

As SHE WENT about her lunchtime front-of-house duties at the Hotel Harbourside restaurant, Kate Parker was only too aware of the ill-concealed interest in her. The too-interested glances quickly averted; the undertones; the murmurs.

Poor Kate.

If she heard—or sensed—that phrase one more time, she'd scream.

Her and her big, big mouth.

Why, oh, why had she made such a big deal of her childhood crush on Jesse Morgan? She wished she'd never told a soul, let alone all and sundry in her home town of Dolphin Bay, that the next time Jesse was back she'd finally let him know how she really felt about him.

Because now he was home, now she had kissed him for the first time since they'd been just kids fifteen years ago, and it had turned out a total disaster. She'd felt nothing. *Absolutely nothing.* Instead of turning her on, his kiss had turned her off. She'd fought the urge to wipe her mouth with the back of her hand.

And Jesse? He'd been as embarrassed and awkward as she'd been. They'd parted, barely able to look each other in the eye.

She cringed at the memory—as she'd cringed a hundred times already—as painfully fresh today as it had been three days ago when it had occurred.

And now everyone in their small community knew she'd made an utter fool of herself by believing there could be anything more between her and Jesse than the affection due to a family friend she'd known since they'd both been in nappies.

Poor Kate.

The air was thick with pity for her. She looked around the restaurant; many of the tables were already full for Sunday lunch.

She wanted to run out the door, down the steps onto the beach below and get home to lock herself in her bedroom with the music turned up loud.

Instead, she girded herself against the gossip. She forced herself to smile. First, because a warm, confident smile was essential to any role in hospitality. And second, because she couldn't bear for any of those too-interested townsfolk to guess how churned up, anxious and panicky she was feeling inside.

It meant nothing, people, she wanted to broadcast to the room in general. *Less than nothing. I walked away from that darn kiss completely unaffected.*

But that wouldn't be completely true.

Because the Great Kiss Disaster had left her doubting everything she'd believed about who was the right man for her. She'd discovered the man she'd thought was Mr Perfect was not, in fact. So where did she go next? How could she ever trust her judgement of men again?

Smile. Smile. Smile.

The restaurant in the award-winning hotel was one of the best places to eat in Dolphin Bay. More people were arriving for lunch. She had a job she valued. She wanted to be promoted to hotel manager and she wouldn't achieve that by moping around feeling sorry for herself.

She took a deep, steadying breath, forced her lips to curve upwards in a big welcome and aimed it at the next customer—a man who had pushed his way through the glass doors that led from the steps from the beach and into the restaurant.

She nearly dropped the bottle of wine she was holding with hands that had gone suddenly nerveless. He caught her smile and nodded in acknowledgement.

Where the heck had he *come from?*

She'd never seen him in Dolphin Bay before, that was for sure.

Dark-haired, tall and powerfully built, his broad shoulders and muscular arms strained against his black T-shirt, his hard thighs against the worn denim of his jeans. His heavy black boots were hardly seaside resort wear, but they worked. Boy, did they work.

No wonder the two young waitresses on duty stampeded past her to show him to the best table in the house. She had to hold herself back from pulling rank and elbowing them out of the way to get to him first.

His stance was easy, confident, as he waited to be shown to a table. Her heart started to pound double-quick time. When had she last felt the kind of awareness of a man that made her ache for him to notice her?

But, when his gaze did turn in her direction, she quickly ducked her head and studiously read the label on the wine bottle without registering a single word.

She looked up again to see the young waitress who had won the race to get to him first looking up at him in open admiration and laughing at something he'd said. Did the guy realise half the female heads in the room had swivelled to attention when he'd strode in?

Not that he looked like he cared much about what people thought. His dark brown hair was several months away from a haircut—shoved back off his face with his fingers rather than a comb, by the look of it. The dark growth on his jaw was halfway to a beard.

He looked untamed. Sexy. And dangerous.

Way too dangerous.

She was shocked by the powerful punch of attraction that slammed her, the kind of visceral pull that had caused her such terrible hurt in the past. That was so different from how she'd felt for safe, familiar Jesse. She never wanted to feel again for any man that wild compulsion. The kind, when it had got out of control, that had led her down paths she never wanted to revisit.

Not now. Not ever.

She let the smile freeze on her face, stepped back and watched the other girl usher the handsome stranger to his table. She would hold off on her obligatory meet and greet to a new customer until she'd got herself together enough to mask her awareness of his appeal with breezy nonchalance. To use the light, semi-flirtatious tone that worked so well in hospitality.

Because, after all, he was just a stranger who'd breezed into town. She'd overreacted, big-time. She didn't need to fear that rush of attraction for an unsuitable man. He was just a customer she would never see again after he'd finished his lunch and moved on. He didn't even seem the kind of guy who would leave a generous tip.

Sam Lancaster knew he should be admiring the glorious view of the Dolphin Bay Harbour with its heritage-listed stone breakwaters, its fleet of fishing vessels and, beyond, the aquamarine waters of the Pacific Ocean. This stretch of the New South Wales south coast was known for its scenic beauty.

But he couldn't keep his eyes off the even more appealing view of the sassy, red-haired front-of-house manager who flitted from table to table in the Hotel Harbourside restaurant, pausing to chat with each customer about their orders.

Sam wasn't in the habit of flirting with strangers. He wasn't the type of man who always had a ready quip for a pretty flight attendant, a cute girl behind a bar or a hot new trainer at the gym. Consequently, he was stymied by his out-of-the-blue attraction to this woman.

She hadn't reached his table yet, and he found himself willing her to turn his way. In his head, he played over and over what clever remark he might utter when she did.

She wasn't movie-star beautiful, but there was a vibrancy about her that kept his gaze returning to her again and again: the way the sunlight streaming through the windows turned the auburn of her tied-back hair to a glorious, flaming halo. The sensual sway of her hips in the modest black skirt. The murmur of her laughter as she chatted to a customer. All were compelling. But, when she finally headed his way, the warmth of her wide smile and the welcome that lit her green eyes made him forget every word he had rehearsed.

Her smile was of the practised meet-and-greet type she'd bestowed on every other customer in the room. He knew that. But that didn't make it any less entrancing. She paused in front of his table. This close, he could see she had a sprinkling of freckles across the bridge of her nose and that her smile was punctuated with the most charming dimples.

What was a woman as sensational as this one doing in a backwater like Dolphin Bay?

Good manners prompted him get up to greet her, stumbling a little around the compact, ultra-modern chair not designed for a man of his height and build. Her startled step backwards made him realise she was just doing her job and a customer would usually remain seated. He gritted his teeth; he really wasn't good at this. Where was a clever quip when he needed one?

But she quickly recovered herself. 'Hi, I'm Kate Parker; welcome to Hotel Harbourside. Thank you for joining us for lunch.' Her voice was low and throaty without being self-consciously sexy and transformed the standard customer greeting spiel into something he'd like to put on a repeat loop.

He thrust out his hand in greeting. 'Sam Lancaster.'

Again she looked startled. He'd startled himself—since when did he shake hands with waitresses? But she took his hand in a firm, businesslike grip. He noted she wasn't wearing a ring of any kind.

'Hi, Sam Lancaster,' she said, her teasing tone making a caress of the everyday syllables of his name. 'Is everything okay at your table?'

He cleared his throat. 'F…fine.'

That was all he managed to choke out. Not one other word of that carefully thought out repartee.

Damn it.

He was a man used to managing a large, successful company. To never being short of female company if he didn't want it. But he couldn't seem to get it together in front of this girl.

He realised he'd gripped her warm, slender hand for a moment too long and he released it.

She glanced down at the menu on the table, then back up at him, the smile still dancing in her eyes. She knew. Of course she knew. A woman like this would be used to the most powerful of men stuttering in her presence. 'Have you ordered lunch yet? I can recommend the grilled snapper, freshly caught this morning.'

'Thank you, no. I'll order when my friend gets to the table.'

One winged auburn eyebrow quirked. 'Oh,' she said. 'A lady friend?' She flushed. 'Forgive me. None of my business, of course.'

'Nothing to forgive,' he said, pleased he'd given her cause to wonder about the sex of his lunch companion. 'While I'm waiting for *him,* I'm admiring the view of the harbour,' he said. 'It's really something.'

But the view of her was so much more enticing.

'No charge for the view,' she said. 'It's on the house.' She laughed, a low, husky laugh that made him think of slow, sensual kisses on lazy summer afternoons.

He couldn't look at her in case he gave away the direction of his thoughts. Instead he glanced to the full-length windows that faced east. 'I reckon it must be one of the most beautiful harbours on the south coast.'

'Hey, just on the south coast? I say the most beautiful in the whole of Australia,' she said with mock indignation.

'Okay. So it's the very best harbour in Australia—if not the world,' he agreed, playing along with her.

'That's better,' she said with a dimpled smile.

'I like the dolphins too.'

'You mean the real ones or the fake ones plastered on every building in town?'

'I didn't see them on *every* building,' he said. 'But I thought the dolphin rubbish bins everywhere had character.'

She put her hand on her forehead in a theatrical gesture of mock despair. 'Oh, please don't talk to me about those dolphin bins. People around here get into fights over whether they should go or they should stay, now Dolphin Bay has expanded so much. It was such a sleepy town when they were originally put up.'

'What do you think?' he asked.

'Me? I have to confess to being a total dolphin-bin freak. I love 'em! I adored them when I was a kid and would defend them to the last dorsal fin if anyone tried to touch them.'

She mimicked standing with her arms outstretched behind her as if there was something she was shielding from harm. The pretend-fierce look on her face was somewhat negated by her dimples.

In turn, Sam assumed a mock stance of defence. 'I'm afraid. Very afraid. I won't hurt your dolphin bins.'

Her peal of laughter rang out over the hum of conversation and clatter of cutlery. 'Don't be afraid.' She pretend-pouted. 'I'm harmless, I assure you.'

Harmless? She was far from harmless when it came to this instant assault on his senses.

'Lucky I said I liked the bins, then,' he said.

'Indeed. I might not have been responsible for my actions if you'd derided them.'

He laughed. She was enchanting.

'Seriously, though,' she continued. 'I've lived here for most of my life and I never tire of it, dolphins and all. April is one of the best times to enjoy this area. The water's still warm and the Easter crowds have gone home. Are you passing through?'

He shook his head. 'I'm staying in Dolphin Bay for the next week. I'll check in to the hotel after lunch.'

'That's great to hear.' She hit him with that smile again. 'I'm the deputy manager. It'll be wonderful to have you as our guest.'

Could he read something into that? Did she feel even

just a hint of the instant attraction he felt for her? Or was she just being officially enthusiastic?

'Let me know if there's anything you need,' she said.

A dinner date with you?

Gorgeous Kate Parker had probably spent longer than she should at his table. There were other customers for her to meet and greet. But Sam couldn't think of an excuse to keep her there any longer. He was going to have to bite the bullet and ask her out. For a drink; for dinner; any opportunity to get to know her.

'Kate, I—'

He was just about to suggest a date when his mobile phone buzzed to notify him of a text message. He ignored it. It buzzed again.

'Go on, please check it,' Kate said, taking a step back from his table. 'It might be important.'

Sam gritted his teeth. At this moment nothing—even a message from the multi-national company that was bidding for a takeover of Lancaster & Son Construction—was more important than ensuring he saw this girl again. He pulled the phone from his pocket and scanned the text.

He looked up at Kate. 'My friend Jesse is running late,' he grumbled. 'I hope he gets here soon. After a four-hour trip from Sydney, I'm starving.'

Kate's green eyes widened. 'Jesse?' Her voice sounded strangled. 'You mean…Jesse Morgan?'

'Do you know him? I guess you do.'

She nodded. 'Yes. It's a small town. I…I know him well.'

So Kate was a friend of Jesse's? That made getting to know her so much easier. Suddenly she wasn't just staff at the hotel and he a guest; they were connected through a mutual friend.

It was the best piece of news he'd had all day.

* * *

Kate was reeling. Hotter-than-hot Sam Lancaster was a friend of Jesse's? That couldn't, couldn't be. What unfair quirk of coincidence was this?

Despite her initial misgiving about Sam, she'd found she liked his smile, his easy repartee. She'd found herself looking forward to seeing him around the hotel. No way was she looking for romance—not with the Jesse humiliation so fresh. But she could admire how good-looking Sam was, even let herself flirt ever so lightly, knowing he'd be gone in a week. But the fact he was Jesse's friend complicated things.

What if Jesse had told Sam about the kiss disaster? She'd thought she'd fulfilled her cringe quotient for the day. But, at the thought of Sam hearing about the kiss calamity, she cringed a little more.

She should quickly back away from Sam's table. The last thing she wanted was to encounter Jesse not only in front of this gorgeous guy, but also the restaurant packed with too-interested observers, their gossip antennae finely tuned.

But she simply could not resist a few more moments in Sam Lancaster's company before she beat a retreat—maybe to the kitchen, at least to the other side of the room—so she could avoid a confrontation with Jesse when he eventually arrived.

'Where do you know Jesse from?' she asked, trying to sound chirpy rather than churning with anxiety.

'Jesse's a mate of mine from university days in Sydney,' Sam said in his deep, resonant voice. 'We were both studying engineering. Jesse was two years behind me, but we played on the same uni football team. We used to go skiing together, too.'

So that made Sam around aged thirty to her twenty-eight.

'And you've stayed friends ever since?' she said.

She'd so much prefer it if he and Jesse were casual acquaintances.

'We lost touch for a while but met up again two years ago on a building site in India, rebuilding the villages damaged in those devastating floods.'

She hadn't put darkly handsome Sam down as the type who would do active charity work in a far-flung part of the world. It was a surprise of the best kind.

'So you work for the same international aid organisation as Jesse?' she asked.

'No. I worked as a volunteer during my vacation. We volunteers provided the grunt work. In my case, as a carpenter.'

That figured. His hand had felt callused when she'd shaken it earlier.

'I'm seriously impressed. That's so…noble.' This hot, hunky man, who would have female hearts fluttering wherever he went, spent his hard-earned vacation working without pay in a developing country in what no doubt were dirty and dangerous conditions.

'Noble? That's a very nice thing to say, but I'd hardly call it that. It was hot and sweaty and damn hard work,' he said. 'I was just glad to be of help in what was a desperate situation for so many people.'

'I bet it wasn't much fun, but you were actually helping people in trouble. In my book, that's noble—and you won't make me think otherwise.'

He shrugged those impressively broad shoulders. 'It was an eye-opener. Sure made me appreciate the life I have at home.'

'I've thought about volunteering, but I've never actually done it. What made you sign up?'

His face tightened and shutters seemed to come down over his deep, brown eyes. 'It just seemed a good thing to do. A way to give back.' The tone of his voice made her wonder if he was telling her everything. But then, why should he?

Sam Lancaster was a guest—his personal life was none of her concern. In fact, she had to be careful not to overstep the mark of what was expected of a deputy manager on front-of-house duty on a busy Sunday.

It was as well to be brought back to reality.

She returned her voice to hospitality impartial. 'I'm so glad it worked out for you.' She glanced down at his menu. 'Do you want to order while you're waiting for Jesse?' It was an effort to say Jesse's name with such disinterest.

'I'll wait for him. Though I'm looking forward to exploring the menu; it looks very good.' Sam glanced around him and nodded approvingly. 'I like the way Ben built this hotel. No wonder it won architectural awards.'

'Ben, as in Jesse's brother? My boss? Owner of Hotel Harbourside?' She couldn't keep the incredulity from her voice.

'I'm friends with Ben as well as Jesse,' he said.

'Of course you would be,' she replied.

If she'd entertained for one moment the idea of following up her attraction to Sam Lancaster, she squashed it right now. She'd grown up with Ben too. The Morgans had been like family. The thought of conducting any kind of relationship with Sam under the watchful, teasing eyes of the Morgan brothers was inconceivable—especially if Jesse had told him about the kiss.

'Do you go way back with Ben, too?'

'He joined Jesse and me on a couple of ski trips to Thredbo,' said Sam. 'We all skied together.'

'More partying and drinking than actual skiing, I'll bet,' she said.

'What happens on ski trip, stays on ski trip,' said Sam with that devastating smile.

Individually, his irregular features didn't make for handsome. But together: the olive skin; the eyes as dark as bitter chocolate; the crooked nose; his sensual mouth; the dark, thick eyebrows, intersected by that intriguing small scar, added up to a face that went a degree more than handsome.

Jesse or Ben had not been hit with the ugly stick, either. She could only imagine what that trio of good-looking guys would have got up to in the party atmosphere of the New South Wales ski slopes. She knew only too well how wild it could be.

She'd gone skiing with her university ski-club during her third year in Sydney for her business degree. The snowfields were only a day's drive away from Sydney, but they might as well have been a world away.

Social life had outweighed skiing. That winter break they'd all gone crazy with the freedom from study, from families, from rules. If she'd met Sam then she would have gone for him, that was for sure. Instead she'd met someone else. Someone who in subsequent months had hurt her so badly she'd slipped right back into that teenage dream of kind, trustworthy Jesse. Someone who had bred the unease she felt at the thought of dating men with untamed good looks like Sam.

'So you're friends with Ben, too; I didn't know. We all went our separate ways during the time you guys must have met each other.' A thought struck her. 'Ah, now I get it. You're in Dolphin Bay for Ben and Sandy's wedding on Saturday.'

'Correct,' he said. 'Though I'm not one for weddings and all the waste-of-time fuss that surrounds them.'

Kate drew herself up to her full five-foot-five and put her hands on her hips in mock rebuke. 'Waste-of-time fuss? I don't know if I can forgive you for that comment as I happen to be the wedding planner for these particular nuptials.'

'Deputy manager of a hotel like this *and* a wedding planner? You're the very definition of a multi-tasker.'

'I'll take that as a compliment, thank you,' she said. 'I like to keep busy. And I like to know what's going on. Jesse calls me the self-appointed arbiter of everyone's business in Dolphin Bay.'

She regretted the words as soon as they'd slipped out of her mouth. Why, why, why did she have to bring up Jesse's name?

But Sam just laughed. 'That sounds like something Jesse would say. You must be good friends for him to get away with it.'

'We are good friends,' she said.

And that was all they ever should have been. When they'd been still just kids, they'd shared their clumsy, first-ever kiss. But it hadn't happened again until three days ago when she'd provocatively asked her old friend why it had been so long between kisses. A suggestion that had backfired so badly.

'What Jesse says is true,' she continued. 'He calls me a nosy parker. I like to call it a healthy curiosity about what's going on.'

'Necessary qualities for all your various occupations, I would think,' he said.

'Thank you. I think so too. I particularly need to be

on top of the details of Ben's wedding which is aaargh...'
she mimed tearing her hair out '...only six days away.'
She mentally ran through the guest list. 'Now I think of
it, there *is* a Sam on the guest list; I've been meaning to
ask Ben who it was. I don't know anything about him—
uh, I mean *you.*'

Sam spread out both hands in a gesture of invitation.
'I'm an open book. Fire away with the questions.'

She wagged a finger in mock-warning. 'I wouldn't say
that to a stickybeak like me. Give me carte blanche and
you might be here all day answering questions.' *What was
she saying?* 'Uh, I mean as they relate to you as a wedding guest, that is.'

'So I'll limit them,' he said. 'Five questions should be
all you need.'

*Five questions? She'd like to know a heck of a lot more
about Sam Lancaster than she could discover with five
questions.*

'Don't mind if I do,' she said.

Do you have a girlfriend, fiancée, wife?

But she ignored the first question she really wanted to
ask and chose the safe option. 'Okay, so my first question is wedding-menu related—meat, fish or vegetarian?'

'All of the above,' he said without hesitation.

'Good. That makes it easy. Question number two: what
do you plan to do in the days before the wedding? Do you
need me to organise any tours or activities?'

With me as the tour guide, perhaps.

He shook his head. 'No need. There's a work problem
I have to think through.'

She itched with curiosity about what that problem could
be—but questioning him about it went beyond the remit
of wedding-related questions.

'Okay. Just let me know if you change your mind.

There's dolphin-and whale-watching tours. Or hikes to Pigeon Mountain for spectacular views. Now for question number three: do you…?'

Something made her look up and she immediately wished she hadn't. *Jesse.* Coming in late for his lunch. She swallowed a swear word. Why hadn't she made her getaway while she could?

Too distracted by handsome Sam Lancaster.

Now this first post-kiss encounter with Jesse would have to be played out in front of Sam.

Act normal. Act normal. Smile.

But her paralysed mouth wouldn't form into anything other than a tight line that barely curved upwards. Nor could she summon up so much as a breezy 'hi' for Jesse— the man she'd been friends with all her life, had been able to joke, banter and trade insults with like a brother.

Jesse pumped Sam's hand. 'Sorry, I got held up.'

'No worries,' said Sam, returning the handshake with equal vigour.

'Kate,' said Jesse with a friendly nod in her direction, though she didn't think she was imagining a trace of the same awkwardness in his eyes that she was feeling. 'So you've already met my mate Sam.'

'Yes,' was all she managed to choke out.

'I see you got the best table in the house,' Jesse said to Sam, indicating the view with a sweep of his hand.

'And the best deputy manager,' said Sam gruffly, nodding to Kate.

'Why, thank you,' she said. For Sam, her smile worked fine, a real smile, not her professional, hospitality smile.

Jesse cleared his throat in a way she'd never heard before. *So he was feeling the awkwardness, too.*

'Yes; Kate is, beyond a doubt, awesome,' he said.

Kate recognised the exaggerated casualness of his tone. Would Sam?

'We're just friends,' Kate blurted out. She shot a quick glance at Sam to see a bemused lift of his eyebrow.

'Of course we're just friends,' Jesse returned, too quickly. He stepped around the table to hug her, as he always did when they met. 'Kate and I go way back,' he explained to Sam.

Kate stiffened as Jesse came near. She doubted she could ever return to their old casual camaraderie. It wasn't that Jesse had done anything wrong when he'd kissed her. He just hadn't done anything for *her*. He was probably a very good kisser for someone else.

But things had changed and she didn't want his touch, even in the most casual way. She ducked to slide away.

Big, big mistake.

Sam frowned as he glanced from her to Jesse and back again. Kate could see his mental cogs whirring, putting two and two together and coming up with something other than the zero he should be seeing.

It alarmed her. Because she really wanted Sam Lancaster to know there was nothing between her and Jesse. That she was utterly and completely single.

'Why don't you join us for lunch?' Jesse asked, pulling out the third chair around the table.

No way did she want to make awkward small talk with Jesse. The thought of using her three remaining questions to find out all about Sam Lancaster was appealing—but only when there was just him and her in the conversation.

She pointed her foot, clad in a black court pump, in the direction of the table. 'Hear the ball and chain rattling? Ben would have a fit if I downed tools and fraternised with the guests.'

Did she imagine it, or did Sam's gaze linger on her leg?

She hastily drew it back. 'Shame,' he said. He sounded genuinely regretful.

Not only did she want to walk away as quickly as she could from this uncomfortable situation but she also had her responsibilities to consider. She'd spent way too much time already chatting with Sam. 'Guys, I have to get back to work. I'll send a waitress over straight away and tell the chef to fill your order, pronto. I'm sure you both must be hungry.'

In an ideal world, she'd turn and walk away right now—and not return to this end of the room until both men had gone—but before she went there was wedding business to be dealt with.

'Jesse, will I see you this evening at Ben and Sandy's house for the wedding-planning meeting? We need to run through your best-man duties.'

'Of course,' said Jesse. 'And Sam will be there too.'

'Sam?' Ben had never mentioned that the Sam on the guest list would be part of the wedding party.

Sam shrugged those impressively broad shoulders. 'I've got business with Ben. He asked me to come along tonight.'

She'd anticipated seeing Sam around the hotel, but not seeing him so soon and in a social situation. She couldn't help a shiver of excitement at the thought. At the same time, she was a little put out she hadn't been informed of the extra person. Didn't her friends realise a wedding planner needed to know these things? What other surprises might they spring on her at this late stage?

Ben hadn't mentioned employing a carpenter. Were they planning on getting Sam to construct a wooden wedding arch on the beach where the ceremony was to be held? She wished they'd told her. They were counting down six days to the wedding.

But she would find that out later. Right now she *had* to get back to work.

'I'll see you tonight, Kate,' said Sam.

Did she imagine the promise she heard in his voice?

CHAPTER TWO

SAM DIDN'T WANT to have anything to do with weddings: whip-wielding wedding planners; mothers-of-the-bride going crazy; brides-to-be in meltdown; over-the-top hysteria all round. It reminded him too much of the ill-fated plans for his own cancelled wedding. Though it had been more than two years since the whole drama, even the word 'wedding' still had the power to bring him out in a cold sweat.

If it hadn't meant a chance to see Kate again he would have backed right out of the meeting this evening.

Now he stood on the sand at the bottom of the steps that led down from the hotel to the harbour beach. Jesse's directions to Ben's house, where the meeting was to be held, had comprised a vague wave in the general direction to the right of the hotel. He couldn't see a house anywhere close and wasn't sure where to go.

'Sam! Wait for me!'

Sam turned at the sound of Kate's voice. She stood at the top of the steps, smiling down at him. For a moment all he could do was stare. If he'd thought Kate had looked gorgeous in her waitress garb, in a short, lavender dress that clung to her curves she looked sensational.

She clattered down the steps as fast as her strappy sandals would allow her, giving him a welcome flash of pale, slender legs. Her hair, set free from its constraints, flowed all wild and wavy around her face and to her shoulders, the fading light of the setting sun illuminating it to burnished copper. She clutched a large purple folder under her arm and had an outsized brown leather bag slung over her shoulder.

She was animated, vibrant, confident—everything that attracted him to her. So different from his reserved, unemotional ex-fiancée. Or his distant mother, who had made him wonder as he was growing up whether she had wanted a son at all. Whose main interest in him these days seemed to be in how well he managed the company for maximum dollars on her allowance.

Kate came to a halt next to him, her face flushed. This close, he couldn't help but notice the tantalising hint of cleavage exposed by the scoop neck of her dress.

'Are you headed to Ben's place?' she asked.

'If I knew exactly where it was, yes.'

'Easy,' she said with a wave to the right, as vague as Jesse's had been. 'It's just down there.'

'Easy for a local. All I see is a boathouse with a dock reaching out into the water.'

'That *is* the house. I mean, that's where Ben and his fiancée, Sandy, live.'

'A boathouse?'

'It's the poshest boathouse you've ever seen.' Her face stilled. 'It was the only thing left after the fire destroyed the guesthouse where the hotel stands now.'

'Yes. I knew Ben lost his first wife and child in the fire. What a tragedy.'

'Ben was a lost soul until Sandy came back to Dolphin Bay. She was his first love when they were teenagers. It was all terribly romantic.'

'And now they're getting married.'

Kate laughed. 'Yes. Just two months after they met up again. And they honestly thought they were going to get away with a simple wedding on the beach with a glass of champagne to follow.'

'That sounds a good idea to me,' he said, more whole-heartedly than he had intended.

She looked at him, her head tilted to one side, curiosity lighting her green eyes. 'Really? Maybe, if you don't have family and friends who want to help you celebrate a happy-ever-after ending. Dolphin Bay people are very tight-knit.'

He wondered what it would be like to live in a community where people cared about each other, unlike the ano-nymity of his own city life, the aridity of his family life. 'Hence you became the wedding planner?'

'Yes. I put my hand up for the job. Unofficially, of course. The simple ceremony on the beach is staying. But they can't avoid a big party at the hotel afterwards. I aim to take the stress out of it for them.'

'Good luck with that.' He couldn't avoid the cynical twist to his mouth.

'Good planning and good organisation, more likely than mere luck.'

'You mean not too many unexpected guests like me?' he said.

Her flush deepened. 'Of course not. I'm glad Ben has invited a friend from outside.'

'From *outside*?'

'I mean from elsewhere than Dolphin Bay. From Syd-ney. The big smoke.'

He smiled. She might see Sydney as 'the big smoke', but he'd travelled extensively and knew Sydney was very much a small player on the world stage, much as he liked living there.

'My business with Ben could be discussed at a different time,' he said. 'I honestly don't know why they want me along this evening.'

'Neither do I.' She immediately slapped her hand over her mouth and laughed her delightful, throaty laugh. 'Sorry. That's not what I meant. What I meant was they hadn't briefed me on the need for a carpenter.'

He frowned. 'Pass that by me again?'

'You said you were a carpenter. I thought they were asking you tonight to talk about carpentry work—maybe an arch—though I wished they'd told me that before. I don't know how we'd secure it in the sand, and I haven't ordered extra flowers or ribbons or—'

'Stop right there,' he said. 'I'm not a carpenter.'

'But you said you worked in India as a carpenter.'

'As a volunteer. Yes, I can do carpentry. In fact, I can turn my hand to most jobs on a building site. My dad had me working on-site since I was fourteen. But my hard-hat days are behind me. I manage a construction company.'

He couldn't really spare the week away from the business in this sleepy, seaside town. But with the mega-dollar takeover offer for the company brewing, he needed headspace free of everyday demands to think.

The idea of selling Lancaster & Son Construction had first formed in India, where he'd escaped to after his cancelled wedding. In a place so different from his familiar world, he'd begun to think of a different way of life—a life he would choose for himself, not have chosen for him.

'So I'm not in the business of whipping up wedding arches,' he continued.

'Oh,' Kate said, frowning. 'I got that wrong, didn't I?' He already had the impression she might not enjoy being found mistaken in anything.

He threw up his hands in surrender. 'But, if they want a wedding arch, I'll do my best to build them one.'

'No, that's not it. That was only something I thought about. I wonder why they wanted you there, then?'

He smiled to himself at her frown. It was cute the way she liked to be in the know about everything.

'I've got business with Ben,' he said. 'I'm not sure if it's hush-hush or not, so I won't say what it is.'

She glanced down at her watch. 'Well, let's get there and find out, shall we?'

Kate started to stride out beside him in the direction of the boathouse. He noticed her feet turned out slightly as she walked. The financial controller at his company had a similar gait and she'd told him it was because she'd done ballet as a kid. Kate moved so gracefully he wondered if she was a dancer too. He'd like to see her moving her body in time to music—some sensual, driving rhythm. He could join her and…

Kate paused. 'Hang on for a minute. The darn strap on the back of these sandals keeps slipping down.'

She leaned down to tug the slender strap back into place, hopping on the other foot to keep her steady. She wobbled, lost her balance, and held on to his shoulder to steady herself with a breathless, 'Sorry.'

Sam wasn't sorry at all. He liked her close—her face so near to his, her warmth, her scent that reminded him of oranges and cinnamon. For a moment they stood absolutely still and her eyes widened as they gazed into each other's faces. He noticed what a pretty mouth she had, the top lip a classic bow shiny with gloss.

He wanted to kiss her.

He fisted his hands by his sides to stop him from reaching for her and pressing his mouth to hers.

He fought the impulse with everything he had.

Because it was too soon.

And he wasn't sure what the situation was between

Kate and Jesse. Earlier today, he hadn't failed to notice the tension between two people who had professed too vehemently that they were just friends.

Kate started to wobble again. Darn sandals; she needed to get that strap shortened. Sam reached out to steady her. She gasped at the feel of his hand on her waist, his warmth burning through the fine knit fabric of her dress. She wanted to edge away but if she did there was a very good chance she'd topple over into a humiliating heap on the sand.

She didn't trust herself to touch him or to be touched. Before she'd called out from the top of the steps, she'd paused to admire him as he'd stood looking out past the waters of Dolphin Bay to the open sea, dusk rapidly approaching. She'd been seared again with that overwhelming attraction.

But that was crazy.

She'd only just faced the reality that Jesse was not the man for her. That she'd been guilty—for whatever reason—of nurturing a crush for way too long on a man whom she only loved like a brother.

Of course, there had been boyfriends in the time between the two kisses. Some she remembered fondly, one with deep regret. But, in recent years, the conviction had been ticking away that one day Jesse and she would be a couple.

That kiss had proved once and for all that Jesse would never, ever be the man for her. There was no chemistry between them.

Could she be interested, so soon, in Sam Lancaster?

He'd changed to loose, drawstring cotton pants in a sludgy khaki and a collarless loose-weave white shirt— both from India, she guessed. The casual clothes made no secret of the powerful shape of his legs and behind, the well-honed muscles of his chest and arms—built up, she suspected, from his life as a builder rather than from hours in the gym.

Now, as he helped her keep her balance, she was intensely aware of the closeness of their bodies: his hand on her waist; her hand on his shoulder; the soft curve of her breast resting lightly against the hard strength of his chest. The hammering of her own heart.

Somewhere there was the swish of the small waves of the bay rushing onto the sand then retreating back into the sea; the rustle of the evening breeze in the trees that grew in the hotel garden; muted laughter from the direction of the boathouse.

But her senses were too overwhelmed by her awareness of Sam to take any of it in. She breathed in the heady aromas of masculine soap and shampoo that told her he was fresh out of the shower.

She was enjoying being close to him—and she shouldn't be. Three days ago, she'd wanted to kiss Jesse. How could she feel this way about a stranger?

She couldn't trust feelings that had erupted so easily. She needed time to get over the Jesse thing, to plan where she went to next. Not straight into another impossible crush, that was for sure.

Having Sam around was a distraction. He didn't look like the man who had battered her young heart—and a good portion of her soul—eight years ago when she'd been twenty, but he was the same type. Sam had that outrageous masculinity; the untamed, 'don't give a damn' look that sang to something wild and feminine and reckless in her—a part of herself she thought she'd long suppressed.

Panic started its heart-stopping, breath-stealing, muscle-tensing attack on her. She took in a deep breath that came out halfway to a sob.

'You okay?' Sam's deep voice was warm with concern.

She pretended to cough. 'F-fine thanks,' she said. 'Just…just a tickle in my throat.'

She dropped her hand from his shoulder and stepped away so his hand fell from her waist. She immediately felt bereft of his touch. With hands that weren't quite steady, she switched her handbag to her other shoulder.

'Let me carry that bag for you,' Sam said, taking it from her, his fingers grazing the bare skin of her arm. It was just a momentary touch but she knew she'd feel it for hours.

'Th-thanks,' she stuttered.

He heaved the bag effortlessly over his own shoulder. 'It weighs a ton; what on earth do you have in it?'

'Anything and everything. I like to be prepared in case anyone needs stuff. You know—tissues, insect repellent, pain-relievers, tamp— Never mind. My bag's a bit of a joke with my friends. They reckon anything they need they'll find in there.'

'And they probably rely on it. I get the impression you like to look after people.'

'I guess I do,' she said. There was no need to mention the accident that had left her sister in a wheelchair when Kate had been aged thirteen, or how her father had left and Kate had had to help out at home more than anyone else her age. How helping other people run their lives had become a habit.

'So what's in the folder?' he asked.

'The master plan for the wedding. The documents are on my tablet too, and my PC, but I've got backup printouts just in case. There's a checklist, a time plan, everyone's duties spelled out to the minute. I want this wedding to run like clockwork. I've printed out a running sheet for you too, to keep you up to speed, as they've made you part of the meeting.'

Schedules. Plans. Timetables. Keep the everyday aspects of life under control, and she'd have a better chance of keeping errant emotions and unwelcome longings under control.

She couldn't let Sam Lancaster disrupt that.

Sam noticed that as Kate spoke her voice got quicker and quicker. She was nervous. *Of him?*

Had she somehow sensed the tight grip he'd had to keep on himself to stop from pulling her into his arms?

He hadn't been looking for a relationship—especially not when everything was up in the air with the business. Selling it would impact not only on his life but also on the lives of the people employed by his company, including the contractors, suppliers and clients. It was important to weigh up the desire to free himself from the hungry corporate identity that had dominated his life since he'd been a child with the obligations due to those loyal to the company. He owed it to the memory of his father to get such a momentous decision right.

But in just the few short hours he'd been in Dolphin Bay Kate Parker had wiggled her lovely, vivacious way under his skin. He hadn't been able to think of anything else but seeing her again since he'd said goodbye to her at the restaurant.

And now he wanted to take her hand and walk her right past that boathouse—past the meeting she'd scheduled for a big wedding the bride and groom didn't seem to want and onto the beach with him, where she could ask him any questions she wanted and he could ask her a few of his own.

But he would not do that while there was any chance she could be involved with his good friend.

Again, she glanced down at the watch on her narrow wrist. 'C'mon, I can't bear to be late for anything—and especially for a meeting I arranged.'

He liked the dusting of freckles on her pale arms, so different from the orange-toned fake tan that was the standard for so many Sydney girls. He liked that she was so natural and unaffected, unlike the girls his mother, Vivien—she'd never liked him calling her Mum—kept trying to foist on him ever since the big society wedding she'd wanted for him had been called off.

'Let's go, then,' he said, trying to inject a note of enthusiasm into his voice. When they started talking flowers, caterers and canapés, he'd tune out.

Dusk was falling rapidly, as it did in this part of the world. The boathouse ahead was already in shadow, the lights from the windows casting a welcoming glow on the sand. There was music and the light hum of chatter. He thought he recognised Ben's laugh.

As Kate walked beside him, he realised she was keeping a distance away from him so that their hands would not accidentally brush, their shoulders nudge. He didn't know whether to be offended by her reaction to his closeness or pleased that it might indicate she was aware of the physical tension between them.

It was torture not knowing where he stood with her.

As they got within striking distance of the boathouse, he couldn't endure not knowing any longer. He wanted to put out his hand and stop her but he didn't trust himself to touch her again. He halted. She took a few more steps forward, realised he'd stopped and turned back to face him, a questioning look on her face.

Before she had time to speak, he did.

'Kate—stop. Before we go any further, I have to ask you something.'

'Sure,' she said, her head tilted to one side. 'Fire away. We've got a few minutes left before we're late.'

He prepared himself for an answer he didn't want to hear. 'Kate, what's the story with you and Jesse?'

CHAPTER THREE

KATE'S FACE FROZE in shock at his question. For a long moment she simply stared at him and Sam waited for her reply with increasing edginess.

'Me and J…Jesse?' she finally managed to stutter out.

Sam nodded. 'You said you were just friends. Is that true?'

'Yes. It is. Now.'

'What do you mean "now"?'

'You mean Jesse didn't say anything?'

'About you? Not a word.'

Kate looked down so her mass of wavy hair fell over her face, hiding it from him. She scuffed one sandal in the sand. Sam resisted the urge to reach out and push her hair into place. She did it herself, with fingers that trembled, and then looked back up at him. Even in the fading light he could see the indecision etched on her face. 'Do you want to hear the whole story? It's…it's kind of embarrassing.' Her husky voice was so low he had to dip his head to hear her.

Embarrassing? He nodded and tried to keep his face free of expression. He'd asked the question. He had to be prepared for whatever answer she might give him.

Kate clutched the purple folder tight to her chest. 'Our mothers were very close and Jesse, Ben and I grew up together. The mums were always making jokes about Jesse and me getting married in the future. You should see the photos they posed of us as little babies, holding hands.'

Sam could imagine how cute those photos would be, but he felt uncomfortable at the thought of that kind of connection being established between Kate and Jesse at such a young age. He had a vague recollection of Jesse once mentioning a red-haired girl back home. What had he said? Something about an ongoing joke in the family that if he and the girl never found anyone else they could marry each other...

Sam had found it amusing at the time. He didn't find it amusing right now. How difficult would it be to break such a long-standing bond?

'So that's the embarrassing bit?' he asked.

Kate pulled a face. 'It gets worse. When I was thirteen and he was fourteen we tried out our first ever kiss together. It was awkward and I ended up giggling so much it didn't go far. But I guess in my childish heart that marked Jesse as someone special.'

Jealousy seared through Sam at the thought of Jesse kissing Kate, even if they had been only kids. He was aware it was irrational—after all he hardly knew Kate—but it was there. It was real.

He had to clear his throat to speak. 'So you dated?'

She shook her head so vehemently her hair swung over her face. 'Never. We both dated other people. As teenagers, we cried on each other's shoulders when things went wrong. As adults, we lived our own lives. Until...'

Her brow creased as though she were puzzling out loud. 'Until a few years ago—I don't know why—I started to think Jesse might be the one for me. After all, everyone else thought so. I developed quite a crush on him.'

'So what's so embarrassing about that?'

She paused. 'Three days ago we kissed—at my suggestion.'

Now that jealousy turned into something that seethed in his gut. He'd always prided himself on being laid-back, slow to anger. He felt anything but laid-back at the thought of her in another man's arms, even one of his friends. Especially one of his friends.

'And?' His hands were fisted.

'Crush completely over. It was an utter disaster. So wrong that words can't describe it. And I speak for him as well as for me.'

Sam's fists slowly uncurled.

'So Jesse doesn't want you as more than a friend?'

'Heavens, no!' Her voice had an undertone of almost hysterical relief. 'We could hardly wait to make our getaways. And we succeeded in avoiding each other until we met in the restaurant earlier today.'

'It seemed awkward between you. Tense.'

'At first. But it's okay now. We've been friends for so long, seems we can both laugh it off as a monumental mistake and move on.'

With no more kissing, if Sam had anything to do with it.

He stepped closer to her. This time he did reach out and smooth an auburn curl from falling over her cheek. She started but didn't step away and he tucked it behind her ear before letting his hand drop back to his side. They stood as close as they could without actually touching.

'So Jesse's right out of the picture,' he said. 'Is there anyone else?'

Anyone else he had to fight for her?

Her face was half in shadow, half in the dim light coming from the boathouse. 'No one,' she said. 'I...I haven't dated for quite some time.' She paused. 'What about you? Question number three: is there any special lady in your life?'

'I was engaged to a long-term girlfriend. But no one special since that ended.'

He'd smarted for months at the way the engagement had been terminated, the wedding cancelled. In fact, he'd been so gutted he'd taken off to India to get away from the fallout. With perspective, he could see ending the engagement had been the right decision. But, while the wounds had healed, he had been wary of getting involved with anyone. Now he was ready. His ex had moved on, but he hadn't met a woman who had interested him. Until now.

'Oh,' she said. 'Would it count as question number four if I asked about what happened—or would that be part of question number three?'

He grinned. 'I'll allow it as part two of question three—but it might have to wait until I have more time to answer it.'

'I'm okay with that,' she said with a return of her dimples.

The last thing he wanted to do was scare Kate off. He had never before experienced this instant attraction to a woman. He had to work through how he handled it.

Kate was so obviously not the kind of woman for a no-strings fling. It wasn't what he wanted either. But his previous relationships had started off slowly with attraction growing. He understood how that worked, not this immediate flaming that might just burn itself out in a matter of days. The kind of flaming that had seen his parents trapped in an unhappy marriage, the consequences of which he had been forced to endure.

That aside, he realised Kate might not feel the same way as he did. If he wanted to get to know her, he knew he had to take things carefully.

'Before Jesse came into the restaurant, I was about to ask you out on a date,' he said. 'What would you have said?'

'I...I... You've taken me by surprise. I would have said—'

Just then the door of the boathouse opened, flooding them with further light. Ben peered through the door and called out. 'Hey, Kate, what are you doing out there? You warned us all to be on time or suffer dire consequences and now *you're* running late.'

Kate immediately stepped back from Sam so fast she nearly tripped. 'I'm coming!' she called in Ben's direction.

Sam cursed under his breath at the interruption. He wanted to shout at Ben to get lost.

Kate looked back up at Sam. 'Sam, I...'

But Ben was now heading towards them. He caught sight of Sam. 'Sam. Mate. I didn't see you there. Come on in.'

Sam groaned. Kate looked up at him in mute appeal. He shrugged wordlessly in a gesture of frustration. But not defeat; he would get Kate's reply sooner rather than later.

Then he was swept along into the boathouse with Kate, Ben walking between them like an old-fashioned chaperone.

An hour later, Kate was pleased at how well the meeting had gone. Everyone who needed to be there had been there—except for Sandy's sister who lived in Sydney, and her five-year-old daughter who was to be the flower girl. Plans had been finalised, timetables tweaked. Now the bridal party had been joined by a few other friends. Snack platters from the hotel kitchen had arrived and the barbecue was being fired up. There wasn't much more she could do to ensure the wedding went to plan on Saturday.

If only she hadn't been so darned conscious of Sam the entire time. It had been more than a tad distracting. She'd found herself struggling to remember important facts, her mind too occupied with Sam. But no one seemed to have noticed the lapse from her usual efficiency.

She just hoped they hadn't noticed the way she'd found herself compelled to check on him every few minutes. He'd met her glances with a smile, even a wink that had made her smother a laugh. It was only too obvious he was bored by the details of the wedding meeting. He'd crossed his long legs and uncrossed them. He'd not-so-subtly checked his mobile phone. He'd even nodded off for a few minutes until Ben had shoved him awake.

But she hadn't had a moment alone with him since they'd been interrupted on the beach.

She'd been just about to say yes to Sam's suggestion of a date. But would it really be a good idea?

Her fears screamed no. Just the light touch of his fingers on her cheek had practically sent her hurtling to the stars. She'd never felt such strong attraction so quickly. She was terrified that it might lead her into the kind of obsession that had nearly destroyed her in the past. It would be wisest to keep Sam at a distance.

But her loneliness urged yes to seeing Sam. Why shouldn't she go out with him on an uncomplicated, everyday date, with no other agenda than to share a meal, enjoy a movie, find out something about what made the other tick? Flirt a little. Laugh a lot. It didn't have to go further than that.

For so long she'd been on her own. Surely she deserved some masculine excitement in her life—even if only temporary? Sam would only be around for a week and then he'd be gone. Where was the harm in enjoying his company?

It was time to say yes to that date.

She'd lost sight of him—difficult in the space of the boathouse, which was basically just one large room converted into luxury living. He must have escaped outside to the barbecue. She'd go find him.

Before she could make the move, the bride-to-be, Sandy, sidled up beside her. 'Sooo,' she said in a teasing tone. 'You and that gorgeous hunk, Sam Lancaster...'

Kate couldn't help it; she flushed again and Sandy noticed. That was the problem with being a fair-skinned redhead: even the slightest blush flamed. 'What about me and Sam?' she said, knowing she sounded unnecessarily defensive.

'You've hardly kept your eyes off him all evening. And he you. I reckon he's smitten. And maybe you are too.'

'Of course he's not. Of course I'm not.'

'Oh, really?' said Sandy in an overly knowing tone.

Kate narrowed her eyes. 'Are you by any chance paying me back for the way I poked my nose in with you and Ben when you first came back to Dolphin Bay?'

Kate had been overprotective of her friend Ben when Sandy had showed up out of the blue after twelve years of no contact. But she'd very soon warmed to Sandy and they'd become good friends.

'Don't be silly,' said Sandy. 'I'm so deliriously happy with Ben, I want you to be happy too. Sam is really nice, as well as being a hunk. I got the lowdown on him.'

'I only met him today. Nothing is happening there, I can assure you.'

Nothing except her heart starting to race every time she caught a glimpse of him towering over the other guests.

'But it might. You know what they say about what happens at weddings.' Sandy smiled. 'The bridesmaid and the groomsman...'

Kate frowned. 'I don't know what you mean. I'm your

bridesmaid. But Sam isn't Ben's groomsman. I should know, as your wedding planner.'

'Uh, think again. Right now, Ben's asking Sam to be just that.'

'What? I thought he only wanted a best man?'

'He's changed his mind. My sister Lizzie, as chief bridesmaid, will be partnered by the best man, Jesse. That means you'd be coming up that beach aisle by yourself. We thought why not even things up by partnering you with Sam? You'll easily be able to readjust your ceremony schedules. That is, if Sam agrees to it.'

Kate tried to tell herself she was being oversensitive but she could sense that echo again: *poor Kate.*

'Sandy, it's so sweet of you, but is this about what happened with Jesse and me three days ago? If so, I—'

Sandy's hazel eyes were kind. 'Kate, I'm so sorry it didn't work out with Jesse. I know how much you've always wanted him.'

Kate swallowed hard. It was so difficult to talk about it. 'Did I really, though, Sandy? I think maybe I dreamed of a kind, handsome man—so different from the men I'd dated—and Jesse was there. I...I fixated on him. It wasn't real.'

'You could be right. To tell you the truth, I didn't ever see any chemistry between you.'

Kate giggled. 'There was no chemistry whatsoever. I can't tell you how much I regretted it. I couldn't run away fast enough.'

'I bet you wouldn't run too far if you were alone with Sam Lancaster. Doesn't he fit the bill? He's handsome, all right—and he must be kind, or he wouldn't have been off volunteering in India, would he?'

Kate sobered. 'All that. But, Sandy, don't try to match-make, will you? I don't want a pity party. I'm not desperate for a man.'

Sandy put her hand reassuringly on Kate's arm. 'Of course you're not. But is it a bad thing for your friends to look out for you? And for you to let them? You've got to admit, it's more fun being a bridesmaid if you have a handsome groomsman in tow.'

'Of course it is. And you're right; you don't get more handsome than Sam Lancaster. And he's interesting, too.' She found herself looking over her shoulder to watch out for him, only to see him coming back into the room with Ben. 'Here he is. I hope he didn't hear me twittering on about how handsome he is,' she whispered to Sandy.

She watched as Sam and Ben approached. Funny; she'd always found Ben so imposing, Jesse so good-looking. But Sam outshone any man she'd ever met in terms of pure, masculine appeal.

'So did Sam say yes to being groomsman, Ben?' asked Sandy.

'Of course he did,' said tall, blond Ben.

Sam stood shoulder-nudging distance from Kate. She could feel his warmth, smell the hint of bourbon on his breath. 'As if I had a choice, when I heard who would be the bridesmaid I was escorting,' he said with a smile that was just for her. She smiled back, glad beyond reason to have him by her side.

She would ask *him* on a date. ASAP.

Now the planning part of the evening was over and her duties done, she could get the heck out of there and take Sam with her, so they could talk in private away from too-interested eyes.

But Ben had other ideas. He turned to Kate. 'I was going to introduce you to Sam tonight, but as you've already met I'll cut straight to the chase.'

Kate sighed inwardly. All she could think of was being alone with Sam. But she was aware that, while Ben was a long-time friend, he was also her boss. He had his boss voice on now; she almost felt she should be taking notes.

'Yes, sir,' she said flippantly, at the same time wondering how a work thing could possibly involve Sam.

'We've finally got planning approval for the new resort,' said Ben with a whoop of triumph.

'Really?' she said, scarcely able to let herself believe the news. 'Really and truly?'

'Really,' said Ben with a huge grin.

'Congratulations, Kate,' said Sandy, hugging her. 'I know how hard you worked with Ben on the submission.'

Momentarily lost for words, Kate hugged Sandy back. Then she looked from Sam to Ben to Sam again. 'That's amazing. After all the hours we put in, I can hardly believe it's actually happening,' she said.

She grabbed hold of Sam's arms and did a little jig of excitement—then realised what she'd done and dropped her hands. She pulled a face. 'Sorry. I got carried away.'

'Don't be sorry,' he said. 'I can see this means a lot to you.'

Ben put up his hand. 'Wait. There's more. Sam's company is going to build the resort. Lancaster & Son Construction is one of the biggest and the best in the country. We're fortunate to have him on board.'

Kate stared, too astounded to say anything. *Why hadn't she known this?*

When she finally got her breath back, Kate turned to Sam. 'So that was the hush-hush business.'

And she'd thought he was a carpenter.

'Not so hush-hush now,' he said.

'I can't tell you how thrilled I am about this project,' she said. 'A luxury, boutique spa resort nestled in the bush on that beautiful spot. It's on land overlooking Big Ray Beach—that's our surf beach—with incredible views. The resort's a big deal for Dolphin Bay.'

'And a triumph for Kate. It was initially her idea,' Ben explained to Sam. 'As her reward for kick-starting it, she has equity.'

Her ownership was only measured in the tiniest of percentages—a token, really—but Kate intended to be a hands-on manager once the resort was up and running. It would be her dream job, something she wanted so much it hurt.

'Congratulations,' said Sam. 'It's great to hear you're such an entrepreneur.'

Kate basked in the admiration she saw in his eyes. At age twenty-eight, she'd had a few false starts to her career; now she was exactly where she wanted to be. 'I'm still a bit dazed that it's actually going to happen,' she said.

Ben turned to Kate. 'I want you to be our liaison person with Sam—starting from now. I'll be away on my honeymoon after next week and this week too caught up with work at the hotel.'

She blinked at Ben. 'Th..that's a surprise.'

'But it makes sense,' said Ben. 'You know more about the project than anyone else but me. You can start by taking Sam to the site for him to take a look at it. That okay with you, Sam?'

'Of course,' said Sam, though Kate thought he looked perturbed.

'I'll leave you to two to discuss the details,' said Ben, ushering Sandy away.

Finally Kate was left alone with Sam, exactly what she'd longed for all evening. She'd never been more aware of his big, broad-shouldered body, his unconventionally handsome face.

Only now she would value a few minutes on her own to think over what had just happened.

Ten minutes ago she'd been ready to drag him outside and arrange a date. Or two. Except now things were very different. She would have to put all such thoughts on hold. Sam was no longer a stranger blown into town for a week, never to be seen again. He was someone with ongoing links to Dolphin Bay. She'd be working with him as a professional in a business capacity.

How could she possibly think she could have any kind of personal relationship with him?

CHAPTER FOUR

SAM HAD BEEN knocked sideways by the news that he'd
be working with Kate on Ben's new resort development.
He'd always enforced a strict rule in the company—no
dating clients. Without exception. Not for his employees,
not for him. He'd amended a number of his father's long-
standing edicts when he'd taken over but not that one. It
made good business sense.

How ironic that it now applied to Kate—and company
protocol was too important to him to have one rule for the
boss and another for the rest of the team.

He felt like thumping the wall with his clenched fist,
right through the tastefully restored wooden boards. He
clenched his jaw and uttered a string of curse words under
his breath.

He had to get out of this room. On top of his frustration,
he felt stifled by all the wedding talk buzzing around him.
When it came to his turn to get hitched—his own derailed
wedding hadn't turned him off the idea of getting married
one day—he thought elopement would be a great idea.

Then there were the overheard murmurs that had him
gritting his teeth. They had all been along the lines of what
a shame it was about Kate and Jesse—immediately hushed
when he'd come near. Whether that was because they saw

him as an interloper, or they could tell he was interested in Kate, he didn't know. But he didn't like it.

Everything he'd heard about the oppressive nature of small-town life was true.

He hated everyone knowing his business. How Kate could bear it was beyond his comprehension. Anything smaller than Sydney, with its population of more than four-and-a-half million, would never be for him.

A middle-aged woman was bearing down on them. No doubt she wanted Kate's opinion on the colour of ribbons on a flower arrangement or some such waste-of-space frivolity.

'I'm going outside for some air,' he muttered to Kate and strode away before the woman reached them.

He realised his departure was being watched with interest by everyone else in the room. Tough. There'd be nothing for them to gossip about now. Kate was strictly out of bounds.

It was dark outside now but the moon was full, reflecting on the quietly rippling waters of the bay. He gulped in the cool evening air, then let out those curse words at full volume as he kicked at the solid base of a palm tree as hard as he could.

His first thought was that after the site inspection tomorrow he would get the hell out of Dolphin Bay. But he'd promised to be Ben's groomsman. He cursed again. He was trapped here—with a woman he wanted but suddenly couldn't have.

The door opened behind him, a shaft of light falling on the deck. He moved away. He was in no mood to talk. To Ben. To Jesse. To anyone.

'Sam?' Her voice was tentative but even without turning around he knew it was Kate.

He turned. There was enough moonlight so he could

see the anxiety on her face. She was wringing her hands together. He ached to reach out to her but he kept his hands fisted by his sides.

'Let's walk out to the end of the dock,' she said. 'You feel like you're on a boat out there. And no one can over-hear us.'

He fell into step beside her. A row of low-voltage sensor lights switched on to light them to the dock. The builder in him admired the electrics. His male soul could only think of the beautiful woman beside him and regret about what might have been.

They reached the end of the dock without speaking. A light breeze coming off the water brought with it the tang of the sea and lifted and played with the soft curls around Kate's face. She seemed subdued, as if the moonlight had sucked all that wonderful vivacity from her.

She turned to him. 'I had no idea you were building the resort.'

'I had to keep it confidential. I didn't know you were involved in any way.'

'It was the first time I heard I was to liaise with you. I hadn't seen that coming.' She looked up at him. Her face was pale in the weak, shimmering light, her eyes shad-owed. 'This…this changes things, doesn't it?'

'I'm afraid it does,' he said, knowing from the regret in her eyes that she was closing the door on him before it got any more than halfway open.

'It…it means I have to say no to that date,' she said.

One part of him was plunged into dismay at the tolling finality of her words, the other was relieved that he hadn't had to say them first.

'It means I have to rescind the offer,' he said gruffly. 'I have an iron-clad no-dating-the-clients rule.'

Her short, mirthless laugh was totally unlike her usual

throaty chime. 'Me too. I've never thought it was a good idea. There can be too many consequences if the dating doesn't work out but you still have to work together.'

'Agreed,' he said. 'There are millions of dollars at stake here.' And his company's reputation—especially at the time of a publicly scrutinised buy-out bid. The company had to come first again—as it always did. This time, it came ahead of him dating the only woman who had seriously interested him since his broken engagement. Again he had that sense of the business as a millstone, weighing him down with protocol and obligation—as it had since he'd been fourteen years old.

Kate laughed that mirthless laugh again. 'Funny thing is, I suspect it's Ben's clumsy attempt at matchmaking and it's totally backfired.'

He gave a snort of disbelief. 'You think so?'

'The groomsman thing? The cooked-up excuse to get me to show you the land when there's no real need for me to?'

'My take on it is that Ben thought you knew more than anyone else about the plans for the new resort. You were the best person for the job. Why would you believe any differently?'

'I guess so,' she said with a self-deprecating quirk of her pretty mouth. 'But the out-of-the blue request to be a groomsman?'

Sam snapped his fingers. 'I get it—you were concerned an extra member of the wedding party would put your schedules out?'

Her smile was forced as she raised her hand. 'Guilty! I guess I *was* a little disconcerted about that. But I mainly felt bad for you being coerced into being a groomsman on such a trumped-up excuse. You don't seem to be comfortable with all the wedding stuff—I saw you yawning during the meeting. Then you get thrown in at the deep end.'

'Ben didn't have to coerce me to be his groomsman. I liked the idea of being your escort at the wedding.'

Wouldn't any red-blooded male jump at the chance to be with such a gorgeous girl? Or had Jesse done such a number on her she didn't realise how desirable she was?

Truth be told, if it hadn't been for the prospect of more time with Kate, he'd rather have stayed a guest and stood apart from the wedding tomfoolery. Now he would have to spend the entire time with Kate, knowing she was off-limits. It would be a kind of torture.

'Thank you,' she said. 'It will be nice to have you there. It might have been awkward with Jesse otherwise. People would have been gossiping. Even though…'

'It has to be strictly business between us now.'

'Yes,' she said. 'I…I realise that.'

The tinkling, chiming sound of rigging against masts from the boats moored in the harbour carried across the water, adding to the charm of the setting. Dolphin Bay was a nice part of the world, he conceded. For a visit, for work—a vacation, perhaps—but not to live here.

'We should be going back to the others,' she said with a notable lack of enthusiasm.

'Yes,' he said, without making a move.

The last place he wanted to be was back in the boathouse. He liked being out here on the dock talking to her, even if the parameters of the conversations they could have had now had been constrained.

Suddenly she slapped her hand on her arm. 'Darn mosquitoes!'

She reached into that capacious shoulder bag, burrowed around and pulled out a can. 'Insect repellent,' she explained.

'You really do have everything stashed in there,' he said, amused.

'Even a single mosquito buzzing its way down the coast will seek me out and feast on my fair skin.' As she spoke, she dramatised her words and mimed the insect dive-bombing her in a totally unself-conscious manner.

Lucky mosquito. Sam could imagine nuzzling into the pale skin of her throat—kissing, nibbling, even a gentle bite...

That was forbidden territory now.

'Want some?' she asked.

Mosquito spray? 'No thanks. They never bother me.'

'Lucky you.' She stood away from him and sprayed her legs and arms with a spray that smelled pleasantly of lavender.

'You're not suited to beach-side living, are you?' he asked when she came close again.

'Not really,' she said. 'Insects adore me and I burn to a frizzle if I'm out in the sun in the middle of the day. But I love to swim, and the mornings and evenings are great for that.'

A moonlight swim: her pale body undulating through the shimmering water, giving tantalising glimpses of her slender limbs, her just-right curves; he shrugging off his clothes and joining her...

This kind of scenario was not on. Not with a client.

He cleared his throat. 'I like to start the day with a swim. Where do you recommend?' he asked.

'The bay is best for quiet water. Then there's Big Ray surf beach—you get to it via the boardwalk. Around from there is an estuary where the freshwater river meets the sea. It's magic. Not many people go there and you can swim right up that river without seeing another soul. Oh, except for the occasional kangaroo coming down to drink.'

'It sounds idyllic,' he said.

'That's a good word for it. I can show you how to get there on the map. I'd offer to take you but that's—'

'Not a good idea,' he said at the same time she did. Not with him in his board shorts and her in a bikini. Or, with that fair skin of hers, did she wear a sleek, body-hugging swimsuit?

A cold sweat broke out on his forehead. Somehow he had to stop himself from thinking of Kate Parker as anything other than a client. She was the Hotel Harbourside client liaison. Nothing more.

'I'll have to have a word with Ben,' said Kate. 'About his matchmaking efforts, I mean—well-meaning but misguided.'

'Ben's an amateur. You haven't seen misguided matchmaking until you've met my mother. She's a master of it.'

Why had he said that?

Why not?

Kate was a client. That didn't mean he couldn't have a personal conversation with her.

'But not successfully?' Kate asked.

What had she called herself? A stickybeak. It was such an Aussie expression but so perfectly summed up a person who couldn't resist sticking their noses into other people's business. He preferred her description of herself as having a healthy curiosity. And right now he could tell it had been piqued.

'I veto all her efforts,' he said. 'I might work in the family firm but I run my own life.'

That hadn't always been the case. His father had been overly domineering. His mother had just wanted him kept out of her hair. There'd been an almighty battle when his mother had planned to send him to boarding school— with his father victorious, of course. As a child he'd had no choice but to go along with the way they'd steered his life. As a teenager he'd rebelled against his father but still had little choice. The real confrontation hadn't come until he'd turned twenty-one, nine years ago.

'Your mother—she's in Sydney?' Kate asked.

An image of his mother flashed before his eyes: whippet-thin in couture clothes, hair immaculate, perfectly applied make-up that could not disguise the lines of discontent around her mouth or the disappointment in her eyes when she looked at her son. Her son who'd chosen to follow his father into the rough and tumble of the construction industry—not a law degree or a specialist medical degree she saw as more socially acceptable. Not that she ever complained about the hefty allowance the company brought her.

He looked at Kate in the moonlight, at her hair, a glorious mass of riotous waves, her simple dress, her eyes warm with real interest in what he had to say. She seemed so straightforward. So genuine. Never had two women been more different.

'Yes. She'd never stray from the eastern suburbs.'

'And your father? I wondered about the "and son" bit in your company name. Are you the son?'

'You realise that's question number four?' he said.

'I guess it is,' she said. Her dimples had snuck back into her smile but now they disappeared again. 'Sorry. I guess I shouldn't ask more questions now…now things have changed.'

'As a business client? Why not? Fire away.'

'And, in fact, it's a three-part question.'

'Well, number two was a two-part question.'

'I start as I mean to continue.'

'So I've got a four-part question to look forward to in the next stage of my interrogation?'

'Maybe. I'll keep you guessing.' Her delightful laughter echoed around the beach. 'But in the meantime, do you want to answer part one of question four?'

'My father died three years ago.'

The laughter faded from her voice. 'I'm so sorry. Was it expected?'

'A sudden heart attack. He was sixty-seven and very fit.'

'How awful for you. And for your mother.'

'It was a shock for her. She was my father's second wife and considerably younger than he was. Didn't expect to be left on her own so soon.'

'And you?' Her voice was gentle and warm with concern. 'It must have been a terrible shock for you too.'

He'd been in Western Australia when he'd got the phone call, a six-hour flight away. He'd never forgiven himself for not being there. He'd been so concerned with proving himself to his father by fixing the problems in Western Australia, he had missed his chance to say goodbye to him.

'Yes. Worse in some ways, because suddenly I had to take over the running of the company. I hadn't expected to have to do that for years to come.'

'That was a truckload of responsibility.'

He shrugged. 'The old man had been preparing me for the role since I'd been playing with my Lego, teaching me the business from the ground up. He was a tough taskmaster. I didn't get any privileges for being the boss's son. I had to earn my management stripes on my own merits.'

'Still, actually taking the reins of such a large company must have been scary.'

'The first day I took my place at the head of the boardroom table was as intimidating as hell. All those older guys just waiting for me to make a mistake.' He had never admitted that to anyone. *Why Kate? Why now?*

'But you won their respect, I'll bet.'

'I worked hard for it.' Too hard, perhaps. He hadn't had time for much else, including his fiancée. That was when she had started accusing him of being an obsessive workaholic who put the company ahead of everything else—particularly her. He'd come to see some truth in her accusations.

'Good for you; that can't have been easy,' said Kate. 'Which brings me back to question four—you're the son in the company name?'

'Actually, the son was my father. My grandfather started the company, building houses in the new suburbs opening up after the Second World War. My dad grew the company far bigger than my grandfather could ever have dreamed. In turn, I've taken it even further.'

'Obviously you build hotels.'

'And office towers and shopping malls and stadiums. All over the country. Even outside the country.'

In the three years he'd been at the helm he'd steered the business through tough economic times. He had pushed it, grown it. He didn't try to hide his pride in his achievements. They'd come at a cost—his personal life.

Kate went quiet again. 'You must have thought I was an idiot for suggesting you were here to build a wedding arch.'

'Of course I didn't think you were an idiot. I'm a builder. I can make arches. Fix drains. Even turn my hand to electrical work if I have to.' He held out his hands. 'With the calluses to prove it.'

She turned away so she looked out to sea and he faced her profile—her small, neat nose, her firm, determined chin. 'But you're also the CEO of a huge construction company. That's quite a contradiction.'

And now she was his client.

He realised the distance their business roles now put between them. Once more his commitment to the company came over his personal happiness. It was a price he kept on paying.

And he wasn't sure he was prepared to do that any longer.

Kate found it difficult to suppress a sigh. *Be careful what you wish for.*

She hadn't wanted to be distracted by Sam while she sorted out her life after the Jesse issue. Now Sam could not be anything more than a business connection.

Her disappointment was so intense she felt nauseous, choked by a barrage of what might have beens. She hadn't been able to get him off her mind since he'd walked into the restaurant. But how did she stop herself from being attracted to him?

Because the more she found out about him, the more she liked him.

Still, she had had practice at putting on a mask, at not showing people what she really felt. At hiding her pain. At being cheerful, helpful, always-ready-to-help-out Kate.

She would simply slip into the impersonal role of client, hide her disappointment that she couldn't spend time with Sam in any other capacity. She must remember to thank Ben for the opportunity to deal with the CEO of the company building her dream hotel.

It was probably for the best, anyway. She wasn't ready for romance, especially with someone who lived so far away. The four hours to Sydney might as well be four hundred as far as she was concerned. One of the reasons Jesse had been appealing was that, although he worked overseas now, he intended to settle in Dolphin Bay.

She looked down at her watch, the dial luminous in the dark.

'We really should be getting back,' she said, aiming for

brisk and efficient but coming out with a lingering, 'don't really want to go just yet' tone that wouldn't fool anyone as smart as Sam.

'I like it out here,' he said. He hunkered down on the very end of the dock then swung his long legs over the edge. He patted the place next to him in invitation. 'No one will have missed us.'

Against her better judgement, she joined him. She was hyper-aware of his warmth, his strength, his masculinity, and she made sure she sat a client-like distance from him so their shoulders didn't touch. The water slapped against the supports of the pier and a fish leapt up out of the water, glinting silver in the moonlight, and flopped back in with a splash.

'You're right; it's like being on a boat,' Sam said.

'Without the rocking and the seasickness.'

'Or the feeling of being trapped and unable to get off exactly when you want to.'

Her eyes widened. 'You feel that way about boats too?'

'I've never much cared for them. Which is at odds with living on the harbour in Sydney.'

'Me neither,' she said. 'I'd rather keep my feet firmly planted on land.'

'*Definitely* not a seaside person.'

'In another life I'd probably live in a high-rise in the middle of the city and go to the ballet and theatre on the nights I wasn't trying the newest restaurants.' Now she did indulge in the sigh. 'Trouble is, I love it here so much. I wasn't joking earlier when I said I thought it was the most beautiful place in Australia.'

'That hasn't escaped my attention,' he said.

'It's familiar and s—' She hastily bit off the word 'safe' and said, 'So relaxed.'

'It's nice, I'll give you that. But have you been to many places to compare?' he asked.

'Do I really sound like a small-town hick?'

'Anything but,' he said. 'I was just interested. I've travelled a lot; we might have been to the same places.'

'Sure, I've been to lots of other places. When I…after I…'

She struggled to find the right words that wouldn't reveal the back story she had never shared with anyone: the reason she'd left university in Sydney without completing her degree. The reason she felt she would always doubt her choice of men. 'I toured all around the country in a small dance company.'

'I thought you might have been a dancer,' he said. She followed his gaze down to where her feet dangled over the edge of the pier.

'Let me guess—because of the duck walk? Years of training in classical ballet tends to do that. Only, we dancers call it "a good turn-out".'

'I was going to say because of the graceful way you move.'

'Oh,' she said and the word hung still in the air.

She blushed that darn betraying blush. She wasn't sure how to accept the compliment. Mere hours ago she might have replied with something flirtatious. But not now. Not when all that was off the agenda.

'Thank you,' was all she said.

'Would I have heard of your dance company?'

'I highly doubt it. It was a cabaret troupe and far from famous. We toured regional Australia—the big clubs, town halls, civic centres, small theatres if they had them. Once we had a stint in New Zealand. We were usually the support act to a singer or a magician—that kind of thing. It was hard work but a lot of fun.'

'Was?'

'A dancer's life is a short one,' she said, trying to sound unconcerned. 'I injured my ankle and that was the end of it.'

She didn't want to add that her ankle had healed—but the emotional wounds from a near-miss assault from a wouldn't-take-no-for-an-answer admirer had not.

During the time the man had had her trapped, he'd taunted her that her sexy dance moves in body-hugging costumes made men think she was asking for it. Coming so soon after her damaging relationship with her university boyfriend, she'd imploded. She hadn't performed since, or even danced at parties.

'I'd like to see you dance some day,' Sam said.

'Chance would be a fine thing. I don't dance at all any more.'

Sadness wrenched at her as it always did when she thought about dance. To express herself with movement had been an intrinsic part of her and she mourned its loss.

'Because of the ankle?' he said.

'Yes,' she lied.

She felt uncomfortable with the conversation focused on her. That was a time of her life she'd sooner forget. She made her voice sound bright and cheery. That was what people expected of her. 'You do realise you've skipped answering part two of question four,' she said.

'I did?'

'You know, about why your engagement ended?' she prompted. 'Unless that's off the agenda now for discussion between business associates.'

'No secrets there,' he said. 'Two weeks before the wedding my former fiancée, Frances, called it off. I hadn't seen it coming.'

'That must have been a shock. What on earth happened?'

Kate really wanted to hear his reply. She couldn't understand how anyone engaged to be married to Sam Lancaster could find any reason to call it off. She could scarcely believe it when—just as Sam was about to answer her—she heard her name being called from the boathouse.

She stilled. So did Sam. 'Pretend you don't hear it,' Sam muttered in an undertone.

She tried to block her ears but her name came again, echoing over the water. Sandy's voice.

'Over here,' she called, then mouthed a silent, 'Sorry,' to Sam.

Sandy rushed along the dock. 'Thank heaven you hadn't gone home. Lizzie, my sister, just phoned. She can't make it to the hen and stag night on Wednesday. We'll have to drive up to Sydney and have it there instead.'

'But I—'

'Don't worry, Kate,' said Sandy. 'I promise it won't be any more work for you.' Sandy turned to Sam. 'Are you okay with the change of plan?'

Sam shrugged. 'Sure.'

Kate cleared her throat against the rising panic that threatened to choke her. She couldn't go to Sydney. She just couldn't. But she didn't want to tell Sandy she wouldn't be going with them. She couldn't cope with the explanations, the reasons. She'd make her excuses at the last minute. They could party quite happily without her.

'Fine by me too,' she said, forcing a smile. 'One less thing for me to have to organise.'

CHAPTER FIVE

UP UNTIL NOW, Sam had never had a problem with the 'no dating the clients' rule. Along the way there had been attractive female clients who had made their personal interest in him clear. But he had had no trouble deflecting them; the business had always come first.

It was a different story with Kate Parker. Kate certainly wasn't coming on to him in any way. In fact, she couldn't be more professional. This morning she had picked him up from the hotel. On the short drive to the site of the proposed resort, the conversation had been completely business-related—not even a mention of the wedding, let alone their thwarted date.

He was the one who was having trouble seeing her purely as a client and not as a beautiful, desirable woman who interested him more than anyone had interested him for a long time. It was disconcerting the way she appeared so easily to have put behind her any thought of a more personal relationship.

The thought nagged at him—if Ben hadn't appointed her as his liaison would she have agreed to that date? Might they have been going out to dinner together tonight?

She was a client. Just a client.

But as she guided him around the site he found her presence so distracting it was a struggle to act professionally.

The way her hair gleamed copper in the mid-morning sun made even the most spectacular surroundings seem dull by comparison. When she walked ahead of him in white jeans, and a white shirt that showcased her shapely back view, how could he objectively assess the geo-technical aspects of the site? Or gauge the logistics of crane access when her orange cinnamon scent wafted towards him?

He gritted his teeth and kicked the sandy soil with its sparse cover of indigenous vegetation, filling his nostrils with the scent of eucalypt leaves crushed underfoot.

Truth be told, he didn't really need to inspect the site. The company had a team of surveyors and engineers to do that. He'd promised Ben he'd take a look more as a courtesy than anything. Now Kate was standing in for Ben and it was a very different experience than it would have been tramping over the land with his old skiing buddy.

'What do you think?' Kate asked.

She twirled around three-hundred-and-sixty degrees, her arms outstretched. Pride and excitement underscored her voice. She'd seemed subdued when he'd said goodnight at the boathouse—thrown by the last-minute change to the stag night. But there was no trace of that today. It appeared she could take change in her stride. He admired that—in his experience, not all super-organised people were as flexible.

'It's magnificent,' he said. *You're magnificent.* 'You're on to a winner.'

The large parcel of land stood elevated above the northern end of what the locals called Big Ray beach, though there was another name on the ordinance surveys. Groves of spotted gums, with their distinctive marked bark, framed a view right out past the breakers to the open sea.

'There was a ramshackle old cottage in that corner,'

Kate said, pointing. 'It had been there for years. It was only demolished quite recently.'

'The great Australian beach shack—that's quite a tradition,' he said. 'No doubt generations of the same family drove down from Sydney or Canberra to spend the long summer holidays on the beach.'

'I wouldn't get too nostalgic about it,' she said. 'It was very basic; just one step up from a shanty. I pitied the mum of the family having to cook in it on sweltering January days.'

'Maybe the guys barbecued the fish they'd caught.'

'You sound like you speak from experience. Did your family have a beach house when you were growing up?'

'We owned a beach house at Palm Beach—it's the most northern beach in Sydney.'

Her eyes widened. 'I know it—don't they call it the summer playground of the wealthy?'

'I guess they do,' he said. 'Our place was certainly no beach shack. And I never went fishing with my father. He was always at work.'

'Your mother?'

'She was partying.'

He shied away from the thinly veiled pity in Kate's eyes. 'Did you have brothers or sisters?' she asked.

He shook his head. 'I was an only child.'

As a little boy he had spent many lonely hours over the long school holidays rattling around the palatial house by himself. Then, when he'd turned fourteen, his father had started him working as a labourer on the company building sites during the holidays. It had been tough—brutal, in some ways, as the old hands had tested the 'silvertail' boss's son from the private school. But he'd been strong—both physically and mentally—and willing to prove himself. He'd won the doubters over.

From then on, the company had dominated his life. And he'd rarely gone back to that lonely Palm Beach house until he'd been old enough to take a group of his own friends.

'I envied the school friends who'd come back from a place like this full of tales of adventure.' He waved his hand towards the demolition site. 'I bet that old shack could have told some stories.'

'Perhaps. But only the one family got to enjoy the views and the proximity to the beach,' Kate said. She looked around the land with a distinctly proprietorial air. 'The owners got a good price for the land and now lots of people will be able to enjoy this magic place.'

'Spoken like a true, ruthless property developer,' he said, not entirely tongue-in-cheek. He had no issue with property developers—the good ones, that was—they were the company's lifeblood.

'I wouldn't say ruthless. More…practical,' she said with an uplifting of her pretty mouth.

'Okay. Practical,' he said.

'And don't forget creative. After all, no one else ever saw the potential of this land.'

'Okay. You're a practical and creative property developer without a ruthless bone in your body.'

'Oh, there might be a ruthless bone or two there,' she said with a flash of dimpled smile. 'But I wouldn't call me a property developer,' she said. 'I just like hotels.'

'Which is why we're standing here today,' he said. 'How did your interest come about?'

'When we were on tour with the dance company we stayed in some of the worst accommodation you could imagine.' She shuddered in her exaggerated, dramatic way that made him smile every time. Her face was so mobile; she pulled faces that on anyone else would be unattractive but on her were disarming.

'Let me count the ways in which we were tormented by terrible bedding, appalling plumbing and the odd cock-roach or two. In one dump out west, we found a shed snakeskin under the bed.'

That made Sam shudder too. He hated snakes.

'Whenever we could manage it, a few of the girls and I scraped together the funds to lap up the luxury of a nice hotel where we lived the good life for a day or two.'

He nodded. 'I did the same thing in India. While we were working, we didn't expect accommodation any bet-ter than the people's homes we were rebuilding. When we were done, I checked in for a night at an extraordinary hotel in an old maharajah's palace.'

Her eyes sparkled green in the sunlight. 'Was it awe-some? I would so love to see those Indian palace hotels.'

'The rooms were stupendous, the plumbing not so much. But I didn't care about that when I was staying in a place truly fit for a king.'

'That's it, isn't it? It doesn't have to be bandbox perfect for a good experience.' She bubbled with enthusiasm. 'It can be something more indefinable than gold-plated taps or feather mattresses. On those tours, I really got to know what made a good hotel or a bad one—regardless of the room rate. When the chance came to work with Ben at Harbourside, I jumped at it. I had to train from the ground up, but knew I'd found the career for me.'

'You've never wanted to work at a different hotel? A bigger one? Maybe somewhere else—one of those Indian hotels, perhaps? Or even Sydney?' He fought a hopeful note from entering his voice when he spoke about the pos-sibility of her moving to his home city. There was no point. She was off-limits.

She shook her head emphatically. 'No. I want to work right here in Dolphin Bay. I couldn't think of anything else I would rather do than manage the new hotel. I want to make it the number-one destination on the south coast.'

She looked out to sea and he swore her dreams shone from her eyes.

But he was perturbed that her horizons seemed so narrow. In his view, she was a big fish in a small pond, too savvy to be spending her life in a backwater like this. And yet, despite that, her vision had been expansionary.

'What gave you the idea for this kind of resort?' he asked, genuinely interested.

She gave a self-deprecating shrug but he could tell she was burning to share her story. 'I saw friends flying to surf and yoga resorts in Bali. Others driving to Sydney to check in for pampering spa weekends. I wondered why people couldn't come to Dolphin Bay for that. We're well placed for tourists from both Canberra and Sydney: we've got the beach, we've got the beautiful natural environment. Get the eco credentials, and I reckon we could have a winner. Ben thought so too when I talked it over with him.'

'You've obviously done your research.' But as he thought about it, he realised there was something vital missing from her impassioned sell.

'You haven't actually visited the surf and spa hotels in Bali and Sydney yourself, by way of comparison?'

'Unfortunately, no.' Her face tightened and he could tell he'd hit a sore spot. 'I'm more of an armchair traveller. I know the best hotels' websites backwards, but I don't have the salary to afford overseas trips.'

He would enjoy showing her the world. The thought came from nowhere but with it the image of showing her some of the spectacular hotels he'd stayed in. Of taking her to the ones she'd dreamed of and ones she'd never imagined existed. But that went beyond the business brief of liaising on the hotel build.

'Maybe you should talk to Ben about your salary.' He couldn't imagine his old mate Ben would rip Kate off. But he knew only too well how tight-fisted some business people could be. His father had believed in rewarding people properly for their work and he'd followed suit. It was one of the reasons the company had so many loyal, long-serving employees.

Those people were why he hadn't immediately accepted the takeover offer. The owners of Lancaster & Son Construction had always prided themselves on being a family company, not only in the sense that it was owned by a family, but also because the people who worked for them were a family of sorts. Many of the staff would see a sale as a personal betrayal on his part. Worry about that was keeping him awake at night.

Kate shook her head. 'You probably know hospitality isn't the highest paying of industries, but Ben pays me fairly. And I've had the opportunity to learn the business from the ground up.'

'Soon you'll get the chance to see a hotel built from the ground up.'

'I can't wait to see it come to life,' she said, bubbling again with the enthusiasm he found so attractive.

She reached down for the clipboard she'd left on the bonnet of the small white van with the Hotel Harbourside logo. 'That's a cue to get down to business.'

'Fine by me,' he said. 'Fire away with any questions you might have.'

'Okay.' She looked up at him. 'Do I have to include the business questions in the questions I've got left with you?' She hastily amended her words. 'I mean, those questions wouldn't be about the actual building but about you. Uh… about you as our builder, I mean.'

'Fair enough,' he said. Her series of questions indicated

that underneath her businesslike attitude she might still be interested in him as a person, not just a contact. Though he doubted they'd be in one another's company long enough for her to ask them all.

'How long do you think it will take to build the resort?' she asked.

'From breaking ground to when you greet your first guests?'

She nodded.

'At least a year, maybe longer. This site is out of the way with a section of unsealed road to complicate matters in bad weather. That might pose problems with transporting equipment and materials. Then there's the fit-out to consider. You've specified a high standard of finish.'

'But you'll give us dates for commencement and completion in the final contract?'

'Of course. But we'll err on the side of conservative.' It was difficult to stay impartial and businesslike when the look of concentration on her face was so appealing; when the way she nibbled on the top of her pen made him want to reach over, pluck it from her hand and kiss her.

She scribbled some notes on her notepad. 'I'll include that in my report.'

Going on what he already knew about Kate, Sam had no doubt the report would be detailed and comprehensive.

'Talking like this makes it all seem very real,' she said. 'I'll be out here every day after work impatiently watching it go up. Will...will you be here to supervise it?'

He shook his head. 'There will be a construction manager on site. The team here will report back to Sydney.'

'So...you're just here for the one week?'

'That's right,' he said.

He wasn't sure whether he saw relief or disappointment in her eyes.

This was just one of many jobs for him but to her it was a big deal. He knew she wanted to do her best for Ben as well as make a mark for her own career. It would be best to be honest with her.

'Actually, there's a chance I won't be involved at all with the company by the time construction starts.' He kept his voice calm, not wanting to reveal the churning angst behind his words.

His obsession with the company had turned him into the worst kind of workaholic. Someone who, once his headspace was on the job, had pushed all other thoughts aside—family, friends, even his fiancée. His obsession had meant he had not been present at his father's deathbed. It had led his fiancée to dump him. To sell the company might free him to become a better person. But it could never be an easy decision.

Kate's eyes widened in alarm. 'What do you mean?'

'There's a serious offer on the table for the company.'

'You mean you're going to sell your family company?' The accusation in her eyes made him regret that he had opened the subject.

'It's an option. A decision I still have to make,' he said, tight-lipped.

She frowned. 'How could you do that when your father and grandfather built it up?' Her words stabbed like a knife in his gut. *Betrayal*—that was how people would see it. Like Kate saw it.

'Businesses are bought and sold all the time. You must know that.'

The words sounded hollow to his own ears. He knew what his father would have said—would have shouted, more like it. But he'd spent too many years trying to live up to his father's ambitions for him. The business was his now, to make the best deal as he saw it.

Her frown deepened. 'But surely not family concerns? It's…it's like the business has been entrusted to you, isn't it?'

What was she, the voice of his conscience?

'You could say that, but a company becomes an entity of its own,' he said. 'The multi-national company making the bid would grow it beyond what I could ever do in the current climate.'

'Bigger isn't always necessarily better, you know.'

He had no answer for that. Not when he couldn't understand why she wanted to lock herself away in a small town. But he *could* cut this conversation short, stop her from probing any further into the uncomfortable truths he had to deal with.

'That's beside the point,' he said. 'What I do with the company is my concern.'

Her mouth twisted. 'So you're telling me it's none of my business?'

'That's right,' he said.

Kate didn't know why she was shocked by Sam's revelation, or his blunt dismissal of the ensuing conversation. After all, her first impression of him was that he looked a tough, take-no-prisoners type of guy.

But then she'd seen a different side to his character with his talk of his volunteer work in India.

Who was the real Sam? Was she not the only one with lurking, unresolved issues?

She had to keep in mind he was a successful businessman. Could he have got where he was without elbowing other people aside, trampling over them, focusing only on the end goal no matter who might get hurt along the way?

But she didn't like the idea of him trampling over someone she cared about. 'What about Ben? That *is* my business. Ben trusts you to build this hotel. How could you be so...so disloyal to him?'

She didn't expect loyalty to her—after all, they were barely strangers—but the fact he could walk away so easily stung just a little.

His face was set rigid. 'There's nothing disloyal about it. It's business, pure and simple. Ben's a businessman himself, he'd understand that.'

'Don't be so sure of that. Ben wants you to build this hotel. Now I've met you, I...I want you to build the hotel. I call it disloyal if you hive it off to some other company we don't know.'

That scowl was back, his eyes bitter chocolate, dark and unreadable. 'Correction,' he said. 'You want the *company* to build your hotel. Not me personally.'

'That's not true. It's the personal connection that won you the tender.'

He towered above her. 'And I thought it was because of my expertise in building hotels.'

'That too, of course.' His glare made her fear she'd overstepped the mark. 'I'm sorry. I should back down.'

She was surprised that he didn't agree with her, remind her again it was none of her business. But she got the impression he carefully considered his next words. 'If—and it's still an "if"—the company is sold, the new owners will honour existing contracts and do exactly the same job as the company would have done under my direction.'

She exclaimed in disbelief. 'How can you say that? When our local deli was taken over by a bigger company, the first thing they did was sack people and the quality declined. Same thing happened with our garden centre. They were never the same. How can you be sure that wouldn't happen with your company?'

He paused. 'I can't be sure. If I sold, the new company would make certain assurances. But once new management was in charge they would do things their own way.'

'As I thought,' she said slowly. She dreaded having to bear this news to Ben.

'But as yet, I haven't made any decisions,' Sam said. 'That's one of the reasons I'm here, to take a break and think about the issue with a clear mind.'

Was that a crack in his armour of business speak?

'I still don't get it,' she said. 'Why would you consider selling, with all that family history invested in your company?'

'Try I'd never have to work again in my life?' His voice was strong and certain but the conviction was missing from his eyes.

She was probably totally out of line but she persisted. 'I don't know you very well, but I wonder if never working again would really satisfy you. What purpose would you have in life? I have the feeling you're not the kind of person who would be happy doing nothing.'

Sam's mouth tightened and his jaw tensed. She got the feeling she'd prodded a raw spot.

'Let me rephrase that,' he said. 'Selling would give me freedom to make my own mark, rather than carry on my father's vision for the company. To forge something new of my own.'

She paused. 'I guess there's that,' she said. She looked up at him. 'I might be speaking out of place here but—'

'But you're going to say it anyway,' he finished, with the merest hint of a smile that gave her the confidence to continue.

'Please think about it really carefully. Not just for Ben's

sake. Or mine. Or, I guess, the people who work for you. But for you.'

'I'll keep that in mind,' he said, his voice studiously neutral.

'Good,' she said. 'I don't know why, but I care about the effect it might have on you. You seem like a good person. And I reckon you might never forgive yourself if what makes your family company so special was to be destroyed.'

Sam swore under his breath. Every word Kate had said had hit home hard where he felt most vulnerable—and then hammered at his doubts and insecurities. How did she know how much he feared wrecking everything that was unique and good about his family company?

He'd known her for barely twenty-four hours yet straight away she seemed to have tuned in to the dilemmas that nagged at him regarding the sale. Yes, he'd seen moral outrage in those green eyes. But he'd also seen genuine understanding.

Frances, his ex-fiancée, would have advised sell, sell, sell. Not for the money, but to rid him of the business that she'd seen as a greedy mistress that had taken him too often from her side.

'You're a workaholic who doesn't care about anything but that damn company, and there's nothing left to give me.' Frances had said that on any number of occasions, the last when she'd flung her engagement ring at him. She'd never understood his compulsion to work that Kate had figured out within hours of meeting him. The compulsion he scarcely understood himself.

But he didn't welcome Kate's naive assumptions about the nature of the company deal. He didn't want to keep the business because of misplaced loyalty to an outmoded 'one set of hands on the steering wheel' management model. *He had to be one hundred per cent sure.*

'Thank you, Kate. You've made some good points and I'll certainly take them on board,' he said in a stiff, businesslike tone. As if the deadline for his decision wasn't already making his gut churn and keeping him awake at night.

'I'm glad you're not offended,' she said. 'I don't want to get off to a bad start for our working relationship.' Her brows were drawn together in a frown and her eyes were shadowed with concern.

'Not offended at all. What you said makes sense. I'm not the type of guy who deals well with time on my hands. I like to be kept busy. A day out from the office and I'm getting edgy already.'

He had started to pace back and forward, back and forward, in the same few metres of ground in front of Kate. It was a habit of his when he was stressed. He was scarcely aware he was doing it.

In silence, she watched him, her head swivelling each time he turned, until eventually she spoke. 'Do you realise you're wearing a groove in the sand?'

He stopped. 'Just making a start on digging for the foundations,' he said in a poor attempt at defusing his embarrassment with humour. As a CEO, as the child of a dominant father who had expected so much of him, he didn't like revealing his weaknesses.

She stared at him for a long moment then laughed. 'Okay. I get it. But if this is what you're like when you're meant to be taking a break, I'd hate to see you when you're on a deadline,' she said.

He halted. 'I need to hit the gym. Or the surf. Get rid of some energy.'

'If you really want to keep busy, I have a job for you that could fill a few hours.'

'A job?'

She shook her head. 'No, sorry, forget I said anything. You don't like waste-of-time wedding things.' She looked up at him, green eyes dancing. 'Do you?'

CHAPTER SIX

SAM GRITTED HIS TEETH. Kate so obviously wanted him to cajole her into telling him about the job she wanted him to do. If he played along with her girly game he could end up with some ghastly wedding-related activity like tying bows on frilly wedding favours, or adding loops and curls to his no-nonsense handwriting on place cards—all activities he'd managed to avoid for his own cancelled wedding. On the other hand, if he called her bluff and didn't cajole her, he'd always wonder if it was a job he might have enjoyed, that would have helped take his mind of the looming deadline for his decision.

'Tell me what you'd like me to do and I—'

'Okay,' she said with delight. 'I'd like you—'

He put up his hand to stop her. 'Before you go any further, please let me finish. I reserve the right to pass on any excessively frivolous wedding duty.'

She pulled one of her cute faces. 'Oh dear. I'm not sure if what I was going to ask you to do would count as frivolous or not.'

He tapped his booted foot on the ground. 'Try me.'

She gave an exaggerated sigh. 'Okay, then. That wedding arch.'

'The wedding arch you thought I'd come here to build?'

'The very same. Only there was never a wedding arch. That was me jumping to conclusions.'

'But now there *is* a wedding arch.'

'The more I thought about it, the more I thought Sandy would love a wedding arch. And, as you told me you could build one, I thought it might be a good idea. As a surprise for the bride and groom.'

He shrugged. 'Why not?'

'You mean you'll do it?'

'Yep.'

'Really?' Her face lit up and for a moment he thought she was going to grab his hands for an impromptu jig, like she had last night. But then she turned away, aware, no doubt, as he was, that it was inappropriate behaviour for a business relationship.

He realised that, again, his devotion to the company and company rules was squashing the development of a potential relationship with a woman. Did it have to be that way? Was there a way he could keep the company and conquer the workaholic ways that had led him to be single at thirty when he had anticipated being happily married at this age? Maybe even with a family?

'But won't it be quite difficult?' she said. Kate's words brought him back to the present.

'For a simple wooden structure? Nah. I reckon I could get everything I need at your local hardware store. Just give me an idea of what you've got in mind.'

'I've looked on the Internet and downloaded some images of beautiful arches for inspiration. I'll show you on my phone.'

'Okay,' he said. He liked to work with his hands. He found the rhythm of sawing, sanding and painting relaxing. Kate's 'little job' might be just what he needed to get the takeover offer into perspective.

'But I'd have trouble getting flowers and ribbons at this stage,' she said.

He frowned. 'Ribbons?'

'Sorry, I'm thinking out loud,' she said.

'Do you need all that stuff? I can paint the arch white.'

'Nice. But not enough. Not for a wedding.' She thought some more. 'I've got it—lengths of white organza draped around the poles. Simple. Elegant. Sandy would love that.'

Sam wasn't too sure what organza was. 'That's some kind of fabric, right?'

'Yes. Fine, white wedding-like fabric.'

'Then we'll have to make sure the arch is anchored firmly in the sand. If it's windy we don't want the fabric to act like sails and pick it up.'

'Oh no. Can you imagine the whole structure taking off and flying into the ocean?' She gracefully waved her arms in her long white sleeves, miming wings, and he could see the dancer in her.

He had been dragged along with his mother to see *Swan Lake* for some charity function; he was struck by the image of Kate in costume as an exquisite white swan. He wished he'd seen her dance on stage.

'Yep. I can see the headlines in the *Dolphin Bay Daily*,' he said. '"Bridal Arch Lost at Sea".'

'Eek! Please don't tease me about it. A wedding planner's nightmare.' She frowned. 'That really would be a disaster, wouldn't it? Maybe we should forget the whole idea of the arch."

'I'll make it work. I promise.' He liked it that his words of reassurance smoothed away her frown.

'Thank you, Sam. You're being such a good sport about this.'

She looked up at him and smiled and there was a long moment of complicity between them.

Working on the project meant more time spent with Kate. He shouldn't be so pleased at the idea but he was. He usually looked temptation in the eye and vanquished it. Not so when it came to the opportunity to spend more time with this woman.

Building a wedding arch was the last thing he wanted to do. Correction—the frilly wedding favours would have been the last thing. But he'd happily make ten wedding arches if it meant seeing more of Kate. He couldn't have her. He couldn't date her. He couldn't think of her in terms of a relationship. But that wouldn't stop him enjoying her company in a hands-off way.

'Okay, now that you've reassured me it will work, I'm so excited we're doing this,' she said. 'I can't wait to see the look on Sandy's face when she walks onto the sand and sees it there.'

'Let's get on with it, then,' he said.

And try not to think about what it would be like to have a hands-on *relationship with Kate.*

'So, show me the pictures on your phone,' he said.

'Sure.' She burrowed into that oversized handbag and pulled out her phone. 'Here they are,' she said, holding it up. He moved towards her so he could stand behind her, looking over her shoulder to her phone. He ended up so close, if she leaned backward she would nestle against him, as if they were spooning. *Not a good idea.*

He took a step back but then he couldn't see. He narrowed his eyes. 'The sun's reflecting off the screen,' he said. 'All I can see is glare.' He reached around her shoulder so he could cup her phone with his hand and shade it from the sunlight.

Bad move. It brought him way too close to her. He had to fight to ignore his tantalising proximity to her slender back, the curves of her behind.

Was she aware too? Her husky voice got even huskier as she chattered on, which made him suspect she was not as unaware as she was trying to seem. 'This one's made with bamboo but I think it looks too tropical,' she said. 'I like the wooden ones best; what do you think?'

She scrolled through the images of fancy wedding arches, but he was finding it too hard to concentrate when he could only think of the way-too-appealing woman so close to him.

'Can you see it?' she asked, swaying back. Now they were actually touching. He gritted his teeth.

'Yes. The wooden one is good,' he said in a strangled voice.

'Might the bamboo be easier for you to make?' she said.

'The wooden is fine. Easy.'

'So you don't like the bamboo?'

'No.' He couldn't care less about the arch. He could easily look up some designs later himself when he got back to the hotel.

'Can you figure out the measurements you need?'

There was only one set of measurements on his mind, and it wasn't for a wooden wedding arch.

'You have to allow room for both bride and groom,' she nattered on, while he broke out in a cold sweat. 'Ben's tall, but Sandy isn't wearing a big skirt, so...'

He couldn't endure her proximity for a moment longer. 'I've got the measurements,' he said abruptly as he stepped back.

He wanted to forget every rule he'd ever made and gather her into his arms.

But he couldn't. She was a client. And, while he still owned the company, he still followed its rules. He was stuck here in Dolphin Bay until after the wedding. He had to get through his friend's ceremony without there being any awkwardness. Kissing Kate right now would be ill-advised. Unwise. Irresponsible.

And he just knew it would be utterly mind-blowing.

He took another step back so she was more than arm's length away, so he could not be tempted to reach out to her.

She turned to face him. 'Are you okay with that? Do you need to see more?' Her face was flushed, her eyes wide, her mouth slightly parted. *She felt it too.* He was sure she did. Maybe she was more disciplined than he was. Because all he wanted to do was kiss her. Claim that lovely mouth, draw her close to him.

'No. I've got it,' he said.

'So, now we've settled on the style we—I mean you—need to start making it happen.'

'I won't be able to do it by myself. You'll need to consult. Approve.'

The flush on her cheeks made her eyes seem even greener. 'Of course,' she said. 'If we want to keep the arch a secret, we'll have to work on it away from the bride and groom. There's a big shed at home. It…it used to be my father's; there are tools in there.'

'Sounds good,' he said.

'I'll give you the address and you can have the timber delivered there.'

She looked around her and then at her clipboard. 'Have we done all we need to do for the site inspection?'

'For the moment.'

'Let's go, then. I'll drop you at the hardware shop. I'll look for the organza but I don't think I'll find it in the quantity we'll need in any of the shops here. I might have to ask Sandy to get it for me in Sydney on Wednesday. I'll tell her it's for the table decorations. She won't question that.'

'Hold on,' Sam said. 'Why wouldn't you buy it in Sydney yourself?'

Kate stilled and didn't meet his gaze. 'Because I...I won't be going to Sydney.'

'What?' He was astounded. 'For the stag night? Hen night? Hag night? Whatever they're calling it.'

Her freckles stood out from her pale skin. 'No.'

'But you organised it.' He'd been looking forward to getting her on his home territory. He'd even been going to propose they all stay at his apartment instead of a hotel. He'd bought the large penthouse in anticipation of getting married. It was way too big for one person; sometimes he felt as lonely there as he had in the palatial Palm Beach house. Kate could have her own room; there would be no question of any more intimate arrangement.

She shook her head. 'I organised a night out in Dolphin Bay. Not Sydney.'

'You're upset that your plans were changed?'

Colour rushed back into her face. 'Of course not. If Lizzie can't come here, you should all go to Sydney. But not me, I'm afraid.'

He drew his brows together. 'I don't get it. Don't you want to be with your friends?' He paused. 'Is it because you don't want to spend time with Jesse? He's the best man. It would be difficult to avoid him.'

'No. Jesse and I are fine with each other now. It's as if the...the incident never happened. He's as relieved as I am.'

'I was going to suggest I show you around the Lancaster & Son headquarters while we're all in Sydney.'

'That would have been nice. Perhaps another time?'

The stubborn tilt of her chin and the no-nonsense tone of her voice made him realise she had no intention of coming to Sydney. To party, to visit his office, even for a change of scene.

'Sure,' he said. 'But this would be a good time for a visit to the office.'

'You mean while you still own the company?'

It felt painful to think there could very well be a time when he had no connection to the company. But how could he keep the business and stop making the mistakes that had blighted his life because of it?

'That too. But at the beginning of the job. You could meet the team who'll be working on the resort build. That way they won't be strangers when they come to Dolphin Bay.'

'By the time we got up to Sydney and back the next day, I'd be away for too long. I'm needed here.'

'At the hotel? Surely Ben can organise someone to replace you?'

'Maybe. But it's late notice. I'm also learning how to look after Sandy's bookshop while she's away on her honeymoon. I love Bay Books.'

Everything she loved seemed to be in Dolphin Bay.

He remembered how she'd referred to Sydney as 'outside'. It had seemed odd at the time.

'I can't believe Ben and Sandy would want you to stay here working and not go to Sydney with them. You're their bridesmaid.'

'It's not just them. I have…other commitments here.'

'Commitments?' He suddenly realised how little he knew about her. She could be a single mother with kids to support. She could have an illness that required regular hospitalisation. She could belong to some kind of sect that didn't allow partying. Who knew?

'I live with my mother and sister,' she said.

Okay, it was unusual to be living at home at twenty-eight years old, but not unheard of.

'And they don't let you leave town?' he quipped in a joke that immediately fell flat.

'Of course they do. I don't let myself leave town because I'm needed here.'

He frowned. He didn't think he was particularly obtuse but he didn't know what she was getting at. 'I don't follow you,' he said.

'My mother and I share the care of my sister,' she said. 'She was injured in a car crash when she was eleven and left a paraplegic. She's confined to a wheelchair.'

For a long moment, Sam was too stunned to speak. That was the last thing he had anticipated. 'I'm sorry,' he eventually managed to say.

'No need to apologise,' said Kate. 'You weren't to know. Mum's a nurse and often works night shift at the Dolphin Bay Community Hospital. My sister, Emily, says she's fine on her own, but we like to be there when we can.'

'I understand,' he said.

Did he really? Sometimes Kate didn't understand herself how she'd ended up at her age living at home with her mother and her twenty-six-year-old sister.

Sam's brow was furrowed. 'But you lived in Sydney and travelled with your dance troupe. Who looked after your sister then?'

She wished he wouldn't ask the awkward questions that made her look for answers she didn't want to find. The more he spoke, the more she could see herself reflected in his eyes. And she wasn't sure she was at ease with what she saw.

'My mother. Then she broke her arm, couldn't manage and asked could I come home for a while.'

'How long ago was that?'

'Five years ago.' Right when she'd fallen apart after the near-assault and had left the dance troupe. She'd been glad for an excuse to run home.

'And you never left again?'

'That's right.'

'That's when you started to work for Ben?'

'Yes. Though it was only casual hours at first. You see, I'd dropped out of university in the final year of my business degree.'

'To join the dance troupe?'

'Yes.' There'd been so much more to it than that. But she wasn't ready to share it with Sam. With anyone. 'So when I came back, I finished my degree part-time at a regional campus not far from here.'

'And here you've stayed.'

'Put like that it sounds so grim. Trust me, it isn't. I'm happy here. This is a fabulous community to live in. And I love my job.' She tried not to sound overly defensive.

'If you say so.' He didn't look convinced. Who would blame him? Even her mother urged her to get more of a life. 'I'm not one for small towns,' he said.

'Dolphin Bay might not be for everyone but it suits me.'

'Sure,' he said. 'But I'm sorry you're not coming to Sydney for the party. Have you told Sandy?'

She shook her head. 'No, I haven't, and I'd appreciate it if you didn't tell her. I'll make an excuse at the last minute so she doesn't waste time trying to convince me to change my mind. Because I won't.'

'*I* can't make you change your mind?'

If anyone could, it would be him. 'Not even you.'

The knots of anxiety that could tie her up for hours were starting to tighten. She could lose control. She had to stop thinking about the trip to Sydney, not get caught up in that vortex of fear.

But right now she had to be cheerful Kate and put a bright face on it.

'Let's get moving, then, shall we? We've got a top-secret wedding arch to build.'

CHAPTER SEVEN

SAM NOTICED THREE things about the home Kate shared with her mother and sister as he approached it the next afternoon. The first was the wheelchair-friendly ramps that ran from the street to the house. The second was the riotously pretty garden and tubs of bright flowers everywhere. The third was the immediate sense of warmth and welcome that enveloped him when Kate opened the door to him.

'Come in,' she said with a smile that sparkled with dimples. 'The delivery from the hardware store has arrived. I got them to stack it in the shed out the back.'

She had only recently finished her shift at the hotel but had already changed into faded jeans and a snug-fitting T-shirt. The simple clothes did nothing to hide her shapely body. That was going to prove distracting. And yet even if she were dressed in an old sack he'd find her distracting.

It was getting more difficult with every moment he spent with Kate to think of her only as a business contact. He shoved his hands in his pockets so he wouldn't be tempted to greet her with a hug.

Inside, the open-plan house was nothing special in architectural terms, comfortably furnished with well-worn furniture in neutral colours. What made it stand out was that it had obviously been redesigned to accommodate a wheelchair—plenty of space left between furniture and the kitchen benches set much lower than was usual.

Framed photographs propped on practically every surface caught his eye: a wedding photo from thirty-odd years ago, baby photos—the adorable infant with the fuzz of ginger hair and gummy smile with tiny dimples already showing must surely have been Kate. There was another of Kate wearing a checked school uniform with her wayward hair tamed into two thick plaits. Kate with her arm around a younger girl with strawberry-blond hair. Kate, graduating in a cap and gown.

But the picture that held his attention was a large, framed colour photograph hanging on the wall of a young Kate in a classical ballet costume. The slender teenager was wearing a white dress with a tight, fitted bodice with gauzy wings at the back and a full translucent skirt. She balanced on pointed toes in pink ballet slippers. Her pale graceful arms were arched above her head to frame her face. Her hair was scraped right back off her face but glowed with fiery colour, and her green eyes sparkled with irrepressible mischief.

Sam gestured to it. 'That's nice.'

'When I was thirteen I was embarrassed when Mum hung it up so prominently. Now I look at that girl and think she was kinda cute.'

Sam's mother didn't like family photos cluttering up the house. There was just one of him as a baby framed in heavy silver on her dressing table. There had been photos of him in the formal blazer and striped tie of his private school, others of him playing football. They used to be in his father's study. He had no idea where they were now. He was gripped by a sudden, fierce desire to get them back. One day, when he had his own family, he wanted the living room to look like this one—not the stark, empty elegance of his mother's.

'You were lovely,' he said, then quickly amended, '*Are* lovely.'

'Thank you,' she said, looking wistfully at the photo. 'It seems so long ago now. I thought I was going to be a prima ballerina. So much has happened since.'

The time the photo was taken must have been around the time she'd shared her first kiss with Jesse. Again jealousy seared him. Unwarranted, he knew; he had no reason to doubt Jesse or Kate. Jesse had taken him aside and explained that, while he loved Kate like a sister, there was absolutely no romance between them. But still he felt uncomfortable at the thought of them kissing.

There was another equally large framed photo of an attractive, strawberry-blond teenager playing wheelchair basketball. 'Is this your sister?' She was holding the ball up ready to shoot a goal with strong, muscular arms, her expression focused and determined.

'Yes. Emily's a champion basketball player.'

He looked around the room. 'She's not home now?'

'No. She's an accountant at the bank in Dolphin Bay, so won't be home until this evening. Though you might meet Mum; she'll be knocking off from the hospital early today.'

'I'll look forward to that,' he said. He was curious about the dynamic between three adult women sharing a house.

'Come on,' said Kate. 'I'll take you out the back to the shed. I'm looking forward to getting started on the *amazing arch*.' She said the last two words with typical Kate exaggeration.

'So it's to be an *amazing* arch now, is it?' he asked as he followed her.

'Of course. After all, you're making it,' she said with that unconsciously flirtatious lilt to her husky voice.

'I'm flattered you're so confident in my abilities,' he said.

She laughed but, as she neared the old wooden shed at the bottom of the garden, her laughter trailed away. She stopped outside the door. 'I…I don't go in here often.'

'You said it was your father's workshop. He's not around?'

Kate looked straight ahead rather than at him. 'He…he was driving the car when Emily was injured. Another car was on the wrong side of the road. Dad swerved to avoid a head-on collision but smashed into a tree.'

For a long moment Sam was too shocked to speak. 'I'm sorry.'

'Emily was trapped inside the car. He…Dad…walked away uninjured. But Emily… Her spine was broken.' Kate's mouth twisted. 'Dad never forgave himself. Couldn't deal with it. Started drinking. Eventually he…he left. Six months later, he died.'

Sam found it hard to know what to say as Kate's family tragedy unfolded. 'When did that happen?'

Her arms were tightly folded across her chest. 'The accident happened not long after that photo of me at my ballet concert was taken.'

'That must have been tough for you.' He knew the words were inadequate but they were the best he could come up with. He had lost his father but it had been to a quick heart attack. He'd gone too soon, and he still mourned him, but the loss hadn't been in the tragic way of Kate's father.

She nodded. 'For me. For my mum. Most of all for Emily. She was in hospital for more than a year. Our lives changed, that's for sure.'

He longed to reach out and draw her into his arms but couldn't bring himself to do it. It would change things between them and he didn't know that she would want that. Or if he did.

Instead he pushed open the door to the shed. Inside it was neat and orderly. Hand tools were arranged on shadow boards. Nails and screws were lined up by size in old glass jars. He whistled his appreciation. 'This is a real man cave. Your dad must have liked spending time here.'

Kate hesitated, only one foot past the doorway. 'He liked making things. Fixing things. I…I spent lots of time in here with him. He taught me how to be a regular young handywoman.'

Just as his father had decided to make a man of him and introduce him to building sites.

Kate adept with hammer and saw? She continued to surprise him. 'That's a good attribute in a girl.'

'He wanted me to grow up as an independent woman who didn't need a man to change a tap washer for her.'

'And did you?'

'He left before he completed my workshop education.' Her voice was underlined with a bitterness he hadn't heard from her before.

'I'm sorry,' he said again. He realised that while he could handle disputes on building sites, or argue the fine points of a multi-million-dollar contract, he was ill-equipped to deal with emotion. Frances had accused him of being so tied up with the company he couldn't care about anything—or anyone—else. Perhaps she'd been right.

'He changed so much,' said Kate. 'Changed towards me. Became angry when he'd always been so even-tempered. I was okay, he was okay, but Emily was lying broken in her hospital bed. Survivor's guilt, I suppose now. But as a kid I didn't know about all that. In a way…in a way I was glad when he went.'

Sam stood silent, not knowing how to comfort her in her still-present grief, raging at himself that he couldn't. He was relieved when she changed the subject.

'Anyway, enough about that,' she said with a forced cheerfulness to her voice. We've got an *amazing* wedding arch to make.'

Kate found it disconcerting to have another man working in her father's shed—and totally distracting because the man was Sam in jeans, work boots and a white T-shirt. Strong, capable and utterly male.

For a moment it seemed like the past and present collided. Yesterday, she was the little girl revelling in being allowed to work with Daddy in his shed, her father kind and endlessly patient. Today the grown-up Kate was acutely aware of tall, broad-shouldered Sam dominating the restricted space. Sam, the successful—and possibly ruthless—businessman. Sam, the man who spent his vacation helping people in need. Sam, who had been so good-natured about agreeing to make the arch she was sure would delight her friends on their special day.

Her dad would have liked him.

She forced the thought away. For so long, her memories of her father had been bitter ones. Not that he had caused Emily's accident—his action in the car had saved her sister's life—but the way he had changed afterward. Had become someone so different he had frightened her.

But being here with Sam was bringing back the happy memories, memories of being loved and cherished.

Sam checked the delivery from the hardware store. 'It's all here,' he said. He looked around him. 'Your dad had a good collection of tools. That orbital saw is in good nick. I'd like to use it.'

'Help yourself,' she said. 'And anything else you need. Nobody else uses the tools.'

'Not even you? Not after what your father taught you?'

'No,' she said, her tone letting him know she didn't want to talk any further about her father.

She stepped back from Sam, though there wasn't much room to move in the confined space of the shed. Wherever she stood, she wasn't far from him. She was aware of his proximity, the way his muscles flexed as he hauled the timber into place, the way he looked so good in those jeans.

She liked the assured way he handled the pieces of timber as he showed her how he intended to construct the arch. 'There will be four sturdy supports and four corresponding brace supports across the top,' he explained, running his hands along the length of the timber. 'Building it with four supports instead of just two will make it much more stable.'

His hands were large and well-shaped, strong but deft. She refused to let herself think about how they would feel cradling her face, stroking her body...

'Tell me where you want to drape your fabric and I'll insert a series of pegs you can wind it around to keep it in place,' he said.

'That sounds perfect,' she said. 'Clever you.'

'The actual structure will be quite big and cumbersome,' he said. 'I'm going to use hinges so we can easily dismantle it to get it to the beach in your van and put it together again.'

'Good idea,' she said. 'We'll have to work on the logistics of that. Like, when do I attach the fabric, and how do we get it to the beach early enough so it's a surprise? We might have to let someone else in on the secret.'

Sam paused and looked searchingly at her. 'Have you spoken to Sandy about getting the fabric yet?'

She couldn't meet his gaze. 'I'll do that tomorrow.'

'Are you sure you won't change your mind about going to Sydney?'

'No,' she said firmly so he wouldn't be aware of the fear thudding through her at the thought of getting in a car and driving to Sydney. 'As I said, it's too inconvenient.'

'You'll be letting your friends down—'

She spoke over him. 'Don't you think I know that?' She wanted her voice to sound firm, even a little angry, at his interference but it came out shaky and unsure.

She turned her back on him and picked up one of her father's pliers from the shadow board. She remembered it was one of his favourite tools and hung it back again on the exact spot where he had so carefully outlined its shape.

She tried to avoid the empty section of shadow board where her set of child-sized tools had hung. Her dad had bought them for the birthday she'd turned eleven. After he'd left, in a fit of anger and grief she'd pulled them down and hurled them to the ground, wanting to destroy them. She didn't know what had happened to them after that.

'I see where you got your organisational skills from,' Sam said in a voice that was too understanding.

A voice that made her want to rest her head on his broad shoulder and confess how confused and scared she was. Tell him she didn't know what was wrong with her, that she was letting her friends down. How she was dreading letting Sandy know she wouldn't be going to Sydney.

Instead, she pasted on her bright, cheery smile and turned back to face him.

'Can I tell you again how much I appreciate you doing this for me?' she said.

'You're welcome,' he said gruffly and she knew she hadn't fooled him one bit. 'Now you've told me your dad taught you some handywoman skills, I guess I can count on you to help.'

'I'm not that great with saws or drills. But I can hammer and use a screwdriver, and I'll put my hand up for sanding.

I'm very good at sanding.' She picked up a sanding block from the bench to prove the point. 'The surface will have to be really smooth. We don't want Sandy's gown catching on it and snagging. Can't have a bride with a snagged gown—not on my watch.'

She was aware she was speaking too rapidly. Aware that it wasn't just from nervousness but acute awareness of Sam—his perceptive brown eyes that saw right through to her innermost yearnings; the heat of his powerfully muscled body that warmed her even without them touching. Just looking at his superb physique and so handsome face made her feel wobbly at the knees.

Towering above her, he seemed to take up every bit of the confined space. When he took a step closer it brought him just kissing distance away. She would only have to reach out her hand to stroke that scar on his eyebrow that she found so intriguing, to trace the high edge of his cheekbone, to explore with trembling fingers his generous, sensual mouth.

Looking intently into her face, and without saying a word, he took the block from her suddenly nerveless fingers and placed it on the bench. 'No need for that right now,' he said. Her breath caught in her throat in a gasp that echoed around the walls of the small space.

She didn't resist when, without another word, he drew her close, cupped her chin in his hand and kissed her. She sighed with pleasure and kissed him right back, her heart tripping with surprise, excitement and anticipation. Hadn't she wanted this from the day she'd first seen him?

His lips were firm and warm and, when his tongue slipped into her mouth, passion—so long dormant—ignited and surged through her. She quickly met his rhythm with her own, slid her hands up to rest on his broad shoulders, delighted in the sensation of their closeness.

This was how a kiss should be. This kiss—Sam's kiss—consigned any other kiss she'd ever had into oblivion.

His breath was coming fast and so was hers. Desire, want, need: they all melded into an intoxicating hunger for him.

He pulled her close to his hard chest and his powerful arms held her there, her soft curves pressed against him. His kiss became harder, more demanding, more insistent. She thrilled to the call of his body and her own delirious response.

They kept on kissing. But the force of his kiss pushed her backwards against the wall of the shed so it pressed hard into her back with no way of escaping the discomfort. Suddenly her mind catapulted her back to the farmer forcing his unwanted attentions on her. He'd backed her into a boot cupboard, confined, airless—like the shed she was in now.

Sudden fear gave her the strength to put her hands flat against Sam's chest and push him away. 'No!' she cried. He released her immediately.

Swaying, she gripped on to the edge of the bench beside her.

His breathing came fast and heavy; her own was so ragged she could barely force out words. 'I'm sorry. I'm so sorry, I—'

'I rushed you,' he said hoarsely.

'No. It wasn't that. Things moved so quickly. I was… scared.'

He drew his dark brows together in a frown. 'Scared? I would never hurt you, Kate.'

'I…I know that. It's just…' There was no easy explanation for her behaviour.

'Just what? Is there something wrong?' His voice was rich with concern, which only made her feel worse.

'No. Nothing wrong,' she lied. But she knew she should tell him that it was nothing he'd done. That it was old fears, old hurts, that were tethering her. 'Sam, I—'

At that moment her mobile phone rang. She picked it up and swore silently at the voice of the panicking staff member at the other end. She put the phone back in her bag and turned to Sam, unable to meet his eyes.

'Th…there's an emergency at the hotel they seem to think only I can solve.' She didn't know whether to be relieved or annoyed at the interruption.

'Go,' he said.

'What just happened—I'm sorry.'

'Nothing to be sorry about,' he said. 'You're needed at work. You have to be there. No one knows that better than I do. Work comes first. It…it always has with me.' There was an edge to his voice that made her wonder what was behind those words. Again she wondered if she wasn't the only one with secret hurts in her past.

'Are you sure you'll be okay here?'

'Sure. It will be good to get stuck into working on the arch. I want to get as much as I can done before I leave for Sydney tomorrow.'

Saying goodbye was awkward. Now there could be no denying their mutual attraction. They were not friends, so no casual kiss on the cheek. Not just business contacts, so shaking hands would be inappropriate.

The kisses they'd shared had changed everything, had broken the barrier of business that they had constructed between them and had left her wanting more kisses—wanting *more* than kisses. But she'd freaked out and pushed him away. What must Sam think of her?

The emergency at work took longer than Kate expected. The glitch in the online reservation system had required rather more than the tweak she'd initially thought. It was more than two hours later before she returned home. She headed for the shed but was disappointed to find it empty.

The pieces of timber Sam had been working on lay across her father's pair of old wooden sawhorses. Wood shavings and sawdust had fallen to the floor and their sharp fragrance permeated the room. Sam's leather work gloves, moulded to the shape of his hands, sat on the bench top. She picked one up. It still felt warm from his body heat. She couldn't resist the temptation to put it to her face and breathe in the scent of the leather and Sam. It was intoxicating.

Where was he? She was surprised at the depth of her disappointment that he hadn't waited for her. Had her reaction to his kiss made him leave?

Her mobile phone rang from her handbag. Her mum. 'We heard you come in. Sam's in the house with me and Emily.'

Of course.

Why hadn't she realised that would happen? She'd told her mother that Sam would be using the shed. Mum, in her hospitable way, would have popped in to see how he was and next thing she'd probably have invited him in for a cup of tea.

Sam looked quite at home on the sofa drinking tea, as predicted, with her mother and Emily. His big boots were propped by the door and he was in socked feet. She drank in the sight of him, looking so relaxed and at ease in her home. Her heart seemed to swell with the pleasure of it.

'Sorry, I got held up, Sam,' she said.

He immediately got up to greet her. His eyes connected with hers, probing, questioning. But his voice was light-hearted. 'As you can see, I'm being well looked after. Dawn's chocolate fudge cake is the ideal fuel for a hungry man.'

There was a tiny smear of chocolate on the top of his lip that she found endearing. She fought the impulse to lean over and wipe it off with her finger. Tried to fight the thought of what it might be like to lick it off, then follow it with a kiss that would show him how much she wanted him and negate the awkwardness of their earlier encounter.

'Sam was working so hard out there, I thought he needed feeding,' said her mother.

'Thanks, Mum,' she said. 'You always think people need feeding.'

'You mean you're going to pass on a piece of chocolate cake?' said her mother.

'Of course not,' Kate said, affecting horror. 'Bring it on, please.'

'Sam's been filling us in on your project,' said Emily. 'I love the idea of the wedding arch.' She laughed. 'Sandy's plan to have just her and Ben and Hobo on the beach with no one else sure isn't going to happen.'

'It will still be simple and intimate, but with just a few more guests and a lot more to eat afterwards,' said Kate, unable to prevent the defensive note that crept into her voice.

'Sandy won't regret it,' said Dawn. 'Your wedding day should be something really special you can always look back on with joy. Sandy will thank you, sweetie, for taking it in hand for her.'

'Did you say Hobo was going to be part of the wedding?' asked Sam. 'You mean Ben's dog?'

As a guest at Hotel Harbourside, he would be familiar with the big, shaggy golden retriever who was often to be found near the reception desk.

'Yes,' said Kate. 'He'll be wearing a wide, white bow around his neck.'

'If he doesn't chew it off first,' said Emily.

'How well trained is Hobo?' asked Sam. 'I'm thinking about the arch.'

'Oh no, you don't think he…?'

Sam shrugged. There was a definite twinkle in those dark eyes. 'Dogs and lamp posts. Dogs and trees. Why not dogs and wedding arches?'

Kate stared at him. 'Noooo! Hobo lifting his leg on our beautiful wedding arch in the middle of the ceremony? Not going to happen. Someone will have to make darn sure he stays on his leash.'

'Another job for the wedding planner,' said Sam. 'Better appoint an official dog minder and write them out a schedule of duties.'

There was a moment of silence. Kate saw her mother and Emily exchange glances. Did they really think she would take offence at Sam's teasing?

Emily laughed, which broke the tension. 'Sam, have you ever got Kate sussed out already.'

Her mother laughed too, then Sam, and Kate joined in. It was warm, friendly, inclusive laughter.

'Kate, we've invited Sam to stay for dinner,' said Dawn. 'If that's okay with you.'

Sam caught her eye. She could see he liked being here, liked her family. But he was waiting for her to give her okay. Had the kiss they'd shared made any difference?

'That's fine by me,' she said.

But she knew she'd have to be on guard all evening. Their passionate encounter had made a difference to her. She could no longer deny how strongly she was attracted to him. And she knew beyond a doubt she was in serious danger of developing deeper feelings for Sam.

CHAPTER EIGHT

TELLING SANDY SHE wouldn't be going to Sydney for the bridal party's night out was every bit as difficult as Kate had dreaded it would be. And then some.

Kate cringed at the hurt in her friend's eyes. Her excuses for why she was dropping out of the trip were weak and didn't stand up well to interrogation.

'I totally don't believe Emily needs you to be here with her tonight,' Sandy said.

Neither would her fiercely independent, mobile sister if she'd known she'd been used as an excuse. In fact, Emily would be furious.

'Is this about Sam?' Sandy asked. 'Are you mad at me and Ben for throwing you together with him?'

'Not at all. I really like him. Seriously, I do.' The cursed blush crept into her cheeks.

'Then *why?*'

I don't know! Tell me and we'll both know.

Kate bit down on her bottom lip to stop it from betraying her with an about-to-cry quiver. She felt so bad about letting Sandy down. But she'd suffered enough humiliation over the Jesse disaster not to want anyone—even Sandy—to know she couldn't even explain to *herself* why she was staying behind.

'I'm sorry but I just can't go. Can we leave it at that?'

Sandy eventually gave up her questioning. But Kate felt more and more miserable by the minute.

The wedding party had decided to go up to Sydney in one car. Kate stood in the driveway of Hotel Harbourside, perilously close to tears, as she watched Sam throw his overnight bag into the boot of Ben's big SUV.

Just as she thought he was about to leave, Sam turned and strode towards her. 'Last chance. Are you sure you won't come with us?' he said in a voice lowered for her ears only.

There was nothing she wanted more than to go with him. To throw herself into his arms and say 'yes.' But she was terrified of what might happen when she tried to get into the car.

Poor Kate.

In her mind, she could hear the shocked exclamations as if they were really happening.

No way would she ruin this moment for her friends, or endure further humiliation for herself.

She looked back up at Sam and mutely shook her head.

He met her gaze for a long moment, then frowned, obviously perplexed by her behaviour. 'Okay,' he said and turned away. 'I'll see you tomorrow when we get back.' He made no attempt to touch her, to kiss her goodbye. But then why would he, when she had so soundly rejected his last kiss?

Would he ever want anything to do with her again?

Shoulders slumped, she watched him head to the car. Ben and Sandy sat in the front and Sam climbed in with Jesse in the back. If she'd gone with them, would they have expected her to sit in the middle between Sam and Jesse? She wouldn't have let that happen. She would have wanted it to be just her and Sam.

As the car pulled away from the hotel driveway she

turned her back on it and dragged one foot after the other, away from the hotel. No way did she want to wave them off. She wished she could have gone with them to celebrate the wedding of two people she cared about, who both deserved their second chance at happiness.

But something she didn't understand was holding her back with a grip she seemed powerless to resist. She knew what would have happened if she'd tried to get into that car—pounding heart, nausea, limbs paralysed.

What was wrong with her?

She left the hotel behind her and kept walking, away from the harbour and along the boardwalk that led to Big Ray beach.

Had she become such a small-town hick she'd developed an aversion to fast traffic and bright lights?

She walked slowly along the beach, mid-week quiet with only a few people enjoying the surf, not taking her usual joy from the sight of the aquamarine water. She didn't even look out for the big, black manta rays for which the beach had been unofficially named.

At the north end of the beach, where the sand ended, she clambered over the rocks that divided Big Ray from the next beach. It was low tide and the rocks were fully exposed, smelling of salt and seaweed and the occasional whiff of decay from some poor stranded sea creature. She climbed down the final barrier of rocks onto the sand of the neighbouring beach, Wild Water, which had waves so violent and rips so dangerous only the boldest of adolescent surfers braved its waters.

Was it because she feared being alone with Sam?

With the rocks behind her, ahead of her was a stretch of white sand, bounded by rocks again at its northern end. To her right was the vast expanse of the Pacific Ocean. To her left was the freshwater river with its clear, cool water.

She slipped off her sandals and scuffed her feet in the sandbar that blocked the estuary of the river from flowing into the sea. The sandbar had appeared after the last big storm to hit the coast. It would just as likely disappear in the next one. In the meantime, the thwarted river pooled into a wide stretch of safe, shallow water. Her parents had taught her and Emily to swim here. She remembered again her father's endless patience and encouragement.

On one side were sand dunes, on the other bush straggled down a slope right down to the banks of the river, stands of spotted eucalypts reflected in the still waters of the lagoon. The beach bordered national park and there wasn't a building in sight. Sometimes kangaroos came down to the surf and splashed in the shallows, much to the delight of visitors, but there weren't any today.

This was one of her very favourite places. When she'd been on tour, tossing and turning in yet another uncomfortable hotel bed, she'd closed her eyes and envisaged its peace and beauty. In the first rapturous weeks of her romance with R—she could only bear to think of him by his initial—she'd told him about this place and suggested he come with her to see it. Thankfully he had scorned the idea, and that meant it was untainted by memories of him.

She inhaled a deep breath of the fresh salt-tangy air. And another. And another. Somehow she had to get herself together. If she couldn't get her thoughts in order here, she couldn't anywhere.

Dolphin Bay was her safe place. This place was her safest of the safe. But had she somehow transformed a safe place into a trap from which she could never escape?

Sam sat in the back seat of Ben's car, headed north to Sydney on the Princes Highway. There should have been laughter and banter as they started to celebrate in time-honoured style Ben and Sandy's last nights of 'freedom' from matrimonial chains.

But an uncomfortable silence had fallen upon the car.

Kate.

No one wanted to mention her. No one wanted to express their worries about why their friend had reneged on part of the wedding arrangements she had so wholeheartedly thrown herself into. He, who had known her for such a short time, was eaten up with concern about her.

How had she become so important, so quickly?

The car passed the last petrol station on the far outskirts of town.

'Stop the car,' Sam said. 'Can you pull over here, please, Ben?'

Ben did as directed, bringing the car to a halt on the side of the road.

'Do you need to visit the little boy's room, mate?' asked Jesse.

'No,' said Sam. 'I'm going back for Kate.'

The sound of the combined intake of three sets of breath echoed through the interior of the car.

'Good,' said Sandy at last. She twisted around from the front seat to face Sam. 'There's something wrong. I'm worried about her. Really worried.'

'Me too,' said Jesse. 'It's unlike Kate to pass on the chance of a party.'

'She wouldn't come to Sydney with me to help me choose my wedding dress, either,' added Sandy. 'At the time I thought she wanted me to have time just with Lizzie. Now I'm not so sure that was her reason.'

'Should we all go back?' asked Ben.

'No,' said Jesse. 'It should be Sam. When it comes to Kate, Sam's the man.'

As he got out of the car, Sam nodded to Jesse in unspoken male acknowledgement of what his words had meant.

'Tell her how much we want her to come,' Ben called after him. 'Kate's been so good to us. It won't be the same without her.'

Sam didn't have to wait long to hitch a ride back into town. Once back at the hotel he dumped his bag and went to look for Kate. Her mobile went to voice mail. Neither her mother nor sister answered the phone at their home. Finally, the girl at the hotel reception told him Kate wasn't on duty but that, after the boss and his fiancée had taken off for Sydney, she had seen her heading in the direction of the beach.

Sam strode out towards the boardwalk to Big Ray beach. The surf beach was practically deserted. He spied a lone set of small, female-looking footprints just above the waterline. The footprints tracked along the length of the beach right to the end where the rocks took over. Shallow, swirling waves were encroaching and starting to obliterate them. He remembered Kate telling him about the idyllic place she loved on the next beach. The footprints turned out slightly, ballet-dancer style. He took a punt they were hers.

Kate sat in the shade of a grove of overhanging gum trees set back from the water's edge. She wished she could have a swim but the one thing her capacious handbag didn't hold was a swimsuit. When she was younger she wouldn't have hesitated to strip off her dress and swim in her underwear in the welcoming waters of the lagoon. She would even swim nude on a day like this when there wasn't another soul in sight.

She wouldn't risk that now, not since R had insinuated into her psyche such doubts about her body, her sexuality, her desires. Not since her attacker had taunted her about her provocative dance moves and her immodest stage outfits.

These days she kept everything buttoned up: her emotions, her desires, her needs. She realised, with a sharp stab of despair, that she had barricaded herself against intimacy, against love, against feeling.

Against allowing herself to admit the depth of her attraction to Sam and enjoy to the full the pleasure of being in his arms.

She sat hunched over with her arms wrapped around her knees, lost in the thoughts that spun around and around in her brain. How had she come to this, sitting alone on a beach, when the life she wanted went on around her?

When she was younger the restrictions of small-town life had chafed her. She'd thought the best view she'd ever see of Dolphin Bay would be in the rear-view mirror as she'd left to go to university in Sydney. Back then, she'd been full of hope and ambition and dreams of seeing the world. She'd never imagined she'd come back to Dolphin Bay as anything other than a visitor to catch up with her family and old friends.

She shut her eyes. The muted rhythm of the waves crashing on the nearby sand was near-hypnotic. A breeze gently rustled the branches of the trees above her. It was like she was going deep inside herself to dark places she had never wanted to see again. Deep. Deep. Deeper.

She didn't know how much time had elapsed before the sound of dried twigs crunching underfoot and a shadow falling across her made her snap back out of the trance and her eyes flew open.

She blinked at the light and then focused on the unexpected intruder in her solitary reverie.

'Sam? What are you doing here?' She shook her head

to clear her thoughts, pasted on her best smile. 'This is a surprise.'

He smiled back—that heart-wrenchingly wonderful smile—as he towered above her, his strong, muscular legs planted firmly in the sand. 'What did I want to go to Sydney for? I live there. I can party in the city any old time.' He'd rolled up his jeans; he was barefoot.

'But…I saw you leave with the others…'

He shrugged. 'So I came back. I thought I'd rather stay in Dolphin Bay and count the seagulls—or whatever you do for fun in this part of the world.'

In spite of herself, she giggled. 'Stay still for a moment and you might see a goanna running up a gum tree. That's nearly as much fun.'

'Yeah. Right,' he said with a grin. 'I forgot to tell you, I don't care much for reptiles, especially huge lizards.'

'So you just happened to come upon me here?' she said. Her heart leapt at the thought he might have sought her out.

'I remembered you told me about this place when I asked you about good spots to swim. I figured I might like to see it for myself.'

'So where's your swimsuit and towel?' she said in mock interrogation.

'If I hadn't encountered a certain redhead, I'd planned on diving in without the benefit of swimsuit or towel.'

She couldn't help a swift intake of breath at the thought of Sam stripping off his clothes and plunging naked into the water. She had to mentally fan herself. 'Oh, really?' she said when she thought her voice would work again.

He threw up his hands in surrender. 'Okay. You got me. I came back for you.' His tone was light-hearted but his eyes were very serious.

'For me?' Her heart started to thud at twice its normal rate.

Now he dropped all pretence at levity. 'To see if I could talk you into driving with me to Sydney. Just you and me. We could join the others later.'

'Why would you do that when I'm just...just a business contact?'

He looked down at her and for a long, still moment their gazes connected so there was scarcely a need for words. 'I think you know we're more than that,' he said finally.

'Yes,' she said. 'I believe I knew that from the get-go.'

She went to get up but she'd been sitting in the same position for so long, her right foot had gone numb and she stumbled. He caught her by both hands and pulled her to her feet. When she regained her balance, he kept hold of her hands. She was intensely aware of his nearness, his scent, his strength. There was no terror, no overwhelming urge to break free from his hold. Not in this safe place. Not with Sam.

'Wh...what did the others think about you coming back for me?'

'They couldn't understand why you didn't want to go with them.'

She gasped and the gasp threatened to turn into a sob. 'Sam, can't you see it's not that I don't *want* to go to Sydney? It's that I *can't*.'

She tried to twist away from him, embarrassed for him to see the confusion and worry that must be only too apparent on her face. But his grip was strong and reassuring and he would not let her go.

Slowly, he nodded. 'I think I can see that now. Can you tell me what's really going on, Kate?'

The concern in his brown eyes, the compassion in his voice, made her long to confide in him, though she scarcely knew him. She couldn't lie to *herself* any longer that there was nothing wrong, so why should she lie to *him*?

She took a deep, steadying breath. 'I've been sitting here for I don't know how long, wondering what the heck has happened to me.'

'You mean, the way you're too frightened to go to Sydney?'

'Is the...the fear that obvious?' So much for her 'nothing bothers me' facade.

'Not immediately. But as I get to know you, I realise—'

'How constricted my life has become?'

'The way you don't seem to want to leave Dolphin Bay.'

She took in a deep intake of breath and let it out as a heavy sigh. 'As I sat here, I came to terms with how my life has become narrower and narrower in its focus. The truly frightening thing is that I realised I hadn't left Dolphin Bay for more than two years.'

He frowned. 'What do you mean?'

She disengaged her hands from his, turned to take a step away so she could think how to explain without him thinking she was a total nut job, then turned back to face him. There was no other way than to state the facts.

'Not just to go to Sydney but to go anywhere outside the town limits. I haven't been to any of the places I used to enjoy. Every time someone wanted me to go to Bateman's Bay for dinner, or to Mogo Zoo to see the white lion cubs, I'd find some excuse. I never made any conscious decision not to leave, it just *happened*.'

'Have you thought about why?'

She could see he was carefully considering his words. Something twisted painfully inside her. Did he think she was crazy? *Maybe she was...*

'I was beginning to suspect I might have some kind of...of agoraphobia. I...I looked it up at one stage. But I don't have full-blown panic attacks, or need someone with me just to go out of the house. I feel absolutely fine until I think about leaving Dolphin Bay.'

'It's not a good idea to label what you're feeling from looking it up the Internet,' he said, more sternly than she had ever heard him speak.

She managed a broken laugh. 'You're right, of course. Self-diagnosis is kinda dumb. But one thing that did give me a light-bulb moment was that agoraphobia—even in its mildest forms—can have had some kind of triggering event.'

'That makes sense. Have you thought back to when your fear started?'

'Yes.'

'Want to tell me about it? I've got broad shoulders.'

She shook her head, unable to speak. Ashamed of how she'd behaved, what she'd become, not so many years ago. 'It's…it's personal. We don't know each other very well.'

'Maybe this is one way to get to know each other better.' That damaged eyebrow gave him a quizzical look. If she ever got the chance, she'd like to ask him how it had happened.

'You might not want to know me better after I've cried all over your shoulder,' she said, trying to turn it into a joke, but her voice betrayed her with a tremor.

'Let me be the judge of that,' he said. 'We've all done things we've regretted, Kate. I certainly have. I reckon whatever it is that's causing your fear could be like a wound that's got infected. You have to lance it to let the poison out or it will continue to fester.'

'Maybe,' she said but didn't sound convinced even to her own ears.

'Look around us,' said Sam, with an all-encompassing wave of his arm. 'There's no one else to hear but me. And I won't be telling anyone.'

She'd held everything inside her so tightly. It might be a relief to let it all out. To Sam. 'Can we sit down? This might take a while.'

'Sure,' he said, casting his gaze around them. 'How about a comfy rock?'

She giggled again, aware of the trill of nervousness that edged it. 'This grassy ledge here might be more comfortable.'

'Much better,' he said, flattening the tall grasses that grew there before he sat down.

She sat down next to him, trying to keep a polite distance, but his shoulders were so broad, his arms so muscular, it was impossible for hers not to nudge them.

'C'mon,' he said. 'Spill.'

She still wasn't at all sure it was a good idea to talk to a man she liked so much about her time with another man. But maybe Sam was right—she needed to release the poison that had been seeping into her soul.

'I...I had a bad experience in Sydney, when I was at university.'

'With a guy?'

She shuddered. 'I can't bear to think about it. I can't even think about his name. In my mind, I only refer to him by his initial.'

Sam tensed. 'Did he... Was it...?'

'No. Not that. I was more than willing to go along with him. That's what makes it so bad, that I could have been so stupid.'

'Or innocent?'

'Maybe that too. I was in my third year of university in Sydney. We met on a vacation ski trip where we were all acting a little wild. He was the handsomest man I'd ever seen.' She snuck a sideways glance at Sam. 'Until now, of course.'

Sam snorted. 'You don't have to say that.'

'But it's true. Seriously.'

'Huh,' he said, but she thought he sounded pleased. 'Go on.'

'I fell for him straight away. Not only was he good-looking, he was funny and kind. Or so I thought.'

'But it was all an act?' Sam's face was grim.

She nodded. 'It was a...a...very physical relationship. I...I hadn't had much experience. He got me well and truly hooked on him and how he could make me feel. I became obsessed with him. It was like...like a drug. Being with him became more important than anything else. I started missing classes, being late with assignments.'

'And then he changed?'

She liked the way he seemed to understand, the way he listened without judging as she finally let it all out. 'It became a...a sexual power game. I wanted love and affection but he wanted something much...much darker than that. He...he had me doing things I'd never dreamed I'd do. Humiliating things. Painful things. But he threatened me that if I didn't go along with what he wanted I'd lose him.'

'And you couldn't bear that,' Sam said slowly.

She looked down at the ground between their bare feet, not wanting to see on his face what he must think of her. 'I thought I loved him. That I couldn't live without him.'

'And you thought he loved you too.'

'That didn't last. He'd been so full-on, but then he became distant. Unavailable. Not answering my calls. But when we saw each other, he'd reassure me nothing was wrong.'

'It was all about control. He wanted to keep you under his thumb.'

She gritted her teeth. No matter what Sam thought about her, she had to tell him the truth. 'I became so anxious that I turned into a person I didn't want to be. I became hysterical if he didn't reply to my texts. Stalked him to see if there was someone else. I dropped out of uni, didn't finish my final semester, just to be at his beck and call. What a fool I was.'

If that wasn't guaranteed to scare Sam off, nothing would be.

He shook his head. 'You were young and vulnerable, he was manipulative.'

'And sadistic,' she said, spitting out the word. 'My suspicions weren't unfounded. I discovered him with another girl. He laughed at my distress.'

'And that was the end?' Sam's voice was gruff.

'He still thought he could pick me up and put me down as he chose. But seeing him with someone else finally knocked some sense into me. To let him get away with that would have been a step too far on a path to self-destruction. I…I walked away.'

'Good for you to find the courage to do that.'

She managed a shaky laugh. 'Oh, I wasn't very courageous. I was scared of how far down I might let myself be dragged. I didn't want to go there.'

'But you did it. You broke the chains. You took the control back.' There was a dark intensity to his eyes as they searched her face.

'Yes. But university was a complete wipe-out. I couldn't stay there to repeat the subjects I'd failed, not when I'd see him around the campus. When the offer came to join the dance troupe, I jumped at it. I got away from Sydney and him and I didn't have to crawl home with my tail between my legs. People thought I'd moved on to something more glamorous and exciting than finishing a business degree. Only I knew what a failure I was.'

He frowned. 'You didn't tell anyone about what had happened?'

'There was a girl at uni who was very supportive. But we lost touch. I didn't really want to be reminded of the person I'd been when I was so obsessed.'

'You didn't tell your mother or your sister?'

'I couldn't bear to tell them I'd failed uni. They thought I'd dropped out because I wanted to dance. They still don't think any different. Still think I threw away my degree.'

'But that meant you didn't ever have to face up to what had happened?'

'That's right. I can't tell you how many times I wished I'd gone home then. Got some help. Because I didn't, it meant I didn't know how to cope with the next situation that made me doubt myself.'

She took a deep breath and edged away from him. 'But I think you've heard enough of my history for one day.'

He put his hand out to draw her back to him but then he hesitated, his dark brows drawn together, and dropped his hand back to his side. She couldn't bear it if he thought she didn't want his touch, his kisses, *him*. She took a step that brought her closer to him, her gaze locked with his. 'Hold me, Sam,' she said. 'Please?'

He put his arm around her shoulder and drew her back closer so her head rested on his shoulder. It was, indeed, broad. And solid, warm and comforting. 'You need to get all that poison out. If there's more, I want to hear it,' he said.

CHAPTER NINE

SAM HAD ALWAYS scorned the concept of love at first sight. In his book, instant attraction was all about sex, not love. The proof had been his parents' disastrous 'marry in haste, repent at leisure' marriage. And yet, although he wanted to kiss her, hold her, make love to her, he felt more than physical attraction for Kate—something that had been there from the first time they'd met. A feeling that was so strong, it made any further pretence at a business-only relationship seem farcical.

He was surprised and pleased, after the way she had pushed him away from their kiss the previous day, that she had actually sought his touch. He held her close to him, her bright head nestled on his shoulder, the folds of her blue dress brushing his legs, her hand resting lightly on his knee. He breathed in her heady, already so familiar scent. And he didn't want to let her go.

But this was no simple boy-meets-girl scenario.

Beneath that open, vivacious exterior Kate seemed to be a seething mass of insecurities, far from the straightforward person he'd thought she was. She'd been hiding secrets for years. Were there more? Could he deal with them?

With every fibre of his being he wanted to help her. But he didn't know how he could, other than being supportive. Nothing in his life experience had prepared him for this.

She shifted back from him, not so that she eluded the protective curve of his arm but so he could see her face.

'Can I tell you how good it is to talk to you like this?' she said.

Shadows from the overhanging trees flickered across her face. It made it difficult to read her eyes.

'If it helps, I'm glad.' He wasn't sure what else he could say. He risked dropping a kiss on her bare, smooth shoulder. She didn't flinch from him—that was progress.

'Are you sure you want to hear more? The second incident wasn't such a big deal. Not nearly as traumatic. I mightn't even mention it if I wasn't trying to find what triggered my aversion to leaving the city limits.'

'Bring it on. Did something happen while you were on tour with the dance troupe?'

Her hair was pulled back in a tie and he could see every nuance of her expression. She pulled a puzzled 'Kate' face. 'How did you know that?'

'Lucky guess,' he said, not adding that as soon as she'd started to talk about it her stilted words had become a dead giveaway.

'The injured ankle wasn't how my career as a cabaret dancer ended,' she said. 'Though I did hurt my ankle in a triple pirouette that collapsed in a less-than-graceful stumble.'

After the story of her abuse at the hands of her university lover, he wasn't at all certain he wanted to hear this double whammy, but he asked anyway. 'So how did it end?'

'After the injury healed, I joined the troupe again. They were about to go to Spain. I was so looking forward to it.'

'You would have gone overseas?' He couldn't keep the surprise from his voice.

'Yes. That's the crazy thing. I was so looking forward to it. Not a trace of this…this current affliction. We'd done a few weeks in New Zealand and I'd loved it. I'd even bought myself a "teach yourself Spanish" CD.'

The best thing, he figured, was to let her talk. 'So what happened to change things?'

'We had an extended stay at a club in a big country town in western New South Wales. There was a guy.' She rolled her eyes. 'Yeah, I know—another guy.'

'I should imagine there were a lot of guys interested in you,' he said drily. Smart. Beautiful. A dancer. She must have been besieged.

'Maybe,' she said with a wobbly smile. 'But I wasn't interested in *them*. In fact, after my experience at uni I'd sworn off men. I…didn't feel I could trust anyone.'

'Understandable,' he said, while thinking of a few choice words to describe the creep who had treated a vulnerable girl with such contempt and cruelty.

'There were often men at the stage door hoping to meet the dancers but I never took any notice of them. This guy seemed different. A gentleman. The Aussie grazier with the Akubra hat, the tweed jacket, the moleskin jeans. Older than the guys I'd dated. We had a drink after the show one evening and he was charming. He bred horses on his property and showed me photos. His historic old homestead, quite a distance out of town, looked amazing. And there were photos of foals. He asked me would I like to come and see the foals.'

'And of course you said yes.'

'Who could resist foals? They looked adorable with their long, baby legs. I couldn't wait to pet them.'

'You let down your guard.'

'He…he seemed so nice…'

'I can hear an "until" in your voice.'

Kate reached down to pick up a fallen eucalypt leaf. She started to tear it into tiny strips, releasing the sharp tang of eucalyptus oil to mingle with the salt of the breeze that wafted over them. 'Until he tried to kiss me and wouldn't take no for an answer. He wanted more than kisses. Got angry when I refused. Told me I was asking for it by dressing in sexy costumes and dancing provocatively onstage.'

Sam surprised himself with the growl of anger that rumbled from his throat and the string of swear words directed at her attacker.

'I used some of those words, too,' she said. 'But I got away, thank heaven. Luckily some sense of caution had made me refuse his offer of a ride to his place. I'd borrowed a car to get out there, so was able to get back under my own steam. The troupe left town the next day. I've never been so glad to get out of a place.'

'Did you report him?'

She shook her head. 'I was strong and agile and very angry—he didn't get anywhere near me.'

'You were lucky.' If he could get his hands on him, the guy would know not to go anywhere near her again.

'I know. I shook for hours when I got back when I thought about how differently it might have ended. He... he'd backed me into a boot room and closed the door.'

'That's why you reacted the way you did in the shed yesterday?'

Mutely, she nodded.

'Please tell me you confided in someone about the attack.'

'I didn't tell anyone. It made me look so stupid. The more experienced girls would never have gone off alone with a stage-door stalker.'

'He was cunning to use baby horses as a lure.'

'I know, which made me look even stupider for falling for it. And again, I began to doubt myself.'

'What do you mean?'

She got up from the ledge, threw the shredded leaf to the ground. 'The farmer guy was right in a way. Our dance costumes *were* form-fitting. Modern dance moves *can* be provocative. For one of our routines we had to dress as white poodles and bark as we danced. Can you imagine?'

She seemed determined to put a light spin to her story. She even took a few graceful, prancing steps on the sandy ground, mimed a dog's paws held out in front of her, her head alert to one side.

'You had to bark like a dog?' It took an effort not to laugh.

'Not just any old dog. A poodle. I listened to how a poodle barked in the interests of authenticity.' She paused. 'Go on—you're allowed to laugh. I get quite hysterical when I remember it. You'd be hysterical too if you saw us in those skin-tight white costumes with pompom poodle-tails on our butts and fluffy poodle ears on our heads.'

'I don't actually think I'd be laughing. It sounds very cute to me.' And very sexy. It wasn't difficult to see how a guy in the audience had got obsessed with her.

'There was a circus ringmaster cracking his whip as we danced and barked, which was kinda weird.'

This time he couldn't stop the laugh. 'I'm sure you made a gorgeous poodle.'

She pulled another of those cute Kate faces. 'You never know, I might do my poodle bark for you some time. I got quite good at it.'

He could only imagine. 'I'd like to see you dance.'

'Wearing a poodle costume?'

'Maybe. Or a white dress, like in that photo in your living room.'

This time the face she pulled was wistful, her eyes shadowed with regret. 'We danced *Swan Lake* that year for the end-of-year concert. I was Odette.'

'How fortunate that *Swan Lake* is the only ballet I've ever seen. So I actually know what you're talking about.'

'You won't see me perform it again. I stopped dancing soon after that near escape, even social dancing. The farmer guy's words kept going around and around in my head. Even though I'd been dancing since I was a child, I suddenly lost it. Became self-conscious, too aware of how I looked. How the men in the audience might perceive me. Scared, I guess.'

'Scared?'

'Scared of the next incident when some weirdo guy might think I was asking for it.' She paused. 'Now you know all my secrets. All my disasters updated.'

Sam jumped up from the ledge and took the few steps needed to reach her. But he didn't hug her close like he wanted to. Not when she'd just been remembering an assault.

'Kate, what that guy did was not your fault. What the guy in Sydney did wasn't your fault.'

Slowly, she nodded. 'I know. But, no matter how many times I told myself that, I didn't quite believe it. Was it something about me that attracted creepy guys? Why didn't I see them for what they were? Whatever; I couldn't get out there onstage and dance any more. I blamed it on my ankle but that didn't fool people for long. When Mum called to say she'd broken her arm and could I come home for a few weeks, I quit the dance company before they had a chance to sack me.'

'And you haven't danced since.'

'Sadly, no. I came back here where I know everyone and they know me. There were no opportunities to dance professionally. I'm qualified to teach dance but I didn't even want to do that.'

'And here you stayed.'

'No one knew what had happened to me—the abusive boyfriend; the scary experience with the farmer guy. Mum and Emily were glad to see me back. I was wanted, I was needed, and I just settled back into life here.'

'You didn't talk to anyone when you got back? Your family doctor, maybe?'

She shrugged. 'There was nothing to talk about. I blamed everything that happened on being away from home. Once I was home, it was okay.

'So you pretended it hadn't happened.'

'That's right. I felt safe here. Unthreatened.'

'I told you, small-town life is not for me. But, after dinner at your place last night, I can see the attraction for you. Your mum is such a nice lady—not to mention an incredible cook. And Emily is delightful. If I had a family like yours, I'd be tempted to stay here for ever too.'

But Kate was of an age when she should be making her own home. Thinking about starting her own family. *So should he.*

He realised with a sudden flash of clarity that the reason he spent so much time in the workplace was that it had become a substitute for family. At work he got recognition, admiration, companionship, security.

'Your family isn't like that?' she said, frowning.

'My family was so far removed from yours, there isn't any comparison. Home was like a battlefield where both sides have made a truce but occasionally resume hostilities. My mother was my father's second wife. He was still grieving his first wife when he met Vivien and—'

Kate put up her hand to interrupt him. 'Who is Vivien?'

'My mother. She doesn't like be called Mum or Mother—says it makes her feel too old.' He hated explaining it, as he'd always hated explaining it. Sitting in Kate's house, with her mother fussing over him with tea and home-baked cake, he had felt a tug of envy. His mother had not been the cake-baking, cosy type.

For once, Kate seemed lost for words. 'That's, uh, unusual. Even when you were a little boy?'

'Even when I was so little I had trouble pronouncing "Vivien".' He made a joke of it, but he'd never liked calling his mother by her name. If she hadn't wanted to be thought of as a mother, what had that meant to his identity as a son?

'You poor little thing,' said Kate. 'I mean you *were* a poor little thing. I don't mean you're a poor little thing *now*. In fact, you're rather big and—'

'I get it,' he said with a laugh.

Kate was back in full stickybeak mode but he had the distinct impression she was using it to distract him. 'You have to tell me more. We should shut up about me now. I still have one more question to go, you know; I've been saving it to find out about—'

He cut across her. 'We can talk about me later. Right now, we need to concentrate on you.'

She fell silent. 'Try to sort me out, you mean?' Her mouth turned downward so far it was almost comical.

'Don't be so hard on yourself. You were young, you had some traumatic experiences. You retreated to the safe place you needed to get over them.' She started to wring her hands together, something he noticed she did when she was upset.

'That safe place seems to have become a comfortable prison,' she muttered.

Without a word, he reached out and stilled her hands with his. 'That you now realise you have to release yourself from.'

He didn't know where these words of comfort came from other than a deep need to connect with her—maybe from his management training. It certainly didn't come from the tough love dished out by his parents. But it seemed to be helping Kate and that was all that counted.

She sighed. 'I'm angry at myself that I took the comfortable option instead of confronting my problems. Problems that, as you said, must have festered away.'

'Don't beat yourself up about it. Sounds like you've had a good life in Dolphin Bay.' He looked around him. 'Idyllic' really was the right word to describe their surroundings. 'There are worse places to be holed up while you heal.'

She slammed one fist into another. 'But it's not enough any more. I feel like I'm in a science fiction story where some big, transparent dome is over the town that only I'm aware of and I can't get past it. Meeting you has reminded me of what I'm missing out on.'

'True. For one thing, there's a whole, wide world of fabulous hotels out there for you to explore.' He kept his tone light, teasing, to defuse the anger she was turning on herself.

'You're right,' she said, after a long pause. 'Starting with that fabulous palace hotel in India. I looked it up after you told me about it. I so want to see it for myself.'

'I studied engineering at university, not psychology. But that seems to make sense. To go see a maharajah's palace is as good an incentive as any for you to break out.'

'I'm going to aim for it—something to focus on.' She looked up at him, her face still and very serious. Then she reached up and touched his cheek with her cool, eucalyptus-scented fingers. 'Sam, thank you for being the first person I've ever told anything about all this.'

Knowing he had helped her felt good. He caught her hand with his. 'Don't let me be the last. Talk to your mother. Perhaps even seek professional help,' he said. 'We really don't want you trapped inside that dome.'

'But only *I* can get over it. No one can do that for me.'
She kept hold of his hand as she spoke.

'You've taken the first step by realising you need help,'
he said.

Her eyes widened. 'Sam Lancaster, how did you get
to be so wise?'

'I'm not wise. I...I just like you.' Maybe that was all it
took—to care enough about another person to help her. It
might transcend everything.

'I'm glad to hear that. Because...because I like you
too,' she said.

Her eyes were in shadow but amazingly green, the
pupils very large as she looked back at him. Again, there
was that long moment of silent communication between
them. She swayed towards him. Before he could think
any further about it, he caught her and lowered his head
to kiss her, first on each of those delightful dimples, then
her pretty mouth. But this time, now he understood where
she was coming from, he held back so the kiss stayed tender and non-threatening.

She gave a gasp of surprise followed by a murmur of
pleasure as she relaxed into the kiss. Her arms slid up
around his neck and she pulled his head closer. The kiss
started as a light brushing of lips, returned tentatively at
first as if she were wary, then more passionately, perhaps
as she realised she was safe with him. Her warm lips,
the cool taste of her tongue, ignited his hunger for her. A
shudder of want ran through him as he deepened the kiss.
But as it became more urgent she broke away, gasping,
her face flushed.

'Sam. Wow. That...that was wonderful. Yesterday was
wonderful. And...and I wasn't scared.'

'You will *never* have cause to be frightened of me,'
he said.

He would do all he could to make sure she trusted him. But the confusion and doubt on her face made him realise it would not be plain sailing.

'Thank you,' she said and squeezed his hand. 'But I...I don't know that I'm ready for...for more yet. I...I haven't got anything to give you when I'm such a mess.'

He had trouble keeping his voice even, still reeling from the impact of her kiss. From knowing he wanted so much more. 'You're not a mess. You're a smart, special woman who just has the one problem to deal with.' He dropped a light kiss on her cheek. 'And I've got the takeover bid for the business looming.'

He should take his cue from her—the last thing he needed right now was the complication of a relationship. Not when he only had a few days to make a decision that would impact on so many other people.

Though wasn't he doing what he always did—using work as an excuse for keeping his distance?

'I guess we both have issues to deal with,' she said. She looked up at him. 'Sam, you've been such a help to me today, I'd love to be able to help you. If you want someone to talk over your business stuff with, well, I'm your girl. Not that I know anything about construction, but I could be a sounding board.'

'Thanks,' he said. He was touched by her offer, but the decision whether or not to sell the company his grandfather, his father and then he himself had invested their lives in rested firmly on his own shoulders.

She made a game of fanning herself with one graceful, elegant hand. 'I'm going to dip my feet in the water to cool off. Want to come with me?'

She walked into the ankle-deep shallows at the river's edge and he fell into step beside her.

Cooling off seemed like a very good idea.

* * *

Sam had kissed her again and Kate had loved every moment of it. There'd been no panic, no fear, just pleasure, comfort and excitement. But now wasn't the time for further kissing—though there was nothing she'd rather be doing. She knew, deep down, that until she sorted out her agoraphobia—if that was what it was—kissing Sam would only complicate things.

When she'd first seen him, her instincts had told her he was dangerous. Now she was convinced he wasn't dangerous in the way she had feared. The real danger was to her heart.

It would be only too easy to fall in love with Sam.

And she couldn't handle that right now.

To talk about all that stuff she'd kept bottled up inside her for so long had been truly liberating. Sam was a wonderful listener and seemed to have an instinct for drawing out her most painful memories. What she'd liked most was that he had given her good advice without judging her.

'When did you realise that Dolphin Bay had become a prison?' he said now as they walked hand in hand in the ankle-deep water at the edge of the lagoon.

'Only recently. The wedding has brought it all into focus. And…and it's only today, here by myself in this place that I love, that I realised how restricted my life had become. That…that it isn't enough any more.'

'You might have to dig down deeper under the scars from the past to find out how to fix it,' he said, obviously choosing his words carefully.

She turned away. 'You must think I'm a neurotic wreck.' She tried to make a joke of it, but her words came out as sounding anything but funny. With a tug to her hand, he pulled her back to face him.

'Of course I don't think you're a neurotic wreck. In fact, I don't know how you've held it together this long.'

'Obviously I didn't hold it together. I'm a recluse.'

'Where do you get these labels from? You're far from being a recluse. You have family and friends who all care for you.'

'I haven't dated for years, you know.'

'That I find very difficult to believe.' The admiration in his eyes took the sting out of her admission.

'I didn't trust my judgement. I couldn't tell the bad guys from the good guys.'

'Have you made a judgement of me?'

'You're...you're definitely one of the good guys.' Of her intuition, she was absolutely certain.

'Good,' he said. 'So where did Jesse fit in?'

'I've been thinking about that too. Trying to analyse how I got it so wrong.'

'Seems to me you got attached to Jesse about the same time as your dad moved out.'

She thought back to that traumatic time. 'Maybe. Everything else got turned upside down but my friend was still there. Stable. Secure. Maybe I got to believe all those family jokes about if we didn't each meet someone else we'd end up together.'

'Maybe that stopped you from getting serious about someone else.'

'You mean, after I came back here I used a crush on Jesse to protect myself from taking risks with other guys?'

'Could be.'

'It...it makes a strange kind of sense,' she said slowly.

Sam glanced down at his watch. 'Talking of Jesse, Ben and Sandy—if we leave now we can meet our friends in Sydney in time for dinner. What do you think?'

She swallowed hard at the sudden constriction in her

throat. 'I want to go. I really do. I feel sick that I've let them down—feel even sicker that I've let myself down with this stupid fear.' She forced bravado into her voice. 'Maybe…maybe I'm ready to try again. With you to hold my hand, that is.'

'I can drive us. But are you sure you want to go?'

She wasn't at all sure. But she was determined to give it a try. For Sandy. For Ben. For Sam, who'd been so patient with her.

She held on to his hand as they made their way back via the quicker route up through the bushland and along the pathways that led past the site for the new hotel. But, as they got closer to the town centre where she'd parked her car, Kate dropped his hand.

'I know it's ironic, as I'm the biggest gossip in town myself, but I've had enough of people talking about me,' she explained. 'I want to keep our…our friendship to ourselves.'

'Fair enough. I don't like people talking about my business either.' He stopped. 'But I do like holding your hand,' he said with a grin that warmed her heart.

Kate was okay getting into her car and driving home with Sam seated next to her. She was okay packing an overnight bag while Sam checked on his carpentry work out in the shed. She only started to get shaky as she drove back to the hotel to transfer to Sam's sports car.

'You okay?' he asked.

'Yep,' she said, pasting on that cheerful smile, hoping it would give her the courage and strength she so severely lacked.

But as soon as Sam opened the passenger door for her to get in she was again gripped by fear. As she went to slide into the seat, her knees went to jelly. Nausea rose in her throat and she started to shake.

She gasped for air. 'I can't do it, Sam. I thought I could, but I can't.'

He pulled her out of the car and held her to him, patting her on the back, making soothing, wordless sounds until the shaking stopped. She relaxed against him, beyond caring who saw her or what they might say.

'Too much, too soon,' he said.

She pulled away. 'Maybe,' she said. 'But I'm so angry with myself, so disappointed…'

'So we don't go to Sydney. What's the fuss?'

'You could still go. You've got plenty of time to get up there.'

'What's the point of a groomsman going out on the town without his bridesmaid?'

'You can still have fun in Sydney. Lizzie booked a really nice venue.'

'No arguments. I can go out in Sydney any time. I'm staying here with you.'

'But—'

He placed his index finger over her lips. 'No buts. We're going to look at this afternoon like it's a bonus. It gives us more time to spend working on the arch.'

She took a few more deep breaths, felt her heart rate returning to normal.

'I haven't shown you yet how good I am as a handy-woman.'

'Now's your chance,' he said. 'Then we're going to go on that date.'

'Wh-what about your no dating rule?'

'I own the company; I make the rules. I say to hell with that rule—as least, as it applies to you. I'm taking you out to dinner. We'll have our own party.'

She laughed with relief and a bubbling excitement. 'As Ben so obviously tried to set me up with you, I don't think there's a "no dating Sam" rule in place. It was more my own...my own fears giving me an excuse.'

'Let's book the best restaurant in Dolphin Bay.'

'The Harbourside is the best restaurant,' she said loyally.

'Okay—the second-best restaurant in Dolphin Bay,' he said. 'Or Thai take-out on the pier. Or fish and chips at the pub. Your choice.'

She smiled, relieved she could feel normal again, excited at the thought of dinner with Sam. 'I'm overwhelmed by the responsibility of the decision. But Thai does sound kind of tempting.'

'Thai it is—and lots of it. I'm starving.'

'Are you always hungry?'

'Always,' he said.

She laughed. 'I'm really getting to know you, aren't I?'

While she kept a happy smile pasted to her face, inside Kate wasn't so happy. The more she got to know Sam, the more she liked him.

But what future could there be for a man who travelled the world and a girl who was too scared to go further than the outskirts of her home town?

CHAPTER TEN

SANDY HAD BEEN RIGHT, Kate realised on the day of the wedding. A wedding *was* more fun for a bridesmaid when she had a handsome groomsman in tow. It was also more fun for a wedding planner when that groomsman had volunteered to be her helper—not only with the construction of the bridal arch, but also with other last-minute jobs along the way.

Not that Sam and she had spent much time together since their Thai take-out dinner. She'd still had her shifts at the hotel. And Sam had seemed to be in one conference call or video call after another. So much for that break from his business.

But, despite his grumbling about waste-of-time wedding fripperies, Sam had not only finished the arch but had also helped Sandy and her with writing the place cards and Emily with counting out the sugared almonds to put in the tulle-wrapped wedding favours. He had, however, point-blank refused to tie pretty pastel ribbons on them.

Now Ben and Sandy's big day was here. Dolphin Bay had, thank heaven, put on its finest weather for the last weekend of daylight saving time—although Kate didn't take the good weather for granted. With a ceremony being held outdoors on the beach, she'd planned alternative arrangements to cover all contingencies, from heatwave to hailstorm.

At noon she was still in the function room at the Hotel Harbourside, where the reception was to be held, making final checks on the arrangements for the buffet-style meal.

Sliding doors opened out onto an ocean-facing balcony that gave a good view of the ceremony site on the beach below. Every few minutes she dashed out to see if the sky was indeed still perfectly blue and free of clouds, the wind still the gentle zephyr that would not make an organza-adorned arch suddenly become airborne as the bride and groom exchanged their vows. Not unnecessary anxiety, she told herself, for a wedding scheduled to start in just four hours.

Everything that could be checked off on her multiple pages of lists had been checked off. Everyone who had needed to be briefed on their wedding duties had been briefed. Now it was time for the hotel staff to take over. And for her to start having fun.

But, as she headed for the door that led into the hotel corridor, she couldn't resist turning back and picking up a silver serving platter to see if it had been polished as directed. She peered closely at it, fearing she saw a scratch.

'Ready to stop being an obsessive wedding planner and start being a bridesmaid? I've been dispatched to find you.' Sam's deep, resonant voice coming from behind her made her jump so she nearly dropped the platter. She hadn't heard him come in.

She turned to face him and halted halfway. Her heart seemed to stop as it always did at the first sight of this man who took up so much space in her thoughts. He'd shaved and had had his hair cut. She smiled. 'You look different,' she said, after a long moment when her heartbeat had returned somewhat to normal. 'Just as handsome, but different.'

And even hotter than when she'd last seen him.

'I'm taking my groomsman duties seriously,' Sam said. 'Ben wanted me clean shaven, so I got clean shaven.'

She was unable to resist reaching up and tracing the smooth line of his jaw with her fingers. She would have liked to kiss him, but two of the waiting staff were polishing champagne flutes at the other end of the room. 'You look more corporate than carpenter and that takes a little getting used to. But I like it. And the haircut. Though, I have to say, I really liked the stubble.'

'I guarantee that'll be back by morning,' he said with a grin.

"Good," she said.

She put her hand on his arm. 'Are you okay with all this wedding stuff? I mean, it isn't weird for you when your own wedding was cancelled? I hate to think it might bring back sad memories.'

'I'm good with it. I wasn't actually there for all my own wedding preparations. I was working in Queensland or Western Australia, or Singapore or somewhere else far away.'

'Your fiancée mustn't have been too happy about that.'

'She wasn't. To the point she accused me of being so uninvolved with the preparations, she didn't think I was interested in the wedding or, ultimately, truly interested in her.'

Kate didn't know what she could say to that other than a polite murmur. 'I see.'

'Her tipping point was when I couldn't make the rehearsal because it clashed with an important business engagement.'

Suddenly Kate felt more than a touch of sympathy for

Sam's unknown fiancée. 'I would have been furious if I were her.'

'She was. That's when she threw her engagement ring at me and told me the wedding was off.'

'And you were surprised?'

'Well, yes.'

'Now that you've had time to reflect about it, are you still surprised?'

He grinned. 'No.'

'Good. I would have had to revise my opinion of you if you had said yes.'

'I've had plenty of time to reflect that I was a selfish workaholic, too obsessed with proving myself to my father to be a good boyfriend or a good fiancé. Certainly, I wouldn't have been a good husband.'

'So you weren't really ready to get married?'

'Probably not. But I've also had time to think about whether Frances was right. Maybe...maybe I just didn't love her enough to make that level of commitment and subconsciously used work as an excuse.' He paused and she could see remembered pain in his eyes. 'I was gutted at the time, though. We'd been together for years.'

'Would you say you're still a selfish workaholic?' Kate asked, unable to stop a twinge of jealousy at the thought of the woman who'd shared Sam's life for so long.

'Probably. That's one reason I'm considering selling the company. I suspect I've given too much of my life to it—given it too much importance at the cost of other more important things.'

Kate was just about to reply when a tall, slender girl with a mop of silvery blonde curls poked her head around the door. 'There you are, Kate. The hairdresser, make-up artist and manicurist are all waiting for us.' Lizzie scowled at Sam. 'You, Sam, were charged with getting Kate up to

Sandy's suite,' she scolded. 'We've got secret bridesmaids' business to attend to.'

Kate put up her hand. 'Just one more minute, Lizzie,' she said.

Lizzie folded her arms in front of her chest and ostentatiously tapped her foot. 'I'm going to wait right here to make sure you don't disappear.'

Kate leaned up to whisper in Sam's ear. 'Is everything okay with the arch?'

'Yes,' he murmured. 'Your mother and a friend from the hospital—some guy named Colin—are going to drive the van down to the beach. I'll slip out at the time we arranged and they'll help me install it.'

'Fantastic. Thank you,' she whispered. 'I can't wait to see it.'

'Hurry up, Kate,' urged Lizzie.

'Okay, okay,' said Kate and fled the room.

Sam hadn't been one hundred per cent honest with Kate. The frenzied wedding activities *had* brought back memories of his own abruptly terminated nuptials nearly two years ago.

Seeing at close quarters the levels of planning that went into even a simple ceremony like Ben and Sandy's made him realise how badly he'd neglected Frances in the months leading up to their big, showy wedding. On many of the times she'd asked for a decision, he'd brushed her aside with his stock replies: 'You decide,' or 'I'll leave it to you.' He hadn't cooperated with his mother, either, who had thrown herself into the elaborate preparations with great gusto. With hindsight, he realised his mother had done a lot to help Frances when it should have been *him* doing the helping.

Thinking about how he'd behaved made him feel

vaguely ashamed. At the time, he had paid lip service to
an apology. But, feeling aggrieved, he hadn't really been
sure what he had done to deserve the cancellation of his
wedding and the dumping by his fiancée.

Being around Kate, her family and friends made him
realise exactly what he'd done wrong. And that he'd be
damned sure he got it right the next time round.

Being around Kate was also making him question how
he'd felt about his former fiancée. After several years together, he had never felt for Frances what he already felt
for Kate. If he were about to marry Kate—and of course
that was purely a hypothetical situation—no way would he
be away in another country. He would want to be with his
bride-to-be every minute, working alongside her to plan
their future together. *Hypothetically, of course.*

Now he stood barefoot on the sand, lined up with Ben
and Jesse under the arch he had built with Kate in her father's shed. It held firm in the breeze coming off the waters of the bay. Ben, in that jesting way of good mates, had
told him that he had a bright future ahead of him making
gimcracks for weddings. Because it was Ben's day, he had
let him get away with it.

The three men waited for the bridesmaids and then the
bride to walk down the sandy aisle that had been formed
between rows of folding white chairs and delineated with
two rows of sea shells.

Suddenly the guests swivelled around to a collective
sigh. 'Oohs' and 'aahs' greeted the sight of Lizzie's five-
year-old daughter, Amy. But, by the time Amy was halfway down the aisle, Sam only had eyes for the beautiful
red-haired bridesmaid who followed her.

He'd never understood the expression 'took his breath
away' until now. In bare feet, Kate moved like the dancer
she was, seeming to glide along the sand towards him.

Her strapless peach dress showed off her graceful shoulders and arms, and clung to her curves before it ended just below her knees. Her hair, pulled up off her face with some of it tumbling down her shoulders, shone like a halo in the afternoon sun.

Her glorious smile captivated him as it had the first time he'd seen her. Only this time her smile seemed only for him. Somehow, with just a glance, she seemed to convey how happy she was to be sharing this day with him. He smiled back, unable to take his eyes off her. When she reached the arch, he stepped forward to offer her his arm to guide her to the bride's side of the area. He had to resist a strong impulse to gather her to him and keep her by his side, an arm planted possessively around her waist.

Kate couldn't help a moment of self-congratulation at how well the shades of the sunset colour-scheme worked. She herself wore apricot, Lizzie a shade that veered towards tangerine and little Amy's white dress had a big bow in a pale tint of magenta. The three men were handsome in chinos and loose white shirts. But Sam was the one who made her heart race, who made her aware of where he was at all times without her even having to look.

She kept sneaking sideways glimpses at him, glances that were often intercepted and ended in secret smiles. Every minute she knew him, he seemed to grow more attractive. Not just in his looks but also in his personality, which was funnier, kinder and more thoughtful than she could have imagined—though she didn't let herself forget there must be a ruthless side to him too.

For a moment, when he had stepped forward to take her arm, she had indulged in a fantasy of what it might be like if she'd been walking up an aisle to meet him as her groom. She had immediately dismissed the thought as impossible but its warmth lingered in her mind. How was she going to endure it when he went back to Sydney the next day?

She forced her gaze away from Sam and straight ahead to where Sandy was about to commence her walk down the aisle.

But first it was Hobo's turn. Ben's mother Maura—officially appointed by Kate as dog-handler—had spent days training Hobo to sedately stroll down the aisle and take his place with Ben under the arch. The big, shaggy golden retriever—wearing a white ribbon around his neck, slightly chewed around the ends—started off fine, sitting as directed at the head of the aisle, giving the guests a big, doggy smile. There was a furious clicking of cameras.

'Good boy, Hobo,' Kate heard Maura whisper. But her praise was premature. Hobo caught sight of Ben, lolloped off down the aisle and came to a skidding halt next to his master's feet, spraying sand around him as he landed.

The guests erupted into laughter and Sandy was laughing too as she started her walk down the aisle. It was a perfect start to the ceremony, Kate thought, the laughter vanquishing any last-minute nerves or tension.

When Ben and Sandy exchanged their vows in front of the celebrant, there wasn't a sound except their murmured 'I do'—and the occasional muffled sob and sniffle from the guests.

As she watched them, Kate was tearing up too. She couldn't help an ache in her heart—not from envy of the bride and groom but a longing for the same kind of happiness for herself one day. She'd never really let herself imagine being married, having children, but of course she wanted all that one day.

She just had to get the man right.

She stole another surreptitious glance at Sam, to find

him looking to her too. Did she imagine a hint of the same longing in his eyes? *If only...*

Weddings seemed to dredge up so many deeply submerged emotions and bring them to the surface. She had to be careful she didn't let her imagination run riot and believe Sam felt in any way the same as she did.

But, when the newlyweds moved off to the small table they had set up for the signing of the official papers, Sam was next to her the first second he could be. He interlinked his fingers with hers and drew her to him for a swift, sweet kiss. 'You outshone the bride,' he murmured.

She protested, of course, but was deeply, secretly pleased. She wondered if anyone had noticed their kiss but decided she didn't care. Forget the 'poor Kate' whispers. She reckoned there was more likely to be whispers of 'lucky Kate'.

She *was* lucky to have met him. And, if tonight was the only time she ever had with Sam, she was going to darn well enjoy every minute of it.

CHAPTER ELEVEN

SAM FELT A certain envy at the newlyweds' obvious joy in each other. Being part of the wedding ceremony had stirred emotions in him he'd had no idea existed. Above all, it had forced him to face up to what he could not continue to deny to himself: he was besotted with Kate. No matter how much he fought the concept, he had fallen fast and hard for her.

From his seat at the bride and groom's table he watched Kate as she flitted her way around the wedding reception like a bright flame; her hair, her dress, her smile made her easy to pick out in the crowd.

'She's a great girl, isn't she?' said Lizzie, who was sitting next to him. Was it so obvious that he couldn't keep his eyes off Kate?

'Yup,' he said, not wanting to be distracted.

Lizzie laughed. 'Don't worry, your secret is safe with me.'

He twisted to face her. 'What do you mean?'

'That you're smitten with Kate.' He started to protest but she spoke over him. 'Don't worry. I don't think too many other people have noticed. They're all still determined to pair her off with the home-town favourite, Jesse Morgan. I don't know how Kate feels about that. I thought that might have been the reason why she didn't come up to Sydney on Wednesday.'

A tightness in her voice made Sam look more closely at Lizzie. 'Kate likes him as a friend, almost a brother, that's all.' He was surprised by the flash of relief that flickered across Lizzie's face. 'But you—you like Jesse?'

She flushed. 'Of course I don't. He's arrogant. A player. Much too handsome for his own good and way too sure of himself.'

Sam stored her excessive denial away to share with Kate later. In the meantime, he had to stick up for his friend. 'Actually, Jesse is a mate of mine and a really good guy. He's confident, not arrogant. And he's not a player.'

Lizzie snorted. 'I'll have to take your word for it.'

Lizzie had an acerbic edge to her and possibly too many glasses of champagne on board. Sam decided he didn't want to engage in any further discussion about Jesse. He was relieved when she excused herself to go and have a word with her sister.

He drummed his fingers on the tabletop and wished Kate would come back to her chair. Ideally, he wanted her to be by his side all evening, but that wasn't going to happen—not with the number of people who were waylaying her for a chat. She knew everyone and they knew her. No wonder she had found it so easy to stay in this town for so long; there was no denying the sense of community.

But could he live here?

Despite his aversion to small-town life, it was a question he had to ask himself. What if Kate was unable to get over her problem, to get out from under that invisible dome? The way he felt about her, he would find it untenable for them not to be in the same town if anything developed between them. If she couldn't come to him in Sydney, might he have to come to her in Dolphin Bay?

If it meant being with Kate, he had to consider it.

When his father had had one too many drinks, he'd

sometimes decided to give his son advice on women. It
had always been the same—telling Sam to be sure he knew
a woman really well before he considered commitment.
The old 'marry in haste, repent at leisure' thing would inevitably come up. His dad had adored his first wife, the
only blight on the marriage being the fact they hadn't had
children. He had been devastated when she'd died, had not
been able to handle being on his own. Quite soon after,
he'd met Vivien and had married her within months. By
the time they'd realised it was a mistake, Sam had been
on the way. They'd never actually said so, but he'd come
to believe his parents had only stayed together for their
child's sake.

Sam wasn't ready to propose to Kate after only a week.
That would be crazy. But he didn't want to wait for ever
to have her beside him, sharing his life.

*He wanted what Ben and Sandy had, and he wanted
it with Kate.*

Kate slid into the chair beside him and hooked her arm
through his. 'My mouth is aching from smiling so much
and I'm not even the bride,' she said. 'Are you having fun?'

'Now you're back with me, the fun is back on track,'
he said.

'The perfect reply,' she said, with the full-on dimpled
smile that was getting such a workout. This was the vivacious, bubbly Kate everyone knew. Looking at her flushed,
happy face, it was difficult to believe she had secrets that
haunted her.

'You must be pleased at how well everything is going,'
he said. 'Congratulations to the wedding planner.'

'Congratulations to the world's best wedding-arch
builder,' she said. 'It was a big hit.'

'I'm glad we made the effort.' He realised he had fallen
into talking about 'we'—and he liked the feeling.

'Clever us.' She sighed. 'I can't believe how fast it's gone. All that work and it's over in a matter of hours. But now the speeches are done, the band is starting up and we can all relax.'

On cue, the band started to play and the MC announced it was time for the bride and groom to dance the first dance to a medley of popular love songs.

Sam noticed Kate go so pale, her freckles stood out. She looked anything but relaxed. 'Are you okay?'

He noticed she was wringing her hands together under the table. 'I didn't think this through,' she said in an undertone. 'According to the order of the reception, the best man and chief bridesmaid will get up to dance next. Then they'll expect you and me to get up.'

'I'm okay with that, if you don't mind my two left feet.'

'It's not that. It's me. I can't dance—I don't dance—especially not in front of all these people.'

Her panicked voice reminded Sam all over again of the way Kate's fears had paralysed her. Lizzie had been correct—he was smitten with Kate. But would he be able to help her overcome those fears so she could move on to a less constricted life? If she couldn't, would there be any chance of a future for them?

He covered her hands with his much bigger ones to soothe their anxious twisting. 'No one is going to force you. But I do think, as you've been such an important part of this wedding, you're expected to get up on the dance floor. I'll lead you on and we can shuffle.'

'Shuffle?'

'Stand there and sway to the music. That way you don't have to dance, I don't have to dance—and you won't let your friends down.'

She took a deep breath and Sam could see what an effort it was for her. 'All those years of dance training and it comes to this,' she said with that bitter twist to her mouth.

'You're in a room full of friends,' he said. 'And do you know what? None of them know you're afraid to dance.'

'You're right,' she said, not looking at all convinced.

But when the MC invited the bridesmaid and grooms-man to get up onto the dance floor, Kate let him pull her to her feet. She was a little shaky but Sam didn't think anyone but he noticed it. He took her by the hand and led her onto the dance floor. She rested one hand on his shoulder and the other around his waist. Only he could feel her shivers of nervousness.

'Now we can shuffle,' he said. 'Just think of it like an ambulatory hug.'

'That's a Sam way of putting it,' she said, but she laughed. And he was glad he could make her laugh.

Kate had dreaded the dancing part of the evening. But standing there with Sam in the circle of his arms she felt safe, protected by his closeness. She trusted him not to let her make a fool of herself.

'I'm stepping my feet from side to side,' he said in an undertone she could only just hear over the music. 'We have to look like we're making an effort to dance. The people who know you're a professional dancer will be feeling sorry for you for being stuck with a shuffler grooms-man like me.'

Wrong! No woman in her right mind would ever pity her for being in Sam's arms. They'd envy her, more like it. She held on to him just a little bit tighter.

After the barefoot wedding ceremony, the bridal party had changed into high-heeled strappy sandals for the girls and loafers for the boys. She felt Sam's shoe nudge her toes.

'Hey, I felt that,' she said. 'Crushed toes aren't part of the deal.'

'I warned you I had two left feet.'

But she did as he suggested and stepped lightly from side to side. Securely held by Sam, as she tentatively started to move, the rhythm of the music seemed to invade her body. First her feet took off in something that was much more than a sideways shuffle, then her body started to sway. The old feeling came flooding back, the joy of her body moving—not just to the beat of the music but in step with Sam, who was also doing more than stepping from side to side.

Before she knew it, he had steered her into the centre of the dance floor and they were whirling around with the other couples. With a start of surprise, she realised she was being expertly led around the dance floor by a man who was light on his feet and perfectly in rhythm. She felt flushed with a relieved triumph that she had overcome her debilitating fear, and warm delight that she was back in the swing of things.

'I thought you said you couldn't dance,' she said to Sam.

'I said I had two left feet. But years of dancing instruction at my private boys' school beat a bit of coordination into them.'

'You had dance lessons at school?'

'It wasn't all rugby and cricket—though I was a far better football player than I ever was a dancer. We had to learn so we could dance with the girls from our corresponding girls' school. And take our place in Sydney society, of course.'

'I wish I'd known you when you were a schoolboy. I bet you were the hottest boy in your class.'

'I wouldn't say that,' he said, obviously uncomfortable

at such flattery—warranted though it was. She couldn't resist teasing him.

'I can imagine all the girls were after you.'

'Think again. I was this tall when I was thirteen. Big, awkward and shy.'

'I don't believe that for a moment.'

'Seriously. The other boys had way better chat-up lines than I did. By the time I'd thought about what I'd say, the girl had danced off with one of them.'

'Who needs chat-up lines when you're as handsome as you? Trust me, you would have been breaking girlish hearts all over the place. You could probably have had three at a time.'

'I hope not,' he said with genuine alarm. 'I'm a one-woman kind of guy.'

Suddenly the conversation had got kind of serious. And important.

'Really?' she said. Her breath caught in her throat.

'I met my first serious girlfriend in the final year of high school. She took a gap year in Europe and we broke up. Then there was a girl I dated at university and then Frances after that.'

'You…you don't have to give me your dating résumé,' she assured him.

'I want you to know you can trust me,' he said. Those bitter-chocolate-dark eyes searched hers.

'I think…I already know that,' she said.

'Good,' he replied and expertly twirled her around the floor until she was exhilarated and laughing. She couldn't remember when she'd enjoyed herself more.

Kate had been dancing for so long the soles of her feet were beginning to burn. All evening she'd regretted she hadn't worn her new shoes in—but then she hadn't anticipated she'd dance every dance. When the band took a break, she was hot and breathless and fanning herself with her hands.

'Some fresh air?' asked Sam.

'Absolutely,' she said, panting a little.

She followed Sam out onto the balcony away from the stuffiness and high chatter levels of the ball room. They virtually had the balcony to themselves, with only one other couple right down the other end.

The full moon reflected on the water of the bay. She took a deep breath of the cool night air. Sam leaned on the railing and looked out to sea. She slid her arms around his waist and rested her cheek against his broad back.

'Thank you for your help back there,' she murmured. 'I can't tell you how it feels to be able to dance again. I wouldn't have dared get up without you. Well, I might have, but maybe not for a long time and maybe—'

He turned around to face her. '*You* did it. Not me. But I'm happy I was able to help. Do you think, now you've danced once, you'll be able to do it again?'

She looked up at him. 'To be honest, I doubt I'll ever again dress up in a white leotard and bark like a poodle.'

He laughed. 'Sorry, but I wish I'd seen you. Do you have any photos?'

'*No.* And, if I did, no one would ever see them. It was hardly the highlight of my career as a professional dancer. A career I won't be reviving any time soon. But now it's not because I *can't,* but because I don't want to.'

'Sounds good to me.'

'It gives me hope I'll be able to get out of Dolphin Bay, too. I finally told Mum some of what happened in Sydney. She gave me the name of a psychologist at the hospital—someone I can speak to in confidence. I've made an appointment to see her next week.'

'That's a step in the right direction,' he said. 'I'm proud

of you. I know how difficult it's been for you to talk about it.'

'It's a small step. You're the one who can take the credit for helping me to get me this far.'

'I was just the shoulder you needed—'

'You were so, so much more than that, Sam.' She reached up and traced a line down his cheek with her fingers. Already his beard was growing and was rough under her fingertips. 'I...I hope I might be able to come and see you in Sydney before too long.'

He caught her hand and briefly pressed his lips to it. 'I wish you could come with me tomorrow.'

Joy bubbled through her that he should suggest it when deep down, in spite of her growing trust in him, she'd feared these few days might be all they'd ever have.

'Me too,' she said with a catch in her voice. 'But I can't. Not just because of...because of the dome but also because I'm looking after the hotel for the next ten days while Ben is on his honeymoon.'

'And helping out at Bay Books in your—' he made quotation marks with his fingers '—spare time.'

'It...it won't give me any time to mope around missing you,' she murmured, turning her head away, not wanting him to see the truth of how deeply she felt about him in her eyes.

With his index finger, he gently turned her chin back so she faced him. 'I'll miss you too,' he said. 'If I didn't have to go back to Sydney tomorrow morning, I wouldn't. But you know it's decision time at the meeting on Monday.'

'I know,' she said. 'I have every faith in you to make the right choice.'

His dark brows slanted. 'What happens if you don't get out from under that dome? If I sold the company, I could live anywhere I wanted. Even here.'

'In Dolphin Bay?' She shook her head. 'I don't think so.'

He cleared his throat. 'What I'm trying to say is that I want to spend more time with you, Kate. If that means moving to Dolphin Bay...'

She could hardly believe what she was hearing. 'I couldn't—wouldn't—ask that of you. You'd hate it here.'

'How can you be so sure of that?' he said. 'It...it's kind of growing on me. The community. The beach. The—'

'The way you'd be bored out of your brain within weeks?'

'I couldn't imagine ever being bored with you,' he said.

'Oh,' was all she managed to choke out in response.

He cradled her face in his two large, warm hands. His deep, brown eyes searched her face. 'Kate, in such a short time you...you've become...important to me.' Behind the imposing adult, the man who was gearing up to do battle in the boardroom over a multi-million-dollar deal, she saw the schoolboy, uncertain of the words he needed to find to win the girl.

'Oh, Sam, you've become so important to me too. But I...I... Until I get myself together I...'

He silenced her protest with a kiss. After a moment's surprised hesitation, she kissed him back and she gave herself up to the sheer pleasure of the pressure of his mouth on hers. Her lips parted on a sigh of bliss and his tongue slipped between them to tease and stroke and thrill. Her breath quickened. She met his tongue with hers and she pulled his head closer, her hands fisting in his hair. His hands slid down to her waist and drew her closer to his hard, muscular body. She could feel the frantic thudding of his heart, answered by the pounding of her own.

As the kiss flamed into something deeper and more passionate, desire ignited in delicious flames of want that surged through her, her breath coming hard and fast and broken. Sam groaned against her mouth and she answered the sensual sound by straining her body tighter to his.

She wanted him desperately—so desperately, she forgot she was on a balcony in close proximity to family and friends. Every sense was overwhelmed by her awakened need for him, the utter pleasure coursing through her body. Making her want more, making her want him at any cost.

She stilled. Her heart pounded harder, now from fear rather than passion as she realised the direction her thoughts had taken. This hunger for him would have her do anything he wanted. It could have her enslaved. It might transport her on a tide of need to an obsession where she lost all sense of herself. She felt like she was choking.

She wrenched away from Sam's arms and staggered backwards. He put out a hand to steady her. 'I...I can't do this,' she said.

He dropped his hand from her arm. His jaw clenched and his dark scowl was back, overlaid with both disbelief and pain.

'Because people can see us?' he growled. 'Because *Jesse* might see us?'

She shook her head. 'Because I want you so much and... it scares me.'

'This is about the guy at university,' he said flatly.

Mutely, she nodded.

His expression was grim as he seemed to gather his thoughts. Her heart sank to somewhere below her shoes. Had she scared him off with her endless fears?

'Kate, do you realise that this might scare me too? I've only known you a week and you're all I can think about. My feelings for you have become an issue in the most important decision I've ever had to make. This...this is new to me. I've laid it on the line for you. But are you ever going to be able to trust me?' He turned so his shoulder was facing her and his face was shrouded by shadow. Terror grabbed at her with icy claws.

He could walk away.

And that would be worse than anything else that could happen.

'Sam, I'm sorry. I...I've been so caught up in me and how I'm feeling, I...I didn't think enough about how it was affecting you.'

To her intense relief, he turned back so she could see his face, illuminated by the pale moonlight. 'I wouldn't break your spirit in the way that guy did. Your feistiness and independence are part of your appeal for me. I'm strong, Kate. I want to be there for you. You need time to sort through your issues and I know that. But it has to be two-way.'

She needed time. But it had been years since she'd fallen into that dark tunnel. Years when she'd hidden herself away, protecting herself against any real relationships by her fixation on Jesse, letting fear inhibit and stultify her emotional growth. She'd been a girl then, now she was a woman. She had to grow up. She had to come to Sam as an adult who considered his emotional needs as well as her own. Be aware that *she* could hurt *him*.

'Sam.' Urgently, she gripped his upper arms to keep him with her. She looked up into his eyes and her heart twisted painfully at the wariness that clouded them. No way could she lose him. 'You're right; I've been so focused on myself. I want a partnership. Me looking after you, as well as you looking after me. My shoulders aren't nearly as broad as yours, but I want them to be there for you like yours are for me.'

He started to say something but she rose up on her toes and silenced him with a kiss. She murmured against his mouth, 'And I want you. Tonight, when the party is over, I want to come with you to your room.'

He pulled back. She could see it was an effort for him but he managed a lopsided imitation of his usual wide grin. 'I want you too, believe me. I can't tell you how tempted I am to pick you up and carry you up to my room right now. But it wouldn't be right. It's too soon. And the whole of Dolphin Bay will know you've stayed with me. Neither of us wants that, especially as I'm going in the morning.'

Her body was still warm with want for him. But, in a way, she was relieved. It *was* too soon. The growing up she needed to do wasn't going to happen overnight. 'Yes. You're right.' But she twined her arms around his neck and drew him down for another kiss. 'But making love with you isn't an easy thing to say no to,' she murmured as she kissed him again.

'Woo-hoo!' Lizzie's voice interrupted them.

Kate pulled away from the kiss, flushed, her breathing erratic. Not only Lizzie, but also Jesse was standing in the doorway. Jesse caught her eye and winked. She knew Jesse so well, she realised that meant he approved of her and Sam getting together. What really surprised her was the knowing look Lizzie sent to Sam and the sheepish smile he sent her in return. What was that about?

'C'mon, you two, Sandy's about to toss her bouquet,' said Lizzie, ushering her and Sam back into the room. 'I'm staying right out of range but you, Kate, might want to be within catching distance.'

Did she?

After the encounter she'd just shared with Sam, was it weird to entertain the thought of marriage for even the briefest moments of wedding-fuelled madness? The groom in her 'walking to the altar' fantasy was tall, dark-haired and with a scowl that transformed into the sexiest of smiles...

For all they'd come to tonight, there was still much

both she and Sam needed to consider before she got carried away by dreams. Even if she did break her way free from the dome, what happened next?

Still, she had to admit to a twinge of disappointment when Sandy's bouquet went sailing over her, and the outstretched arms of all the other single ladies vying to catch it, to land fairly and squarely in Emily's lap. Kate was surprised by Emily's blushes and protests at the chants of, 'You're next,' 'Emily is next.' Hmm. She might have to quiz her little sister on the reason for those blushes.

But she forgot all about that as Sam put his arm around her to lead her over to the table that was serving coffee and slices of chocolate wedding cake.

'I hate fruit cake,' he said, picking up the biggest piece on the platter. 'When I get married, I'll want a chocolate cake.'

He said it so casually, seemingly without even being aware of the significance of his words, it made her wonder if Sam had a few dreams of his own.

CHAPTER TWELVE

SAM WOKE UP and for a long moment wasn't sure where he was. Then he realised he was sprawled across the sofa in Kate's living room. Kate was asleep, snuggled into his side, her head resting on his chest, her sweetly scented hair spilling over his neck. She was breathing deeply and evenly.

There were sooty smudges around her eyes where her make-up had smeared. Her lips were free of lipstick—it had been thoroughly kissed away. Her bridesmaid dress was rumpled up over her slender thighs. She'd kicked off her sandals and he noticed her toenails were painted the same pretty colour as her dress. He was fascinated by how pale her skin was, how he could see the delicate traceries of veins. Such a contrast to his own olive skin.

With her colouring, she certainly hadn't been made to live by the sea where so much activity was played out on the water or the sand under the blazing Australian sun. She loved her home town, but he suspected she was a city girl at heart. He thought she'd be happy in Sydney.

His Sydney was very different from the student haunts where she'd played out the relationship that had so traumatised her. The waterfront penthouse apartment he owned was part of a redeveloped wharf complex and was right next to some of the best restaurants in town. It was only a walk into the centre of the city. He reckoned she'd love it.

His arm was around her shoulder and he cautiously adjusted it to make himself more comfortable. She made a little murmur of protest deep in her throat and nestled in tighter, one hand clutching on to his chest. He dropped a light kiss on the top of her head.

He knew he should go, but he could not resist a few more moments of having her so close to him.

After the bride and groom had left the reception last night, he and Kate, along with Jesse, Lizzie and a group of their other friends, had adjourned to the bar at the Harbourside. Eventually it had ended up with just Kate and him left. There'd been nothing he wanted more than to take her up to his room and make love to her. But he had known, much as he'd wanted her, that wasn't going to happen. That *mustn't* happen. Instead he'd taken her home, she'd invited him in for coffee and they'd made out like teenagers on the sofa until they must have fallen asleep.

Sam smiled as he remembered how they'd kept talking until the time between each other's responses had got longer and longer until finally there had been silence. He hadn't wanted to let her go, hadn't wanted to say goodnight. And he didn't want to now.

The pale light of dawn was starting to filter through the blinds. He couldn't stay any longer. Not only would it be awkward for Dawn and Emily to come in and find him there, but he had to get on the road.

He edged his way into a sitting position and pulled Kate upright. He stroked her hair. 'Kate,' he whispered. 'I have to go.'

Her eyes opened, then shut again, then finally opened wide. She blinked as her eyes came into focus. 'Sam! Wh-where...? Oh. I remember now.' She stretched her arms languorously above her head, which made the top of her breasts swell over the edge of her strapless dress. She put her hand over her mouth as she yawned.

He averted his eyes to look over her head. Waking up with her pressed so intimately close was bad enough; seeing her skirt all rucked up around her thighs and the top starting to slide right off was more than a man could be expected to endure.

'C'mon, Kate.'

She planted her arms around his neck and pouted. 'No. Don't want you to go.' Her hair was all tousled and the smudged make-up around her eyes gave her a sultry air. The effect was adorable. She kissed him, her mouth soft and yielding, her tongue teasing the seam of his lips.

He groaned softly and kissed her back. Then he summoned every ounce of self-discipline he had to push himself up from the sofa, which in turn tipped her back against the cushions. She still looked groggy, a little bewildered and quite possibly half-asleep. Leaving her there was one of the most difficult things he had ever done.

He slipped into his shoes and picked up his car keys from the coffee table. Then he crouched down to the level of the sofa. 'Kate, listen. I'm leaving for Sydney as soon as I pick up my bag from the hotel. Do you understand?'

Her eyes widened and she nodded. 'Yes.' She pulled a sad, funny Kate face. 'I don't know when I'll next see you, but I hope it will be soon.'

'Me too,' he said. He kissed her gently on the mouth. 'Bye, Kate. You try to get some more sleep.'

''Kay,' she murmured.

He pulled a throw over her and tucked it around her bare legs. Then he let himself out of the door. He suspected she was asleep again before the door had closed behind him.

He forced his brain to change gears from thinking about making love to Kate to corporate responsibility and business pros and cons. And what would be the decision he would communicate to the potential purchaser of his company.

Her lingering perfume and the imprint of her body against his made his old workaholic tricks the least effective they'd ever been.

Kate had to put up with much teasing from her sister and mother when they discovered her dishevelled and asleep on the sofa, with two empty cups on the coffee table.

'I don't have to ask who you had here until all hours,' said Emily, her eyes dancing.

There was no point in denying it. Half of Dolphin Bay had probably seen her kissing Sam on the balcony of the hotel. And Emily had been among the group who'd congregated in the bar after the wedding reception. Kate and Sam had held hands the entire time.

As she showered, she thought that over breakfast might be a good time to talk through a few things with her mother and Emily.

The thought of their Sunday favourite of scrambled eggs and bacon made her gag. Not that she was feeling ill; it was just that her stomach was tied in knots of tension. She missed Sam already. It was devastating to think that when she started her shift at the hotel this afternoon he wouldn't be there. And she was also coming down from the high of all those frantic wedding preparations.

She waved away the eggs and instead nibbled on the platter of fruit Emily had cut up. Clearing up and doing the dishes was her breakfast task for today. As three adults sharing a house, they also shared the chores.

'So,' said her mother, sipping a cup of tea. 'Have you got something you want to say to us?'

'Something about someone?' said Emily. She broke into

the childish chant the sisters had used since they'd been tiny and still did. 'Someone whose name begins with *S*?'

Kate put down her own cup of herbal tea. 'Yes. I do. And it *is* about me and Sam.'

'Tell all,' said Emily, leaning forward on her elbows, her eyes avid.

'There's not a lot to tell yet, but there might be,' said Kate.

'We really like Sam, don't we, Mum?' asked Emily. Her mother nodded.

'I like him, too,' confessed Kate, the accursed blush betraying her. 'But he lives in Sydney and I live here. Which could be a problem.'

'Sweetie, there is that major issue for you to overcome before you can think about going to Sydney,' said her mum, raising her eyebrows in the direction of Emily. 'You know…'

'Don't worry, Mum, I've told Emily about the dome,' Kate said. She'd found visualising her issue as 'the dome' made it easier somehow to imagine herself breaking out of it. She wondered if the psychologist she was seeing on Tuesday would think it was a good idea.

'Good,' said her mother.

Kate took a deep breath. 'But there's another problem—one that doesn't just involve me. When I'm able to, I'll want to drive to Sydney fairly often. Who knows, I might end up living there one day before too long so I can date Sam, if I can afford exorbitant city rents. But…but I know I'm needed here. With you two.'

Her mother and Emily exchanged glances that Kate couldn't quite read.

She hastened to reassure them. 'Don't worry. If you want me to stay, we can work things out and—'

'Don't even *think* of giving up Sam for my sake,' said

Emily. 'A guy like him only comes along once in a million years. Grab on to him and don't let him go.'

'Er, Emily, that's not quite the way to put it,' said her mother. 'But we know what you mean and I echo the sentiment.'

Dawn reached out to give Kate a comforting pat on her arm. 'Don't worry about us, sweetie. It's been wonderful having you here with us all these years, and don't think I don't appreciate it. But things change. For all of us. You need to get your wings back and start to fly.'

'Actually, I have something to say too, Kate,' ventured Emily, an edge of excitement to her voice. 'I'm moving out next month. I didn't want to announce anything until it was certain. I've only just told Mum.'

Emily had talked about moving out on her own often enough but it was a big step. Kate was disconcerted it was actually happening. 'Where are you moving to?'

'To Melbourne. I'm going to share with some other basketball players in a house that's set up for wheelies. The bank has organised a transfer for me to a branch down there. I'm all set.'

Kate narrowed her eyes. 'And are all your new roomies female?'

'Um, no,' said Emily. 'But that's all very new and I don't want to jinx it by talking about him.'

'Okay,' said Kate, determined she would get all the details out of her sister before the end of the day. 'I'm really pleased for you. And visiting you will give me a good excuse to get to Melbourne.' Another reason to get out from under that dome.

She could feel her major tie to Dolphin Bay stretching and snapping. Emily didn't need her any more—though, if she was honest with herself, Emily hadn't needed her for a long time. *Had she needed to be needed?*

'So that just leaves you and me, Mum,' Kate said.

'I'm not pushing you out, Kate, but it will do you good to go when you're ready. I never imagined I'd have my great big girls of twenty-eight and twenty-six still living at home with me. It's time for me to have my independence too.'

Kate had inherited her tendency to blush from her mother and she was surprised at the rising colour on her mother's cheeks.

'I didn't know Colin's other name was "independence", Mum,' teased Emily.

Kate looked from her mother to Emily and back again. 'Colin?'

'My friend from the hospital—he's new in the admin department. He was the one who helped me and Sam put up the wedding arch. He...he's very nice.'

'And why didn't I know this?' demanded Kate.

'You're losing the plot, sister dear,' replied Emily. 'Too caught up with handsome Sam to keep your finger on the pulse of everyone else's business as you usually do.'

'And the wedding planning. And the resort stuff...' began Kate, and realised she was being overly defensive. She laughed. Maybe she didn't need to keep such a rigid control on things any more. Maybe there were fewer fears to keep at bay.

She'd ask Sam what he thought.

CHAPTER THIRTEEN

ON MONDAY MORNING, Sam sat behind the imposing desk that had once been his grandfather's in his office at the Sydney headquarters of Lancaster & Son Construction. He was aware if he went ahead with the sale of the family company that the name Lancaster & Son, founded by his grandfather, carried on by his father and then nurtured by him, would disappear into the history books.

That would be inevitable. But if he didn't have a son— or had a son who didn't want to go into the construction industry—would the name be such a loss?

In many ways it would be a relief—the burden of living up to that name and to his father's expectations would be finally lifted. He remembered back to the day he'd turned twenty-one when he'd demanded some autonomy from his father. Grudgingly, it had been given. But, even though his father had gone, there was still that feeling of having stepped into his shoes without having forged shoes of his own. He'd worked for the company since he'd been fourteen years old. Surely he deserved the chance for some cashed-up freedom?

Still, it was gut-wrenching to think of pulling the plug on so much of his family's endeavours. Thanks to his canny management, the company had been successful through all the ups and downs of the market. The balance sheet was very healthy with profits consistently rising—which was what made it so attractive to the company wanting to buy it. And the Lancaster reputation for quality and reliability was unsurpassed.

The money the sale would earn him was a mind-boggling amount, more than enough for him to start a business that was just his own. As well as the luxury of time to decide what that new venture might be.

It was a compelling reason to sell.

Again he flipped through the document that answered his questions about what the multi-national company intended to do if he accepted their offer. With the turn of each page, his gut clenched into tighter and more painful knots. Whatever labels you put on a business strategy, be they 'process re-engineering', 'shifting paradigms' or 'amalgamating cost centres', the truth of the matter was that the sale would result in downsizing. And not one member of his crew deserved to lose their job. There were the clients to consider too—clients who trusted him. Clients like his friend Ben Morgan.

He thought about what Kate had said—and knew there was much truth in her words. With his inheritance had come responsibilities. His father had been fond of that old-fashioned word 'duty'. In the contemporary world of dog-eat-dog business, did words like 'responsibility' and 'duty' have a place—or were they just remnants of a more honourable past?

Then there was his personal life to consider. His workaholic devotion to the company had lost him a fiancée. Now he'd fallen for a woman who might not be able to leave her small, coastal home town in the short-term; perhaps not for a long time. If he wanted to be with her, he might have to live there too. What had she said? *You'd be bored out of your brain within weeks.*

He'd started to be seduced by Dolphin Bay but now he was back in Sydney the thought of living in a backwater became less and less appealing. Even with Kate by his side, a ton of money in the bank and freedom from corporate responsibility, he suspected he would find it stifling.

If he took that path, might he come to resent her? Might that resentment become a poison that would destroy their relationship before it would have time to flourish?

There was such a short time left for him to make his momentous decision. He leaned back in his big leather chair, linked his hands behind his head, closed his eyes and reviewed again his options.

It seemed like no time at all had elapsed before his PA buzzed him that his meeting was about to start.

He picked up the folder with all the relevant documents and headed for the boardroom.

Kate was on edge all morning. From the time Sam's meeting was scheduled, she had started checking her mobile phone for messages. Whatever decision he made it would be life-changing for him—and possibly for her.

When the call finally came, she found her hands were shaking as she picked up her phone. 'Well?' she asked him. She held her breath for his answer.

'I didn't sell,' he said. 'The company is still mine.'

She let out her breath in a sigh. 'Congratulations. I'm proud of you. It must have been difficult but I think you made the right decision.'

'Me too. I did that "make a choice and live with it for an hour" exercise—and decided to sell. But as I headed to the meeting, and realised it would be the last time I would have a say in the business, I knew there was nothing I'd rather do than run Lancaster & Son Construction. I finally understood that my inheritance had never been a burden but a privilege. And that it was entirely up to me how I chose to direct it—my vision, my future. So I changed my mind.'

'Which means everyone gets to keep their jobs and Ben gets to keep his builder.'

'All that.'

'I'd like to give you a big hug.'

'A big Kate hug is just what I need right now. I didn't realise just how stressful the whole process would be.' She could sense the weariness in his voice.

'I wish I...'

'You wish what?'

'Oh, I wish I could hop in the car and drive up to Sydney to be with you to celebrate. But obviously that can't be.'

'You'll get there, just give it time,' he said. It still amazed her that this big, sexy hunk of a man could be so considerate.

She took another deep breath. 'I've got a new goal to aim for—besides seeing the Indian palace hotel, that is. When Ben comes back from his honeymoon, I plan to drive up to Sydney to see you.'

There was silence at the other end of the line. 'You're sure that's not too ambitious?'

She shook her head, even knowing he couldn't see her. 'No. I'm going to drive a little further every day until I can point that car in the direction of Sydney and go for it. And hope I don't drive smack into the dome, of course.'

'Okay. But don't beat yourself up about it if the practice proves more difficult than the theory.'

'I won't,' she promised.

There was a pause on the line before Sam spoke again. 'Unfortunately, the decision to hold on to the company means it's unlikely I'll make it down to Dolphin Bay. Not before the time Ben gets back, anyway.'

Disappointment, dark and choking, constricted her

voice but she forced herself to sound cheerful. 'That's okay. I'll...I'll be so flat out with everything here. Not to mention the daily get-out-of-town driving goals I've set myself that—'

'It's not okay,' he said. 'But because I've been away for a week, and because I've got to be seen to be taking the reins with confidence, that's the way it's got to be. There are changes I want to make straight away. This is seen as a turning point for the company.' She suspected his words were accompanied by a shrug. 'I'm sorry,' he added.

Her voice was too choked to reply immediately and she nodded. But of course he couldn't see that. She donned her 'everything is just fine' voice. 'Sure. We can call or text. Maybe even video calls.'

'It won't be the same as seeing you but, yes, that's what we'll do. Now, I have to go for the first of a long line-up of meetings. The start of the new era.'

'Where the company is truly yours—in your mind, anyway.'

There was silence at the end of the line and Kate thought he might have hung up. But he spoke again. 'You're very perceptive. That's exactly what the decision has meant to me.'

When Kate put down the phone she was more than ever determined to get out of that dome so she could take more control of her life—and choose when she wanted to see Sam, rather than waiting for him to come to her.

By Wednesday afternoon, Kate had driven further away from Dolphin Bay town centre than she had for two years. While being aware there was such a thing as overconfidence, she felt buoyed by the knowledge that she had got into the car without shaking or nausea. By the end of the ten days, she was sure she would make it onto the Princes Highway and away.

The initial meeting with the psychologist had gone well. She'd been surprised that the thoughtful, middle-aged woman hadn't wanted to talk much about the past. Rather, she'd acknowledged that Kate—thanks to her talks with Sam—already had a level of insight into what had caused her problems. Then the psychologist had gone straight into examining and challenging Kate's thoughts and feelings. At the second session on Wednesday morning, she'd given her strategies for coping in trigger situations, like getting into cars. Kate had found the breathing techniques and visualisations particularly helpful.

She'd been amazed that she could progress so quickly when she'd thought it might take months—even years— to get to the bottom of things. Why on earth hadn't she admitted to herself long ago that she'd needed help, when the solution seemed so straightforward?

By the following Tuesday, on her morning off, she drove all the way south to the larger town of Bateman's Bay nearly an hour away. She strolled up and down the water-front, revelling in her freedom. Then she sat in a café right on the water and congratulated herself for having pushed the boundary of the dome so far back. She was confident that by Friday she'd be on the road north to Sydney, count-ing down the minutes until she saw Sam.

After she finished her coffee, she decided to phone Sam on her mobile to share the good news. She'd be in Sydney on Friday in time to meet him for dinner.

'I'm so proud of you, you're doing amazingly well,' he said. 'But there's going to be a change of plan.'

Kate swallowed hard against that same lump of disap-pointment that seemed to rise in her throat when she talked to Sam about her plans to visit him in Sydney. But she refused to listen to the nagging, internal voice that taunted her that she had, once again, been a bad judge of a man's character. That maybe, just maybe, Sam would hedge and defer and change dates until it ended up that she would never see him again.

Trust him, trust him, trust him, she chanted to herself.

'A change of plan?' she repeated, desperately fighting a dull edge to her voice.

'Not such a bad one,' he said. 'At least, I don't think you'll find it so bad. In fact, I'm sure you'll think it's good news.' There was a rising tone of restrained excitement to his voice that made her wonder.

'Okay, so enough with the torture,' she said. 'Tell me what it is.'

'I have to fly to Singapore tonight for a series of meetings that will go on until the weekend.'

'And that's good news?' she said, her heart sinking.

'The good news is I want you to meet me there. Now that you've told me you'll be in Sydney, I'm confident you can do it. I'll send you an email with the details.'

She had to pause to get her thoughts together. 'In Singapore? You want me to meet you in Singapore?' She wasn't sure if the churning in her stomach was dread or excitement.

'Yes.'

'When I've only just managed Bateman's Bay?'

'You can do it, Kate. I know you can. Especially when you hear where we'll be staying in Singapore. Remember the hotel you told me about that shared top spot with the Indian palace one on your list of must-see hotels?'

'The huge new one with the mammoth towers and the world's highest infinity pool, fifty-seven floors up?'

'The very one.'

'The one with the amazing spa on the fifty-fifth floor?'

'Yup,' he confirmed.

'And the luxury shopping mall underneath, and the casino, and what they say are the best views in Singapore?' By now she was practically screeching with excitement. A couple at the next table looked at her oddly and she lowered her voice.

'I've booked a suite on the highest floor I could,' he said. 'With a butler.'

'A butler? You're kidding me.'

'No. Nothing short of the lap of luxury for Ms Parker.'

'But...but you'll already be there and I'll have to get there by myself. I don't know that I—'

'If you can get to Sydney, all you have to do is get to the airport. There'll be a first-class ticket waiting for you. You'll hardly know you're in the air.'

She lowered her voice to a note above a whisper. 'But, Sam, what if I can't do it? What if I don't get as far as Sydney?'

'Then we cancel it all and wait until I can get down there to see you.'

'Okay. So I have an escape route.'

'If you like to see it as that, yes,' he said. 'But Kate, here's the deal: to make it easier for you, I'll send down a chauffeur-driven limo to pick you up from home. He'll drive you to Sydney International Airport so you don't actually have to worry about driving. That will be one less pressure on you. The driver—who is on my staff—will escort you into the first-class lounge where you can check in. Then I'll meet you at the other end.'

'Sam, I so want to see you. I...I miss you. And this all sounds terribly exciting. Like a dream, really.'

'So you'll do it?'

'Just give me a second.' She took a few of the controlled, calming breaths she had been practising. 'Yes. I'll do it.

Mum told me I needed to get my wings back but I didn't know that she meant aeroplane wings.'

'Great,' he said and she was surprised at the relief in his voice.'

'Sam?' she ventured. 'Thank you. This might just be the incentive I need to get me out of that dome once and for all. I'll see you in Singapore.'

CHAPTER FOURTEEN

I CAN DO THIS. Kate kept repeating the words like a mantra as the ultra-smooth limousine, way too big for one person, left Dolphin Bay behind. She realised she was sitting rigidly on the edge of the seat and she made herself sink back into its well-upholstered comfort.

She'd only had a light breakfast, but felt a little queasy, so she made herself take the controlled, calming breaths the psychologist had taught her. Buried deep in her handbag was some prescription medication she'd got from her doctor, as insurance in case she got overwhelmed by panic. But she was determined it would not come out of its wrapping. She wanted to be with Sam. To be with Sam, she had to stay in this car and not beg the driver to take her home. She was determined to find the strength to turn her life around. *I can do this.*

She pulled out her phone from her bag and flicked through to the photos of the wedding. There was a lovely one of Sam and her, she smiling up at him, him with his dark head bent to hear what she was saying. She pressed a kiss to her finger and transferred the kiss to the photo. All this was worth it.

It didn't seem long before coastal bushland made way for rolling green farmland. She gazed out the window and marvelled that she had not been along these roads for five years. But that self-imposed isolation was behind her now. She'd smashed through the dome.

The previous night she'd had a broken sleep, kept awake by alternate bouts of churning excitement and worry. Three times she'd got out of bed to check that her passport and travel documents were packed. By the time the car was driving through the picturesque town of Berry, she was fast asleep.

The driver woke her as they approached Sydney International Airport. She looked around her, bewildered, until she realised where she was. A wave of exultation surged through her. *I've done it!*

The last time she'd flown, it had been with the dance troupe. That had involved a bus ride to the airport and the cheapest of bargain airline seats right down the back of the plane.

Being ushered into the first-class lounge was a different experience altogether. She tried not to look too awestruck at the level of elegant luxury that surrounded her. Customers waiting for their flights could enjoy anything from a snack to a three-course meal. There was even a day spa where she could book in for a facial—all part of the service. It was like a six-star hotel on a smaller scale. But she couldn't enjoy it—even if she tried looking on it as research.

Everyone else seemed to know where they were going, what they were doing. The staff bustled around, greeting frequent flyers by name but not paying her any attention. Kate felt awkward and alone and unable to pretend she fitted in. She sat huddled on the edge of an ultra-contemporary leather sofa with a plate of gourmet snacks uneaten on the small table beside her.

She was wearing slim black trousers, a silk tank top and a loose, fine-knit black jacket trimmed with bronze metallic studs. Teamed with black ballet flats, she thought her outfit looked fine and would be comfortable for the flight.

But there wasn't a designer-label attached to any of it.

And this was designer label territory.

Was this Sam's world? She hadn't thought of him being super-wealthy but the personal chauffeur and the first-class travel indicated otherwise.

How well did she actually know him?

Every so often, boarding calls went out over the sound system. Each time she thought it might be for her. Each time she realised she'd forgotten her flight number and had to fumble in her bag to pull out her boarding card. Each time she got more and more flustered.

She began to dread the thought of actually boarding the plane—seven hours cooped up with no possibility of escape. Seven hours of escalating worry. What if Sam wasn't there to meet her at the other end? What if she had to find her own way to the hotel in a foreign city? What if she got lost?

Dread percolated in the pit of her belly. She started to shake and tried to control it by wringing her hands together. Her heart thudded wildly. Perspiration prickled on her forehead. *She couldn't do this.*

She used her breathing techniques to slow down the panic—then started to feel angry. This wasn't about an unresolved issue in her past. It was about Sam.

Sam should not have expected this of her. This was forcing her to run before she was even sure she could walk. He knew her problems only too well—and she'd thought he understood them. She should not be expected to fly to Singapore on her own. This was the first time she had been able to venture out of her home town for five years. To pop her on a plane all by herself like a first-class parcel and expect her to cope was nothing short of cruel.

It dawned on her that, not only hadn't she seen Sam since he'd gone back to Sydney, she hadn't really talked to him that much either. He was always preoccupied with the company he had taken charge of with renewed vigour. What had he said about the reason for his cancelled wedding? *I was a selfish workaholic.*

Obviously things hadn't changed. *He* hadn't changed.

Maybe Sam in Dolphin Bay and Sam in Sydney were two different people. Away from stress and the pressure of his job, he'd been the kind, thoughtful man she'd fallen in love with. But back on the city treadmill he'd become that ruthless, selfish person she'd always suspected might be there beneath the surface—a man whose woman would always come second to his business, who would have to fit in around him when it suited him.

She didn't want that kind of man.

It had been a classic holiday romance, she supposed with a painful lurch of her heart. Only he had been the one on holiday and she had been the one left behind when he'd gone home. He had been more than generous with dollars in organising this trip for her. But he had been exceedingly stingy with his time.

Sure, she'd wanted to see that wonderful hotel in Singapore. But most of all she'd wanted to see *him.* Now, on top of the shaking and shivering and cold sweats, she felt tears smarting. *She could not get on that plane.*

No way could she risk a public meltdown high in the sky somewhere between Sydney and Singapore. Only to be met at the other end —if he wasn't too busy in a business meeting—by someone she was no longer certain she wanted to see.

Kate swallowed the sob that threatened to break out, got up from the sofa and picked up her bag. She couldn't go home, that was for sure. Instead she'd march out to the taxi rank and get a ride to one of the glamorous new Sydney hotels she'd explored only on their websites. There she'd lock herself away for a few days, cry her eyes out, order room service and figure out where she went from there.

But as she headed towards the exit she was blocked by a tall, dark-haired man wearing a crumpled business suit, sporting dark stubble and an expression of anguish. 'Kate. Thank heaven. What was I thinking of, to expect you to fly by yourself?'

Her heart starting pounding so hard she had to put her hand to her chest. Sam. Gorgeous, wonderful, sexy Sam. She desperately wanted to throw herself into his arms. But that wouldn't work.

Kate looked at him with an expression of cold distaste in her beautiful green eyes. How could Sam blame her? He'd been nothing short of inept in the way he'd gone about this whole trip, a trip that was supposed to give her a treat and cement their relationship.

He could blame the pressures of the sale decision and subsequent reassurances to the staff, many of whom had been unsettled by the reports in the press about the potential takeover. But that was no real excuse.

By the time he'd finally got some time to himself on the plane to Singapore, he'd realised what he'd done. He'd reverted to the same old bad, work-obsessed ways that had destroyed his relationships before. After all that angst over the sale of the company, the new direction he wanted to take, he hadn't changed a bit. He'd expected a girl struggling to overcome a form of agoraphobia to do what must have seemed impossible to her. What kind of fool was he?

Kate went to move away from him and he realised she was heading towards the exit. 'Kate, where are you going? We have to board the plane in ten minutes.'

She spun back on her heel. '*We?* Sam, what are you doing here? I'm confused, to say the least.' He realised she was dangerously close to tears—tears caused by him. The knowledge stabbed him with pain and guilt for hurting her.

'I got to Singapore and realised what an idiot I was to expect you to get on a plane by yourself. So I got another plane back here as soon as I could so we could fly together.'

Her brow furrowed. 'You *what?*'

'I just flew back from Singapore. My plane landed here at this terminal. I wanted to be here to meet you when you arrived by limo, but the plane was late and there was a hellish crowd in the arrivals hall. Thankfully, I got here in time.' He would never have forgiven himself if he had missed her.

A smile struggled to melt her frosty expression. 'I don't believe what I'm hearing.'

'I booked another ticket for me so we could fly together, like we should have in the first place.'

'But what about your meetings in Singapore?'

'I rearranged them.'

'Weren't they important?' she asked.

'Nothing is more important than you, Kate.'

He didn't blame her for the scepticism that extinguished that nascent smile. He put his hands on her shoulders and this time she didn't move away. 'Seriously. I had a lot of time to think on that plane coming back to Sydney. I realised I had to change my obsessive, destructive, workaholic ways or I'd lose you. And I couldn't bear that.'

'So what do you intend to do?' she asked.

'Delegate. Give some of the really good people I have in my organisation more chance to manage. My father's old right-hand man has been seriously under-utilised because I saw him as a threat rather than a help. Most of all, I'm going to build in time for the woman I love.'

Her eyes widened with astonishment. 'Did…did you just say you…?'

'That I loved you? Yes, I did. And I'll say it again—I love you, Kate Parker.' He gathered her into his arms and kissed her on the mouth.

After the frantic dash from the plane to the lounge, Sam had been so engrossed with making sure Kate would be getting on the plane with him that he had completely forgotten about his surroundings. He was brought back to reality by a polite smattering of applause and turned around to see that they had attracted a smiling audience.

He looked at Kate and she blushed and laughed, her dimples flirting in her cheeks. She turned to face the people applauding and dipped a deep, theatrical, dancer's curtsey. He joined her in a half-bow of acknowledgement. Then he took her hand and tugged her towards him. 'C'mon, we've got a plane to catch.'

Travelling first class was an adventure all on its own, Kate thought as they disembarked in Singapore. She'd enjoyed a fully flat bed, pillows, blankets, luxury toiletries, even pyjamas. And the food had been top-class-restaurant standard delivered with superlative service.

The best thing of all had been Sam's company. After his frantic dash from Sydney to Singapore and back again, he'd drowsed for much of the flight, but every moment they'd both been awake they'd been together. She'd even managed to ask her final question, number five—how had he got that scar on his eyebrow? The prosaic answer related to an unfortunate encounter with a sharp metal window frame being moved around on a building site. She would have preferred something more romantic but, as he'd said in his practical way, he was lucky he hadn't lost an eye.

And now was her first sight of exotic Singapore.

Another limousine was there to pick them up. As she waited for her suitcase to be loaded into the boot, she sniffed the warm, humid air, tinged with a fragrance she didn't recognise. She asked Sam what it was.

'I call it the scent of Asia—a subtle mix of different plants, foods, spices. I find it exciting every time I smell it—and it's intoxicating when it's the first time.'

She couldn't agree more. *She was in Asia!*

It was night-time, and Singapore was a city sparkling with myriad fairy-tale lights that delighted her. As they drove across a bridge, her first sight of their hotel made her gasp. Brightly lit, its three tall towers seemed to rear up out of the water, the famous roof-top pool resort slung across the very top.

'I can't wait to get up there and swim on the top of the world,' she said. She clutched Sam's arm. 'Oh, thank you for bringing me here. This is the most amazing place I've ever seen.'

'I'm happy to be sharing it with you.' He smiled his slow, sexy smile. 'Around here is the really modern part of Singapore. Most of this area is built on reclaimed land—it's an engineering marvel. Tomorrow I'll take you to the old part. There's a mix of gracious buildings from the co-lonial past and temples I think you'll find fascinating.'

'I'll look forward to it,' she said. 'You know, I'm hav-ing to pinch myself to make sure this is all real and I'm not dreaming.'

He laughed. 'It's real, all right.' He looked down at her. 'But the best part is having you here with me.'

'Agreed,' she said happily, squeezing his hand.

Thank heaven, she thought, as she had thought a hun-dred times already, she hadn't walked out of that exit back at Sydney airport.

Inside, the hotel didn't disappoint. The atrium was so

mind-bogglingly spacious she got a sore neck from looking upwards. And the interior design was like nothing she'd ever seen—upmarket contemporary, with Oriental highlights that made it truly unique.

'Considering your interest in hotels, I've arranged for you to have a private tour,' Sam said as they went up in the elevator to their room. 'You just have to decide on a time that suits you.'

'You've thought of everything,' she replied with a contented sigh.

'Except the most important thing,' he said with a wry twist to his mouth. 'I'll never forgive myself for expecting you to get on that plane by yourself.'

Kate silenced him with a halt sign. 'I've forgiven you, so you have to forgive yourself. Really. You realised your mistake and remedied it with the most marvellous of gestures.'

'So long as you're okay with it,' he said. 'I shocked myself at how easily I relapsed into work-obsessed ways.'

'So, I'm going to police this workaholic thing,' she asserted more than half-seriously. 'It's not good for you. Or me.'

'You can discipline me whenever you like,' he shot back with a wicked lift of his eyebrow.

'Count on it,' she said, smiling as the elevator doors opened on their floor.

The first thing she noticed when they walked into their spacious suite wasn't the smart design or the view across the harbour. It was the fact that in the open-plan bathroom the elegant, free-standing bathtub was full of water and had sweetly fragrant rose petals scattered across the surface. When she looked across to the bed, rose petals had also been scattered across it.

'How romantic!' she exclaimed, clapping her hands in delight. 'Did you organise this too?'

'I can't take the credit,' he said. 'The hotel staff…uh… they seemed to think we were on our honeymoon.'

'Oh,' she said. 'Well, I hope… That is, I'd like to think this will be a…a honeymoon of sorts.' She wound her arms around his neck. 'Sam, this hotel is wonderful. Singapore is wonderful. All the stuff you've got planned for us is wonderful. But just being alone with you is the most wonderful thing of all.'

She kissed him, loving his taste, the roughness of his beard, the hard strength of his body pressed close to hers.

'I'd have to argue that you're the most wonderful of the wonderful,' he murmured against her mouth.

'I've never been so lonely as those days in Dolphin Bay after you went home. I ached to be with you,' she confessed.

'One night, after a business dinner, I got into the car and decided to drive down just to see you for an hour or two,' he said.

'So why didn't you?'

'Because I figured I'd end up driving home at night without sleeping at all and thought there was a good chance I'd crash the car.'

She stilled as she thought of the accident that had injured Emily and ultimately, because of its repercussions, taken her father's life too. 'I'm so glad you stayed put,' she said. 'Although I probably wouldn't have let you go back if you'd come.'

He kissed her and she eagerly kissed him back. Then she broke away to plant hungry little kisses along the line of his jaw, and came back to claim his mouth again in a deep kiss that rapidly became urgent with desire.

Without breaking the kiss, he slid her jacket off her shoulders so it fell to the floor. She fumbled with his tie, and when it didn't come undone easily she broke away from the kiss with a murmur of frustration so she could see what she was doing.

'Did I tell you how incredibly sexy you look in a suit?' she asked, her breath coming rapidly as she pulled off his tie and started to unbutton his shirt so she could push her hands inside. His chest was rock-solid with muscle, his skin smooth and warm. 'But then you look incredibly sexy in jeans too. Maybe you look incredibly sexy in anything—or maybe nothing.'

Her body ached with want for him. And this time there was no reason to stop—except *he* stopped. 'Wait,' he said.

'I don't want to wait,' she urged breathlessly. 'We're in the honeymoon suite.'

He stepped back. 'Seriously. I have to tell you something,' he said, the words an effort through his laboured breathing.

'Okay,' she replied, thinking of the bed behind her and how soon she could manoeuvre him onto it.

'Kate, listen—I can see where this is heading.'

'Good,' she said.

'And I don't think you're ready for it.'

Her eyes widened. 'Let me be the judge—' she started to say.

'Please,' he broke in. 'This is important. I've told you before, I want you to be able to trust me.'

'Yes,' she said.

'I want you to be sure of me before we…we make love.'

She wasn't certain what he was trying to say but she sensed it was important. Very important.

'What I'm trying to say is that if we wait until we're married you'll have no doubts about how committed I am to you. And it will give you the security I think you really need.'

She stared at him, lost for words, but with a feeling of intense joy bubbling through her.

'I'm asking you to marry me, Kate,' he said hoarsely.

'And…and I'm saying yes,' she whispered.

He gathered her into his arms and hugged her close. They stood, arms wrapped around each other for a long moment, when all she was aware of was his warmth and strength, the thudding of his heart and their own ragged breathing.

'I love you, Sam,' she said. 'I…I couldn't say it at the airport in front of all those people. It's too…too private.'

'I didn't mean to say it there; no one was more surprised than I was. I was just so relieved you hadn't flown away already, never to speak to me again, when you discovered I wasn't in Singapore to meet you.'

Then and there, she resolved never to tell him that she'd been on her way out of the airport when he'd found her.

'There's another thing,' he said, reaching into his pocket and pulling out a little black velvet box. 'I want to make it official.'

She drew a sharp intake of breath. It couldn't be. *It just couldn't be.* That would be too, too perfect.

With a hand that wasn't quite steady, she took the box from him and opened it. Inside was an exquisite ring, set with a baguette-cut emerald surrounded by two baguette-cut diamonds. 'Sam. It's perfect.'

'I thought it went with the colour of your eyes,' he said, sounding very pleased with himself in a gruff, masculine way. 'There's a good jewellery shop in the shopping arcade attached to the hotel.'

'I love it,' she whispered as Sam slipped it on to the third finger of her left hand. 'I absolutely love it.' She held her hand up in front of her for them both to admire. 'It's a perfect fit.'

'Lucky guess,' he said. 'Though, we builders are good with measurements.'

'Clever you,' she said, kissing him.

'I'd like to get married as soon as possible,' he declared. 'So we can…?'

'Not just because of that. Because I want you to be my wife.'

'And I love the idea of you being my husband,' she murmured. 'My husband,' she repeated, liking the sound of the words.

'Obviously, with the business, there's no way I can live in Dolphin Bay—though we can buy a holiday house there if you like. We'll have to live in Sydney. If that's okay with you.'

'Yes,' she said. 'I'd like that. Though, there are things we need to sort out. Like Ben. My job.'

'I don't think Ben will be at all surprised to be losing you, and you'll still be involved with the new resort as a part owner.'

'And through my connection with the owner of the construction company,' she said.

'I was thinking of setting up a hotel development division in the business,' he told her. 'What do you think?'

'That I could work with?' she asked.

He nodded. 'Of course, that would involve necessary research visiting fabulous hotels all around the world with your husband.'

'That seems a sound business proposition,' she said.

'Starting with a certain palace hotel in India where we can have our real honeymoon.'

'And write it off on expenses,' she said with a giggle.

'I like your thinking,' he said. 'Welcome to Lancaster & Son Construction, Mrs Lancaster-To-Be.'

'We…we might have a son,' she said. 'The name would live on.'

'Or a daughter. Or both. I want at least two children, if that's okay by you. I hated being an only child.'

'Quite okay with me,' she said on a sigh of happiness.

She wound her arms around his neck, loving it when her ring flashed under the light. 'Sam? I feel like I really trust you now. And I'm very sure of your commitment.'

'Yes,' he murmured, kissing the soft hollow at the base of her throat.

'And I want you to be sure of my love and commitment.'

'Thank you,' he said.

'We're officially engaged now, aren't we? You're my fiancé, right?'

'Yes,' he replied, planting a trail of little kisses up her neck to the particularly sensitive spot under her ear. It was almost unbearably pleasurable.

'So do you think we could start our practice honeymoon now?'

She looked meaningfully across at the enormous bed, covered in pink rose petals.

'Good idea,' he said as he picked her up and carried her towards it.

* * * * *

THE WEDDING
PLANNER AND
THE CEO

ALISON ROBERTS

CHAPTER ONE

'*No?*'

The smile was sympathetic but the head-shake emphasised the negative response and the receptionist's raised eyebrows suggested that Penelope must have known she was dreaming when she thought her request might be considered reasonable.

'There must be *someone* I could speak to?' It was harder to say no face to face than over the phone, which was, after all, why she'd taken time out of her crazy schedule to fight London traffic and come to the company's head office in person.

In desperation?

'There's really no point.' The receptionist's smile faded slightly. 'You might be able to engage a cowboy to let off a few fireworks on a week's notice but to get the kind of show the best company in the country has to offer, you have to book in advance. *Months* in advance.'

'I didn't have months. My bride only decided she wanted fireworks this morning. I'm talking Bridezilla, here, you know?'

There was a wary edge to the receptionist's gaze

now. Was she worried that Penelope might be capable of following her client's example and throwing an epic tantrum?

'I understand completely but I'm sorry, there's still nothing I can do to help. For future reference, you can book online to make an appointment to talk to one of our sales reps.'

'I don't want to talk to a sales rep.' Penelope tapped into the extra height her four-inch heels provided. 'I want to talk to your manager. Or director. Or whoever it is that runs this company.'

The smile vanished completely. 'We have a chief executive officer. All Light on the Night is an international company. An *enormous* international company. We do shows like the Fourth of July on the Brooklyn Bridge in New York. New Year's Eve on the Sydney Harbour Bridge in Australia.' Her tone revealed just how far out of line Penelope had stepped. 'You might very well want to talk to him but there's no way on earth Ralph Edwards would be interested in talking to *you*.'

'Really? Why not?'

The curiosity sounded genuine and it came from a male voice behind Penelope. The effect on the young woman in front of her was astonishing. The receptionist paled visibly and her mouth opened and closed more than once, as if she was trying to recall all the vehement words that had just escaped.

Penelope turned to see a tall man and registered dark hair long enough to look tousled, faded denim jeans and…cowboy boots? One of the sales reps, perhaps?

'She…doesn't have an appointment.' The receptionist was clearly rattled. 'She just walked in and wants to book a show. A *wedding*...'

The man's gaze shifted to Penelope and made her want to smooth the close fit of her skirt over her hips even though she knew perfectly well it couldn't be creased. Or raise a hand to make sure no errant tresses had escaped the French braiding that described a perfect crescent from one side of her forehead to meet the main braid on the back of her head.

'Congratulations.' His voice had a rich, low timbre. It made Penelope think of gravel rolling around in something thick and delicious. Like chocolate.

'Sorry?' Was he congratulating her on her choice of this company?

'On your engagement.'

'Oh...it's not *my* wedding.'

That was a dream too distant to be visible even with a telescope at the moment. And there was no point even picking up a telescope until she knew what it was she was looking for, and how could she know that until she discovered who she really was and what she was capable of? Come to think of it, this was the first step towards that distant dream, wasn't it? The first time she was taking a leap out of any known comfort zone. Doing something *she* wanted—just for herself.

'I'm an event manager,' she said, after the barely perceptible pause. 'It's my client who's getting married.'

'Ah...' The spark of polite interest was fading rapidly. 'You've come to the right place, then. I'm sure Melissa will be able to help you with whatever arrangements you want to make.'

Melissa made a choked sound. 'She wants the show next Saturday, Mr Edwards.'

Mr Edwards? The terribly important CEO of this huge international company wore faded jeans and cow-boy boots to work? Penelope was clearly overdressed but she couldn't let it faze her enough to lose this un-expected opportunity.

One that was about to slip away. She saw the look that implied complete understanding and went as far as forgiving the company receptionist for her unprofes-sional exchange with a potential client. She also saw the body language that suggested this CEO was about to retreat to whatever top-floor executive sanctuary he'd unexpectedly appeared from.

'I'll give her a list of other companies that might be able to help,' Melissa said.

'I don't want another company.' The words burst out with a speed and emphasis that took Penelope by sur-prise. 'I...I have to have the best and...and you're the best, aren't you?'

Of course they were. The entire wall behind the re-ceptionist's desk was a night sky panorama of explod-ing fireworks. Pyrotechnic art with a combination of shape and colour that was mind-blowing.

The man's mouth twitched. Maybe he'd been sur-prised, too. 'We certainly are.' Amusement reached his eyes with a glint. Very dark eyes, Penelope noticed. As black as sin, even. Her pulse skipped and sped up. There was only one thing to do when you found your-self so far out of your depth like this. Aim for the sur-face and kick hard.

'It might be worth your while to consider it.' She snatched a new gulp of air. 'This is a celebrity wedding. The kind of publicity that can't be bought.' She managed a smile. 'I understand you specialise in huge shows but New Year's Eve and the Fourth of July only happen once a year, don't they? You must need the smaller stuff as well? This could be a win-win situation for both of us.'

An eyebrow quirked this time. Was he intrigued by her audacity? Was that a sigh coming from Melissa's direction?

'You have a managerial board meeting in fifteen minutes, Mr Edwards.'

'Give me ten,' Penelope heard herself saying, her gaze still fixed on him. 'Please?'

She looked like some kind of princess. Power-dressed and perfectly groomed. The spiky heels of her shoes looked like they could double as a lethal weapon and he could imagine that the elegant, leather briefcase she carried might be full of lengthy checklists and legally binding contracts.

She was the epitome of everything Rafe avoided like the plague so why on earth was he ushering her into his office and closing the door behind them? Perhaps he was trying to send a message to the junior staff that even difficult clients needed to be treated with respect. Or maybe there had been something in the way she'd looked when he'd suggested it was her own wedding she'd come here to organise.

A flicker of...astonishment? He'd probably have the

same reaction if someone suggested he was about to walk down the aisle.

Maybe not for the same reasons, though. The kind of people he had in his life were as non-conformist as he was, whereas this woman looked like she'd already have the preferred names picked out for the two perfectly behaved children she would eventually produce. One girl and one boy, of course. She might have them already, tidied away in the care of a nanny somewhere, but a quick glance at her left hand as she walked past him revealed an absence of any rings so maybe it had been embarrassment that it was taking so long rather than astonishment that had registered in that look.

No. More likely it was something about the way she'd said 'please'. That icy self-control with which she held herself had jarred on both occasions with something he'd seen flicker in her face but the flicker that had come with that 'please' had looked like determination born of desperation and he could respect that kind of motivation.

'Take a seat.' He gestured towards an area that had comfortable seating around a low coffee table—an informal meeting space that had a wall of glass on one side to show off the fabulous view of the Wimbledon golf course.

Not that she noticed the gesture. Clearly impressed to the point of being speechless, she was staring at the central feature of the penthouse office. A mirror-like tube of polished steel that was broken in the middle. The layer of stones on the top of the bottom section had flames flickering in a perfect circle.

He liked it that she was so impressed. He'd designed this feature himself and he was proud of it. But he didn't have time for distractions like showing off.

'Ms...?'

'Collins. Penelope Collins.'

'Rafe Edwards.' The handshake was brief but surprisingly firm. This time she noticed his invitation and he watched her seat herself on one of the couches. Right on the edge as if she might need to leap up and flee at any moment. Legs angled but not crossed.

Nice legs. Was that subtle tug on the hem of her skirt because she'd noticed him noticing? Rafe glanced at his watch and then seated himself on the opposite couch. Or rather perched on his favourite spot, with a hip resting on the broad arm of the couch.

'So...a celebrity wedding?'

She nodded. 'You've heard of Clarissa Bingham?'

'Can't say I have.'

'Oh... She's a local Loxbury girl who got famous in a reality TV show. She's marrying a football star. Blake Summers.'

'I've heard of *him*.'

'It's a huge wedding and we were lucky enough to get the best venue available. Loxbury Hall?'

'Yep. Heard of that, too.'

Her surprise was evident in the way she blinked— that rapid sweep of thick, dark eyelashes. He could understand the surprise. Why should he know anything about a small town on the outskirts of the New Forest between here and Southampton? Or an eighteenth-century manor house that had been used as a function venue for the last decade? He wasn't about to tell her that this location did, in fact, give him a rather close connection to this upcoming event.

'It could be the last wedding ever held there because the property's just been sold and nobody knows whether the new owner will carry it on as a business venture.'

'Hmm.' Rafe nodded but his attention was straying. This Penelope Collins might not be remotely his type but any red-blooded male could appreciate that she was beautiful. Classically beautiful with that golden blonde hair and that astonishing porcelain skin. Or maybe not so classical given that her eyes were brown rather than blue. Nice combination, that—blonde hair and brown eyes—and her skin had a sun-kissed glow to it that suggested an excellent spray tan rather than risking damage from the real thing. She was probably no more than five feet three without those killer heels and her drink of choice was probably a gin and tonic. Or maybe a martini with an olive placed perfectly in the centre of the toothpick.

'Sorry...what was that?'

'It's the perfect place for a fireworks show. The terrace off the ballroom looks down at the lake. There'll be six hundred people there and major magazine coverage. I could make sure that your company gets excellent publicity.'

'We tend to get that from our larger events. Or special-effects awards from the movie industry. There are plenty of smaller companies out there that specialise in things like birthday parties or weddings.'

'But I want this to be spectacular. The *best*...'

She did. He could see that in her eyes. He'd had that kind of determination once—the need to get to the top and be the very best, and it hadn't been easy, especially that first time.

'Is this your first wedding?'

Her composure slipped and faint spots of pink appeared on her cheeks. 'I run a very successful catering company so I've been involved in big events for many years. Moving to complete event design and execution *has* been a more recent development.'

'So this *is* your first wedding.'

She didn't like the implied putdown. Something like defiance darkened her eyes and the aura of tension around the rest of her body kicked up a notch.

'The event is running like clockwork so far. Everything's in place for the ceremony and reception. The entertainment, decorations and catering are locked in. Clarissa is thrilled with her dress and the photographers are over the moon by the backdrops the venue offers. We even have the best local band playing live for the dancing. You must have heard of Diversion?'

Rafe's breath came out in an unexpected huff. Another connection? This was getting weird.

'It was all going perfectly until this morning, when Clarissa decided they had to have fireworks to finish the night. She had a complete meltdown when I told her that it was probably impossible to organise at such late notice.'

Rafe had dealt with some meltdowns from clients so he knew how difficult it could be, especially when your reputation might be hanging by a thread. Maybe Penelope was reliving some of the tension and that was what was giving her voice that almost imperceptible wobble. A hint of vulnerability that tugged on something deep in his gut with an equally almost imperceptible 'ping'.

'When it got to the stage that she was threatening to pull the plug on the whole wedding, I said I'd make some enquiries.'

'So you came straight to the top?' The corner of Rafe's mouth lifted. 'Have to say your style is impressive, Ms Collins.'

He'd done the same thing himself more than once.

'I know I'm asking a lot and it probably is impossible but at least I can say I tried and…and maybe you can point me in the direction of an alternative company that might be able to do at least a reasonable job.'

There was a moment's silence as Rafe wondered how to respond. Yes, he could send her hunting for another company but nobody reputable would take this on.

'Have you any idea what's involved with setting up a professional fireworks show?'

She shook her head. She caught her bottom lip between her teeth, too, and the childlike gesture of trepidation was enough to make Rafe wonder just how much of her look was a front. And what was she trying to hide?

'Long-term planning is essential for lots of reasons. We have to have meetings with the client to discuss budgets and the style and timing of the show.'

'The budget won't be an issue.'

'Are you sure? We're talking over a thousand pounds a minute here.'

'I'm sure.' She sounded confident but he'd seen the movement of her throat as she'd swallowed hard.

'The show gets fired to music. That has to be chosen and then edited and correlated to the pyrotechnic effects. The soundtrack has to be cued and programmed into a computer.'

Once upon a time, Rafe had done all these jobs himself. Long, hard nights of getting everything perfect on an impossible schedule. The memories weren't all bad, though. That kind of hard work had got him where he was today.

'The fireworks have to be chosen and sourced. The site has to be mapped and the display layout planned for firing points. There are safety considerations and you have to allow for a fallout range that could be over a hundred metres. You have to get permits. And this all has to happen before you start setting up—fusing all the fireworks together in the correct sequence, putting electric matches in each fuse run, and then testing the whole package to make sure it's going to work.'

'I understand.' There was a stillness about her that suggested she was preparing to admit defeat. 'And you were right. I had no idea how much work was involved. I'm sorry...' She got to her feet. 'It was very kind of you to take the time to explain things.'

The door to the office opened as she finished speaking. Melissa poked her head around the edge.

'They're waiting for you in the boardroom, Mr Edwards.'

Rafe got to his feet, too. Automatically, he held out his hand and Penelope took it. It was a clasp rather than a shake and, for some bizarre reason, Rafe found himself holding her hand for a heartbeat longer than could be considered professional.

Long enough for that odd ping of sensation he'd felt before to return with surprising force. Enough force to be a twist that couldn't be dismissed. A memory of what it was like to be struggling and then come up against a brick wall? Or maybe articulating all the steps of the challenge of delivering a show had reminded him that he'd been able to do all that himself once. Every single job that he now employed experts in the field to do on his behalf.

He could do it again if he wanted. Good grief, he ran one of the biggest pyrotechnic companies in the world—he could do whatever he wanted.

And maybe...he wanted to do *this*.

He had everything he'd always dreamed of now but this wasn't the first time he'd felt that niggle that something was missing. Wasn't the best way to find something to retrace your footsteps? Going back to his roots as a young pyrotechnician would certainly be retracing footsteps that were long gone. Had he dropped something so long ago he'd forgotten what it actually was?

'There is one way I might be able to help,' he found himself saying.

'A personal recommendation to another company?' Hope made her eyes shine. They had a dark outline to their pupils, he noticed. Black on brown. A perfect ring to accentuate them. Striking.

'No. I was thinking more in terms of doing it myself.'

Her breath caught in an audible gasp. 'But...all those things you said...'

'They still stand. Whether or not it's doable would depend on cooperation from your clients with any restrictions, such as what fireworks we happen to have in stock. The site survey and decisions on style and music would have to be done immediately. Tomorrow.'

'I could arrange that.' That breathless excitement in her voice was sweet. 'What time would you be available?'

'It's Saturday. We don't have any major shows happening and I make my own timetable. What time would your clients be available?'

'We'll be on site all day. They have a dance lesson in the morning and we're doing a ceremony rehearsal in the afternoon. Just come anytime that suits. Would you like me to email you a map?'

'That won't be necessary. By coincidence, I'm familiar with the property, which is another point in favour of pulling this off. The site survey wouldn't be an issue.'

The massive image of exploding fireworks was impossible to miss as Penelope left the office but it was more than simply a glorious advertisement now. For a heartbeat, it felt like she was actually *there*—seeing them happen and hearing the bone-shaking impact of the detonations.

Excitement, that was what it was. Ralph Edwards might look like a cowboy but he was going to help her get the biggest break she could ever have. Clarissa's wedding was going to finish with the kind of bang that

would have her at the top of any list of desirable wedding planners. On her way to fame and fortune and a
lifelong career that couldn't be more perfect for her.
She would be completely independent and then she'd
be able to decide what else she might need in her life.

Who else, maybe…

Thanks to the traffic, the drive back to Loxbury was
going to take well over two hours, which meant she
would be up very late tonight, catching up with her
schedule. She could use the time sensibly and think
ahead about any potential troubleshooting that might
be needed.

Or she could think about fireworks instead. The kind
of spectacular shapes and colours that would be painted
against the darkness of a rural sky but probably seen
by every inhabitant of her nearby hometown and have
images reproduced in more than one glossy magazine.

As the miles slid by—despite an odd initial resis-
tance—Penelope also found herself thinking about the
tousled cowboy she would have to be working with in
the coming week to make this happen. He had to be
the most unlikely colleague she could have imagined.
Someone she would have instinctively avoided like the
plague under normal circumstances, even. But if he
could help her make this wedding the event that would
launch her career, she was up for it.

Couldn't wait to see him again, in fact.

CHAPTER TWO

'No, no, Monsieur Blake. Do not bend over your lady like that, or you will lose your balance and you will both end up on the floor. Step to the side and bend your knee as you dip her. Keep your back *straight*.'

Blake Summers abruptly let go of his bride-to-be but Clarissa caught his arm. 'Don't you dare walk out on me again. How are we ever going to learn this dance if you keep walking away?'

He shook his arm free. 'I can't do it, babe. I told you that. I. Don't. Dance.'

'But this our *wedding* dance.' The tone advertised imminent tears. 'Everyone will be watching. Taking photos.'

'This whole thing is all about the photos, isn't it? I'm up to *here* with it.' Muscles in the young football star's arm bunched as he raised a fist well above head level. 'You know what? If I'd had any idea of how much crap this would all involve I would have thought twice about asking you to marry me.'

'Oh, my God…' Clarissa buried her face in her hands and started sobbing. Penelope let out a long sigh. She felt rather inclined to follow her example.

The dance teacher, Pierre, came towards her with a wonderfully French gesture that described exactly how frustrated he was also becoming.

'It's only a simple dance,' he muttered. 'We've been here for an hour and we have only covered the first twenty seconds of the song. Do you know how long Monsieur Legend's "All of Me" goes for?' He didn't wait for Penelope to respond. 'Five minutes and eight seconds—that's how long. *C'est de la torture.*'

Blake's expression morphed from anger to irritation and finally defeat. 'I'm sorry, babe. I didn't mean it. Really.' He put his arms around Clarissa. 'I just meant we could have eloped or something and got away from all the fuss.'

'You did mean it.' Clarissa struggled enough to escape his embrace. 'You don't want to marry me.' She turned her back on him and hugged herself tightly.

'I do. I love you, babe. All of me, you know, loves all of you.'

Clarissa only sobbed louder. This was Penelope's cue to enter stage left. She walked briskly across the polished wood of the floor and put an arm around her client's shoulders.

'It's okay, hon. We just need to take a break.' She gave a squeeze. 'It's such an emotional time in the final run-up to such a big day. Things can seem a bit overwhelming, can't they?'

Clarissa nodded, sniffing loudly.

'And we've got a whole week to sort this dance out. Just a few moves that you can repeat for the whole song, isn't that right, Pierre?'

Pierre shrugged. 'As you say. Only a few moves.'

Penelope turned her most encouraging smile on the groom-to-be. 'You're up for that, aren't you, Blake? You do know how incredibly sexy it is for a man to be able to dance, even a little bit, don't you?'

'Dancing's for pansies,' Blake muttered.

Penelope's smile dimmed. She could feel a vibe coming from Pierre's direction that suggested she might be about to lose her on-call dance teacher.

'How 'bout this?' she suggested brightly. 'We'll put the music on and Pierre will dance with Clarissa to show you what you'll look like on the night. So you can see how romantic it will be. How gorgeous you'll both look.'

Blake scowled but Clarissa was wiping tears from her face with perfectly French-manicured fingertips. The sideways glance at the undeniably good-looking dance teacher was flirtatious enough for Penelope to be thankful that Blake didn't seem to notice.

'Fine.' He walked towards the tall windows that doubled as doors to the flagged terrace. Penelope joined him as Pierre set the music up and talked to Clarissa.

'Gorgeous view, isn't it?'

'I guess. The lake's okay. I like those dragons that spout water.'

'The whole garden's wonderful. You should have a look around while the weather's this nice. There's even a maze.'

The notes of the romantic song filled the space as Pierre swept Clarissa into his arms and began leading her expertly through the moves. Blake crossed his arms and scowled.

'It's easy for her. She's been doing salsa classes for years. But she expects me to look like *him*? Not going to happen. Not in this lifetime.'

Penelope shook her head and smiled gently. 'I think all she wants is to be moving to the song she's chosen in the arms of the man she loves.'

A sound of something like resignation came from Blake but Penelope could feel the tension lift. Until his head turned and he stiffened again.

'Who's that?' he demanded. 'I told you I didn't want anyone watching this lesson. I feel like enough of an idiot as it is. If that's a photographer, hoping to get a shot of me practising, he can just get the hell out of here.'

Penelope turned her head. The ballroom of Loxbury Hall ran the length of the house between the two main wings. There were probably six huge bedrooms above it upstairs. Quite some distance to recognise a shadowy figure standing in the doorway that led to the reception hall but she knew who it was instantly. From the man's height, perhaps. Or the casual slouch to his stance. That shaft of sensation deep in her belly had to be relief. He'd kept his word.

She could trust him?

'It's Ralph Edwards!' she exclaimed softly. 'I told you he was coming some time today. To discuss your fireworks?'

'Oh...yeah...' Blake's scowl vanished. 'Fireworks are cool.' He brightened. 'Does that mean I don't have to do any more dancing today?'

'Let's see what Pierre's schedule is. We'd have time

for another session later. After the meeting with the florist maybe. Before the rehearsal.'

It was another couple of minutes before the song ended. Clarissa was following Pierre's lead beautifully and Penelope tried to focus, letting her imagination put her client into her wedding dress. To think how it was going to look with the soft lighting of hundreds of candles. The song was a great choice. If Blake could end up learning the moves well enough to look a fraction as good as Pierre, it was going to be a stunning first dance.

Details flashed into her mind, like the best places to put the huge floral arrangements and groups of candles to frame the dance floor. Where the photographers and cameramen could be placed to be inconspicuous but still get great coverage. Whether it was going to work to have the wrist loop to hold the train of Clarissa's dress out of the way. She scribbled a note on the paper clipped to the board she carried with her everywhere on days like this so that none of these details would end up being forgotten.

The dress. Candles. Flowers. There was so much to think about and yet the thing she was most aware of right now was the figure standing at the ballroom doorway, politely waiting for the music to finish before interrupting. Why did his presence make her feel so nervous? Her heart had picked up speed the moment she'd seen him and it hadn't slowed any since. That initial twinge of relief had shattered into butterflies in her stomach now, and they were twisting and dancing rather like Clarissa was.

Not that the feeling was altogether unpleasant. It reminded her of the excitement that strong physical attraction to someone could produce.

Was she physically attracted to Ralph Edwards?

Of course not. The very idea was so ridiculous she knew that wasn't the cause. No. This nervousness was because the fireworks show wasn't a done deal yet and there could be another tantrum from Clarissa to handle if the meeting didn't go well.

It had to go well. Penelope held the clipboard against her chest and clutched it a little more tightly as the music faded.

Rafe was quite content to have a moment or two to observe.

To bask in the glow of satisfaction he'd had from the moment he'd driven through the ornate gates of this historic property.

A property he now owned, for heaven's sake.

Who would have thought that he'd end up with a life like this? Not him, that's for sure. Not back in the day when he'd been one of a busload of disadvantaged small children who'd been brought to Loxbury Hall for a charity Christmas party. He'd seen the kind of kingdom that rich people could have. People with enough money to make their own rules. To have families that stayed together and lived happily ever after.

Yes. This was a dream come true and he was loving every minute of it.

He was loving standing here, too.

This room was stunning. A few weeks ago he'd had to use his imagination to think of what it might be like with music playing and people dancing on the polished floor. Reality was even better. He was too far away to get more than a general impression of the girl who was dancing but he could see enough. A wild cascade of platinum blonde waves. A tight, low-cut top that revealed a cleavage to die for. Enhanced by silicone, of course, but what did that matter? She was a true WAG and Blake Summers was a lucky young man.

What a contrast to Ms Collins—standing there clutching a clipboard and looking as tense as a guitar string about to snap. You'd never get her onto a dance floor as a partner, that's for sure. His buoyant mood slipped a little—kind of reminding him of schooldays when the bell sounded and you had to leave the playground and head back to the classroom.

Never mind. As she'd pointed out herself, this could well be the last time the reception rooms of Loxbury Hall would be used as a public venue and there was a kind of irony in the idea that he could be putting on a fireworks show to mark the end of that era for the house and the start of his own occupation.

Remarkably fitting, really.

Rafe walked towards her as the music faded. Was her look supposed to be more casual, given that it was a weekend? If so, it hadn't worked. Okay, it was a shirt and trousers instead of a skirt but they were tailored and sleek and she still had that complicated rope effect going on in her hair. Did she sleep like that and still not have a hair out of place in the morning?

Maybe she didn't sleep at all. Just plugged herself in to a power point for a while.

Good thing that he was close enough to extend a hand to the young man standing beside Penelope. That way, nobody could guess that his grin was due to private amusement.

'I'm Rafe Edwards,' he said. 'Saw that winning goal you scored on your last match. Good effort.'

'Thanks, man. This is Clarissa. Clarrie, this is Ralph Edwards—the fireworks guy.'

'Rafe, please. I might have Ralph on my birth certificate but it doesn't mean I like it.' His smile widened as Clarissa batted ridiculously enhanced eyelashes at him and then he turned his head.

'Gidday, Penny. How are you?'

'Penelope,' she said tightly. 'I actually like the name on *my* birth certificate.'

Whoa…could she get any more uptight? Rafe turned back to the delicious Clarissa and turned on the charm.

'How 'bout we find somewhere we can get comfortable and have a chat about what I might be able to do for you?'

Clarissa giggled. 'Ooh…yes, *please*…'

'Why don't we go out onto the terrace?' Penelope's tone made the suggestion sound like a reprimand. 'I just need to have a word with Pierre and then I'll join you. I'll organise some refreshment, too. What would you like?'

'Mineral water for me,' Clarissa said. 'Sparkling.'

'A cold beer,' Blake said. 'It's turning into a scorcher of a day.'

'I'm not sure we've got beer in the kitchen at the moment.'

Blake groaned.

'My apologies,' Penelope said. 'I'll make sure it's available next time.' She scribbled something on her clipboard.

'Coffee for me, thanks,' Rafe said. 'Strong and black.'

The look flashed in his direction was grateful. 'That we *can* do. Would you like a coffee, too, Blake?'

'Have to do, I s'pose. At least we're gonna get to talk about something cool. Do we get to choose the kind of fireworks we want?'

'Sure. We need to talk about the music first, though.' Rafe led the way through the French doors to the terrace. 'I'm guessing you want something romantic?'

Music wasn't being discussed when Penelope took the tray of drinks out to the group. Rafe had a laptop open and Blake and Clarissa were avidly watching what was on the screen.

'Ooh…that one. We've got to have that. What's it called?'

'It's a peony. And this one's a chrysanthemum. And this is a golden, hanging willow. It's a forty-five-shot cake so it goes for a while.'

'Nice. I like them loud.' Blake was rubbing his hands together. 'Man, this is going to be epic.'

'With it being your wedding, I was thinking you might want something a bit more romantic.' Rafe tapped his keyboard. 'Look at this for an opening, maybe.'

'OMG.' Clarissa pressed a hand to her open mouth. 'You can do love hearts? For *real*?'

'Sure can. And look at this. Horsetails look a lot like bridal veils, don't you think?'

Clarissa hadn't looked this happy since the first fitting of her wedding dress. Before she'd started to find tiny imperfections that had to be dealt with.

'I want it to be romantic,' she breathed. 'And I've got the perfect song. Whitney Houston's "I Will Always Love You".'

Blake rolled his eyes and shook his head. Rafe lifted an eyebrow. 'Nice, but the tempo could be a bit on the slow side. Maybe a better song to dance to than accompany fireworks?'

'It's soppy,' Blake growled. 'We need something loud. Fun. Wasn't the whole idea to end the night with a bang?'

Clarissa giggled. 'Oh...we will, babes, don't you worry about that.'

Blake grinned. 'You're singing my song already.'

Rafe's appreciative grin faded the moment he caught Penelope's gaze. He took a sip of his coffee.

'What about Meat Loaf?' Blake suggested. '"I'd Do Anything For Love"?'

'Not bad. Good beats to time to effects.'

'No.' Clarissa shook her head firmly.

Penelope was searching wildly for inspiration. 'Bon Jovi? "Livin' On A Prayer"? Or the Troggs? "Wild Thing"?'

'Getting better.' Rafe nodded. The look he gave her this time held a note of surprise. Did he think she wasn't into music or something? 'Let's keep it going. Bon Jovi's a favourite of mine. What about "Always"?'

The words of the song drifted into Penelope's head. Along with an image of it being passionately sung. And even though it was Rafe she was looking at, it was no excuse to let her mind drift to imagining him with wild, rock-god hair. Wearing a tight, black singlet and frayed jeans. Saying he would cry for the woman he loved. Or die for her…

Phew…it was certainly getting hot. She fanned herself with her clipboard and tried to refocus. To push any image of men in frayed jeans and singlets out of her head. So not her type.

She liked designer suits and neat haircuts. The kind of up-and-coming young attorney look, like her last boyfriend who'd not only graduated from law school with honours but was active in a major political party. Disappointing that it had turned out they'd had nothing in common—especially for her grandparents—but she didn't have time for a relationship in her life right now anyway.

She didn't have time to pander to this group's inability to reach an agreement either, but she couldn't think of any way to speed things up and half an hour later they were still no closer to making a definitive choice.

Further away, perhaps, given that both Clarissa and Blake were getting annoyed enough to veto any suggestion the other made and getting steadily snarkier about it. Any moment now it would erupt into a full-blown row and the hint of annoyance in Rafe's body language would turn into disgust and he'd walk away from a job he didn't actually need.

Penelope was increasingly aware that time was running out. They had a meeting with the florist coming up, Pierre was going to return for another dance lesson and there was a rehearsal with the celebrant in the garden at four p.m.

'Did you have anything else you needed to do while you're here?' she asked Rafe.

'A bit of a survey.' He nodded. 'I need to get a feel for the layout and check where I'd position things. I'm thinking a barge on the other side of the lake but I'll be able to get a good view if I go upstairs and—' He stopped abruptly. 'Is that a problem?'

'We're not allowed upstairs,' Clarissa confided. 'Apparently it's one of the biggest rules about using this venue.'

'Is that right?'

It was no surprise that Rafe wasn't impressed by a set of rules and his tone suggested he wouldn't hesitate in breaking them. She could imagine how well it would go down if she forbade the action and she certainly didn't want to get him offside any more than he was already, thanks to the sparring young couple.

If he had to go upstairs in order to be able to do his job, maybe she'd just have to turn a blind eye and hope for the best. At least she could plead ignorance of it actually happening if word got out and she could probably apologise well enough to smooth things over if the owners were upset.

'How long will your survey take?' The words came out more crisply than she'd intended.

'Thirty-nine minutes.' He grinned. 'No, make that forty-one.'

He wasn't the only person getting annoyed here. 'In that case, let's meet back here in forty-five minutes,' Penelope said. 'Blake—take Clarissa to the Loxbury pub and you can get your cold beer and a quick lunch and see if you can agree on a song. This fireworks show isn't going to happen unless we lock that in today. Isn't that right, Ralph?'

His look was deadpan.

'Sorry. Rafe.'

'That's right, Penelope. We're on a deadline that's tight enough to be almost impossible as it is.' He smiled at Clarissa. 'You want your red hearts exploding all over the sky to start the show. What if I told you we could put both your names inside a love heart to finish?'

Clarissa looked like she'd just fallen in love with this new acquaintance. She tugged on Blake's arm with some urgency. 'Come on, babes. We've *got* to find a song.'

'I'll have a think, too,' Penelope called after them. 'I've got my iPod and I need a bit of a walk.'

There was a third-floor level on each of the wings of the house, set back enough to provide an upstairs terraced area. Rafe fancied one of these rooms as his bedroom and that was where he headed. He already knew that he'd have the best view of the lake and garden from that terrace. It took a few minutes to get there. Was he crazy, thinking he could actually live in a place this big?

By himself?

He had plenty of friends, he reminded himself as he stepped over the braided rope on the stairs marking the boundary of public access. The guys in the band would want to make this place party central. And it wasn't as if he'd be here that much. He had his apartments in New York and London and he was looking at getting one in China, given that he spent a lot of time there sourcing fireworks. He'd need staff, too. No way could he manage a house this size. And he'd probably need an entire team of full-time gardeners, he decided as he stepped out onto the bedroom terrace. Just clipping the hedges of that maze would probably keep someone busy for weeks.

In fact, there was someone in there right now. Rafe walked closer to the stone pillars edging the terrace and narrowed his eyes. The figure seemed to know its way through the maze, moving swiftly until it reached the grass circle that marked the centre.

Penelope. Of course it was. Hadn't she said she needed a walk? She stopped for a moment with her head down, fiddling with something in her hand. Her iPod? And then she pressed her fingertips against her ears as though she was listening carefully to whatever music she had chosen.

Rafe should have been scanning the grounds on the far side of the lake and thinking about positioning things like the scissor lift he'd need to hold the frame for the lancework of doing the names in fireworks to end the show. Instead, he found himself watching Penelope.

She was kicking her shoes off, which was probably sensible given that heels would sink into that grass. But then she did something that made Rafe's jaw drop.

Blew whatever it was he'd been thinking of her right out of the water.

She started dancing.

Not just the kind of unconscious jiggle along with the beat either. She was dancing like she thought no one could see her which was probably exactly what she did think, tucked into the centre of that maze with its tall, thick hedges.

Rafe leaned into the corner of the terrace, any thoughts of planning a show escaping irretrievably. His eyes narrowed as he focused on the slim figure moving on her secret stage.

An amused snort escaped him. No wonder she needed to hide herself away. She was rubbish at dancing. Her movements were uncoordinated enough to probably make her a laughing stock on a dance floor.

But then his amusement faded. She was doing something she believed was private and she was doing it with her heart and soul. Maybe she didn't really know how to dance but she was doing more than just hearing that music—she was a part of it with every cell of her body.

Rafe knew that feeling. That ability to lose yourself in sound so completely the rest of the world disappeared. Music could be an anaesthetic that made even the worst kind of pain bearable.

Impossible not to remember wearing headphones and turning the sound level up so loud that nothing else existed. So you couldn't hear the latest row erupting in the new foster home that meant you'd be packed up before long and handed around again like some unwanted parcel.

Impossible not to still feel grateful for that first set of drums he'd been gifted so many years ago. Or the thrill of picking up a saxophone for the first time and starting the journey that meant he could do more than simply listen. That meant he could become a part of that music.

It was another world. One that had saved him from what this one had seemed doomed to become.

And he was getting the same feeling from watching Penelope being uninhibited enough to try and dance.

What was that about?

He'd sensed that what you could see with Penelope Collins wasn't necessarily real, hadn't he? When she'd admitted she knew nothing about setting up a fireworks show. Watching her now made him more sure that she was putting up a front to hide who she really was.

Who was the person that was hiding?

Or maybe the real question here was why did he want to know?

He didn't.

With a jerk, Rafe straightened and forced his gaze sideways towards the lake and the far shore. Was there enough clearance from the trees to put a scissor lift or two on the ground or would the safety margins require a barge on the water? He'd bring one of the lads out here first thing tomorrow and they could use a range finder to get accurate measurements but he could trust his eye for now. And he just happened to have an aerial photograph of the property on his laptop, too. Pulling a notepad and the stub of a pencil from the back pocket of his jeans, he started sketching.

By the time he'd finished what he'd wanted to do he

was five minutes late for the time they'd agreed to meet back on the terrace. Not that it made him hurry down the stairs or anything but he wouldn't have planned to stop before he turned into the ballroom and headed for the terrace. The thought only occurred to him when he saw the iPod lying on the hall table, on top of that clipboard Penelope carried everywhere with her.

If he took a look at what she'd played recently, could he pick what it was that she'd been dancing to? Get some kind of clue to solve the puzzle of who this woman actually was?

Clarissa and Blake were late getting back from lunch and, judging by the looks on their faces, they hadn't managed to agree on the music to accompany their fireworks show.

Which meant that Rafe would most likely pull the plug on doing it at all.

He came through the French doors from the ballroom at the same time as the young couple were climbing the stairs from the garden.

'Did you decide?' Rafe asked.

'We tried,' Clarissa groaned. 'We really did...' Her face brightened. 'But then we thought you're the expert. We'll let you decide.'

Penelope bit back the suggestion she'd been about to make. Throwing ideas around again would only take them back to square one and this was a potentially quick and easy fix.

But Rafe lifted an eyebrow. 'You sure about that? Because I reckon I've found the perfect song.'

'What is it?'

'Doesn't matter,' Blake growled. 'You promised you wouldn't argue this time.'

'Have a listen,' Rafe said, putting his laptop on the table and flipping it open. He tapped rapidly on the keyboard. 'I think you might like it.'

It only took the first two notes for Penelope to recognise the song and it sent a chill down her spine. The very song she'd been about to suggest herself. How spooky was *that*?

'Ohhh…' Clarissa's eyes were huge. 'I *love* this song.'

'Who is that?' Blake was frowning. 'Celine Dion?'

Rafe shook his head. 'This is the original version. Jennifer Rush. She cowrote "The Power of Love" in 1984.'

It was the version that Penelope preferred. The one she had on her iPod. The one she'd been dancing to in her private space in the centre of the maze only half an hour or so ago, when she'd taken that much-needed break.

'It's got some great firing points. Like that…' Rafe's hands prescribed an arc as the crescendo started. 'And we can use the extended version to give us a good length of time. Fade it away to leave your names in the heart hanging over the lake.'

He wasn't looking at Penelope. He didn't even send a triumphant glance in her direction as Clarissa and Blake enthusiastically agreed to the song choice.

Which was probably just as well. Penelope had no idea what her expression might look like but it had to include an element of shock. Surely it had to be more than coincidence and she didn't believe in telepathy but it was impossible not to feel some sort of weird connection happening here. How awful would it be if she looked like Clarissa had when he'd told her he could finish the show by putting their names in a love heart? As though she'd just fallen head over heels in love with the man?

Not that it really mattered. The *pièce de résistance* of the wedding that was going to launch her new career was starting to come together and the choice of song was perfect.

With a lot of hard work and a little bit more luck, this whole wedding was going to be perfect.

CHAPTER THREE

SO FAR, SO GOOD.

They couldn't have wished for a better day weather-
wise for what the local media was already billing the
wedding of the year. The blue stretch of summer sky
was broken only by innocent cotton-wool puffs of cloud
and it was warm enough for the skimpy dresses most of
the women seemed to be wearing. More importantly,
the breeze was gentle enough not to ruin any elaborate
hairdos or play havoc with a bridal veil.

The vintage champagne every guest had been offered
on arrival was going down a treat and people were now
beginning to drift towards the rows of chairs draped
with white satin and tied with silver bows. Penelope saw
someone open the small gauze bag she'd found on her
seat and smile as she showed her partner the confetti
that was made up of tiny, glittery silver stars.

How much bigger were those smiles going to be
when they were watching the kind of stars that would
explode across the sky as the finale to this event? Rafe
had arrived as early as Penelope had, driving onto the
estate in the chill mist of a breaking dawn. She'd seen

him and the technicians he'd brought with him, in their fluorescent vests, working in the field on the far side of the lake at various times over the hectic hours since then. Just orange dots of humanity, really, at this distance, but she was sure it was Rafe who was directing the forklift manoeuvring the pallets from the back of a truck at one point and, much later, the towing of a flat barge to float on the lake.

Because that was the kind of job a boss would do, she told herself. It had nothing to do with that odd tingle of something she had no intention of trying to identify. A tingle that appeared along with that persistent image of the man in frayed jeans and a black singlet she had conjured up. An image that had insisted on haunting her dreams over the last week, leaving her to wake with the odd sensation that something was simply not *fair*...

Heading back inside the house, she popped into the kitchen to check that her team was on top of the catering. Judging by the numerous silver platters of hors d'oeuvres lined up ready for the lull while photographs would be taken after the ceremony, they were right on schedule.

'Any worries, Jack?'

'Apart from an eight-course sit-down dinner for two hundred and supper for six hundred? Nah...it's all good.' The older man's smile was reassuring. 'I've got this side of the gig covered. Go and play with your bride.'

'I do need to do that. But I'll be back later. Keep an apron for me.'

'Are you kidding? That dress is far too fancy to get hidden by any apron.'

'It's not too much, is it?' Penelope glanced down at the dark silver sheath dress she had chosen. A lot of effort had gone into what she hoped would be her signature outfit as she occupied an unusual space in a wedding party that was more than simply hired help but less than invited guest. The dress was demure with its long sleeves and scooped neckline that only showed a hint of cleavage. The skirt was ballet length and fell in soft swirls from thigh level but it did fit like a glove everywhere else and it had a soft sparkle that would probably intensify under artificial or candle light.

Jack grinned. 'You look like the director of the nation's most successful event managing company. Make sure they get some photos of you for one of those flash magazines. Now—stop distracting me. Get out of my kitchen and go and keep our first event ticking. Isn't Princess Clarissa about due for another meltdown?'

'Oh, God, I hope not.' With a worried frown, Penelope headed for a ground-floor room in the west wing that had been set aside for the bride and bridesmaids to get dressed in. A room in the east wing was where the groom and his entourage were waiting. That would be the next stop, to make sure they were in position on time. Penelope checked her watch. Only twenty minutes away. The countdown was on.

She took a deep breath. At least she didn't have to worry about the catering side of things. Jack—her head chef—had worked with her ever since she'd advertised for someone to come on board with a fledgling catering company nearly ten years ago. His own restaurant might have failed despite his talent with food but together they'd built a company to be proud of and it had been his idea for her to take the risky move of taking on event management.

Dreaming about something and even making endless lists of the things that she'd have to keep on top of hadn't really prepared her for the reality of it, though. The catering was only one aspect. Had the celebrant arrived yet? Were the photographers behaving themselves? How were the band going in setting themselves up? She'd seen the truck parked around the back an hour or more ago and people unloading a drum kit and amplifiers but what if they couldn't find enough power points? There was a lighting expert who was coming to supervise the safe positioning and lighting of all those candles and would then be in charge for any spotlighting of key people. He hadn't arrived as far as she knew but they weren't due to meet until after the actual ceremony.

At some point, she would have to find Rafe, too, and make sure that he was happy with his set-up. The fireworks were scheduled to go off at one a.m. to mark the end of the party and there was plenty of security personnel discreetly in place to make sure nobody went into forbidden areas and that everybody left Loxbury Hall when they were supposed to.

It was possible that this was the moment when the tension was at its highest. The moment before the carefully timed show that was going to be the wedding of the year kicked off. With her heart in her mouth, Penelope opened the door of the bride's dressing room. Clarissa—in a froth of white—was standing serenely in the centre of the room with a champagne flute in her hand.

She was surrounded by her six bridesmaids who were in same shade of orange as one of the colours of Blake's football club. One of the girls sent another champagne cork hurtling towards the ceiling with a loud pop and the shriek of happy giggles was deafening. The flash of the camera from the official photographer showed he was capturing every joyous moment.

The hairdresser and make-up artists and their teams were packing up an enormous amount of gear. Hair straighteners, heated rollers and cans of spray went into one set of suitcases. Pots of foundation, dozens of brushes and cards of false eyelashes were heading for another. Penelope smiled at the women.

'I think you deserve to join the celebration. They all look fabulous.' She stepped closer and lowered her voice, although it was hardly necessary as the chatter and laughter as the glasses were being refilled were enough to make any conversation private. 'Any problems?'

Cheryl's smile said it all. 'Bit of a mission to get every one of Clarissa's curls sitting just right but we got there in the end. Thank goodness for industrial-strength hairspray.'

The spirals of platinum blonde hair hung to the bride's waist at the back, easily visible through the sheer mist of an exquisitely embroidered veil. Tresses at the front had been twisted and clipped into a soft frame that supported the tiara holding the veil, as well as offering an anchor for a dozen or more small silver stars. A star made of diamonds sparkled on the perfect spray tan of Clarissa's décolletage—a gift from Blake that had inspired one of the themes for the wedding. Beneath that, the heavily beaded corset bodice of the dress made the most of what had to be close to the top of the bride's assets.

'What d'ya think, Penelope?'

'I think you couldn't look more perfect, Clarrie. It's just as well Blake's got all those groomsmen to hold him up when he sees you walking down the aisle.' She took another quick glance at her watch. 'Five minutes and we'll need you all in position in the reception hall. I'm just going to make sure the boys are out of the building and that those photographs as you come out will be the first glimpse of your dress that the world gets.'

It was Penelope who waited with Clarissa in the main entrance, signalling each pair of bridesmaids when it was their turn to walk out of the huge doorway, down the sweep of wide steps and start the journey along the carpet that led to the raised gazebo where the celebrant was waiting, flanked by the males of the wedding party. Clarissa's song choice of Whitney Houston that had been rejected for the fireworks show was perfect for this entrance but it needed careful timing to make sure the bride arrived beside her groom before the song finished.

Penelope waited until all the heads turned to watch Clarissa take her final position, facing Blake and holding both his hands. Nobody saw her as she quietly made her way to the shade of an ancient oak tree, well away from the audience but close enough to hear the ceremony, thanks to the lapel microphone the celebrant was wearing.

A brief respite from the tension of the day was more than welcome. A private moment to collect her thoughts and remember to breathe.

Except it didn't stay private for long. A figure materialised beside her in the shade. A dark figure. And Penelope forgot to breathe for rather too long.

Had Rafe dressed up for the occasion? He was wearing black jeans today, and a black T-shirt that had a faded image of what was probably an album cover from a forgotten era. The cowboy boots were the same, though, and they were in harmony with a battered, wide-brimmed leather hat that any cowboy would have treasured.

He was dressed for his work and clearly comfortable with being on the hired-help side of the boundary Penelope was balancing on but right now her position in this gathering was unimportant. This short period of time was a limbo where nothing mattered other than the vows the wedding couple were exchanging. This tiny patch of the famous Loxbury Hall gardens was a kind of limbo as well. An island that only she and Rafe were inhabiting.

He was as dark as she was pale. As scruffy as she was groomed. As relaxed as she was tense. Black and white. Total opposites.

It should be making her feel very uncomfortable but it wasn't.

There was a curl of something pleasant stealing through Penelope's body. Try as she might to deny it, the surprise of his company was sprinkled with a condiment that could—quite disturbingly—be delight.

* * *

He'd had something on the tip of his tongue to justify the choice of joining Ms Collins in the shade of this tree. Had it been something about it being the best vantage point to observe the ceremony and that he had the time because everything else that could be a distraction in the background had to be put on hold for the duration? Not that his team had much else to do. Everything was in place and all that was needed between now and about midnight was a rehearsal to check that all the electronic components were in functioning order.

Or maybe it had been something about how well the event was going so far. That it was everything the perfect wedding should be.

No wonder the ability to produce words seemed to have failed him for the moment. This was everything the perfect wedding *shouldn't* be. The epitome of the circus that represented conforming to one of society's expected rules of declaring commitment and faithfulness. A rule that was rarely kept, so why bother with the circus in the first place?

Or perhaps the loss of a conversational opening had something to do with being this close to Penelope?

He'd spotted her discreet position from the edge of the lake where he'd initially positioned himself to be out of sight of the guests. That silvery dress she was wearing shone like a new moon in the dense shade of this ancient tree and…and it was possibly the most stunning dress he'd ever seen. Weird, considering there was no more cleavage to be seen than a tiny, teasing line just where that sun-kissed skin began to swell.

Rafe dragged his gaze away, hopefully before she was aware of his appreciation because the glance had been so swift. Her hair looked different today, too. Softer. She still had those braids shaping the sides of her head but the length of it was loose at the back, falling in a thick ringlet instead of another braid. It was longer than he remembered, almost touching the small of her back in that second, silver skin. What would happen, he found himself wondering, if he buried his fingers in that perfect silky spiral and pulled it apart? Would her whole back get covered with golden waves?

What was more likely to happen was that he would infuriate this would-be queen of event management by messing up her hair. She might not be holding a clipboard right now but the tension was still palpable. She was in control. On top of every moment and ready to troubleshoot any problem with the efficiency of a nuclear blast.

Clarissa's breathlessly excited whisper was being amplified by strategically placed microphones. 'I, Clarissa Grace Bingham, take thee, Blake Robert Summers, to be my lawfully wedded husband. To have and to hold...'

Finally, he found something to say.

'Sounds like she's the happiest girl on earth right now.'

'Of course she is. This is her wedding day. Every girl's dream.'

'Really?' Rafe couldn't help the note of scepticism. 'Does anyone really believe that those vows mean anything these days?'

Uh-oh… Maybe he should have ruffled the spiral of hair down her back instead of dropping some kind of verbal bomb. The look he received made him feel like he'd just told a kid that Santa Claus didn't really exist.

'I believe it,' Penelope said.

She did. He could see it in her eyes. A fierce belief that it meant something. Something important. He couldn't look away. He even found himself leaning a little closer as a soft word of query escaped his lips.

'Why?'

Oh, help… His eyes weren't really as black as sin, were they? The mottled light sifting down through the leaves of the tree was enough to reveal that they were a dark brown, with flecks of gold that made them more like a very deep hazel. And the way he was looking at her…

The eye contact had gone on far too long to be polite but Penelope couldn't break the gaze. It felt physical—almost as though he was holding her in his arms. No… it went deeper than that. He was holding something that wasn't physical. Touching something that was deep inside. The part of her that couldn't be seen.

But Rafe was seeing it and it made her feel… vulnerable?

Nobody had ever looked at her like this. As if they could see that dark, secret part of her. As if the world wouldn't end if the door got opened and light flooded in.

And he wanted to know why she believed in something he clearly had no time for. Marriage. Could he see that she *had* to believe in it? Because there was something about it that held the key to putting things right?

The exchange of vows had been completed on the stage of the gazebo and the applause and raucous whistling told her that the first kiss was happening. The flash of cameras going off was there, like stars in the periphery of her vision, but Penelope still couldn't look away from Rafe's gaze.

'It's about the promise,' she found herself saying softly. 'It's not about the dress or the flowers or…or even the fireworks.'

He raised an eyebrow.

'I don't mean they're not important. That's what weddings are all about. Celebrating the promise.' Penelope drew in a breath. She'd said enough and she should be using the time to make sure the photographers had everything they needed for the next part of the programme. And that Jack was ready to keep the guests entertained with food and wine for as long as it took. 'I can't wait to see the show,' she added with a placating smile. 'I know it'll be fabulous.'

'Oh, it will.' Rafe nodded. 'I'll make sure you get the best spot to watch it, shall I?'

'Won't you be busy? Pushing buttons or something?'

'There's pretty much only one button to push. On my laptop. The rest is automatic.'

'No problems setting up? It is all done?'

'Yes, ma'am.' He tipped his hat. 'We're about to double-check everything and that'll be it until show time.'

'That's great. Thank you so much.' Penelope could see guests starting to move. Reaching for those bags of confetti stars and preparing to shower the bride and groom as they went down the aisle together. She stepped away to move closer but Rafe's voice stopped her.

'That promise,' he said quietly. 'The one you believe in. What is it, exactly?'

Startled, she turned her head. 'Security,' she responded. 'Family. It's the promise of a safe place, I guess. Somewhere you know you'll always be loved.'

There was something soft in his eyes now. Something sad?

'You're one of the lucky ones, then.'

'Because I believe in marriage?'

'Because you know what it's like to have a family. Parents. You know what it's like to live in that safe place.'

And he didn't? Something huge squeezed inside her chest and made her breath come out in a huff. She understood that yearning. Her life might look perfect from the outside but she wanted him to know that she understood. That they had a connection here that very few people could have. They might be complete opposites but in that moment it felt like they were the opposite sides of the same coin.

'I've never had parents. My mother abandoned me as a baby and then died. I have no idea who my father is.' Good grief...why on earth was she telling him this much? She backed off. 'You're right, though. I *was* lucky. My grandparents brought me up. I had everything I could possibly want.'

She saw the change in his eyes. He was backing off, too. Had he thought she understood but now saw her as one of the privileged? One who couldn't possibly have any idea of what it was like not to have that safe place?

Penelope didn't want to lose that tiny thread of connection. She was the one who needed that understanding, wasn't she? Because nobody had ever understood.

'Almost everything,' she added, her voice no more than a sigh. She swallowed past the tightness in her throat. 'Maybe if my parents had believed in marriage they could have looked after each other and things would have been different.' She bit her lip as the admission slipped out. 'Better...'

'You don't know that.' That softness in his gaze had changed. There was a flash of anger there. A world of pain. 'Things could have been worse.' Rafe tugged on the rim of his hat, blocking off his gaze. 'Catch you later,' he muttered as he turned away. 'When it's show time.'

The next hours were a blur. Penelope felt like she needed to be in six places at once to make sure everything was flowing smoothly but the adrenaline of it all kept her going without pause. A reporter from the magazine that had the exclusive, first coverage of the event even asked for a quick interview and photographs.

'You do realise you're going to be inundated with work after this, don't you? Every celebrity who's planning a wedding in the foreseeable future is going to want something this good.'

There was fear to be found hiding in the excitement of how well it was all going.

'We're a boutique company. I'm not ever going to take on more clients than I can personally take care of.'

'You've organised this all yourself?'

'I have a partner who's in charge of the catering today. Come and meet Jack. With dinner over, he should have a minute or two to spare. You could get a great picture of him in his chef's whites in the kitchen. He deserves the publicity as much as I do.'

'Let's get one of you two together.' The journalist made a note on her pad. 'Are you, like, a couple?'

Penelope shook her head as she smiled. 'No. Jack has a family. I'm happily single. Career-woman, through and through, that's me.'

That was certainly the image she wanted to portray, anyway. There was no reason for anybody to ever feel sorry for Penelope Collins.

Not any more.

By midnight, the band had been playing for two hours and the party in the ballroom was still in full swing. The drums pulsed in Penelope's blood and the music was so good it was an effort not to let her body respond. It was just as well she was kept too occupied to do more than make a mental note to download some of Diversion's tracks so she could listen again in private.

People were getting drunk now. Emergency cleaning was needed more than once in the restrooms and an ambulance was discreetly summoned to the service entrance to remove one unconscious young woman. Another one was found sobbing in the garden and it fell to Penelope to sit and listen to the tale of romantic woe and calm the guest enough to rejoin the revelry. Then she escaped to the kitchens for a while and insisted on an apron so she could spend a few minutes helping to prepare the supper that would be served on the terrace, timed to finish as the fireworks started.

And then it would all be over, bar the massive job of clearing up, most of which would happen tomorrow. All the tension and exhaustion of the last weeks and days and hours would be over. What was that going to feel like? Would she crawl home and crash or would she still be buzzing this time tomorrow?

Her head was spinning a little now, which suggested that it might be a good thing if she crashed. Maybe that glass of champagne with Jack a few minutes ago to toast their success had been a bad thing. At least it was quieter in the vast spaces of Loxbury Hall. The dance music was finished and people were crowded onto the terrace, enjoying a last glass or two of champagne, along with the delicious canapés on offer. The bride and groom had gone off to change into their going-away outfits and the vintage car, complete with the rope of old tin cans, was waiting at the back, ready to collect them from the front steps as soon as the fireworks show ended.

It was almost time for those fireworks. Penelope hadn't seen Rafe since that weirdly intense conversation under the tree. She hadn't even thought of him.

No. That wasn't entirely true. That persistent image of him was never far away from the back of her mind. And hadn't it got a bit closer right about the time she'd described herself as 'happily single' to that journalist?

And now he was here again, still wearing that hat, with a laptop bag slung over his shoulder. Right outside the kitchen door, when Penelope had hung up her apron and slipped back into the entrance hall so that she could go and find a place to watch the show.

'Ready?'

Words failed her. She could hear an echo of his voice from that earlier conversation.

I'll make sure you get the best spot to watch...

He'd kept his word. Again. She'd known she could trust him, hadn't she, when he'd turned up for that first meeting here?

Having that trust confirmed, on top of being drawn back into where she'd experienced the feeling that they were somehow connected on a secret level, was a mix so powerful it stole the breath, along with any words, from Penelope's body.

All she could do was nod.

A corner of his mouth lifted. 'Come on, then.'

He held out his hand.

And Penelope took it. His grip was strong. Warm. A connection that was physical. Real, instead of the one that was probably purely only in her own imagination, but if she hadn't already been sideswiped by that visceral force, she would never have taken his hand.

Who in their right mind would start holding hands with a virtual stranger? One who had a 'bad boy' label that was practically a neon sign? What good girl would be so willing to follow him?

Not her. Not in this lifetime. She could almost hear her grandmother's voice. The mantra of her life. Her greatest fear.

'You'll end up just like your mother, if you're not very careful.'

How could it feel so good, then? Kind of like when she knew no one could see her and she could let loose and dance…

No one could see her now. Except Rafe. It was like being in one of her dreams, only she wasn't going to end up feeling that something wasn't fair because she didn't have to wake up any time soon. She had to almost skip a step or two to keep up with his long stride but then she tugged back on the pressure. Silly to feel fear at breaking such a little rule when she was already doing something so out of character but maybe it was symbolic.

'We can't go *upstairs*.'

'We have to. I need to get the best view of the show. I've got people on the ground I can reach by radio if there's any problem but I have to be able to see.' He stepped over the thick red rope. 'It's okay. I'm not really breaking the sacred rules. I've cleared it with the owner.'

He sounded completely convincing. Maybe Penelope just wanted to believe him. Or perhaps the notion of going somewhere forbidden—in his company—was simply too enticing. She could probably blame that glass of champagne for giving in so readily. Or maybe it was because she was letting herself give in to the pulse of something too big to ignore. It might not look like it from the outside, but she was already dancing.

Up the stairs. Along a wide hallway. Past an open door that revealed a luxurious bathroom. Into…a *bedroom*? Yes, there was a four-poster bed that looked about as old as Loxbury Hall itself. It also looked huge and…dear Lord…irresistibly inviting. As if it was the exact destination she'd been hoping this man would lead her to.

Shocked, Penelope jerked her hand free of Rafe's but he didn't seem to notice. He was opening French doors with the ease of knowing exactly where the latches were and then he glanced over his shoulder as they swung open.

'Come on, then. You won't see much in there.'

Out onto the flagged terrace, and the chill of the night air went some way to cooling the heat Penelope could feel in her cheeks. Hopefully, the heat deeper in her body would eventually cool enough to disappear as well.

Rafe checked in with his team by portable radio. Some were as close as it was safe to be to the action, with fire extinguishers available if something went seriously wrong. They would be working alongside him when the show was over, checking for any unexploded shells and then clearing up the rubbish of spent casings and rolling up the miles of cables to pack away with the rest of the gear.

For the next ten minutes, though, there was nothing to do but watch and see how the hard work of the last few days had come together. Rafe set up his laptop, activated the program that synched the music and effects and kept the radio channel open to have the ground team on standby for the countdown. Speakers had been set up along the terrace and the first notes of the song caught everybody's attention.

And then the first shells were fired and the sky filled with expanding, red hearts. The collective gasp from the crowd on the terrace below was loud enough to hear over the music for a split second before the next shell was detonated. The gasp from the woman in the silver dress beside him shouldn't have been loud enough to hear but, suddenly, it was Penelope's reaction that mattered more than anything else.

For the first time in his life in professional pyrotechnics, Rafe found he wasn't watching the sky but he could still gauge exactly what was happening. He could feel the resonance of the explosions in his bones and he could see the colours reflected on Penelope's face. He could see much more than that as well. He could see the amazement, a hint of fear and the sheer thrill of it all. He could feel what it was that had sucked him into this profession so long ago with an intensity that he hadn't realised had become blurred over the years.

And he was loving it.

Penelope had seen fireworks before. Of course she had. She'd always been a little frightened of them. They were so loud. So unpredictable. Too dangerous to really enjoy.

But she felt safer here. She was with the person who was controlling the danger so she could let go of that protective instinct that kept her ready to run in an instant if necessary. She could let herself feel the boom of the explosions in her body instead of bracing herself against them. She could watch the unfurling of those astonishing colours and shapes against the black sky.

She could even watch the new shells hurtling upwards with an anticipation that was pure excitement about what was about to come.

She didn't want it to end. This was the ultimate finale to the biggest thing she had accomplished so far in her life. The wedding was done and dusted and it had been all she had hoped and dreamed it would be. She could let go of all that tension and bask in the satisfaction of hard work paying off.

It had to end, though. The music was beginning to fade. The huge red heart that looked as if it was floating in the middle of the lake came alive with the names of Clarrie and Blake appearing in white inside. The cheering from the crowd below was ecstatic and Penelope felt the same appreciation. Unthinking, she turned to Rafe to thank him but words were not enough in the wake of that emotional roller-coaster.

She stood on tiptoe and threw her arms around his neck.

'That was *amazing*. Thank you *so* much…'

The silver dress felt cool and slippery as his hands went automatically to the hips of the woman pressed against him but he could feel the warmth of her skin beneath the fabric.

This was the last thing Rafe had expected her to do.

He'd been reliving the passion of his job through watching her reaction to the show. Now, with this unexpected touch, he was reliving the excitement of touching a woman as if it were the first time ever. Was this the thing he'd lost? It was a sensation he hadn't even known he'd been pursuing so he couldn't have known it had been missing for so long, but surely it couldn't be real? If he kept on touching her, it would end up being the same as all the others. Or would it?

She drew back and she was smiling. Her eyes were dancing. She looked more alive than Rafe had ever seen her look.

She looked more beautiful than any woman had the right to look.

He had to find out if there was any more to this magic. If he kissed her, would it feel like the first time he'd ever kissed a woman he'd wanted more than his next breath?

He was going to *kiss* her.

Penelope had a single heartbeat to decide what she should do. No. There was no decision that needed to be made, was there? What she should do was pull away from this man. Apologise for being overly effusive in her thanks and turn and walk away.

It wasn't about what she should do. It was about what she *wanted* to do. And whether—for perhaps the first time in her life—she could allow herself to do exactly that. Were the things she had denied herself for ever *really* that bad? How would she know if she never even took a peek?

It was just a kiss but waiting for it to happen was like watching one of those shells hurtle into the darkness, knowing that it would explode and knowing how exciting it would be when it did.

The anticipation was unbearable. She *had* to find

out. Had to open the door to that secret place and step inside.

And the moment his lips touched hers, Penelope knew she was lost. Nothing had ever felt like this. Ever. The softness that spoke of complete control. Gentleness that was a glove covering unimagined, wild abandon.

Not a word was spoken but the look Rafe gave her when they finally stopped kissing asked a question that Penelope didn't want to answer. If she started thinking she would stop feeling and she'd never felt anything like this. It wasn't real—it had to be some weird alchemy of exhaustion and champagne, the thrill of the fireworks and the illicit thrill of an invitation to go somewhere so forbidden—but she knew it would never happen again and she couldn't resist the desire to keep it going just a little longer.

It was bliss. A stolen gift that might never be offered again.

Maybe it wasn't really so astonishing that this woman was capable of such passion. He'd seen her dancing, hadn't he? When she'd thought no one could see her. By a stroke of amazingly good fortune he was sharing that kind of space with her right now. Where nobody could see them. Where whatever got kept hidden so incredibly well was being allowed out to play. Maybe it was true that he wouldn't have chosen a woman like this in a million years but it was happening and he was going to make the most of every second.

Because the magic was still there. Growing stronger with every touch of skin on skin. It was like the first time. Completely new and different and…and just *more*. More than he'd ever discovered. More than he'd ever dreamed he could find.

He took Penelope to paradise and then leapt over the brink to join her. For a long minute then, all he could do was hold her as he fought to catch his breath and wait for his heart to stop pounding. As he tried—and failed—to make sense of the emotions tumbling through his head and heart. Ecstasy and astonishment were mixed with something a lot less pleasant. Bewilderment, perhaps?

A sense of foreboding, even?

What the hell had just happened here?

And what on earth was going to happen next?

CHAPTER FOUR

THE HOUNDS OF HELL were chasing Penelope's car as she drove away from Loxbury Hall.

How awful had that been?

What an absolute, unmitigated train crash.

She'd felt the moment of impact and it had been, undoubtedly, the most shocking sensation of her life. There she'd been, lying in Rafe's arms, floating in a bubble of pure bliss—knowing that there was no place in the world that would ever feel this good.

This safe…

And then she'd heard it. Her grandmother's voice.

'What have you done, Penelope? Oh, dear Lord…it's your mother all over again…you wicked, wicked girl…'

Her worst fear. She'd spent her whole life resisting the temptation to give in to doing bad things and she'd just thrown it all away.

For *sex*… Lust. One of those deadly sins.

Her partner in crime hadn't helped.

'It was only sex, babe.' The look on his face hadn't helped. *'Okay, it was great sex but, hey…it's still no big deal. Don't get weird about it.'*

He had *no* idea how big a deal it was for her.

'It's not as if you have to worry about getting pregnant.'

As if using a condom made it okay. Maybe it did in the world he came from. The world she'd avoided for ever. Sex, drugs and rock 'n' roll.

Her mother's world.

Oh, she'd held it together for a while. Long enough to get her clothes on and retreat from that bedroom with some dignity at least. She'd gone to the downstairs cloakroom, relieved to find that the only people around were the clean-up crew and members of the band, who were still dismantling their sound system. She'd sat in a cubicle for a long time, hoping that the shaking would ease. That the memory of what it had been like in Rafe's arms would fade. Or that she would be able to reassign it as something as horrible as it should be instead of the most incredible experience she'd ever had.

One that she knew she might desperately want to have again.

No-o-o...

She couldn't be that girl. She wouldn't let herself.

Jack had taken one look at her face when she'd gone to the kitchen and simply hugged her.

'It's over, love. You get to go home and get some sleep. I'll finish up here. I've already packed the leftovers into your car. Those kids at the home are going to get a real treat for Sunday lunch this week.' He'd tightened his hug. 'You've done it. Awesome job. You can be very proud of yourself.'

Jack had no idea either, did he?

Somehow, she got home to the small apartment over the commercial kitchen that had been the base for her business for those first years. It was more of a test kitchen now and a back-up for when they needed things they didn't have the time or space to produce in the bigger kitchens that were Jack's domain, but it was full of memories and Penelope loved it with a passion. She transferred the containers of food to the cool room and then slammed the door to the street shut behind her and locked it, hoping to shut those hounds outside. But they followed her upstairs and she could see them circling her bed, waiting to move in for the kill.

One of them had her grandmother's face. Cold and disgusted. With sharp teeth ready to shave slivers of flesh from her bones with every accusation.

One of them had Rafe's face. With eyes that glowed with desire and a lolling tongue that promised pleasures she'd never dreamed of. It stopped and gave her what looked like a grin as she unzipped the silver dress and it felt like it was Rafe's hands that were peeling the fabric from her body all over again.

Where did that heat come from? Coursing through her body like an electric shock that was delicious instead of painful?

Oh, yeah…it was the bad blood. Of course it was. How else could it move so fast and infuse every cell of her body?

Penelope balled the dress and threw it into the corner. So much for it being her trademark wedding outfit. She'd never be able to wear it again.

She'd never be able to sleep if she got into her bed

either. The thought of lying there in the dark with those mental companions was unbearable. Even exhaustion wouldn't be enough protection.

Pyjamas were a good idea, though. Comfortable and comforting. Her current favourites were dark blue, with a pattern of silver moons and stars. A soft pair of knitted booties on her feet and Penelope was already feeling better. All she needed now was a cup of hot chocolate and the best thing about making that was that she could be in her kitchen and that was a comfort zone all of its own.

Or was it?

Encased in the upright, clear holder on the gleaming expanse of the stainless-steel bench was a recipe for cake. Red velvet cake. The cake she'd promised her grandmother she would provide for the dinner party tomorrow night to celebrate Grandad's birthday. No, make that tonight because Sunday had started hours and hours ago.

Before the fireworks. Before she'd blown up the foundations of her life by doing something so reckless she had no idea how to process any possible repercussions.

Easier not to think. To go on autopilot and do what she could do better than anyone. Opening cupboards, Penelope took out bowls and measuring cups and cake tins. She turned an oven on and went to the cool room and then the pantry to collect all the ingredients she would need.

Flour and cocoa. Unsalted butter and eggs and buttermilk. Caster sugar and red paste food colouring. She could think about the icing later. Cream cheese for between the layers, of course, but the decoration on top would have to be spectacular to impress her grandmother. Maybe a whole bouquet of the delicate frosted roses that she was famous for.

It would take hours. Maybe so long she would have to leave her kitchen and go straight to her Sunday gig of making lunch for the residents of the Loxbury Children's Home. Another comfort zone.

How good was that?

It wasn't easy to identify the prickle of irritation because it had been a long time since Rafe Edwards had felt...guilty?

He didn't *do* guilt. He'd learned at a very young age that it was only justified if you hurt somebody intentionally and that was something else he never did. He refused to feel guilty for breaking rules that weren't going to damage anything bar the egos of people who thought they had the right to control what you did because they were more important. Better educated, or richer, or simply older.

The snort that escaped as he pulled his jeans back on was poignant. The age factor hadn't mattered a damn since he'd been sixteen. Nearly two decades since anyone had been able to make his life unbearable simply because they were old enough to have authority.

Back then, he'd get angry at being caught rather than feel guilty about what rule he'd broken. And maybe there was a smidge of anger to be found right now. Annoyance, for sure. Penelope had wanted it as much as he had, so why had she looked as if the bottom had fallen out of her world the moment her desire-sated eyes had focused again?

Yep. Annoyance had been why he'd baited her. Why he'd made no attempt to cover himself as he'd lain there with his arms hooked over the pillows behind him. Why he'd tried to dismiss what had happened as nothing important. Had he really said it was no big deal because she hadn't been in danger of getting pregnant?

It had been lucky he'd found that random condom in his pocket. Would either of them have been able to stop what had been happening by the time he'd gone looking? That was a scary thought. Unprotected sex was most certainly one of the rules that Rafe never broke because there was a real risk of someone getting hurt. A kid. Someone so vulnerable it was something he never even wanted to have to think about. Didn't want to have to remember...

Robot woman had returned as she'd scrambled into her clothes. Man, Penelope Collins was uptight. No wonder he'd avoided her type for ever. This aftertaste was unpleasant. A prickle under his skin that didn't feel like it was going to fade any time soon.

He didn't bother straightening the bed before he left the room. He owned the room now. And the bed, seeing as he'd bought the place fully furnished. It was the room he intended on using as his bedroom when he moved in but...dammit...would he ever be able to sleep in there without remembering that astonishing encounter?

And maybe that was where that irritation was coming from. Because he knew it was an encounter he was never going to get the chance to repeat.

Which was crazy because he didn't want to. Why would anybody want to if it left you feeling like this?

It was probably this disturbance to his well-being that made it take a second glance to recognise the man coming out of the ballroom when he got downstairs.

Or maybe it went deeper than that?

More guilt?

This was an old friend. One of the few good mates from the past that he hadn't spent nearly enough time with in recent years because his life had taken him in such a different direction. Such an upward trajectory.

This felt awkward. Was there a chance of being seen as completely out of their league? Too important to hang out with them any more?

But there was relief to be found here, too, being drawn back into a part of his past he would never choose to abandon. A comfort zone like no other, and that was exactly what he needed right now.

And it appeared as if he was welcome, judging by the grin that split the man's face as he caught sight of Rafe.

'Hey, man... What the heck are you doin' here?'

'Scruff. Hey... Good to see you. Here, give me that.' Rafe took one of the huge bags that held part of the drum kit. 'I heard you and the boys. You're still sounding great.'

'Thanks, man. Still missing your sax riffs in some of those covers. Like that one of Adele's. If we'd known you were going to be here we would have hauled you on stage.'

The tone was light but there was a definite undercurrent there. Rafe hadn't been imagining the barrier he'd inadvertently erected with his neglect. Or maybe it was more to do with how successful he'd become. How rich…

'I was a bit busy. That fireworks show? Put that together myself. Haven't done the hands-on side of the business for years. It was fun.'

'It was awesome.' Scruff dumped the gear he was carrying beside the van parked on the driveway. He leaned against the vehicle to roll a cigarette and when it was done he offered it to Rafe.

'Nah, I'm good. Given it up, finally.'

'For real? Man…' Scruff lit the cigarette and took a long draw, eyeing Rafe over the smoke. The awkwardness was there again. He was different. Their relationship was different. 'Given up all your other vices, too?'

'Nah…' Rafe grinned. 'Some things are too good to give up.'

Like sex.

Scruff's guffaw and slap on the arm was enough to banish the awkwardness. And then other band members joined them and Scruff's delight in rediscovering a part of Rafe that he recognised was transmitted—unspoken—with no more than a glance.

Rafe was only too happy to take the rebukes of how long it had been. To apologise and tell them all how great it was to see them. Reunion time was just what he needed to banish that prickle.

The one that told him sex was never going to be anything like the same again.

Unless it was with Penelope Collins?

The enthusiasm of the other members of Diversion gained momentum as they finished packing their gear into the truck. 'Bout time you got yourself back where you belong. Party tomorrow night… No, make that *to-night*. You up for it?'

'You bet.'

Diversion's lead singer, Matt, grinned. 'We'd better send out some more invites. I can think of a few bods who'll want to see you again.'

Scruff snorted. 'Yeah…like the Twickenham twins.'

The sudden silence let him know that the boys were eyeing each other again. Still wondering how different he might be. It seemed important to diffuse that tension. To get into that comfort zone more whole-heartedly.

'Oh, no…' Rafe shook his head. 'They're still hanging around? Do they still dress up as cowgirls?'

'Sure do.' Scruff gave him a friendly punch on the arm. 'And they're gonna be mighty pleased to see you, cowboy.'

The prickle was fading already. With a bit of luck, normal service was about to be resumed. 'Bring it on. Just tell me where and when.'

The Loxbury Children's Home, otherwise known as Rainbow House, was on the opposite side of the city from Loxbury Hall and its style was just as different as the location. The building had no street appeal, with the haphazard extensions that had taken place over time and maintenance like painting that was well overdue, and the garden was littered with children's toys and a playground that had seen better days.

But it felt like home, and Maggie and Dave, the house parents, welcomed Penelope with the same enthusiasm as they'd done years ago—that very first time she'd turned up with the tentative offer of food left over from a catering event. The same age as her grandparents, Maggie and Dave were the parents Penelope had never had. The house, noisy with children and as messy and lived in as the garden, was so different from where she'd grown up that, for a long time, she'd felt guilty for enjoying it so much.

She'd gone back, though. Again and again. Maggie hadn't discovered for a long time that she actually cooked or baked things when there weren't enough leftovers to justify a weekly drop-off. When she did, she just gave Penelope one of those delicious, squishy hugs that large women seemed to be so good at.

'It's you we need more than free food, pet. Just come. Any time.'

It wasn't enough to just visit. Helping Maggie in the kitchen was the time she loved the best. Cooking Sunday lunch with her favourite person in the world was a joy and what had become a weekly ritual was never broken.

She'd got to know a lot of the children now, too. The home offered respite care to disabled children and temporary accommodation to those in need of foster homes. There were the 'boomerang' kids who sadly bounced between foster homes for one reason or another and some long-term residents that places could never be found for. The home was always full. Of people. And love.

'Oh, my… Is that fillet steak?'

'It is. Jack over-catered for the wedding last night. It came with wilted asparagus and scalloped potatoes but I thought the kids might like chips and maybe peas.'

'Good idea. What a treat. Well, you know where the peeler is. Let's get on with it. Don't you have some special do at your folks' place tonight?'

'Mmm. Grandad's birthday. There's no rush, though. I'm only doing dessert and I've made a cake. I don't need to turn up before seven-thirty.'

Maggie beamed. 'Just as well. The kids have got a play they want to put on for you after lunch. Have to warn you, though, it's a tad tedious.'

'Nothing on how tedious the dinner party's going to be. I'm almost thirty, Maggie, and I still get 'the look' if I use the wrong fork.'

Penelope rinsed a peeled potato under the tap and put it on the chopping board. She reached for another one from the sack and her damp hand came out covered in dirt. With a grimace, she turned the tap back on to clean it. Dusting the particles that had fallen onto her jeans only turned it into a smear but that didn't matter. She'd probably be rolling around on the floor, playing with one of the toddlers, before long. This was the only place she ever wore jeans and it was an illicit pleasure that fitted right in with not worrying about the mess or the noise. She'd just have to make sure she left enough time to shower and change when she went home to collect the cake.

'So, how was the wedding?' Maggie sounded excited. 'Did you know we could see the fireworks from here? A couple of the boys sneaked out to watch them and we didn't have the heart to tell them off for getting out of bed. They were so pretty.'

'Weren't they? I got the best view from upstairs at the hall.'

'Upstairs? I thought that was out of bounds?'

'Hmm. The guy doing the fireworks show had permission, apparently. He needed to be where he could see everything in case there was a problem.'

'And he took you upstairs, too?'

'Mmm.' Penelope concentrated on digging an eye out of the potato she was holding. 'Upstairs' was the least of the places Rafe had taken her last night but, no matter how much she loved and trusted Maggie, she couldn't tell her any of that.

She knew what happened when you did things that disappointed people.

They stopped loving you.

This time, when she picked up a new potato, the mud on her hand got transferred to her face as she stifled a sniff.

'You all right, pet?'

'Mmm.' Penelope forced a smile. 'Bit tired, that's all. It was a big night.'

'Of course it was.' Maggie dampened a corner of a tea towel and used it to wipe the grime off Penelope's cheek. 'Let's get this food on the table. You can have a wee snooze during the play later. It wouldn't go down too well if you fell asleep during dinner, would it? Your folks are going to want to hear all about everything that happened last night. They must be very proud of you. I certainly would be.'

Penelope's misty smile disguised a curl of dread. Imagine what would happen if she told her grandparents absolutely everything? But could she hide it well enough? Her grandmother had always had some kind of sixth sense about her even thinking about something she shouldn't and she'd always been able to weasel out a confession in the end, and a confession like this one would make the world as she knew it simply implode.

Oh, for heaven's sake. She hadn't been a child for a very long time. Wasn't it about time she stopped letting her grandparents make her feel like one?

It was one of the classic saxophone solos of all time. 'Baker Street' by Gerry Raffety. Rafe had first heard this song when he'd been an angry, disillusioned sixteen-year-old and it had touched something in his soul. When he'd learned that it had been released in 1978, the year he was born, the connection had been sealed. It was *his* song and he was going to learn to play the sax for no other reason than to own it completely.

And here he was, twenty years later, and he could close his eyes and play it as though the gleaming, gold instrument was an extension of his body and his voice. A mournful cry that had notes of rebellion and hope. So much a part of him that it didn't matter he hadn't had time to take the sax out of its case for months at a time. It was always there. Waiting for an opportunity that always came when it was needed most.

And, man, he'd needed it tonight, to exorcise that prickle that had refused to go away all day. Even walking the expanse of amazing gardens he could now call his own, as he'd collected the last of the charred cardboard that had enclosed the shells fired last night, hadn't been enough to soothe his soul. Or floating on his personal lake to retrieve the barge. Memories of the fireworks display that had been intended to celebrate his ownership of Loxbury Hall would be inextricably linked to other memories for ever.

Of a woman he'd never expected to meet and would never meet again.

But never mind. He could let it go now. 'Baker Street' had worked its magic again.

'That was awesome, dude.' Scruff had given his all to his drum accompaniment to the song. So had the guitarists and Diversion's keyboard player, Stefan. Now the beer was cold and there was plenty of comfortable old furniture in this disused warehouse that was the band's headquarters for practice and parties.

'As covers go, it's one of the best,' Stefan agreed. 'But it's time we wrote more of our own stuff.'

'Yeah…' Rafe took a long pull of his beer. 'You know what? I've been toying with the idea of setting up a recording company.'

Stefan's beer bottle halted halfway to his mouth. His jaw dropped and his gaze shifted from Rafe to Scruff, who shook his head. Was it his imagination or did the boys take a step further away from him? Okay, so he had more money than he used to have. More money than most people ever dreamed of, but it didn't change who he was, did it? Didn't change how much he loved these guys.

He shrugged, trying to make it less of a big deal. 'I could do with a new direction. Blowing things up is getting a bit old.'

So not true. But there had been a moment today, when memories of the fireworks and of Penelope had seemed so intertwined, that the idea of taking a break from his profession had seemed shockingly appealing.

'Get a whole new direction.' Scruff had recovered enough to grin. 'Join the band again. Come and experience the delights of playing covers at birthday parties and weddings. You too could learn every ABBA song in existence.'

The shout of laughter echoed in the warehouse rafters. He was forgiven for any differences and it felt great. A cute blonde with a cowboy hat on her bouncy curls and a tartan shirt that needed no buttons fastened between an impressive cleavage and the knot above a bare midriff came over to sit beside Rafe on the ancient couch. One of the Twickenham twins. He knew they'd been watching him closely all evening and their shyness had been uncharacteristic enough to make him feel the barriers were still there. Apparently, he'd just broken through the last of them.

'Nothing wrong with ABBA.' She pouted. 'It's great to dance to.'

'Yeah, baby...' Her identical sister came to sit on his other side. Somehow she moved so that his arm fell over her shoulder as if the movement had been intended. And maybe it had been. 'Let's dance...'

Lots of people were dancing already, over by the jukebox that had been the band's pride and joy when they'd discovered it more than a decade ago—when Rafe had been part of the newly formed band. A pall of smoke fog hung under the industrial lights and, judging by what he could smell, Rafe realised he could probably get high even if he didn't do stuff like that any more. The party was getting going and it was likely to still be going when dawn broke.

The thought brought a wave of weariness. Good grief...was he getting too old for this?

'Can't stay too long,' he heard himself saying. 'Got a board meeting first thing tomorrow. We're making a bid for New Year's Eve in London again this year. It's big.'

'Oh...*man*...' Scruff groaned. 'We just find you and you're gonna disappear on us again?'

'No way. I've bought a house around here now.'

'For real?'

'Yeah...' Rafe wiped some foam from above his top lip. 'Given my advancing years, I reckoned it was time to settle down somewhere.' Not that he was going to tell them where the house was yet. That would put him back to square one by intimidating them all with his wealth and success.

The laughter of some of his oldest friends was disquieting. Stefan couldn't stop.

'House first, then a wife and kids, huh?'

Rafe snorted. 'You know me better than that, Stef.'

The twins snuggled closer on both sides. 'You don't wanna do that, Rafey. A wife wouldn't want to play like we can.'

So true. The connotations of a wife brought up images of a controlling female. Someone who made sure she got everything precisely the way she wanted it.

Someone like Penelope Collins?

The soft curves of the twin cleavages that were close enough to touch and inviting enough to delight any man were curiously unappealing right now. There would be no surprises there. It might be nice but it would be old. Jaded, even, knowing that it was possible to feel like sex was brand-new and exciting again.

Rafe sighed. He had to get out of there. The prickle had come back to haunt him.

'You're not the only one with something big coming up,' Scruff said into the silence that fell. 'We're gonna be a headline act at the festival next month.'

'The Loxbury music festival?' Rafe whistled. 'Respect, man.' Then he frowned. 'I thought they'd wound that gig up years ago. Too much competition from the bigger ones like Glastonbury.'

'They did. It's been nearly ten years but this year is the thirtieth anniversary. The powers that be decided it would be a great blast from the past and put little ol' Loxbury back on the map.'

'Sounds fun. You'll get to play some of your own stuff.'

'You could be in on it, mate. You'd love what we're doing these days. Kind of Pink Floyd meets Meatloaf.'

The other band members groaned and a general argument broke out as they tried to define their style.

One of the twins slid her arm around Rafe's neck. 'There's going to be a big spread in one of the music mags. That's Julie over there. She's a journo and she's going to be doing the story. Did you know a girl died at the very first festival?'

'No… Really?'

'That's not true,' the other twin said. 'She collapsed at the festival. She didn't die until a couple of days later. It was a drug overdose.' She raised her voice. 'Isn't that right, Julie?'

'That's not great publicity to rake up before this year's event.'

'There's a much better story.' Julie had come over to perch on the end of the couch. 'There's Baby X.'

'Who the heck is Baby X?'

'The baby that got found under a bush when they were packing up. A little girl. They reckoned she was only a few days old.'

'She'll be nearly thirty now, then.' The twins both shuddered. 'That's old.'

'Not as old as me.' But Rafe was barely listening any more. Penelope's words were echoing in his head.

My mother abandoned me as a baby and then died. I have no idea who my father is.

Holy heck… Was it possible that *she* was Baby X?

The idea that the renewed curiosity of this journalist could expose a personal history that had to be painful was disturbing.

He should warn Penelope. Just in case.

Not his business, he told himself firmly. And that would mean he'd have to see her again and that was the last thing he wanted.

He drained his beer and then stood up, extracting

himself with difficulty from the clutches of the twins. If he was going to believe what he was telling himself, he needed to get a lot more convincing.

He had to get out of there. He wasn't having fun any more.

The resolution to keep an adult poise along with any secrets she might wish to keep lasted all the way to the elegant old house in one of Loxbury's best suburbs. Her shower might have washed away the effects of so many sticky fingers but the glow of the cuddles and laughter was still with her. Her jeans were in the washing machine and she knew her new outfit would meet with approval. A well-fitted skirt, silk blouse and tailored jacket. There were no runs in her tights and she'd even remembered to wear the pearls that had been a twenty-first birthday gift from her grandparents, along with the start-up loan to start her small bakery.

A loan that was about to be paid off in full. Another step to total independence. She was an adult, she reminded herself again as she climbed the steps carefully in her high heels. The same shoes she'd worn the day she'd gone to the office of All Light on the Night. The same shoes that Rafe had tugged off her feet last night shortly after he'd unzipped that silver dress...

Penelope needed to take a deep, steadying breath before she rang the bell. She had a key to the kitchen door but rarely used it. By implicit agreement, being granted admission to the house she'd grown up in was the 'right' thing to do.

As was the kiss on her grandmother's cheek that

barely brushed the skin and, instantly, she was aware of the child still hidden deep inside. Having skinny arms peeled away from their target with a grip strong enough to hurt.

'Don't hug me, Penelope. If there's anything I detest, it's being hugged.'

'How are you, Mother?'

'Fabulous, darling. And you?' She didn't wait for a response. 'Oh, is that the cake? Do let me see. I do hope it's Madeira.'

'Red velvet.'

'Oh...' The sound would have seemed like delighted surprise to somebody who didn't know Louise Collins. Penelope could hear the undertone of disapproval and it took her back instantly to the countless times she had tried so hard to win affection instead of simply acceptance. Why did it still matter? You'd think she would have given up long before this but somehow, beneath everything, she loved her grandmother with the kind of heartfelt bond she'd had as a tiny child, holding her arms up for a cuddle.

It was a relief that the beat of silence was broken by the arrival of another figure in the entranceway. Maybe this was why she'd never been able to let go. Why it still mattered so much.

'Grandad! Happy birthday...' This time the kiss was real and it went with a hug. A retired and well-respected detective inspector with the Loxbury police force, the happiest times of Penelope's childhood had been the rare times alone with her grandfather. Being hugged. Being told that she was loved. Being taken fishing, or on a secret expedition to buy a gift for her grandmother.

The grandmother who'd never allowed the real relationship to be acknowledged aloud.

'For goodness' sake, Penelope. I was only forty-three when you turned up on our doorstep. Far too young to be called a grandmother.'

'I'll take the cake into the kitchen, shall I?'

'Let me have a peek.' Douglas Collins lifted the lid of the box. 'Louise, look at these roses. Aren't they fabulous?'

'Mmm.' Louise closed the box again. 'Don't stay nattering to Rita in the kitchen, Penelope. The champagne's already been poured in the drawing room.'

Rita always made you remember the old adage of 'never trust a thin cook'. Even bigger than Maggie, her hugs were just as good and her praise of the cake meant the most.

'Red velvet? Oh…I can't wait to taste it. Make sure there's some left over.'

'You should get the first piece, Rita. You're the one who taught me to bake in the first place.'

'Never taught you to do them fancy roses. I always said you were a clever girl.'

'I only *felt* clever when I was in here. It's no wonder I ended up being a baker, is it?'

'You're a sight more than that now. How did the wedding go?'

'It was fabulous. As soon as the magazines come out with the pictures, I'll bring some round for you.' The tinkle of a bell sounded from well beyond the kitchen and the glance they exchanged was conspiratorial. Penelope grinned. 'I'll pick a time when the olds are out and we can have a cuppa and a proper natter then.'

'I'd love that, sweet. You go and have them bubbles and enjoy your family time now. Go on...scoot before her ladyship rings that bell again.'

How ironic was it that 'family time' had already been had today. First with Maggie and Dave and then with Rita in the refuge of her childhood.

The messy places that were always warm and smelled of food.

The drawing room should have been overly warm thanks to the unnecessary coals glowing in the enormous fireplace, but somehow the perfection of every precisely placed object and the atmosphere of a formal visit created a chill. Tasting the champagne as they toasted the birthday didn't help either, because it made Penelope remember the taste in her mouth last night, when she'd emerged from the kitchen to take Rafe's hand and let him lead her upstairs.

The spiral of sensation in her belly at the memory couldn't have been less appropriate in this setting. Closing her eyes with a silent prayer, Penelope took another gulp.

'You look tired.' Her grandmother's clipped tones made it sound like she was excusing her lack of manners in drinking too fast. 'I hope you got some rest today instead of playing cook at that orphanage place.'

'Orphanages don't exist any more, Mother. Not like they used to.'

'I know that, Penelope.'

Of course she did. She'd probably gone searching for one as an alternative to doing the right thing and claiming their baby granddaughter.

'Charity work is to be commended, Louise. You know that better than anyone.' That was Grandad in a nutshell. Trying to keep the peace and protect his beloved wife at the same time. He'd always done that. Like the way he'd explained away some of the endless punishments and putdowns meted out by Louise.

She's only trying to keep you safe, sweetheart. We know what it's like to lose a precious little girl.

And now it was her turn to be soothed. 'Good on you, Penelope, if you went and helped when you were tired.'

'I wouldn't call it charity.' Oh, help. Why was she contradicting everything being said? She took another gulp of champagne and found, to her horror, that she'd drained her glass.

'Of course it's charity. Those children are riff-raff that nobody wants. With no-good parents that probably spend all their money on cigarettes and alcohol and have no idea how to set boundaries for themselves, let alone their offspring.'

'Mmm…' Penelope was heading for the ice bucket that held the champagne bottle. 'Bad blood,' she murmured.

'Exactly.'

The long pause was enough for the silent statement that was as familiar as a broken record.

You can't help having bad blood. You just have to fight against it. Otherwise you know what can happen.

Yep. Penelope knew.

She'd end up just like her mother.

Funny that the ice bucket was on the occasional table right beside the fireplace. And that family photos were positioned artfully on the top of the mantelpiece. There was Penelope in a stiff, ruffled dress, aged about three, clutching a teddy bear that the photographer had had available in his studio.

A not dissimilar professional portrait of another small girl was to one side of an equally posed portrait of her grandparents' wedding. This girl had the same blonde hair as Penelope but her skin was much paler and her eyes were blue. One of the few pictures of her mother, Charlotte—before she'd gone off the rails so badly.

It wasn't that the Collins blood was bad, of course. Charlotte had been led astray by the person who'd really had it. The unknown father whose genes had overridden her mother's to give Penelope her brown eyes and more olive skin. A permanent reminder to her grandparents of the man who'd destroyed their perfect little family.

Louise Collins rose gracefully to her feet. 'I'll go and let Rita know we're ready for the soup. Come through to the dining room, Penelope.'

'On my way.' Or she would be, when she'd filled her glass again. Heaven knew, she needed some assistance to get through the next hour or so of conversation without causing real trouble. Falling out with her grandmother any more than she had already this evening would only distress Grandad.

The worst thing about it all was that she had just learned what it was like when you lost the fight with the 'bad blood'.

And it was a lot more fun than she was having right now.

CHAPTER FIVE

NEARLY THREE WEEKS.

It should have been plenty of time to put any thoughts of Penelope Collins to bed—so to speak.

No...wrong choice of expression. Rafe Edwards closed his eyes for a moment to try and quell that surge of sensation that was inevitable whenever thoughts of Penelope and beds collided.

Maybe this was a mistake. He eyed the old building in the heart of Loxbury's industrial area with deep suspicion. Why had it even occurred to him that it might be a *good* idea?

Karma?

The amusement that was inherent?

Or was he being pulled along by some cosmic force he couldn't resist?

Fate.

With a dismissive snort, Rafe slammed the door of his four-by-four behind him. He didn't believe in any of that kind of rubbish. You made your own fate unless you were rendered powerless by youth or natural disaster or something. And success was sweet when it was earned.

Perhaps that was why he had grudging respect for Penny.

Oops…*Penelope.*

From the outside they were total opposites but there was a driving force at a deeper level that they both shared. Judging by the magazine and newspaper coverage of that wedding, Penelope was now poised for extraordinary success and she'd earned it. For whatever reason, she was carving her own niche in the world and she was doing it exceptionally well.

Plus…

Rafe rapped on the iron door that was the only entrance the building had to the street. No doubt there was a sparkling commercial kitchen behind the door with a team of loyal employees who could do their jobs with the kind of military precision Ms Collins would demand. Given how late in the day it was, however, it would be disappointing if the door was opened by someone other than the woman he'd come to see.

He wasn't disappointed. It was Penelope who opened the door.

'G'dday…' Rafe let his grin build slowly. 'I think you might owe me a favour.'

Oh…*no…*

She'd assumed it was Jack, who'd said he might drop in the new menus he was working on. She would never have opened the door otherwise. Not when she was wearing her pyjamas and slipper socks, with her hair hanging loose down her back. Funny how she'd never thought it might be a problem, with the only windows

facing the street being on the next level where her apartment was.

How stupid was it not to have bothered using the
peephole in the door? Not only stupid, but dangerous.
It could have been anyone demanding entrance. A drug
addict, for instance. Or an axe murderer.

Or…or…*Rafe*…

And he was calling in a favour?

He was still grinning at her. 'I realise you're probably
beating off clients after getting so famous.'

'I… Ah…' Yes. Potential bookings were pouring in
in the wake of the Bingham-Summers wedding. And
part of that success had been down to its glorious finale with the fireworks. And, yes…Rafe had made that
happen when he hadn't had the slightest obligation to,
so she did owe him a favour.

But what on earth could he want from her?

The thought of what she might *want* him to want
from her was enough to make her knees feel distinctly
wobbly and that was more than a little disturbing. She'd
got past that lapse of character. It had been weeks ago.
Her life was back on track. More than back on track.
Penelope tried to pretend that she was wearing her suit
and high heels. That her hair was immaculate. She
straightened her back.

'The thing is, All Light on the Night is booked to
blow up a car on a movie set the day after tomorrow
but the gig's about to be postponed, which doesn't suit
us at all.'

Penelope had no idea where this conversation was
going so she simply stared at him. Which was possibly

a mistake. Beneath that battered hat she could see the tousled hair that her treacherous fingers remembered burying themselves in and below that there was a glint in those dark eyes that made her think he was finding this amusing. More than that—he was quite confident that she might find it amusing, too. Because he knew what she liked and he was more than able to deliver?

Penelope dragged her gaze away from his eyes. Dropped them to his mouth. Now, that really was a mistake. Staring at his lips, she could almost feel her body softening. Leaning towards him. Hastily, she straightened again.

'Sorry, what was that?'

'The catering company. It went on a forty-eight-hour strike today. Something to do with the union. Your workforce doesn't belong to a union, does it?'

'Um…not that I know of.' They'd started with only herself and Jack. Other employees had come via word of mouth and the company had grown slowly. They were like a family and there'd never been a hint of an industrial dispute.

'So you could take on the job? It's not huge. Just an afternoon and there'd only be a couple of dozen people to cater for, but film crews do like to eat and they like the food to be on tap. Catering for a movie set could be a whole new line of business for you. Could be a win-win situation for both of us, even.'

'In a couple of days?' Initial shock gave way— surprisingly—to a flicker of amusement at the way he was using the exact turn of phrase she'd tried on him in his office that day. Had he remembered that

visit in the same kind of detail she had? 'We usually
book that kind of job well in advance. *Months* in advance sometimes.' Her lips twitched. 'I could certainly
give you a list of other companies that might be able to
help.'

Rafe put an elbow up to lean against the doorframe.
It pulled the front of his leather jacket further apart and
tightened the black T-shirt across his chest. 'But I don't
want another company,' he said. 'I have to have the best
and…and I suspect that might be *you*.'

Penelope swallowed hard. She knew what was under
that T-shirt. That smooth skin with just enough chest
hair to make it ultimately masculine. Flat discs of male
nipples that tasted like honey…

Taste. Yes. He was talking about food, she reminded
herself desperately. *Food*…

'Have…have you got any idea what's involved with
setting up a commercial catering event?'

'Nope.' He quirked an eyebrow and tilted his head.
He could probably see into the huge kitchen area behind her anyway so did he really have to lean closer
like that? Was he waiting for an invitation to come inside and discuss it?

Not going to happen. It was no help trying to channel thoughts of being dressed in something appropriate.
She was in her pyjamas, for heaven's sake. At seven-
thirty p.m. Any moment now and she might die of embarrassment.

'There's meetings to be had with the client.' Her tone
was more clipped than she had intended. 'Menus and
budgets and so forth to be discussed.'

'The budget won't be an issue.'

Another turn of phrase she'd used herself that day in his office. When she'd been desperately trying to persuade him to help her. Impossible not to remember that wave of hope when he'd said he might be able to do it himself.

She could do the same for him. Already, a part of her brain was going at full speed. Mini samosas and spring rolls perhaps—with dipping sauces of tamarind and chili. Bite-sized pies. Sandwiches and slices. It wouldn't be that hard. If she put in a few hours in her kitchen tonight, she could get all the planning and a lot of the prep done. She could use the old truck parked out the back that had been her first vehicle for getting catered food to where it was needed.

It might even be fun. A reminder of her first steps to independence and how far she'd come.

'Will you be there?' The query popped out before she could prevent it. What did it matter?

'Oh, yeah…' That wicked grin was back. 'I love blowing things up. Wouldn't miss it. The real question is…' The grin faded and there was something serious about his face now. 'Will *you* be there?'

That flicker of something behind the amusement told her that he wanted her to be there, but was it only about the food?

Penelope couldn't identify the mix of emotions coming at her but it was obvious they were stemming from that place she thought she'd slammed the door on. It would be a struggle to try and contain them and…and maybe it wouldn't be right.

Even her grandmother would tell her that she had an obligation to return a favour.

'Okay.' She tried to make it sound like it wasn't a big deal. 'Give me the details and I'll see what I can do.'

'How 'bout I email them through to you tomorrow?' He tugged on the brim of his hat and she could swear he was smirking as he turned away. 'Don't want to be keeping you up or anything.'

The flood of colour heated her cheeks so much that Penelope had to lean against the cool iron door after she swung it closed. Nobody knew that she liked to wear her pyjamas in the evenings when she wanted to relax. It would have been okay for Jack to find out but... *Rafe*?

Good grief. Penelope tried to think of something to make her feel less humiliated and finally it came to her.

At least he hadn't caught her dancing.

The thought was enough to get her moving. She needed to check supplies in the cold room and the freezers and start making a plan. The way to get over this humiliation was crystal clear. Even if it was only for an afternoon, this was going to be the best damned catering this movie company—and the visiting pyrotechnicians—had ever experienced.

Man, the food was good.

Rafe wasn't the only person on set to keep drifting back to the food truck and the long table set out beside it. Those delicious little triangles of crispy filo pastry filled with potato and peas in a blend of Indian flavours, along with that dark, fruity sauce, were irresistible. Just as well the platter kept getting replenished and he'd arrived just in time to get them at their hottest.

Just in time for Penelope to be putting the platter on the table, in fact.

'Definitely my favourite,' he told her. 'Good job.'

It was more than a good job. She'd not only made it possible for everyone to keep to schedule, there were a lot of people saying they'd never been so well fed on set. His praise brought out a rather endearing shyness in Penelope. She ducked her head and wiped her hands on her apron.

'Samosas are always popular. Try the spring rolls, too, before they run out. These guys sure do like to eat, don't they?'

She wasn't meeting his gaze. Maybe that shyness was left over from the other night when he'd caught her wearing her PJs.

And hadn't that been totally unexpected? About as strange as seeing this uptight woman dancing in the middle of his maze. There were layers to Penelope Collins that just didn't fit. It wasn't the things that were opposite to him that intrigued him. It was the opposites that were in the same person. Did she actually know who she really was herself?

Not that he was going to embarrass her by mentioning the PJs or anything. She'd returned his favour and he was grateful. And that would be the end of it.

'Won't be for much longer. We're all set for the filming and we only get one take.'

'Really? They seem to have been filming the same scene for ages.'

Rafe glanced behind him. They were in a disused quarry and the road had already been used for the sequence of the car rolling off the road.

'That was the hero getting the girl out of the car. I think they've nailed it now. He gets to help her run away from it next and when they hit a certain point is when we blow up the car. My boys are just getting the explosives rigged. It'll look like they're close enough to be in danger but they won't be, of course. All smoke and mirrors but we need the shot of them with the explosion happening behind them and that'll be it for the day.' He glanced upwards. 'Which is just as well. Those thunderclouds are perfect for a dramatic background but nobody wants their expensive camera gear out in the rain.'

'Is it going to be really loud?'

'Hope so. Should be spectacular, too, but you won't see much from here. Want to come where you will be able to get a good view?'

What was he thinking? The flash in her eyes told him she remembered agreeing to that once before and she hadn't forgotten where they'd ended up. The way her pupils dilated suggested that it had been an experience she wouldn't be entirely averse to repeating.

This was supposed to be the end of their association. Favours given and returned but, heaven help him, Rafe felt a distinct stirring of a very similar desire.

'No.' The vigorous shake of her head looked like she was trying to persuade herself. 'I can't. I'm here to do a job.'

'You can just leave it all on the table. Everybody's going to be busy for a while, believe me. Have you ever seen a car being blown up before?'

'N-no...'

'There you go, then. An opportunity missed is an opportunity wasted.'

It was more than a bit of a puzzle why he was trying to persuade her. It was even more of a puzzle why he felt so good when she discarded her apron and followed him to a point well out of shot to one side of the set. He used his radio to check in.

'You all set, Gav? Can you see the point they have to cross before you hit the switch?'

'All good to go, boss.' The radio crackled loudly. 'Reception's a bit crap. ...are you?'

'Other side. Raise a flag if you need me.'

'Roger...' The blast of static made him turn the volume down. 'Something to do with the quarry walls, I guess. They won't need me. I don't usually even come to gigs like this any more.'

Oops. Why had he let that slip? Not that Penelope seemed to notice. She was watching the actors being positioned for the take. Make-up artists were touching up the blood and grime the accident and extrication had created. Cameras were being shifted to capture the scene from all angles. The director was near a screen set up for him to watch the take on the camera filming the central action and the guy holding the clipboard moved in front, ready for the command to begin the take.

'Places, please,' someone shouted. 'Picture is up.'

* * *

This was a lot more exciting than Penelope had expected it to be. So many people who seemed to know exactly what they were doing. There were cameras on tripods, others being held, one even on top of a huge ladder that looked rather too close to the car, which must be stuffed full of explosives by now. A sound technician, with his long hair in a ponytail, was wearing headphones and holding a microphone that looked like a fluffy broomstick. The actors were waiting, right beside the car, for the signal to start running.

'That door's going to blow off first,' Rafe said, his tone satisfied. 'With a bit of luck it'll really get some air at about the same time both ends of the car explode.'

'I hope they're far enough away by then.' Penelope kept her voice down, although they were probably far enough away for it not to matter if they talked.

'See where that camera on the tracks is? There's a white mark on the ground well in front of that. When the actors step across that, it's the signal to throw the switch. There's no chance of them getting hit by anything big.' He shielded his eyes with his hand as he stared across the open ground between them and the car. 'There might not be that many rules I regard as sacred but safety is top of the list.'

Penelope's gaze swerved to his face. The anticipation of waiting for a huge explosion was making her feel both scared and excited. The notion that even her safety was important to Rafe did something weird and, for a heartbeat, it felt like she was falling.

But it also felt like she *was* safe.

Rafe was right beside her. He would catch her before she could get hurt.

As if he felt the intensity of her gaze, his head turned and that weird feeling kicked up several notches. A split second before the eye contact could get seriously significant, however, a loud clap of wood on wood and the shout of 'Action' distracted them both.

Game on.

The actors were doing a good job of making it look like a panicked struggle to get away from the crashed vehicle as flames flickered behind them. The girl was only semi-conscious, blood dripping down her face, and the guy was holding her upright and pleading with her to try and go faster.

Penelope could feel Rafe's tension beside her. He had his hand shielding his eyes again and was looking beyond the actors, who were getting closer to the white mark.

The vehement curse that erupted from his lips made her jump.

'What's wrong?'

But Rafe ignored her. He grabbed his radio and pressed the button.

'Gav? Abort…abort… There's a bloody *kid* behind the car.'

The only sound in return was a burst of static. With another curse, Rafe took off, taking a direct line from where they stood to the side towards the car.

The car that was about to explode…

'Oh, my God…' Penelope couldn't breathe. She stood

there, with her hands pressed to her mouth. Should she do something? Run towards the director and shout for help, maybe?

But Rafe was almost at the car now and surely someone had seen what was happening?

Her feet wouldn't move in any case. She'd never felt so scared in her life. With her heart in her mouth she watched Rafe reach the car. He vanished for a moment behind it and then reappeared—a small figure in his arms and half over one shoulder. Incredibly, he seemed to run even faster with his burden. Off to the side and well away from the line the actors had taken.

Were still taking.

In absolute horror, Penelope's gaze swung back to see them cross the white mark and then the first explosion made her cry out with shock. From the corner of her eye she could see the door of the car spiral into the air just the way Rafe had said it would, but she wasn't watching. Another explosion—even louder—and the car was a fireball. Big, black clouds of smoke spread out and she couldn't see Rafe any longer.

Couldn't think about how close he'd been to that explosion and that something terrible had just happened.

She was safe but—dear Lord—she didn't *want* to be safe in that moment. She wanted to be with Rafe. To know that *he* was safe...

And suddenly there he was. Emerging from the cloud of smoke, still well to the side of the set. Still with the child in his arms.

There was no missing what was happening now. All hell broke loose, with people running and shouting, coming towards Penelope from one side as Rafe came from the other. She was right in the middle as they met.

'What the hell's going on?' The director sounded furious. 'What in God's name is that kid doing here? Where'd he come from?'

'He was hiding behind the car.' The director's fury was nothing on what Penelope could hear in Rafe's voice. His face was grimy from the smoke and his features could have been carved out of stone as he put the boy down on his feet.

And Penelope had never seen a man look more compelling. Then her gaze shifted to the boy and she was shocked all over again. She'd seen this child before.

'Billy?' The name escaped in a whisper that no one heard but the boy's gaze flew to meet hers and she could see the terror of a child who knew he was in serious trouble.

A man in a fluorescent vest, holding a radio, looked as white as a sheet.

'Tried to call you to abort firing, Gav,' Rafe snapped. 'Reception was zilch.'

'We had security in place. Nobody got into the quarry without a pass.'

'He was with me.' Penelope cleared her throat as every face swung towards her, including Rafe's. 'In the food truck. I'm sorry...' She turned towards the boy. 'You knew you were supposed to stay inside, didn't you, Billy? What were you *thinking*?'

Billy hung his head and said nothing but Penelope could see the tremor in his shoulders. He was trying very hard not to cry.

Lifting her gaze, she found Rafe glaring at her with an intensity that made her mouth go dry. He knew she was lying.

'He was thinking he might want to get himself killed,' Rafe said quietly. 'He very nearly succeeded.'

'But he didn't.' Penelope gulped in a new breath. 'Thanks to you.'

'I'll have to file an incident report,' the director said, his anger still lacing every word. 'I should call the police. The kid was trespassing.'

'No.' Penelope took a step towards the boy and put her arm around his shoulders. 'Please, don't call the police. I take full responsibility. It's not Billy's fault. It's mine. I should have stayed in the truck with him.'

'You shouldn't have brought him on set in the first place.'

'I know. I'm sorry. But he knew a car was going to get blown up and it was too exciting an opportunity to miss.' She flicked a glance at Rafe. Would he hear the unspoken plea to get him on side by repeating the words he'd used to persuade her?

As if to underline her plea, a distant clap of thunder unrolled itself beneath boiling clouds. And then raindrops began to fall. Heavy and instantly wetting.

The director groaned. 'This is all we need.'

'Shall we start packing up, chief?' someone asked.

There was a moment of hesitation in which it felt like everyone was holding their breath.

'I'll deal with it,' Penelope offered. 'I'll see that Billy gets the punishment he deserves.'

'I think that's *my* call.' Rafe's voice had a dangerous edge. 'Don't you?'

The heat of his glare was too intense to meet but Penelope nodded. So did Billy.

'Fine.' The director held both hands up in surrender. 'It's your safety regulations that got breached. And it was you that brought this flaky caterer on set. You deal with it.' He turned away, making a signal that had the crew racing to start getting equipment out of the rain, but he had a parting shot for Rafe. 'You have no idea how lucky you are that no harm was done. You'd be out of the movie business for good if it had.' He shook his head. 'You're also lucky that your heroics didn't show up on screen or we'd have to be reshooting and you'd be paying for it, mate.'

The last person to leave was Gav.

'I'll pack down and clear the site,' he said. He cast a curious glance at Penelope and Billy. 'Guess you'll be busy for a while.'

The rain was coming down steadily now. The kid was visibly shivering in his inadequate clothing and the look on his face was sullen enough to suggest he was used to getting into trouble.

Rafe saw the way Penelope drew him closer. For a moment the kid resisted but then he slumped as if to-tally defeated. He wasn't looking at either of the adults beside him but Penelope was looking and she didn't look at all defeated. Her chin was up and she looked ready to go into battle. What was it with this kid? How on earth did Penelope even know his name?

'Want to tell me what this is all about?' Rafe wasn't about to move and any sympathy for how uncomfortable either of these people felt hadn't kicked in yet. 'There's no way this kid was in your truck when you got here.'

'The kid has a name,' Penelope shot back. 'It's Billy.'

'How did you get anywhere near that car, Billy?'

He got no response.

'He didn't know you were going to blow it up. He—'

'Billy's not a puppet,' Rafe snapped. 'Stop talking for him.'

Penelope's mouth opened and closed. She glared at Rafe.

'Billy? Or is your real name William?'

A small sound from Penelope told him that she got the reference to her own name preference. The kid also made a sound.

'What was that?'

'Billy. Only rich kids get called William.'

'And how do you know Penelope?'

'I don't.'

That made sense. Billy looked like a street kid.

Like he'd looked about the same age? Rafe pushed the thought away. He didn't want to go there.

'How does she know your name, then?'

'Dunno.' Billy kicked at the ground with a shoe that had a hole over his big toe.

'I help out at a local children's home.' Penelope's tone was clipped, as if she expected to get reprimanded for speaking again. 'I've met Billy there a couple of times in the last few years when things haven't been so good at home.'

That also made sense. A bit of charity work on the side would fit right in with the image that Ms Collins presented to the world. The image that hid the person she really was?

Rafe stifled an inward sigh. 'So, is that why you sneaked into the quarry? Trying to find a place away from home?'

'I was playing, that's all.' The first direct look Rafe received was one of deep mistrust. 'I saw them doing stuff to the car and I wanted a closer look. You didn't have to come and get me. It was none of your business, man.'

Whoa…did this kid know that he'd almost got killed and didn't care? The anger was still there. In spades.

'You don't get to make decisions like that,' he told Billy. 'Not at your age.'

An echo of something unpleasant rippled through him. People making decisions for him because he was too young. People making rules. Making things worse.

But this was about safety. Keeping a kid alive long enough for him to get old enough to make his own decisions—stupid or otherwise.

'I'm taking you home,' he said. 'I want a word with your parents.'

'No *way*…' Billy ducked under Penelope's arm and took off. If the ground hadn't become slippery already from the rain, he might have made it, but Rafe grabbed him as he got back to his feet. And he held on.

'Fine. If you don't want to go home, we'll go and have a chat to the cops.'

'*No.*' Penelope looked horrified. 'Don't you think

he's got enough to deal with, without getting more of a police record at his age?'

More of a police record? Good grief.

'I'll take him to Maggie and Dave. They'll know what to do.'

'Who the heck are Maggie and Dave?'

'They run Rainbow House—the children's home. They're the best people I know.'

There was passion in her voice. Something warm and fierce that made Rafe take another look at her face. At her eyes that were huge and...vulnerable?

'And how do you think you're going to get him to this home? In the back of your truck that he could jump out of at the first set of traffic lights?' The tug on his arm confirmed his suspicions so he tightened his grip.

Penelope faced Billy. 'You've got a choice,' she said. 'You can either come with me and see Maggie and Dave or go to the police station. What'll it be?'

Billy spat on the ground to show his disgust. 'You can't make me go anywhere.'

'Wanna bet?' Rafe was ready to move. It was easy to take the kid with him. 'Let's go back to your truck, Penelope. We can call the police from there.'

'No.' Billy kicked Rafe's ankle. He stopped and took hold of the boy's other arm as well, bodily lifting him so that he could see his face.

'That's enough of that, d'you hear me? We're try-ing to *help* you.'

'That's what they all say.' There was a desperation in Billy's voice that was close to a sob as he struggled for freedom. 'And they don't *help*. They just make everything worse...'

Oh, man... This was like looking into some weird mirror that went back through time.

'Not Maggie and Dave...' Penelope had come closer. Close enough to be touching Rafe's shoulder. Was it just the rain or did she have tears running down her cheeks? 'They can help, Billy. I know they can.'

'Then that's where we'll go.'

'*We?*'

'I'm coming with you.' He couldn't help his exasperated tone. 'You can't do this by yourself.'

Which was a damned shame because Rafe could do without a trip to some home for problem kids. Could do without the weird flashbacks, thanks very much. But he'd only get more of them if he left this unresolved, wouldn't he?

And this was supposed to be the end of his association with Penelope Collins. It would be a shame to leave it on such a sour note.

'Let's get going,' he growled, as another clap of thunder sounded overhead. 'Before we all catch pneumonia.'

CHAPTER SIX

IF PENELOPE HAD been a frightened child with a home she was scared to go back to, then Rainbow House was exactly the place she'd want to be. She knew she was doing the right thing here, but the vibes from the two males in the front seat of her little food truck told her they didn't share her conviction.

Penelope was driving and Billy was sandwiched between the two adults to prevent any attempt to escape. A sideways glance as they neared their destination revealed remarkably similar expressions on their faces. It could have been a cute 'father and son' type of moment, except that the expressions were sullen. They were both being forced to do something that ran deeply against the grain. Being punished.

Her heart squeezed and sent out a pang of…what? Sympathy? There was something more than the expressions that was similar. Had Rafe been a kid who had broken every rule in the book to get some attention? He still broke rules—look at the total lack of appreciation for the stated boundaries at Loxbury Hall. Not that he needed to do anything to attract attention now. He was the most gorgeous man she'd ever seen. He was clever and passionate about his work. And he'd just risked his life to save a child.

The memory of the wave of emotion when she'd seen him emerge from the smoke unharmed made her grip the steering-wheel tightly. It gave her an odd prickly sensation behind her eyes, as though she was about to cry—which was disturbing because she had learned not to cry a long time ago.

'Don't cry, for heaven's sake, Penelope. The only difference it makes is that your face gets ugly.'

There was no denying that Rafe Edwards stirred some very strong emotions in her and the fact that he clearly thought she was punishing Billy by taking him to Rainbow House was annoying. Hadn't he been prepared to deliver Billy to the police? He'd soon see that she was right.

His expression certainly changed the moment Dave opened the door and welcomed them in. They must have just finished dinner judging by the rich smell of food. Most of the children were in the playroom, watching television, and the sound of laughter could be heard. Maggie was on the floor in front of the fire, dressing a small baby in a sleep suit. She scooped up the infant and got to her feet in a hurry.

'Oh, my goodness. What's happened? Billy? Oh...' She handed the baby to Dave and enveloped Billy in a hug that was not returned. The boy stood as still as a lamppost.

'This is Rafe Edwards,' Penelope told her. 'He's the

pyrotechnician I told you about—the one who did the fireworks at the wedding?'

'Oh...' Maggie held out her hand. 'Welcome to Rainbow House, Rafe,' she said. 'I'm Maggie. This is Dave. And this is Bianca.' She dropped a kiss on the baby's head. Then it was Penelope's turn to be hugged. 'Good grief, darling. You're soaked. Come upstairs with me while I get baby Bi to bed. We'll find you some dry clothes.' She glanced at Rafe. 'I'm not sure there'd be anything in the chest to fit you, but Dave could find you something.'

'I'm fine.' The sullen expression had given way to... nothing. It was as if the Rafe that Penelope knew had simply vanished. This was a man with no opinion. No charisma. No hint of mischief.

'Stand over by the fire, then, at least. Dave'll get you something hot to drink. Billy? You want to come and find some dry clothes?'

'Nah.' Billy's head didn't move but his glance slid sideways. 'Reckon I'll stand by the fire, too.'

Maggie shared a glance with Penelope, clearly curious about the relationship of the stranger to the boy she knew, but she wasn't going to ask. Not yet. Best let her visitors settle in first. Penelope knew she'd accept them no matter what story had brought them here, and she loved Maggie for the way you became a part of this family simply by walking through the door. When Dave handed her the baby, she was more than happy to take her and cuddle her as she followed Maggie out of the room. Pressing her lips to the downy head was a delicious comfort. It eased the worry of glancing back to see Rafe and Billy both standing like statues in front of the fire.

Rafe had the curious feeling that he'd fallen down one of those rabbit holes in Alice's wonderland.

Had he really thought that Penelope came here occasionally as her contribution to society to read stories to the children or something? She was a part of this family. In this extraordinary house that felt exactly like a *real* home. It even smelt like one. The aroma of something like roast beef made his stomach growl. The heat of the fire was coming through his soaked clothing now, too. A sideways glance showed steam coming off Billy's jeans and the kid had finally stopped shivering. He kind of liked it that Billy had chosen to stay with him, instead of disappearing with the others to find dry clothes. Maybe he felt the connection. Felt like he might have an ally.

Not that Rafe had any qualms about leaving him here, if that was possible. This wasn't like any children's home he'd ever experienced. Hell, it wasn't even like any foster home he'd been dumped in. No point in wondering what kind of difference it might have made if there'd been a place like Rainbow House in his junior orbit. Water under the bridge. A long way under the bridge, and he still didn't want to go swimming in it again. The sooner he got out of here, the better.

Dave had gone to the kitchen and the silence was getting noticeable.

'So you've been here before?'

'Yeah…'

'Not bad, is it?'

'Nah...I guess.'

Dave reappeared with two steaming mugs. 'Soup,' he announced. 'Lucky we always have a pot on the back of the stove.'

Maggie and Penelope appeared by the time he'd taken his first sip and he almost slopped the mug as he did a double-take. What was Penelope wearing?

An ancient pair of trackpants, apparently. And a thick, oversized red woollen jersey that had lumpy white spots all over it. She was still rubbing at her hair with a towel and when she put it down he could see damp ringlets hanging down her back. She had *curly* hair?

She looked so young. Kind of like the way she'd looked in her PJs, only a bit scruffier.

Cute...

The power-dressing princess seemed like a different person. Of course she did. It *was* a different person. Just part of the same, intriguing package that had so many layers of wrapping.

A teenaged girl with improbably blue hair walked through the living room on her way to the kitchen.

'Hey, Billy. How's it going?' She didn't wait for an answer. 'Dave—John's got the remote and he's not sharing.'

A shriek was heard coming from the playroom. Dave shook his head. 'Excuse me for a moment.'

Maggie clucked her tongue as the blue-haired girl came back. 'Charlene, go back and get a spoon. It's bad manners to eat ice cream with your fingers.'

A snort of something like mirth came from Billy

and Penelope caught Rafe's gaze as she came closer to the fire. *This is good*, the glance said. *This is where this kid needs to be.*

She was right. Eventually, there was time to explain why they were here. They were listened to and questions were asked that got right to the heart of the matter.

'You live near the quarry, don't you, Billy? Is that where you go when you need to get away from home?'

Billy shrugged.

'You know it's breaking the law, don't you? The quarry's a dangerous place and that's why there's no public access allowed.'

Another shrug.

'Breaking rules just gets you into trouble, Billy,' Penelope added quietly. 'You *know* that.'

'We'd love to have you back here,' Maggie said, 'And, if you want, Dave'll give Social Services a ring in a minute. Do you think you'd like that to happen?'

The silence was broken by a sniff. Billy scrubbed at his nose, his head still bent so his face couldn't be seen.

'Yeah…I guess.'

'You'd have to follow our rules. Not like last time, okay?'

''Kay.'

'Any knives in your pocket?' Dave's voice was stern.

This time Billy glanced up. Rafe frowned at him.

A pocket knife came out of a back pocket and was handed to Dave.

'Matches?'

The packet of matches that was produced and handed over was too soggy to be a danger but the message was clear. Rules were to be followed and, if they weren't, there would be consequences.

But these were good rules. Rules that kept kids safe. Rafe nodded approvingly.

With a phone call made and permission given to keep Billy at Rainbow House for the time being, the chance to escape finally arrived. Weirdly, Rafe wasn't in a hurry any more. He stayed where he was, as Maggie bundled Penelope's wet clothes into a plastic shopping bag and farewells were made.

Penelope spoke quietly to Billy. 'I'll see you when I'm back on Sunday. Don't tell the others but I'll make a cake that's especially for you. What sort do you like?'

'Chocolate.'

'No problem. And, Billy...?'

'What?'

She was speaking quietly but Rafe could hear every word. 'You don't have to break rules to get people to notice you. It's when you follow the rules that people like you and the more people like you, the more likely you are to get what *you* want.'

What? At least the astonished word didn't get spoken aloud but Rafe had to step away and take a deep breath. Did she really believe that?

Probably. It might explain why this woman was such a complicated mix of contradictory layers. Whose rules was she following? And why did it matter so much that she was liked by whoever was setting those rules? Hadn't she learned by now that what really mattered was whether you liked yourself?

Self-respect. Self-belief.

Obviously not. Man…someone must have done a good job on her self-esteem at some point in her life.

Not his problem. None of what was going on here was his problem and he didn't want to get any more involved. He pulled a phone from his pocket.

'What's the address here?' he asked Dave. 'I'll just call a taxi.'

'No…' Penelope turned away from Billy. 'I can drop you home. It's the least I can do. You saved Billy's *life*…'

A look flashed between Maggie and Dave. A look that suggested she thought there was more going on between him and Penelope than met the eye. Oh, help… Had she heard *all* about the night of the fireworks?

'That's a much better idea,' Maggie said, turning her gaze on Rafe.

He almost grinned. It would be a brave man who went against what this loving but formidable woman thought best.

'Fine.' It came out sounding almost as grudging as Billy had about getting something he was lucky to be offered. He put an apologetic note in his voice. 'I'm a bit out of town, though.'

'No problem.' Penelope stuffed her feet into her damp shoes and picked up the bag of clothing. 'We've still got some samosas in the back if we get hungry.'

Penelope followed the directions to take the main road out of town and then the turn-off towards the New Forest.

'I've been here before. It's the way to Loxbury Hall.'

'Mmm.'

The only sound for a while then was the rough rumble of the old truck and the swish of the windscreen wipers. The heater still worked well, though, and Penelope was starting to feel too warm in Maggie's old jersey. The T-shirt she had on underneath wasn't enough to stop the itch of the thick wool. She couldn't wait to get home and put her own clothes on. Fire up her straighteners and sort out her hair, too.

Good grief…she must look an absolute fright. This was worse than being caught wearing her pyjamas. At least her hair had been smooth and under control.

'What was that for?'

'What?'

'That groan. I did tell you I was out of town a bit.'

Penelope cringed inwardly. And then sighed aloud. 'It's not that. I'm just a bit over you seeing me at my worst, that's all. A girl thing.'

There was another silence and then Rafe spoke quietly.

'Maybe I'm seeing you at your best.'

She tried to figure that out. Couldn't. 'What's that supposed to mean?'

'You do realise you broke the rules, don't you?'

'What rules?'

'The safety regulations that are a legal obligation for anyone who runs a business like mine. I should be filing a "Near Miss" incident report. Billy should have been charged with trespass.'

'And you think that would have helped him? For God's sake, Rafe. He's a kid whose home life stinks.'

'And you stood up for him. You were prepared to break the rules to stand up for him. I'm impressed.'

Impressed? With *her*?

Should she feel this pleased that she'd impressed a pyrotechnician cowboy her grandparents would probably consider riff-raff?

Moot point. The pleasure was irresistible and felt inexplicably genuine. And then he went and spoiled it.

'What were you thinking, telling him that people only like you if you follow all the rules?'

'It's true.'

But she could hear the note of doubt in her voice and this man, sitting beside her, was responsible for that. Rafe didn't automatically follow anybody's rules but he had the kind of charisma that no doubt had women falling at his feet with a single glance. He'd won over a small, troubled boy who had probably never trusted anyone in his short life so far. And even Maggie had fallen for him, judging by the way she'd acted when she'd taken Penelope away to find those dry clothes.

Instead of opening the old chest, she'd sat on the top and fanned her face with her hand, giving her a glance that had made Penelope feel she was in the company of young Charlene instead of the warm-hearted and practical woman who was in charge of Rainbow House.

'I'm not a bit surprised you went upstairs at Loxbury Hall with *him*. I'd have been more than a bit tempted myself.'

'Like' was far too insipid a word to describe how Penelope felt about Rafe but she wasn't going to try

and analyse those strong emotions. They were dangerous. The kind of emotions that led to trouble. Shame.
Sometimes, even death…

Rafe's voice brought the wild train of her thoughts
to a crashing halt.

'Did you follow all the rules today? Do you think I
like you less because you didn't?'

She didn't respond. There was a note in his voice that
suggested he didn't like her much anyway.

'Turn in here.'

'Are you kidding?' But Penelope slowed as the iron
gates of Loxbury Hall came up on the left.

Rafe pulled out his phone, punched in a few numbers and the gates began to swing open.

She jammed on the brakes and they came to a grind-
ing halt.

It was quite hard to get the words out. 'When you
said you'd cleared it with the owner about going upstairs, you hadn't actually talked to anyone, had you?'

'Nope.'

'Because you *are* the owner?'

'Yep.'

Oh, no… Penelope let her head drop onto the steering-wheel on top of her hands. Now she felt like a complete idiot. Someone who'd been played like a violin.

'Um…Penny?'

She didn't bother to correct the use of the loathed
diminutive. 'Yeah…?'

'Do you think you could get us off the road properly
before someone comes along and rear-ends us? Just to
the front steps would be grand.'

* * *

The front steps belonged to the property he'd acquired by not following all the rules. He'd got to where he was in life because he'd believed in himself, not because he'd made other people like him.

Billy could do with a message like that.

Not that he wanted to go anywhere near Rainbow House again. It was sorted. This was it. Time to say goodbye to Ms Penelope Collins.

He turned towards her to do exactly that but then he hesitated. Rain beat a steady rhythm on the roof of the truck and it got suddenly heavier. A flash of lightning made Penelope jump and her eyes got even wider at the enormous crack of thunder that came almost instantly.

'The storm's right on top of us. You can't drive in this.' Without thinking, Rafe leaned over and pushed back a stray curl that was stuck to Penelope's cheek. 'Come inside till it blows over.'

She wasn't looking at him. And she shook her head.

He should have left it there but he couldn't. He knew an upset woman when he saw one. Had it been something he'd said? His hand was still close to her face and his fingers slipped under her chin to turn her head towards him. At the same time he was racking his brains to think of what it was that had sent her back into her shell. Revealing that he owned Loxbury Hall? No. That had nothing to do with her. Ah… As soon as Penelope's gaze met his, he knew exactly what it was.

'I still like you,' he murmured. 'Breaking the rules only made me like you more.'

Her lips parted and the tip of her tongue appeared

and then touched her top lip—as though she wanted to say something but had no idea how to respond. The gesture did something very strange to Rafe's gut. The look in her eyes did something to his heart.

She looked lost. *Afraid*, even?

He had to kiss her. Gently. Reassuringly. To communicate something that seemed very important. And, just in case the kiss hadn't got the message across, he spoke quietly, his lips still moving against hers.

'You're beautiful, Penny. Always believe that.'

A complete stillness fell for a heartbeat. There was nothing but the butterfly-wing softness of that contact lingering between their lips. A feeling of connection like nothing Rafe had ever felt in his life.

And then there was a blinding flash of light. A crack of thunder so loud it felt like the van was rocking. Penelope's body jerked and she emitted a stifled shriek.

That did it. Rafe moved without thinking, out of his seat and running to the driver's side of the van. He wrenched open the door and helped Penelope out. He held her against his body and tried to shelter her inside his jacket but even in the short time it took to get across the driveway and up the steps to the front door of his house was enough for them both to be soaked all over again.

Thank goodness for the efficient central heating in this part of the vast old house. But it wasn't enough. Penelope was shivering.

'I could get a fire started.' He was feeling frozen himself.

'Th-that would be n-nice...'

Was the fire already set or would he have to go hunting for kindling and wood?

'It could take a while.' Which wasn't good enough. And then inspiration struck. 'How 'bout a hot bath?'

'Oh...' She looked for all the world as if he'd captured the moon and was offering it to her in his hands. 'I haven't had a bath in...in for ever. I've only g-got a shower at my p-place.'

Rafe felt ten feet tall. With a decisive nod, he walked towards the staircase. 'You'll love my bath,' he said. 'It's well big enough for two people.'

At the foot of the stairs, he had to stop. Why wasn't she following him? Turning his head, he smiled encouragingly and held out his hand.

'You're quite safe. I wasn't actually suggesting that I'm intending to *share* your bath. I just meant that it would be big enough.'

When she took his hand, hers felt like a small block of ice. Weird that it made him feel so warm inside.

As if he was the one who was being given the moon?

CHAPTER SEVEN

HAVING RAFE IN a bathtub with her was crazy.

It also seemed to be the most natural thing in the world.

How had it happened? Penelope had been sitting there, on the closed lid of the toilet, with a big, fluffy towel around her like a shawl while Rafe supervised the filling of the enormous tub. The tap was one of those old-fashioned, wide, single types and the water rushed out with astonishing speed, filling the room with steam. Steam that became very fragrant when Rafe upended a jar of bath salts into the flow. Then he found a bottle of bubble bath and tipped that in as well.

'You may as well use them up,' he said. 'I'm not likely to.'

So the steam smelled gorgeous and the room was warm but Penelope could see that Rafe was shivering.

'You need that bath as much as I do. More... You've been in wet clothes for hours.'

'I'll go and have a shower in another bathroom.' But Rafe had turned his head on his way out and met her gaze and it felt like time had suddenly gone into slow motion. 'Unless...?'

And so here they were. Sitting at either end of this wonderful old, claw-footed bathtub, with Rafe slightly lopsided to avoid the tap and Penelope's legs between his. The bubbles covered her chest enough to be perfectly decent and she kept her knees slightly bent so that her toes didn't touch anything they shouldn't.

For the longest time they simply sat there in silence, soaking up the delicious warmth.

'I've never done this before,' she finally confessed. 'As soon as I got old enough, I wouldn't even let my nanny stay in the bathroom with me.'

'You had a *nanny*?'

Penelope swept some bubbles together with her hands and shaped them into a hill. 'Only because my grandmother didn't want to be a mother again. She'd done it once, she said, and that was enough.'

'I hope it was a nice nanny.'

'She was okay. Rita—our housekeeper—was better. She's the one who taught me to cook and bake, and by the time I was about eight I was spending so much time in the kitchen Mother decided that the nanny was superfluous so they fired her.'

'A housekeeper and a nanny. Your folks must be pretty well off.'

'We only had one main bathroom and my grandparents' room had an en suite that had a shower.' Penelope didn't want to talk about her family any more. Another scoop of bubbles made the hill higher. It wobbled but still provided a kind of wall and it meant she didn't have to look at Rafe directly. 'How many bathrooms have you got?'

'Haven't really counted.' He sounded vaguely discomforted by the query. 'A few, I guess.'

Penelope laughed. 'I'd say so.' Her laughter seemed to diffuse the awkwardness. 'What made you want to live here?'

Rafe tipped his head back to rest on the curved rim of the bath. 'I came here once when I was a kid. To a Christmas party. I thought it was the kind of house that only people with a perfect life could ever live in.'

'Were your parents friends of the owners?'

It was Rafe's turn to laugh. 'Are you kidding? I was one of a busload of what they called "disadvantaged" kids. The ones that went to foster homes because they wanted the extra money but then they'd get found out and the kid would get "rescued" so that somewhere better could be found. Somewhere they wouldn't get so abused.'

Shocked, Penelope slid a little further into the water. Her mind was back under that tree, as Clarissa and Blake's vows had been pledged. Seeing that sadness in Rafe's eyes as he'd told her she was one of the lucky ones.

'You know what it's like to have a family. Parents. You know what it's like to live in that safe place...'

Had he thought that a mansion was that kind of safe place when he'd been a little boy? That it would automatically give him a family and mean he was loved?

Penelope wanted to cry. She wanted to reach back through time and take that little boy into her arms and give him the kind of hug that Maggie would give.

She wanted to scoop him up and take him to Rainbow House—the way they'd taken Billy today.

That explained the hero-worship, didn't it? Had Billy sensed the connection? Somehow realised he was looking at a role model that he could never have guessed could understand what his life was like?

Maybe her thoughts were hanging in a bubble over her head.

'There weren't any places like Rainbow House back in my day,' Rafe said quietly. 'I wish there had been.' Something like a chuckle escaped. 'Maybe then I wouldn't have broken so many rules.'

Penelope's smile felt wobbly. 'Something went right along the way. Look at where you are now. *Who* you are...'

Her foot moved a little and touched Rafe's leg. His hands must have been under the water, hidden by the layer of foam, because his fingers cupped her calf.

'I'm wondering who *you* are,' he said softly. 'Every time I think I have it figured out, you go and do something else that surprises the heck out of me.'

'Like what?'

'Like breaking the rules. Not shopping Billy in to the cops. Going upstairs with me when you thought it wasn't allowed.'

Oh...help. His fingers were moving on her calf. A gentle massage that was sending tendrils of sensation higher up her leg. More were being generated deep in her belly and they were meeting in the middle in a knot that was both painful and delicious.

'Is not dancing in public one of your rules, too?'

'What?' The exclamation was startled.

'I saw you that day. Dancing in the maze. I was up on the balcony.'

Penelope gasped as something clicked into place. 'How did you know what song I was listening to?'

'You left your iPod on the table in the hall. It wasn't rocket science to check what was played most recently.'

'You were *spying* on me.' Penelope pulled her leg away from his touch. She gripped the side of the bath, stood up and climbed out.

Rafe must have climbed out just as fast because he was right there as she wrapped herself in a towel and turned around. Water streamed off his naked body, taking tiny clumps of bubbles with it. He caught her arms.

'Not *spying*,' he said fiercely. 'I was…intrigued.'

The nearness of him was overwhelming. Nearness and nakedness. She could feel the heat coming off his skin. Smell something masculine that cut through the perfume of the bath salts and bubble bath. His hair hung in damp tendrils and his jaw was shadowed by stubble. And the look in his eyes was…

'I still am,' he murmured. 'You intrigue me, Penelope Collins. No…when you get beneath the layers, I think it would be fairer to say you *amaze* me.'

Penelope forgot how to breathe.

She *amazed* him? On a scale of approving of somebody that was too high to be recognisable. Penelope had never amazed anybody in her life. The highest accolade had been her grandad being proud of her. A nod and even a smile from her grandmother.

Rafe had the world at his feet. He ran a huge, successful company. He'd just bought a house that very few people could ever dream of owning. What did he see in her that could possibly amaze him? It was true, though. She could see the truth of it in the way he was looking at her.

Was it possible for bones to actually *melt* for a heartbeat or two? She was still managing to stand but her fingers were losing their grip on the edges of the towel she had clutched in a bunch between her breasts.

Rafe was still dripping wet. His fingers felt damp enough to leave a cool trail as he reached out and traced the outline of her face but coolness turned into enough heat to feel like her skin was being scorched. Across her temple and cheekbone, down the side of her nose and then over her lips, and still they hadn't looked away from each other's eyes. She could feel the dip to trace the bow of her top lip and then his finger seemed to catch on the cushion of her lower lip.

She saw desire ignite in Rafe's eyes and his face came closer. She could feel his breath on her skin. Could feel his mouth hovering over hers—no more than a hair's breadth from touching—but it couldn't be called kissing.

This was something much deeper than kissing. Something that felt spiritual rather than physical. The waiting was agony but it was also the most wonderful thing Penelope had ever felt. The closeness. The knowing what was coming. The feeling of...*safety*? How amazing was that, that she could feel safe when she was so close to something that she knew could explode with all the ferocity and beauty of one of Rafe's fireworks.

The towel slipped from her fingers as his lips finally made contact. This wasn't just one kiss. It was a thousand kisses. Tiny brushes. Fierce bursts of pressure.

He caught her shoulders as her knees threatened to give up the struggle of keeping her upright. He lifted her. Carried her to where they needed to be.

In his bed.

Rafe didn't turn the bedside light off after he'd ripped the duvet back and placed Penelope in his bed. He wanted to see the look in her eyes as he made love to her. To see if he could catch an expression as extraordinary as the way she'd looked when he'd told her that she amazed him.

And he wanted this to be slow. To last as long as he could make it last because—incredibly—it felt like last time, only better. Still as new and exciting as if it had been the first time ever but familiar, too.

Safe...

She smelled like heaven. She *tasted* like heaven and it had nothing to do with all the stuff he'd tipped into that bath.

It was sex but not as he'd ever known it. This was a conversation that went past anything physical. It felt like simply a need to be together.

And even when the passion was spent, it didn't have to end, did it? He could hold her for a while longer. As long as she was willing to stay?

'Oh, Penny...' Rafe drew her more closely to his body, loving the way her head tucked in against his shoulder. 'Sorry.' His words were a murmur that got buried in her hair. 'Penelope. I forgot how much you hate that.'

'I don't hate it when you say it.' The husky note in her voice was full of the lingering contentment of supreme satiety.

'It's more you.' Rafe could feel his lips curl into a smile and it felt odd—as if he'd never smiled quite like that before. 'It's how I'm going to think of you from now on.'

'How do you mean?'

'It's like "Penelope" has extra layers of letters that hide the real stuff. And it sounds kind of...I don't know...stilted? All professional and polished, anyway. Like you were when you came into my office that day. And how you looked in that silver dress at the wedding.' His breath came out in a soft snort. 'Who knew I'd end up seeing you wearing your PJs? And trackpants and a jersey with big fluffy spots on it?'

'Don't remind me.'

He could feel the way her body tensed. He pressed his lips against her hair and willed her to relax. And it seemed to work. She sounded amused when she spoke again.

'I was so embarrassed when you caught me in my pyjamas. I only do that when I think no one's going to see me.'

'When you're being Penny instead of Penelope.'

He felt her breasts press against his arms as she sighed. 'My best friend at school called me Penny for a while but I made her stop.'

'Why?'

'There were some older kids there who knew more about me than I did. They told me I'd been called Penny because they're not worth anything any more. That nobody wanted me. That my mother had died because even she didn't want me.'

'Kids can be so cruel.' Rafe stroked her hair. 'What did you say?'

'That my name was Penelope and not Penny. And then I told the teacher about them breaking the rules and smoking behind the bike sheds and they got into a whole heap of trouble.'

'Did it make you feel any better?'

'Not really. And then I went home and started asking questions and that got me into a whole heap of trouble. My mother got one of her migraines and had to go to bed for three days and Grandad told me not to talk about it again. It became a new rule.'

'Sounds like you grew up with a lot of rules.'

'Yep.'

'Like what?'

'Oh, the usual ones. Doing what I was told and not talking back, getting good marks in school, not smoking or drinking. Only going out with nice boys that they approved of.'

Rafe snorted again. 'Would they approve of me?'

Penelope sounded like she was smiling but her tone was wry. 'After what we've just been doing? I doubt it very much.'

'Breaking another rule, huh? Lucky me.' He pressed another kiss to her tangled hair. 'Guess I'm a bad influence.'

'More likely it's my bad blood finally coming out. And you know what?' Penelope turned in his arms before he could answer. 'Right now, I don't even care.' She lifted her face and kissed him.

It was true. How could something that felt this right be so wrong, anyway? She waited, in that moment of stillness, to hear the old litany about her turning out just like her mother but, strangely, it didn't come. Maybe it would hit her on the way home, in which case she might as well stay exactly where she was for a bit longer. Maybe she could just go to sleep here in his arms. How perfect would that feel?

But Rafe didn't sound sleepy.

'Bad *blood*? What the heck is that?'

'Oh, you know. A genetic tendency to do bad stuff. Like take drugs or have wild sex with strangers.'

'I'm pretty sure you don't have "bad" blood.' He sounded amused now. 'It was probably one of the rules you grew up with. No bad blood allowed.'

'Pretty much. Nurture had to win over nature. Which is why I was never allowed to ask any questions about my father. That's where I got my bad blood from. He was the one who led my mother astray. Got her into drugs. Got her pregnant at sixteen. Made her run away from home so my grandparents never saw her again. Until she was dead.'

'I don't do drugs,' Rafe said quietly. 'And you're not going to get pregnant if I can help it. I do have a few rules of my own. In my case, nature probably won out over nurture.'

'I'm not sixteen. I get to do what I choose now.' It had been true for a very long time but this was the first time it *felt* true. She was choosing to be here and stay here for a bit longer because…because it felt so good.

'But you wouldn't tell your grandmother.'

'No. Only because it would hurt Grandad so much. He loves her. He loves me, too, but his priority has always been to protect Mother. And I get that. I think their lives got ruined when they lost their daughter. My mother.'

'What was her name?'

She hesitated for a long moment. She never talked about this. She'd never told anyone her mother's name. But this was Rafe and she felt safe. The word still came out as a whisper.

'Charlotte.'

There was a long silence then. Penelope was absorbing how it made things seem more real when you spoke them. How weird it was to have had a mother who'd never existed in reality as far as she was concerned.

Rafe seemed content to leave her in peace. Had he fallen asleep?

No. He must have been thinking about her. About her unusual parentage.

'Have you ever wanted to find out who your father was?'

'I know his name. It was on my birth certificate.'

'What was it?'

'Patrick Murphy. How funny is that?'

'Why funny?'

'They're probably the two most common Irish names there are. Imagine trying to search for him.'

'Have you…imagined, at least?'

'Of course. But maybe it's better not to know anything more.'

'What *do* you know—other than his name?'

'That he played a guitar in a band. Took drugs and got girls pregnant and then left town and never saw them again. Doesn't sound like a very nice person, does he?'

'There are always two sides to every story, darling.'

Darling…nobody had ever called her that before. It sent a weird tingle through Penelope's body. Embarrassingly, it made her want to cry. Or maybe there was more to the prickle behind her eyes than the endearment.

'He didn't want me,' she whispered. 'Any more than my mother did. She *left* me…under a bush. Who does that to their baby?'

'Maybe she had no choice.' Could he hear the imminent tears in her voice? Was that why he was holding her so close? Pressing his cheek against her head as if he could feel her pain? And more…as if he wanted to make it go away.

Nobody could do that. It was ancient history.

'There's something I should tell you. It happened a few weeks ago. The night after we…the night after the wedding here.' The pressure on her head was easing—as if Rafe was creating some distance because he was about to tell her something uncomfortable. 'I went to a party with some old mates. A band I used to be part of. There was a girl there…'

Oh, *no*... Was he about to tell her he was in a relationship with someone? That this was nothing more than a bit on the side? Penelope braced herself for something huge. Something that had the potential to hurt her far more than she had a right to let it.

'She was a journalist. Julie, I think her name was.'

Penelope didn't need to know this. Her muscles were bunching. Getting ready to propel her out of Rafe's bed.

Out of his life.

'Anyway, she's interested in a story. About a baby they called Baby X.'

Penelope went very, very still. There was relief there that he didn't seem to be telling her about a woman who was important in his life but there was fear, too. This was something that was supposed to be hidden. Long forgotten.

'Apparently Baby X was found under a bush. At the Loxbury music festival, nearly thirty years ago.'

There were tears running down Penelope's cheeks. 'That was me,' she whispered. 'It's going to be my thirtieth birthday in a couple of weeks.'

'I'm guessing you wouldn't want someone turning up on your doorstep, asking questions?'

'*No*...' Penelope squeezed her eyes shut. 'Or, even worse, chasing my folks. They'd *hate* that.' She swallowed hard. 'You don't think they'll be able to find out, do you?'

'I don't know. I'm surprised it's been kept such a secret for so long. It's the kind of story people love to know there's a happy ending to.'

'Grandad was pretty high up in the police force back

then. He might have pulled a few strings to have things kept quiet. People knew that my mother had died, of course, and that I was an orphan. But I'm pretty sure no one got told *how* she died or where she was at the time.'

'So there's no way to connect her to Baby X, then. You should be safe.'

But there was a note of doubt in Rafe's voice and Penelope felt it, too. Why hadn't anyone made what seemed like an obvious connection?

More disturbingly, what would happen if they did?

'I should go,' she said. 'Maybe I should have a word with Grandad and warn him.'

'Don't go. Not yet.' Rafe's arms tightened around her. 'It's still raining out there. Why not wait till the morning?'

How good would it be to push that all aside and not worry about it yet? If she stayed here and slept in Rafe's arms, would he make love to her again in the morning?

'Julie's actually coming to see me at the office tomorrow. I've offered to do a fireworks show at the close of the festival as a contribution to the charity they're supporting. I could find out how much she knows already. Whether there's a chance they'll find out who you are. I could try and put her off even, if you'd like. Warn her that she could do some damage to people if she pursued a story that would be better left alone.'

He'd do that? For her?

'Thank you. I'd owe you a big favour if you could do that.'

'You wouldn't owe me anything.' Rafe was smiling. 'I told you, Penny. I like you. I like you a lot.'

'I like you, too.'

She gave herself up to his kiss then, and it was easy to put any other thoughts aside. So easy to sink into the bliss of touching and being touched.

Except that one thought wasn't so easy to dismiss. Again, 'like' was too insipid a word to have used when it came to Rafe.

She felt protected. Chosen. Loved—even if that was only a fantasy on her part.

It was no fantasy in the other direction. God help her, but she was in love with Rafe Edwards. She probably had been ever since he'd chosen the song she'd been dancing to for his fireworks show. Knowing that he had done so after seeing her dancing had shocked her, but now it made it all seem inevitable. How could you not fall in love with a man who'd chosen a song he knew would make you dance?

A man who was amazed by you?

The potential fallout of having her past and her family's shame made public was huge. And frightening.

But it wasn't nearly as big as how she felt about Rafe, so she could still feel safe while she was here. She could catch this moment of a happiness she'd never known existed.

Tomorrow would just have to take care of itself.

CHAPTER EIGHT

PENNY WAS GONE from his bed long before dawn broke. It was a downside of working in the food industry, apparently. If they had a large gig to cater, the kitchens opened for work by four a.m. She didn't go in this early very often now, because her role was changing to event management, but she'd told Jack she wanted to be in charge of this particular event.

It was a special occasion, apparently. Something to do with the Loxbury City Council and her grandfather would be there so she wanted everybody to be impressed.

'And I have to go home first. Can you imagine what people would think if I turned up in track pants and a spotty jersey, with my hair looking like *this*?'

She actually giggled and it was the most delicious sound he'd ever heard. No…that prize had to go to that whimper of pure bliss he'd drawn from her lips not so long ago.

But, yeah…he could imagine. They'd be blown away by seeing a side of their boss they'd never seen before. A glimpse of Penny instead of Penelope.

But she never let people see that side, did she?

Maybe he was the only person who'd ever got this close to her?

That made him feel nervous enough to chase away the possibility of getting back to sleep.

And his bed felt oddly empty after she'd gone anyway, so he shoved back the covers and headed for the shower.

The bath was still full of water from last night. The bubbles had gone, leaving only patches of scum floating on the surface of a faintly green pond. With a grimace, Rafe plunged his arm into the icy-cold water and pulled the plug.

Just like he'd have to pull the plug on whatever was happening between himself and Penny at some point down the track? His nervousness morphed into something less pleasant. He avoided looking in the mirror as he moved to the toilet because he had a feeling he wouldn't like the person he'd see.

Somebody who'd let someone get close and then leave town and never see her again?

The puddle of the towel on the tiled floor was in the way of getting to the shower cubicle. Rafe stooped and picked it up, remembering the way it had slipped from Penny's body as he'd been kissing her last night. He could almost swear a faint scent of her got released from the fabric as he dropped it into the laundry basket. He heard himself groan as he reached into the shower and flicked on the taps.

It wasn't that he was setting out to hurt her. He just didn't do anything long-term. What was the point of making promises that only ended up getting broken? That was when people got really hurt.

She was too vulnerable for him. And her belief that marriage was some sacred promise that made everything perfect was downright scary. She would probably deny it—he'd seen that magazine article where she'd said she was a happily single career-woman—but the truth was she was searching for 'the one.' The man who'd marry her and give her a bunch of babies.

And that man wasn't him.

No way.

Funny how empty his house felt when she'd gone. How empty *he* felt.

Well, that was a no-brainer. How had they completely forgotten to have any dinner last night? A fry-up would fix that. Bacon and eggs and some mushrooms, along with some thick slices of toast and a good slathering of butter.

By the time he'd finished that, he might as well go into work himself. He'd promised a show to remember for the anniversary Loxbury music festival and the pressure was on to get it planned and organised.

It was a weird twist of fate that the original festival had such significance in Penny's life but a seed of something that felt good came in thinking about that connection. He might not be able to give her what she wanted in life but he could do something to protect her right now. To stop other people hurting her.

Yes. By the time Rafe locked the door of his vast, empty house behind him and walked out into the new dawn, he was feeling much better.

He could fix something. Or at least make sure it didn't get any more broken than it already was.

Julie the journalist was young—probably in her early twenties—and she had an enthusiasm that made Rafe feel old and wise in comparison.

She was also cute, trying to look professional in her summery dress and ballet flats, with her hair up in a messy kind of bun.

Compared to Penny in professional mode, she looked like a child playing dress-up. She was a bit of a chatterbox, too, and giggled often enough for it to become annoying. Was she flirting with him?

If so, she had no idea how far off the mark she was. He couldn't be less interested but he kept smiling. He might need her cooperation on something important if the opportunity arose to put her off chasing the Baby X story. No, make that when. He'd make sure that opportunity arose.

There was plenty to show her and talk about before that. Video clips of old shows, for instance.

'This was the Fourth of July in Times Square. A bigger show than the one we're planning for the festival but we'll be using a lot of the same kind of fireworks. And this is a much more recent one.'

'Oh...isn't that the Summers wedding? I've seen that already. Love the hearts. And it's a cool song...' Julie's head was swaying and her hands were moving. He couldn't imagine any inhibitions about dancing in public with this girl. Any moment now she'd probably jump onto his desk and start dancing.

An image of Penny dancing in the maze moved in the back of his mind. Awkward. Endearing...

'That's one of the early challenges, picking the right song for a show. And it's important to get it locked in because that's when the planning really starts. Hitting the right breaks with the right shells. Making it a work of art instead of just a lot of noise and colour.'

'So have you chosen the song for the festival?'

'Mmm. Did that first thing this morning.'

'What is it?'

'I can't tell you that. If word got out, it wouldn't be a surprise and it would lose a lot of its impact.'

'Oh...*please*...?' Julie's eyes were wide as she leaned closer. 'I cross my heart and hope to die promise that I won't tell *anybody*.'

She was desperate to know. And if he gave her what she wanted, would she be more likely to return the favour?

'Okay...but this has to be a secret. Just between us.'

Her nod was solemn. Rafe made his tone just as serious.

'The first festival was held in 1985. The first thing I did was search for all the number-one hits for that year. And then I looked for ones that would work well with fireworks.'

'And...?'

'Strangely enough, Jennifer Rush's "Power of Love" was one of them.' And hadn't that hit him like a brick. How long had he sat there, the list blurring on the screen in front of him, as he relived watching Penny watching his fireworks that night. That first kiss...

'But you've already used that recently, yes?'

'Yeah...then I found another one and remembered something big that happened in 1985. In May. Only a few months before the festival so anyone who was there would remember it very well.'

'Bit before my time.' Julie smiled. 'You'll have to enlighten me.'

'The Bradford stadium fire? Killed a bunch of people and injured a whole lot more. It was a real tragedy.'

Julie frowned. 'Doesn't sound like a good connection to remind people of.'

'That's the thing. A group that called themselves The Crowd released a song to help with the fundraising effort and it's a song that everybody knows. An anthem that's all about exactly that—connection between people and the strength that they can give each other.'

'Wow...so, are you going to tell me what this magic song is?'

'Better than that.' Rafe clicked his mouse. 'Have a listen...'

A few minutes later and Julie was looking misty. 'That's just perfect...' She sniffed. 'I'd love to use it in my story but it'll still make great copy for a follow-up review.'

'There should be lots of great stuff to follow up on. Did you know that they've got a lot of the original artists playing again?'

'And current ones—like Diversion. Are you going to play with them? Matt really wants you to.'

Was there something going on between Diversion's lead singer and Julie? Rafe made a mental note to ask his mate what he thought he was doing when he saw the guys at the pub straight after this. Julie was too young. She'd end up getting hurt.

'I'm thinking about it. It'd be fun but I'll be pretty busy setting up the show.'

Julie folded her notepad and picked up her shoulder-bag. She looked like she was getting ready to leave.

'It can't be just the fireworks you're checking up on for your piece about the festival,' he said casually. 'What else is interesting?'

'Well, there's some debate about what charity is going to benefit from the profits. Last time it was the Last Wish Foundation for terminally sick kids and the time before that it was cancer research, but they want something local this time. It's all about Loxbury.'

'Mmm.' Rafe tried to sound interested instead of impatient. 'What about that other story? The girl who died?'

'Oh…' Julie's face lit up and she let her bag slip off her shoulder to land on the floor again. 'Now, that's *really* interesting. I had to call in a few favours to get any information but I finally tracked it down through someone who had access to old admission data at Loxbury General's A and E department. There were a few girls to choose from that day but only one who was really sick.'

'From a drug overdose?'

'That's the interesting bit. It was a bit of a scandal at the time because everyone assumed it *was* a drug overdose.'

'And it wasn't?'

'No. Apparently there was no trace of drugs. The coroner listed the death as being from natural causes. The poor girl had a brain aneurysm. She got taken off life support a few days after she'd collapsed at the festival.'

Why didn't Penny know that? Why had she been allowed to think that her mother had been some kind of drug addict who'd abandoned her in favour of finding a high? He'd suggested that maybe she'd had no choice other than to leave her baby under a bush. Having a brain haemorrhage certainly came under that category, didn't it? Wouldn't it have caused a dreadful headache or something? Scrambled thoughts enough for the sufferer to not be thinking straight?

'I got lucky.' Julie tapped the side of her nose. 'I got her name. Charlotte Collins. I've been trying to contact her family but do you know how many Collinses there are in Loxbury?'

She didn't wait for him to guess, which was just as well because Rafe was still thinking about Penny. How it might change things if she knew the truth. But, then, why hadn't she already been told? What kind of can of worms might he be opening?

'A hundred and thirty-seven,' Julie continued. 'And this Charlotte might not even have been local.' She paused for a breath. 'Mind you, I did get an odd reaction of this dead silence with one call. And then the phone got slammed down. The number was for a Douglas Collins. He got an OBE for service to the police force and now he's got some important job in the city council. I might follow that up again.'

'Don't you think it would be kind of intrusive to have someone asking about the death of your child?'

'But it was thirty years ago.' Julie looked genuinely surprised. 'I'd think they might like to think that someone remembered her. I might suggest some kind of tribute at the festival even, if I can find out a bit more.'

'I wouldn't.' Rafe summoned all the charm he could muster. 'I'd let the poor girl just rest in peace.'

'Oh…' Julie was holding his gaze. 'Really? But doesn't it strike you as too much of a coincidence that a girl died *and* there was an abandoned baby found? There's got to be a connection, don't you think?'

'Is that why you're chasing the story of the dead girl?'

'It's the only lead I've got. I can't find anything out about the baby. All I've got to go on is that they thought it was a few days old and there was a mention in the news that it had been reunited with family a short time later. Nobody ever said *why* it got left under a bush, though.'

'I guess the family wanted privacy. Maybe that should be respected.'

Julie didn't seem to hear him. 'Do you know how many babies get born in Britain?' She had a habit of asking questions she intended to answer herself. 'One every forty seconds or so. That's a lot of babies. Even if you have an approximate birth date you've got hundreds and hundreds to choose from, but guess what?'

'What?'

'Last night, I found one with the surname of Collins.

Born in London but guess what the mother's name on the birth record is?'

Rafe didn't want to guess. He already knew.

'Charlotte,' Julie whispered. 'But that's just between us, okay? I'll keep your secret about the song and you can keep mine.'

'So you're looking for this daughter now?'

'You bet. But I've got a long way to go. What if she got adopted and has a completely different name now?'

'What if she's adopted and doesn't know about it? You could damage a whole family.'

'She's all grown up now. I'm sure she could cope. She might even like her five minutes of fame.'

Rafe stood up. He couldn't say anything else but he needed to move. He wasn't doing a very good job of putting Julie off the scent, was he? How could he protect Penny?

He really, really wanted to protect her.

Somehow.

'As you said, it's a common name. I suspect you'll find a dead end.'

'No such thing in journalism.' Julie beamed at him. 'It just means there's a new direction to try. And I've got one to go and try right now. Thanks for the interview, Rafe. I'll look forward to seeing the fireworks.'

There might be fireworks of an entirely different kind well before the festival, Rafe mused, leaving his office to get to the pub where his old mates were waiting to have a beer and talk about whether he was going to join the band for a song or two on the day.

As soon as he'd had a beer or two he'd get away. At least he and Penny had exchanged phone numbers now. He could call her and warn her about how close Julie was getting to the truth. Apologise for not being more effective in throwing her off the scent, but how could he when she was so far down the track already? He could do it now, in fact, before he went somewhere noisy. Stopping in the street, he pulled his phone from his pocket. He dialled her number but, as it began to ring, another thought struck him.

Maybe he should also tell her that the truth was not what she believed it to be. But that wasn't something he could tell her over the phone. Cutting the call off, he shoved his mobile back into his pocket. It was a good thing he knew where she lived. A smile tugged at his lips as he pushed his way into a crowded Irish bar. Maybe there was a chance she'd be wearing those PJs again when she opened her door. If he stayed a bit longer at the pub with his mates, the odds of that being the case would only get stronger.

There was a good band playing and the beer was even better. Telling Scruff and Matt and the others that he'd like to get up on stage with them for old times' sake led to a lot of back-slapping and a new round of beer, this time with some whisky shots as well.

'You'll love it, man. Can't wait to tell the Twickenham twins. Bet they'll turn up with their pompoms as well as their cowboy hats. Hey, let's give them a call. They might like a night out, too.'

'I can't stay too long. Somewhere to be soon.'

'You can't leave yet. Band's not bad, eh? For a bunch of oldies.'

Rafe took another glance at the group on stage. 'They're no spring chickens, are they? Best place for Irish music, though. They wouldn't sound half as good at an outdoor gig.'

'Don't let them hear you say that. They'll be playing at the festival. They're one of the original acts that's being brought back.'

Rafe peered at the set of drums. 'What's with the name? The *Paws*?'

'Bit of a laugh, eh? I hear it got picked because it's the nickname of the lead guitarist but it got a lot funnier after the Corrs came along.'

'What kind of a nickname is Paws?' Rafe had another look as a new round of drinks got delivered to their corner. 'His hands look perfectly normal to me.'

'That's not normal. Listen to him—the guy's a genius. Paddy's his real name. Good name for an Irish dude, eh?'

'Don't tell me,' Rafe grinned. 'His surname's Murphy?'

Scruff's jaw dropped. 'You knew all along, didn't you?'

'No.' This time Rafe couldn't take his eyes off the guitarist. Paws. Paddy. Patrick. A Patrick Murphy who played the guitar. Who'd been at the Loxbury music festival thirty years ago? What were the odds?

Maybe Julie was right. Dead ends only led to a new direction. If the truth was going to come out, maybe the best thing he could do for Penny was to make sure that the *whole* truth came out. And this was too much of a coincidence to ignore.

Maybe he'd wait until the band finished for the night. Buy the guy a beer and at least find out if he'd ever known a girl called Charlotte Collins. Get a feel for whether there was any point in going any further.

In the meantime, there were drinks to be had. Conversations to be had along with them.

'Hey, Scruff? What did you do with that old set of drums I gave you way back? The ones I got given before I took up the sax?'

'They're still in the back of my garage. Bit of history, they are.'

'D'you really want to keep them?'

'Hadn't thought about it. Guess I should clean out the garage some time so I can fit my car back into it? Why?'

'Just that I met a kid the other day who looks like he could use a direction in life. A set of drums is a good way to burn up a bit of teenage angst, if nothing else.'

'True. Come and get them any time, man. They were yours in the first place, anyway.'

It was the buzzing in his pocket that finally distracted him from what was turning out to be a very enjoyable evening. He would never have heard his phone ringing but he could feel the vibration. When he saw that Penny was the caller, he pushed his way out of the bar again. Out into the relative peace of an inner-city street at night.

'Penny...hey, babe.'

'How *could* you, Rafe? When you knew how important it was...'

Good grief...was she *crying*?

'I trusted you...and then you go and do *this*...'

Yep. She was crying. Either that or she was so angry it was making her words wobble and her voice so tight he wouldn't have recognised it.

'What are you talking about? What am I supposed to have done?'

'Julie.' The word was an accusation. 'You *told* her.'

'Told her what?' But there was a chill running down his spine. He had a bad feeling about this.'

'About me. About my grandparents. She turned up on their doorstep, asking all sorts of questions... Oh, my God, Rafe... Have you any idea what you've *done*?'

'I didn't tell her anything. She'd already figured it out. I was going to tell you...'

'You really expect me to believe that? You told her and then she turned up and now...and now Grandad's probably going to die...'

'*What?*'

'They got rid of her but Mother was really upset. Rita called me. By the time I got there, all I could do was call an ambulance.' There was the sound of a broken sob on the other end of the line. 'He's had a heart attack and he's in Intensive Care and they don't know if he's even going to make it and...and this is...this is all... Oh, *God*... Why am I even talking to you about this?'

The call ended abruptly. What had she left unsaid? That it was all his fault?

It wasn't true. It wasn't even fair.

But standing there, in the street, with the echoes of that heartbroken voice louder than the beeping of the terminated call, it felt remarkably like it was, somehow, *his* fault.

CHAPTER NINE

THEY WERE TAKING him away.

Penelope watched the bed being wheeled towards the elevator, flanked by a medical team wearing theatre scrubs, the suddenly frail figure of her beloved grandfather almost hidden by the machines that were keeping him alive.

The elevator doors closed behind the entourage and Penelope pressed her hand against her mouth. Was this going to be the last time she saw him alive? He was the only person in her life she could believe still loved her, even when she messed up and broke a rule. Someone who could see some value in what Rafe called Penny instead of Penelope.

Oh, God…she didn't want to think about Rafe right now. About that shock of betrayal that had felt like a death and only made it so much worse as she'd watched the paramedics fighting to stabilise Grandad before rushing him to hospital.

A sideways glance showed her own fear reflected on her grandmother's face but the instinct to move closer and offer the comfort of a physical touch had to be suppressed.

'I'll take you to our family waiting room.' The nurse beside them was sympathetic. 'Someone will come and find you as soon as we know anything.'

'How long is this procedure going to take?' Louise spoke precisely and it sounded as though she was asking about something as unimportant as having her teeth whitened but Penelope knew it was a front. She'd never seen her grandmother looking so pale and frightened.

Lost, even...

'That depends,' the nurse said. 'If the angioplasty's not successful, they'll take Mr Collins straight into Theatre for a bypass operation. We should know whether that's likely within the next hour or so. Here we are...' She opened the door to a small room that contained couches and chairs, a television and a coffee table with a stack of magazines. 'Help yourself to coffee or tea. Milk's in the fridge. If you get hungry, there's a cafeteria on the ground floor that stays open all night.'

The thought of food was nauseating.

The silence, when the nurse had closed the door behind her, was deafening.

Louise sat stiffly on the edge of one of the chairs, staring at the magazines. Was she going to pick one up and make the lack of conversation more acceptable?

'Can I make you a cup of tea, Mother?'

'No, thank you, Penelope.'

'Coffee?'

'No.'

'A glass of water?'

'*No*... For heaven's sake, just leave me alone.' Her voice rose and shook and then—to Penelope's horror—

her grandmother's shoulders began shaking. She was *crying*?

'I'm sorry,' she heard herself whisper.

What was she apologising for? Telling Rafe her story, which had been passed on to that journalist who'd been the catalyst for this disaster? How *could* he have done that? She'd felt so safe with him. Had trusted him completely. The anger that had fuelled that phone call had evaporated now, though, leaving her feeling simply heartbroken.

Or was she apologising for being the person her grandmother had to share this vigil with? For all the years that her grandparents had had to share their lives with her when they could have been enjoying their retirement together? Was she apologising for having been born at all?

Or was she just sorry this was happening? Sorry for herself and for Mother and most of all for Grandad.

Maybe it was all of those things.

'He's in the right place,' she said softly. 'And he's a fighter. He won't give up.'

Louise pulled tissues from the box beside the magazines. 'You have no idea what you're talking about, Penelope. This is precisely what *could* make him give up. Being reminded...'

Of what? Losing their daughter and getting the booby prize of a grandchild they hadn't wanted? Penelope didn't know what to say.

Louise blew her nose but kept the tissue pressed against her face so her voice sounded muffled. 'He gave up then. He was in the running for the kind of job that would have earned him a knighthood eventually. A seat in parliament, even, where he could have achieved his life's dream of law reform that would have made a real difference on the front line. There were two things Douglas was passionate about. His job. And his daughter.'

'And you.' Penelope sank onto the couch, facing her grandmother. Louise had never talked to her like this and it was faintly alarming. This was breaking a huge rule—talking about the past. Maybe that was why she was crossing a boundary here, too, in saying something so personal. 'He loves you, too, Mother.'

Louise had her eyes closed as she slumped in her chair. 'I gave him Charlotte,' she whispered. 'That was my biggest accomplishment…but I couldn't stop it happening. I tried *so* hard…'

Penelope's mouth was dry. Was Louise really aware of who she was talking to? It felt like she was listening to someone talking to themselves. Someone whose barriers had crumbled under the weight of fear and impending grief.

'What…?' The word opened a door that was supposed to be locked. 'What was happening?'

'The violin lessons. That was what should have been happening.' The huff of breath was incredulous. 'But, no…we found out she'd given up the lessons. It wasn't hard to have her followed and that's how we found out about the boy.'

Penelope's heart seemed to stop and then deliver a painful thump. 'My…father?'

'Patrick.' The name was a curse. 'A long-haired Irish

lout who'd given up his education to be in a band that
played in pubs. He was living in a squat, along with his
band and their friends—the drug dealers.'

'Oh…' She could understand how distressing that
must have been. What if she had a sixteen-year-old
daughter who got in with a bad crowd? A reminder
of the anger she'd felt towards Rafe surfaced but this
time it was directed at the mother she'd never known.
A drug addict. Someone who'd made her parents unhappy and then gone on to abandon her own baby. There
was something to be said for the mantra she'd been
brought up with. Penelope didn't want to end up like
her mother. No way.

'She threatened to run away and live with the boy
if we tried to stop them seeing each other. They were
"in love", she said. They were going to get married
and live happily ever after.' For the first time since
she'd started talking, she opened her eyes and looked
directly at Penelope. 'How ridiculous was that? She
barely knew him.'

Penelope had to look away, a confusing jumble of
emotions vying for prominence. She barely knew Rafe
but there'd been more than one occasion with him when
she'd thought there was nowhere else in the world she'd
ever want to be. A wave of longing pushed up through
the anger. And then there was that hurt again and somewhere in between there was a flash of sympathy for her
mother. A connection born of understanding the power
of that kind of love?

'Douglas was in the final round of interviews for the
new government position. Can you imagine how help-

ful that would have been? How could anyone think that
he could contribute to law and order on a national level
when he couldn't even keep his own house in order?
When his daughter was living in a drug den?'

Penelope was silent. Maybe it could have been a
point in his favour. Didn't a lot of people become doc-
tors because they hadn't been able to help a loved one?
Have the motivation to help because they understood the
suffering that could be caused? Look at the way Rafe
had been with Billy. He'd known what that boy was
going through and he'd had to step up and help, even
when it had clearly been difficult for him. There was
something fundamentally good about Rafe Edwards. It
was hard to believe he would ever do anything to hurt
someone else deliberately. She didn't *want* to believe
it but how could she not, when the evidence was right
there in front of her?

'It wasn't hard to have the house raided with our police connections. Arrests made.' Louise sounded tired
now. 'There wasn't anything that the boy or his band
friends could be directly charged with but association
was enough. They got warned to get out of town and
stay out. *He* was told in no uncertain terms that if he
tried to contact Charlotte again, charges could still be
laid and they could all find themselves behind bars.'

'So he just left? Even knowing that he was going to
be a father?'

Louise fluttered a hand as if it was unimportant. 'I
don't imagine he knew. I'm not sure Charlotte knew.
Either that or she kept it hidden until it was too late to
do anything about it.'

Somehow this was the most shocking thing she'd heard so far in this extraordinary conversation and the words came out in a gasp.

'An abortion, you mean?'

She might not have existed at all and that was a weird thought. She would never have known the satisfaction of being successful, doing something she loved. Or felt the pleasures that creating beautiful food or listening to wonderful music could provide. She would never have danced. She would never have experienced the kind of bliss that Rafe had given her, albeit so briefly.

There was something else she could feel for her mother now. Gratitude at being protected?

'Of course.' The clipped pronouncement was harsh. 'Not that your mother would have cooperated. She became extremely…difficult. She stopped eating. Stopped talking. Your grandfather was beside himself. It was the psychiatrist we took her to who guessed she was pregnant.'

The long silence suggested that the conversation was over as far as Louise was concerned, but Penelope couldn't leave her story there.

'What happened then?'

'I found a boarding school that specialised in dealing with situations like that. She was to stay there and continue her schooling and then the baby would be adopted.'

That baby was *me*. Your grandchild…

But the agonised cry stayed buried. Instead, Penelope swallowed hard and spoke calmly. 'Was Grandad happy about that?'

Louise had her eyes shut again. 'It was a difficult time for all of us but there was no choice. Not if he wanted that promotion.'

A promotion that had clearly never happened.

The silence was even longer this time. Maybe they would hear soon about what was happening with Grandad. No doubt someone would come and talk to them in person but it was an automatic gesture to check her phone. Nothing.

Except a missed call from Rafe.

Hours ago now. Well before she'd called him.

The wash of relief was strong enough to bring the prickle of tears to her eyes. So he had been telling the truth? He had tried to call her? To confess he'd said something he had promised not to and revealed the identity of Baby X?

But why had those questions Julie had been asking had such an effect? Why was it still such a big deal, given that her grandfather had retired so long? This was only getting more confusing.

'How did I end up at the music festival? Do you know?'

Louise shrugged. 'There was a letter that came to the house. From him. Full of ridiculous statements like how he couldn't live without her. That he'd be at the festival and if she felt the same way she could find him there. I didn't forward it, of course, but I presume Charlotte found out somehow. She was in the hospital then, instead of the school, so it was probably wasn't hard to escape.'

Escape… As though she'd been sent to prison. How

hard would it still have been to get away? To take her newborn baby with her?

Penelope felt the ground shifting beneath her feet. She hadn't been abandoned. Her mother could have left her at the hospital but she'd taken her. To the festival. To meet her father?

'We got the call later that day to say she was in the intensive care unit. Right here, in almost the same place as Douglas. How ironic is that? It was obvious she'd recently given birth so we had no choice but to make enquiries about what had happened to the baby. It was your grandfather who insisted on bringing you home. You were the only thing that he cared about after Charlotte died. He gave up on his job and he…he blamed me for sending our daughter away…'

'He still did well. He got an OBE.'

'Hardly a knighthood.'

'He's a well-respected councillor.'

'Not exactly a seat in parliament or a mayoralty, is it? And the passion was never there any more.' Louise was struggling not to cry again. 'I tried to make the best of it. We pulled strings and managed to keep the story out of the papers. I did my best for you but the reminders were always there. And now there's a reporter trying to turn it all into tabloid fodder. Asking questions about why people had been allowed to assume it was a drug overdose when it wasn't. And it's all—'

All what? *Her* fault? Her own fault? What had caused her mother's death if it wasn't a drug overdose? Something that she could have had treated and survived? Had guilt been the poison in her family rather than shame?

The unfinished sentence was an echo of her call to Rafe. And he probably knew that she'd been about to tell him it was all *his* fault. But how could Julie have known it hadn't been a drug overdose? She hadn't told Rafe that because she hadn't known herself.

This was all a huge, horrible mess. And maybe none of it really mattered at the moment, anyway. The door to the room opened quietly to admit the nurse who had brought them here.

'It's all over,' she said. 'And it went very well. Mr Collins is awake now. Would you like to come and see him?'

Louise seemed incapable of getting up from her chair. She had tears streaming down her face. When she looked at Penelope there was an expression she'd never seen before. A plea that could have been for reassurance that she had just heard what she most wanted to hear.

Or could it be—at least partly—a plea for forgiveness?

Penelope held out her hand. 'Let's go,' she said quietly. 'Grandad needs us.'

'So that's about it. The rehearsal starts at five tomorrow. Let's all work together and make this a really family-friendly occasion.'

Rafe glanced at his watch. The meeting of all the key people involved in the organisation and set-up of the Loxbury music festival had filled an impressive section of the town hall. Scruff and Matt were here and he'd noticed Patrick Murphy at the back, no doubt here to find the time his band was expected to turn up for the rehearsal. Surprising how strong the urge still was to seek him out after the meeting and talk to the man who could well be Penelope's father, but he'd already done enough damage as far as she was concerned and he had no desire to get any more involved.

It was over. Or it would be, when he could shake this sense of...what was it? He hadn't done anything wrong in the first place and he hadn't even tried to contact Penny since she'd hung up on him so why did he feel like he was still doing something wrong? Making a monumental mistake of some kind?

'One other thing...' The chairman of the festival committee leaned closer to his microphone. 'We still haven't made a final decision about the charity that will be supported by the festival. If anyone has any more suggestions, they'll need to talk to a committee member tonight.'

Rafe found himself getting to his feet. Raising his arm to signal one of the support crew who'd been providing microphones for the people who'd wanted to ask questions during the briefing.

'I have a suggestion,' he said, taking hold of the mike.

'And you are?'

'Rafe Edwards. My company is providing the fireworks to finish the festival.'

A ripple of interest turned heads in his direction. The chairman was nodding. 'You've made a significant contribution to the event,' he said. 'Thank you.'

The applause was unexpected. Unnecessary. Rafe cleared his throat. 'The message we've been hearing to tonight is that you want this to be a family-friendly event. A mini-festival that isn't a rave for teenagers but something that could become an annual celebration that will bring families together.'

'That's right.'

'So I have a suggestion for the charity that you might like to consider supporting.'

'Yes?'

'The Loxbury Children's Home—Rainbow House— is a facility that this town should be very proud of. It's changing the lives of the most vulnerable citizens we have—our disadvantaged children—and, with more funding and support, it could do even more good for the community.'

A murmur of approval came from the crowd and the chairman was nodding again, after exchanging glances with the other committee members on the stage.

'It's local,' the chairman said. 'And it's about family. It's certainly a good contender.' A nod signalled that the evening's agenda was complete. 'Thanks, everybody. You'll find some refreshments in the foyer. I look forward to seeing you all again on Saturday evening. And, Mr Edwards? Come and see me before you go. I'd like to provide some free passes for the children at Rainbow House to come to the festival.'

Rafe hadn't intended staying to drink tea or eat any of the cake the Loxbury Women's Institute was providing, but there seemed to be a lot of people who wanted to shake his hand and tell him how appreciated the contribution of his fireworks show was and what a good idea he'd had for the charity to be supported.

One of them was Paddy Murphy.

'Kids are everything, aren't they?' He smiled. 'They're the future. Biggest regret of my life was not having any of my own.'

Close up for the first time, there was no doubt in Rafe's mind that this man *was* Penny's father. Those liquid brown eyes were familiar enough to twist something in his chest. About where his heart was. But he had to return the friendly smile. Say something casual.

'I'll probably have the same regret one day.' Oops. That wasn't exactly casual, was it? He shrugged. 'It's a hard road, finding the right woman, I guess.'

'Oh, I found her.' The Irish brogue was as appealing as the sincerity in Paddy's gaze. 'But then I lost her.' He slapped Rafe on the shoulder and turned away but then looked back with a shake of his head. 'Truth be told, *that's* really the biggest regret of my life. Always will be.'

Rafe watched him disappear into the crowd.

And it was right about then that he realised why he couldn't shake that nagging feeling of making some huge mistake.

He knew what that mistake was.

He just didn't have any idea of how to fix it.

CHAPTER TEN

WHAT ON EARTH was she going to do with all these cakes?

Chocolate and banana and carrot and red velvet. All iced and decorated and looking beautiful, and Penelope had no desire to eat a bite of any of them. The baking marathon had been therapy. Something comforting to do while she tried to sort through the emotional roller-coaster of the last couple of days.

She could take one of them in to the hospital for the lovely nurses who were caring for her grandfather so well. Maggie and Dave were always happy to have a cake in the house and her grandmother might like to take one home to help Rita cater for the stream of well-wishers that were turning up at their door. And maybe—the thought came as a gleam of light at the end of a dark tunnel—she could take one to Rafe.

To say sorry. Of course it couldn't make things right again but...it would be something, wouldn't it?

An excuse to see him one last time, anyway.

She chose the chocolate cake for the nurses in the cardiology ward of Loxbury General.

'You didn't need to,' the nurse manager told her. 'It's been a pleasure, caring for your grandad. We'll be sorry to see him go home tomorrow. But thank you...we *love* cake.'

She gave her grandmother the choice of the other cakes.

'Could I take the red velvet? I know your Grandad loved his birthday cake and it *was* rather delicious.'

'Of course. I'm sorry—I didn't think to make a Madeira one.'

'Do you know, I think I'm over Madeira. Such a boring cake, when you come to think of it.'

There was no farewell hug or kiss after handing over the cake but Penelope still felt good. There was something very different about her relationship with her grandmother now. Something that had the promise of getting better. Just like Grandad.

The smile stayed with her as she drove to Rainbow House. How good had it been to sit and hold Grandad's hand in the last few days? To talk to him about things they'd never discussed and even to tell him about that extraordinary conversation with her grandmother.

'She did do her best with you, you know. And she does love you, even if she doesn't let herself admit how much. She got broken by your mother's death, love. We both did. Nobody's perfect, you know. We all make mistakes but what really counts is who's there to hold your hand when it matters.'

'I know.' It was a poignant thought to realise whose hand she would want to be holding hers in a crisis.

Only she'd want more than that, wouldn't she? She'd

want her whole body to be held. So that she could feel the way she had when Rafe had held her.

'Loving people carries such a risk of getting hurt, doesn't it?' There had been an apology in her grandfather's voice as he'd patted her hand. 'Maybe neither of us was as brave as we should have been.'

Penelope's smile wobbled now as she turned into a very familiar street. How brave was she?

Brave enough to take one of those cakes to Rafe's office? To ask that receptionist if there was a chance that the terribly important chief executive officer of All Light on the Night might have the time to see her?

Not that he'd be at work this late in the day.

Maybe it would be better to take the cake to Loxbury Hall? To the place where she had fallen in love with him...

The place where he'd made *her* feel loved...

Phew... Just as well she had a visit to make to Rainbow House first. Some time with Maggie and Dave and the kids was exactly what she needed to centre herself before taking a risk like that.

How awful would it be if he didn't want to see her?

'Cake... And it's not even Sunday.' Maggie's hug was as warm as ever. 'Come in, hon. How's your grandad?'

'Going home tomorrow. His arteries are full of stents and probably better than they've been for a decade or more. Good grief, Maggie...what's that terrible noise?'

A naked, giggling toddler trotted past, with Dave in pursuit. 'I think we have you to thank for that racket.' He shook his head but he was grinning.

Charlene's hair was orange today. She went past with her fingers in her ears.

'I can't stand it,' she groaned. 'Someone tell him to stop.'

'Maggie?'

'Go and see for yourself. Out in the shed.' Maggie looked at the wet footprints on the hall floor. 'I'd better give Dave a hand with the baths.'

Bemused, Penelope put the cake in the kitchen and kept going through the back door to the old shed at the far end of the garden. The noise got steadily louder. A banging and crashing that had to be a set of drums, but they weren't being played by anyone who knew what they were doing.

Sure enough, opening the door and stepping cautiously into the cacophony, she saw it was Billy who was surrounded by the drum set. He was giving it everything he had—an expression of grim determination on his face. And then he stopped and the sudden silence was shocking.

'That was rubbish, wasn't it?'

Penelope opened her mouth to say something reassuring but someone else spoke first.

'Better than my first attempt.'

Rafe… She hadn't seen him in the corner of the dimly lit shed, sitting on a bale of the straw kept to line the bottom of the rabbit's hutch. Billy had his back to her but if Rafe had noticed her entrance he didn't show it. His attention was on the young boy he'd rescued from that imminent explosion.

'You're doing well all round, Billy. Maggie's told me how hard you're trying.'

Maybe she was interrupting something private. Penelope turned. The door was within easy reach. She could slip out as unobtrusively as she'd come in.

'I'm following the rules,' Billy said. 'Like Penny told me to. So that—you know—people'll like me.'

'Penny's an amazing lady,' Rafe said.

The tone of something like awe in his voice captured Penelope so instantly that there was no way she could make her feet move. Was it possible his feelings went further than merely being impressed by her? A smile tugged at her lips but then faded rapidly as Rafe kept talking.

'What she said, though…well, it's absolute rubbish, Billy.'

That stung. Without thinking, Penelope opened her mouth. 'How can you say that?'

Rafe must have seen her come in because he didn't seem nearly as surprised as Billy that she was there. The boy's head jerked around to face her but the shift in Rafe's gaze was calm.

'You've always followed all the rules,' he said. 'How's that worked out for you?'

'Just fine,' Penelope said tightly. What sort of example was Rafe giving Billy by saying this?

She glared at him. He had his cowboy hat on and the brim was shading his face but he was staring back at her just as intently. She could *feel* it.

'Sometimes you haven't followed all the rules. How's *that* working out?'

Oh…maybe he was providing a good example after all. What were those rules she'd broken? The only one she could think of right now was the time she'd gone upstairs at Loxbury Hall when she'd thought it was forbidden. When she'd given herself to Rafe.

She dropped her gaze to try and shield herself from the intensity of that scrutiny. 'Not so good.'

'You sure about that?' The quiet voice held a note of…good grief…*amusement*? As if he knew very well how well it had worked out.

Billy's foot went down on the pedal to thump the bass drum. 'I don't get it,' he growled. 'One minute you're telling me to follow the rules and then you say stuff about *you* guys breaking them. It doesn't make sense.'

Rafe leaned forward on his straw bale, his hands on his knees, giving Billy his full attention again.

'There are a lot of rules that are important to follow, Billy, but people will like you for *who* you are. You just have to show them who that really is and not hide behind stuff.'

'What kind of stuff?'

'Some people try to hide by being perfect and following all the rules.'

Penelope winced.

'And some people try to hide by making out they're tough and they don't care.'

Billy was twisting the drumsticks he still held. 'I *don't* care.'

'Yeah, you do.' The gentle note in Rafe's voice made Penelope catch her breath. 'We *all* care.'

'You don't know anything.' Billy's head was down. The drumsticks were very still.

'I know more than you think. I *was* you once, kid. I was tough. I didn't give a damn and I broke every rule I could and got into trouble all the time. And you know why?'

It took a long time for the reluctant word to emerge. 'Why?'

'Because I didn't *want* to care. Because it was too scary to care. Because that was how you got hurt.'

The long silence then gave the impression that Billy was giving the matter considerable thought but when he spoke he sounded offhand.

'Is it true we're all going to go and see the fireworks tomorrow night?'

Rafe didn't seem to mind the subject being changed. 'You bet.'

'You got us the tickets,' Billy said. He paused. 'And the drums.'

'The tickets are for everybody. The drums are just for you.'

'For real?'

'For real.' Rafe was smiling. 'And you know why I gave them to you?' He didn't wait for a response but he did lower his voice, as though the words were intended only for Billy. He must have known Penelope could hear, though. Without the drums, it was utterly quiet in there.

'Because I care. It's okay to care back, you know. It's quite safe.'

He got to his feet and took a step towards Penelope. But his words had been directed at Billy just then.

Hadn't they? Her stupid heart skipped a beat anyway. A tingle of something as wonderful as hope filling a space around it that had been very empty.

Billy's sideways gaze was suspicious. 'Do you care about her, too?'

The brim of that hat made it impossible to read the expression in Rafe's eyes but she didn't need to. She could hear it in the sound of his voice.

'Oh, yeah…'

Billy made a disgusted sound. 'You gonna get married, then? And have kids?'

'Um… Bit soon to think about anything like that. And I might have to find out how Penny feels first, buddy.'

Billy's tone was accusing now. 'You care, too, don't you?'

Penelope couldn't drag her gaze away from Rafe. 'Oh, yeah…'

The delicious silence as the mutual declaration was absorbed finally got broken by a satisfied grunt from Billy that indicated the matter was settled. 'Can I go and tell the other kids that the drums are just for me?'

'How 'bout telling them that they're going to have the best time ever at the festival tomorrow? And tell Maggie and Dave that you'll help look after the little ones. Fireworks can be a bit scary close up and I'm going to make sure you have the very best place to watch.'

It was still hard to tell if his words were just for Billy or whether he was reminding Penelope of when he'd taken her to the best place to watch his fireworks.

Billy was on his feet now, though—his skinny chest

puffed with pride. 'I can do that.' He put his drumsticks on the stool. 'I'm one of the biggest kids here.'

He had to walk between Rafe and Penelope to get to the door but neither of them seemed to notice because he was below the line of where they were looking—directly at each other.

His steps slowed. And then stopped. The suspense was getting unbearable. Rafe was going to kiss her the moment Billy disappeared and Penelope didn't want to have to wait a second longer.

But Billy turned back. He went back to the stool and picked up the drumsticks. 'I'm gonna need these.'

Rafe grinned. 'Practise on a cushion for a bit. That way you won't drive anyone crazy.'

'I think I might be going crazy,' Penelope murmured, as Billy disappeared through the door of the shed.

'Me, too.' Rafe pushed the door closed. 'Crazy with wanting you.'

But he didn't move any closer. They stood there, for the longest time, simply looking at each other.

'Me, too.' The words escaped Penelope on a sigh. 'I love you, Rafe...'

He held out his hand. Without saying a word, he led her over to the straw bale and sat down beside her. Then he took off his hat and held it in his hands.

Penelope swallowed hard. She'd said it first and he hadn't said it back. He hadn't uttered a single word since she'd spoken.

He could have kissed her instead. That would have been enough. But he hadn't done that either.

She was standing on a precipice here.

Teetering.

Feeling like she might be about to fall to her death.

She'd said she cared.

Not just the way you could care about a lost kid and want to do something to help put him on the right path, even though that kind of caring could be so strong you had to put yourself out there and maybe face stuff that you thought you'd buried a long time ago.

Penelope had gone further. She'd said she *loved* him. She'd just gone right out there and said the scariest thing in the world. Put herself in the place where you could hurt the most.

The weight of how that made him feel had crushed his ability to form words. To form coherent thoughts even, because what he said next could be the most important thing he ever said in his life.

No pressure there…

That weird weight seemed to be too much for his body as well as his brain. He had to sit down, but he wasn't going anywhere without Penny and she seemed happy enough to take his hand and follow along.

But now he had to say something. He heard the little hitch in her breath in the silence. A sound that made him all too aware of how scared she was.

He was scared, too. His hands tightened on his hat, scrunching the felt beneath his fingers.

'You know why I bought Loxbury Hall?' His voice sounded rusty.

From the corner of his eye, he saw Penelope nod. 'You told me. That night—in the bath. You said it was the kind of house that only people who had perfect lives could live in.'

'Yeah… That's what I thought through all those rough years when my life was like Billy's. If you were rich enough, you could make your own rules. Live in a place like that and have a family that stayed together. You called family a safe place once and I guess that's what a huge house that cost a bucket of money represented to me. That safe place. But you know what?'

Her voice was a whisper. 'What?'

'I was wrong. So, so wrong.' The whole hat was twisted in his hands now. It would never be the same. Dropping it, he turned his head to look at Penelope. His empty hands caught hers.

'The safe place isn't a place at all, is it? It's a person.'

Her eyes were huge. Locked on his, and it felt as if something invisible but solid was joining them.

'But it's a place, too. Not a place you can buy. Or even find a map of how to get there. It's the place that you're in when you're with *that* person.'

Her eyes were shining now. With unshed tears? Was he saying something that she understood? That she wanted to hear?

Even if she didn't, it felt right to say it. Maybe so that he could understand it better himself.

'It's a place that only that person can create with you. You can't see it but it's so real that even when you're not together you can still feel safe because you know where that place is.' He had to pause to draw in a slow, steadying breath.

This was it.

The thing he really had to say.

'You're my person, Penny.'

Yep. They had been unshed tears. They were escaping now.

Her voice was the softest whisper but he could hear it as clear as a bell and it felt just as good as if she were shouting it from a rooftop.

'You're my person, too, Rafe. For ever and always.'

CHAPTER ELEVEN

THE WEATHER GODS smiled on Loxbury for the thirtieth anniversary of their first music festival and the lazy, late-summer afternoon morphed into an evening cool enough for people to enjoy dancing but still warm enough for the ice-cream stalls to be doing a brisk business.

The gates had opened at five p.m. and the fireworks show timed for ten p.m. had been widely advertised as something people wouldn't want to miss—an exciting finale to a memorable occasion.

It was a music festival with a difference. Artists who'd been at the original festival were given star billing, of course, but there were many others. New local groups, soloists, dance troupes, a pipe band and even the entire Loxbury symphony orchestra. The appreciative crowd was just as eclectic a mix as the entertainment on offer. Teenagers were out in force, banding together far enough away from parents to be cool, but there were whole families there as well, staking out their picnic spots on the grass with blankets and folding chairs, prams and even wheelchairs.

Between the musical performers, the MC introduced the occasional speaker. At about eight p.m., when the crowd had swelled to record numbers, the person who came out to speak was the mayor of Loxbury, resplendent in his gown and chain.

'What a wonderful event this is,' he said proudly. 'A credit to the countless people who have given up so much of their time both to organise and perform. Thank you, all.'

The cheer that went up from the crowd expressed their appreciation.

'I came to the very first festival,' the mayor continued. 'And I remember how much opposition there was to it even happening. There was even a petition taken to the council to try and prevent it corrupting our young people.'

There was laughter from the crowd now. Penelope caught Maggie's glance and shared a smile. Rainbow House had several rugs on the grass. The younger children had all visited the face-painting booths and even Billy had been persuaded to have his face painted white with a black star around his eye to look like the lead singer of Kiss. Right now, he was sitting with the youngest children, righting the occasional ice-cream cone that threatened to lose its topping.

'I can't see any dangers here,' the mayor smiled. 'Just a heart-warming number of our families having a great time together.'

It was a poignant moment for Penelope. She'd never dreamed of attending such an event in her life because she'd grown up with the belief that terrible things did, in fact, happen at music festivals. She'd considered herself living proof of exactly that.

'I see parents and grandparents,' the mayor continued. 'And I see many of our youngest citizens, who represent the future of Loxbury. Some of you know the story of Baby X—the baby that got found when they were cleaning up after that first festival that we're celebrating again today. That baby got returned to its family but we all know there are some children that aren't always that lucky, and it's my pleasure to tell you that the charity chosen to benefit from this festival is a place that cares for those children. Rainbow House...'

The clapping and cheering were deafening this time but Maggie burst into tears. Dave took her into his arms and Penelope suspected he shed a few tears as well. She had to blink hard herself because she knew what this could mean. The roof getting fixed, along with a dozen other much-needed repairs. All sorts of things that could make life more comfortable and enable these people she loved to keep doing something so wonderful. She might suggest a minibus so that they could transport the children more easily when they had somewhere special to go.

Like the festival today, which had presented a logistical challenge. And the Christmas party that was going to take place this year at Loxbury Hall. It had been a joy planning that with Rafe last night, and she knew it would happen. She was going to talk to Jack this week about the catering they would be doing for it.

The other crazy schemes they'd come up with might need some adjustment. Turning a wing of Loxbury Hall into offices so they could both work at home might be a waste because he'd still want to travel to his big shows. And she might want to go with him. Making the hall and gardens available as a wedding venue again needed thinking about, too. It was very likely to become their home and would they want to share that with strangers—especially when they had their own family to think about?

But how much happiness could it bring? Maggie and Dave had never hesitated to share their home and some of the people cheering so loudly right now were probably those teenagers who had come to find Maggie and Dave from amongst the gathering just to say hello. Young people who had needed shelter at some time in their lives and had a bond that would never fade. They seemed to be heading in this direction again to share the joy of this announcement and her bonus parents were going to be busy giving and receiving hugs for quite some time. She made sure hers was the first.

How lucky had she been to find that bond herself?

How lucky was Billy?

And something else made her feel that she could never become any luckier. After what Rafe had whispered in her ear last night, maybe the next wedding she was going to manage was going to be her own. That would certainly happen at Loxbury Hall. And there was her birthday in a couple of days. Not that she needed any gifts because she had everything she could possibly want in her life now, but a small party would be nice. One that could be an invitation for her grandparents to share her new life in a meaningful way?

The mayor had finished speaking and the MC was introducing one of Loxbury's newer talents. Penelope recognised the group instantly as Diversion—the band that had played at the Bingham wedding. Were Clarissa and Blake here somewhere? If they were, they were probably dancing with the growing number of people in front of the stage. It was starting to get darker and there were glow sticks in abundance as well as headbands that had glowing stars or flashing lights on them.

Billy was on his feet now, jiggling a little on the spot as he listened to the music with his whole body. Penelope could see his hands twitching as if he was holding imaginary drumsticks. But then he stopped to stare at the stage, his black lipstick making his open mouth rather comical.

'Is that…*Rafe*?'

The band was playing a cover of Billy Joel's 'Just the Way You Are'.

Penelope could only nod in response. She'd known that Rafe would be joining the band for this song. He'd told her about it last night, when they'd left the shed in the garden, excused themselves from sharing cake and had gone to the best place in the world to celebrate the declaration of their love—where it had first begun—at Loxbury Hall. The most magnificent place that wasn't as important as the place he'd found with her.

The tears were too close again now. He'd told her what song he was going to be playing. He'd whispered the words as if they'd been written for him to say and it was his voice she could hear now, rather than Diversion's lead singer as he sang that he would take her just the way she was. That he wanted her just the way she was. That he loved her just the way she was.

And each time these lyrics led to a saxophone riff from the black-clad figure in the cowboy hat that had Penelope's total attention. Every bend and sway of his body ignited an all-consuming desire that she knew would never fade. The words were exactly how she felt. This love would never fade either.

The jab of Billy's elbow prevented her from turning into a mushy puddle.

'What's that thing he's playing?'

'A saxophone. He started learning it after he stopped playing on those drums he gave you.'

'That's what I'm gonna do, too.'

'Good idea.' Penelope took a deep breath as the song finished. 'I'll see you later, Billy. I told Rafe I'd meet him after this song to see how it's going with setting up the fireworks.'

'Can I come, too?'

'You promised to help look after the little ones, remember? You're in the best place to watch and it's not that far away.'

It was just as well there was an acceptable excuse not to take Billy with her. The setting up of the fireworks had been finished by lunchtime today. She was meeting Rafe near the stage simply so that they could be together and she couldn't have kissed him like this if there'd been anyone around to watch.

Couldn't have been held so close and basked in the bliss of all those feelings she'd had during the song that were magnified a thousand times by being pressed against his body. Being able to touch him—and kiss him—just like this.

But Rafe wanted to do more than kiss her.

'Come and dance with me.'

'No-o-o... I can't dance.' Penelope could feel the colour rising in her cheeks. 'You know that. You *saw* me trying to dance in your maze...'

'Ah, but you weren't dancing with *me*...'

And there they were. Among a hundred people dancing in front of the stage to the music from an Irish band that had been announced as one of the original festival artists, and it *was* easy. All she had to do was follow Rafe's excellent lead. They danced through the entire set the band played and then they stood and clapped as the band members took their turns accepting the applause.

The lead guitarist leaned in to the microphone and held up his hand to signal a need for silence.

'It's been thirty years since we played here,' he said. 'But my heart has always been in Loxbury.'

He waited for the renewed applause to fade.

'The love of my life was a Loxbury girl.'

Rafe's hand tightened around Penelope's and she felt an odd stillness pressing in on her. She was still in a crowd but she felt as conspicuous as if a spotlight had been turned onto her. Alone.

No, not alone. She had Rafe by her side.

'Who is he?'

'His name's Paddy Murphy.'

'*Patrick* Murphy?'

'I came to that first Loxbury festival hoping to find

her again but I didn't.' Paddy shook his head sadly. 'There's never been anyone else for me but that's just the way things worked out, I guess. Maybe you're out there tonight, Charlie, my darlin'. If you are, I hope you're happy. Here's one more song—just for you...'

People around started dancing again but Penelope was standing as still as a stone. 'Oh, my God...' she whispered.

Rafe led her away from the dancers before anyone could bump into them. Right away from any people. He took them into the area fenced off as the safety margin for the pyrotechnic crew by showing his pass to a security guard. Off to the edge of field that was criss-crossed with wires leading to the scissor lifts.

'Watch your feet. Don't trip...'

The music was fainter now and the people far enough away to be forgotten. Except for one of them.

'He's my father, isn't he?'

'I think he probably is. He looks a lot like you, close up. And he's a really nice person. Special...'

'Did you know about him being here?'

'I knew his name and that his band was going to be playing. And then I met him a couple of nights ago and he told me that losing the woman he loved was the biggest regret of his life.' Rafe drew Penelope close to kiss her. 'That was the moment I realised that I'd be making the biggest mistake of my life if I lost you. That you were the love of *my* life.'

'He doesn't know about what happened to my mother, does he?'

'Apparently not.'

'You know what I think? I think that she brought me here to meet him. That he was the love of *her* life, too.'

'He told me something else, too. That his other huge regret was never having kids of his own.'

Penelope had a lump in her throat the size of a boulder. 'Do you think he'd want to meet me?'

'How could anyone not want to?' Rafe kissed her again. 'To be able to claim a connection to you would make him feel like the luckiest man on earth. No...make that the *second* luckiest man.'

Oh...the way Rafe was looking at her right now. Penelope wanted to be looked at like that for the rest of her life.

'I think I'd like to meet him,' she said softly. 'But it's pretty scary.'

'I'd be with you,' Rafe told her. 'Don't ever be scared. Hang on...'

The buzz of the radio clipped to his belt interrupted him and Penelope listened as he talked to his crew. The countdown to the fireworks was on. The orchestra was in position.

'This is a show to live music,' Rafe told her. 'It's a complicated set-up with manual firing.'

'Don't you need to be there?'

'That's what I train my crew to do. I'm exactly where I need to be.'

'And the orchestra's going to play it?'

'Along with the bagpipes. Can you hear them warming up?'

The drone of sound was getting louder. The lights set up around the field were suddenly shut down, plunging the whole festival into darkness. Glow sticks twinkled like coloured stars in a sea of people that knew something exciting was about to happen. Penelope and Rafe were standing behind the stage, between the main crowd and the firing area. Rafe turned Penelope to face the scissor lifts and stood behind her, holding her in his arms.

An enormous explosion sent a rocket soaring into the night sky and the rain of colour drew an audible cry from thousands of throats. And then the music started, the bagpipes backed up by the orchestra.

'Oh…' She knew this music. Everybody did.

'You'll Never Walk Alone'. An anthem of solidarity.

Penelope had never been this close to fireworks being fired before. The ground reverberated beneath her feet with every rocket. The shapes and colours were mind-blowingly beautiful but flaming shards of cardboard were drifting alarmingly close to where they were standing.

And yet Penelope had never felt safer.

Here, in Rafe's arms.

They would never walk alone. They had each other.

'Wait till you see the lancework at the very end,' Rafe told her. 'It took us a long time to build.'

The intensity of the show built towards its climax. Blindingly colourful. Incredibly loud. How amazing was it to still hear the crowd at the same time? Surely every single person there had to be singing at the tops of their voices to achieve that.

Penelope wasn't singing. Neither was Rafe. She could feel the tension in his body as the final huge display began to fade and something on the highest scissor lift came to life.

The biggest red love heart ever. And inside that was a round shape with something square inside that. Chains and a crown on the top. It was a coin. An old-fashioned penny. It even had the words 'One Penny' curving under the top.

'For you,' Rafe whispered. 'For my Penny.'

It was too much. Something private but it was there for the whole world to see. Penny. The person she really was. The person she'd tried to hide until Rafe had come into her life. Her smile wobbled precariously.

'A penny's not worth much these days.'

'You couldn't be more wrong. My Penny's worth more than my life.'

Rafe turned her in his arms so that he could kiss her. Slowly. So tenderly she thought her heart might break, but it didn't matter if it did because she knew that Rafe would simply put the pieces back together again.

Every time.

* * * * *

THE WEDDING TRUCE

KERRI CARPENTER

For Carlene, my dear friend and fellow Mermaid. Thank you for always being there for me and for bringing your sunny San Diego sparkles into my life. That's why you're MY hero!

Chapter One

"I love you, Grace Harris."

Grace grinned at the words she'd wanted to hear her entire life. Of course, she'd been waiting for a devastatingly handsome and charming prince to utter them. Instead, she was hearing them from Katie Mason, a client engaged to her own Prince Charming.

"I'm serious, I could kiss you."

Grace laughed. "I'm not sure how George would feel about that."

Katie shook her head. "I don't think he would care one bit when he learns you've figured out how to finally make this wedding come together. I never thought our styles would mesh, but you came up with the perfect plan."

Blending family traditions at a wedding wasn't a novelty—though it wasn't always easy. Grace had worked on hundreds of weddings and there was often some negotiating involved, but everything was always resolved in time to give the bride and groom their perfect day.

She rose from her desk. "It's all in a day's work, Katie. I'm just happy that you're happy. The ceremony is going to be beautiful, and the reception will be extraordinary."

Katie stood as well and scooted around the antique desk to give Grace a quick hug. "And thanks for staying late to help me work all of this out. I know our appointment was supposed to end forty-five minutes ago. You're the best wedding planner ever."

"What a great testimonial to add to my website," Grace said with a wink.

They began walking toward the door, a subtle move Grace hoped wouldn't suggest she was running late due to Katie's earlier meltdown about the logistics of her wedding. She had a date to get ready for, but at the same time, her business was important to her.

"Don't worry. I'll be giving you testimonials, bouquets of flowers, my undying love..."

"All of which are unnecessary. I just want to make your special day amazing."

"I've already recommended you to two of my friends. They're both newly engaged."

Grace stifled the happy dance Katie's words incited. She'd started her wedding-planning business less than two years ago. Only recently had she begun to see a steady profit, so word of mouth between brides was definitely a boost she could use.

The two women said goodbye, and Grace hurried back to her office to tidy up the space before calling it a day. She paused as she picked up a bridal magazine. The issue boasted Florida weddings, and the cover showed a bride wearing the most gorgeous princess ball gown at one of the Disney parks in Orlando.

Two of Grace's favorite things on the planet: wedding dresses and the town where she grew up. Of course, she also loved everything about weddings, too, but she'd always believed that a great wedding began with the gown. That's why she'd loved working at Kleinfeld Bridal in New York City one summer during college. She'd been a lowly intern dashing off on coffee runs, but at least she got to be surrounded by exquisite dresses every day.

She took another look at the bridal magazine, paying close attention to the gown. One of her current clients was a traditional bride throwing a black-tie wedding. She would absolutely love this ball gown.

She ran her hand over the glossy publication and allowed herself a moment to dream about her own wedding. Her own happy ending. Her own Prince Charming.

Grace had wanted to be a wedding planner ever since she planned her first Barbie wedding when she was a little girl. Setting up her dolls' special day had been a great way to drown out the real world. While she prepared her dolls to say their "I do's" in the corner of her cramped bedroom, she didn't have to think about her irresponsible mother, their cold trailer, or the unpredictable and scary life they lived.

When yet another of her mother's new boyfriends came by, she could escape into the happy world where people fell in love and got married. Even if her mother didn't follow that path, Grace knew she would no doubt get the same happy ending as her dolls.

She had to.

And everything would be perfect.

Luckily, later in life, she'd been accepted into Disney's internship program, where she'd been able to learn how to plan their famous nuptials with real live people instead of plastic dolls.

Grace shook her head, her long hair falling over her shoulder. She needed to stop daydreaming, so she threw down the magazine and quickly finished cleaning up the space. With a final glance to check that everything was in place, she shut down her laptop, locked her drawers and turned off the lights.

Then she closed the French doors that led to her office and walked up the stairs to the second floor of the town house she shared with her best friend, Emerson. The first floor of the traditional row home had been converted to offices for both herself and Emerson. The second floor was their living room, dining area and kitchen, and both of their bedrooms and bathrooms were on the third floor.

Not only was it the best commute ever, but Grace also loved living right in the center of Old Town, the historic and trendy area of Alexandria that welcomed tourists, families and locals. She loved the energy of the area with its cobblestone streets, plethora of bars, restaurants and shops, and proximity to the Potomac River and Washington, DC.

Of course, she was also thrilled she got to live with her best friend. Emerson first suggested the arrangement after Emerson's fiancé had broken up with her—and left her with a huge mortgage to pay.

Grace shuddered as she remembered the pain her best friend had endured at the betrayal.

The silver lining—and Grace always looked for the silver lining—was that the two of them got to live together. And the home office space was a perk they both loved.

Grace entered her bedroom and threw her bag onto the frilly eyelet bedspread. She immediately stalked to her closet, rifled through the hangers and grabbed a dress. Then she crossed to her dressing table and began fixing up her makeup. She didn't have much time to get ready for her date.

She didn't have much enthusiasm, either. Which seemed to be a habit with her lately.

Grace Harris was in love with love. Well. The *idea* of love. She'd yet to experience it for herself, after all. In her line of work, though, she got to help others achieve that dream— which only made her long for it even more… The anticipation of a crush. The rush of first love. The enduring comfort of long-term love.

Or, what she assumed would be an enduring comfort.

"You'll get there," she said to her reflection.

Yet, as she ran a brush through her long, black hair and applied her favorite matte red lipstick, there was a niggling thought in the back of her mind. Something that was warning her that she wasn't quite as excited about her date tonight as she should be.

A sigh escaped her painted lips. This would be her fourth date with Derek and if she was being honest with herself, she'd had to talk herself into seeing him again. Which didn't make sense.

Derek Whittaker was successful, handsome and driven. Any woman would kill to go out with him.

She changed into her dress and shoes.

He was also a bit egotistical, kind of full of himself and sort of a bore, too.

She did a little turn in front of her full-length mirror. Her nose crinkled as she took in her shoes. They weren't right.

"Definitely the strappy ones," Emerson said from the doorway.

Grace nearly jumped out of her skin. "Oh, my god, you scared me! I didn't know you were back from that meeting yet." She took a minute to catch her breath. "Which strappy ones? It's not like I only have one pair," she said, laughing.

Completely at home amid her friend's things—which made sense, since they constantly perused each other's wardrobes—Emerson walked to the closet, rummaged around and produced a pair of nude heels. Grace put them on, then did another spin for her best friend.

Emerson whistled. "Grace, you look gorgeous." She tilted her head. "Does Derek deserve this?"

"I'm not dressing for Derek. I dress for one person only and that's myself. If he enjoys it, too, well, that's a bonus."

Emerson flopped down on Grace's bed. "To be honest, I'm surprised you're going out with him again."

"You know my rule." Grace added her favorite pair of silver heart earrings.

"I know, I know. You have to give every guy three chances. But if I remember correctly, you're past three dates."

Grace held up four fingers. She faced Emerson and frowned. "To be perfectly honest, I didn't really want to go out again. But he has this work thing and practically begged me to accompany him." She shrugged one shoulder. "I felt bad not giving it one more chance, so I said yes."

"Of course you did." Emerson rolled her eyes dramatically. "You are too nice, Grace Harris."

"As all wannabe princesses should be."

"Forget about Derek. We have more important things to discuss."

"We do?" Grace spritzed herself with her favorite perfume.

"Yes. You may not be aware, but I am getting married," Emerson announced.

"What?" Grace played along. "You're engaged? When did that happen?"

Of course, Grace was aware of her best friend's recent engagement to Jack Wright. The two of them were beyond perfect for each other. She'd seen the sparks flying from the first time she'd witnessed them together.

Emerson threw one of the twenty throw pillows from Grace's bed at her.

"Don't make me mad at you or I won't ask you to be my maid of honor."

"Em, are you serious? Me?"

"Of course, you." Emerson rose and crossed to Grace. "What do you say? Will you do it?"

"OMG, Em. Yes! I will!"

Emerson's eyes were shining with happiness. "I mean, I'm going to boss you around and claim it's 'my day' and all the usual crap brides say."

"I think I can handle it," she said, rolling her eyes and grinning.

"Will you be able to handle planning the wedding and being in it?" Emerson asked with concern.

Grace nodded emphatically. "Oh, hells yes. I've actually carved out some time around your big day so you will be getting all my personal attention as your wedding planner. And now your maid of honor." She squealed.

Suddenly, her gaze fell on a framed picture that had been taken of her, Emerson and Emerson's sister, Amelia, sitting on the dresser. She picked it up and handed it to her friend. "What about Amelia? I don't want to upset her. Shouldn't *she* be your matron of honor, or, um, I mean your maid of honor."

Amelia had just ended her own marriage after only six months. And from what Grace had heard, she wasn't having an easy time.

Emerson looked at the photo for a moment before returning it to the dresser. "You're going to be co-maids of honor. The only thing is, Amelia isn't in a great place, and I don't want to put her under a lot of pressure. So if it's okay, I'm going to rely on you for most of the traditional maid-of-honor duties."

"No problem. I completely understand." Grace glanced once more at the picture of Amelia. "Poor thing. How's she doing?"

"She's getting by. I know she's making the right decision, and I think she's going to be fine. Amelia's tougher than she realizes."

That was a relief to hear. Grace had known Emerson for years now and she was close with the entire Dewitt family.

As Grace put the finishing touches on her outfit, they continued talking about the wedding. It was interesting to watch her best friend, the calm and cool event planner, become frustrated over the details of her own wedding.

"What are you so worried about?" She grabbed Emerson's shoulders. "Everything is going to be fine. It'll be perfect. You'll see."

Emerson rolled her eyes. "You, my friend, are far too optimistic."

"Hey, that's supposed to be a good quality."

Grace's cell phone went off, and she saw a text message from Derek. He was outside. She could feel her smile fading. "Derek's here."

"Just remember that everything is going to be fine. No, perfect," Emerson said with fake enthusiasm, as she flung Grace's words back at her.

"Gee, thanks." Sometimes being optimistic took a lot of effort.

It took thirty minutes to get to the party in traffic and find street parking in congested Old Town.

"We really should have walked or taken an Uber," Grace said as they *finally* found a parking spot.

Clearly oblivious to the slight annoyance in her voice, Derek put the car in Park and actually stroked the steering wheel. "But then I wouldn't be able to show this baby off. I just got her on Saturday."

"So you told me already." Twice.

When Derek finished petting his new car, he finally turned it off, got out and came around to Grace's side. At least he opened doors. That was something.

It's not enough.

Grace accepted his hand as she got out of the car. But when she tried to pull away, Derek held on tight.

"Come on, honey. You're the other thing I want to show off."

Gross. "I'm not an object, Derek."

"What?" He looked down at her. "Oh, right. Of course, not," he said with zero conviction.

They walked to the party and were greeted by their hosts, a lovely couple who had recently built the house. After exchanging pleasantries, Derek made a beeline for the bar, steering Grace in that direction.

It took ten minutes to get a glass of wine in the packed house. Derek ordered a whiskey and practically downed it in one large gulp.

"Might as well get another while we're here," he said and gestured to the bartender. Grace subtly slipped a five-dollar bill into the bartender's tip jar.

They moved away from the bar and made their way into the living room. Derek draped his arm across her shoulders. Grace wiggled, dislodging his arm.

"Hey, did I tell you about my golf game the other day?"

"Yep, you sure did." Another boring story she'd had to endure on the way over. Grace seriously needed to reconsider her rule about giving dates multiple shots. Sometimes you just knew after the first date.

"I was on fire," Derek said, ignoring her reply. Then he went on to recount the "epic round" for a second time. Grace took the time to familiarize herself with her surroundings.

The house was very tastefully decorated in beige tones. The recessed lighting was turned low and jazz music was playing softly in the background. If Grace had to guess, the host had quite the budget at Williams-Sonoma. She'd noticed much of the furniture and decor from the recent catalog.

She craned her neck to get a look at the food table, which was overflowing with different kinds of cheeses and crackers, fruit and crudité plates. She noticed oysters, fresh shrimp and flank steak, and a guest walked by holding a plate with what looked and smelled like lobster mac-and-cheese.

In other words, the party was picture-perfect.

And she was miserable.

When some of Derek's colleagues sidled up to him and

began telling lame, questionable jokes, she excused herself and headed for the food table.

"Hey, aren't you Derek's girlfriend?"

Grace dropped the carrot she was putting on her plate and turned to find a petite woman with long blond hair and a stylish black dress pointing at her.

Grace wouldn't have been surprised if a big, blinking neon sign that said Warning Sign Number One had been hanging over her the woman's head. Before Grace could correct the blonde, she continued.

"I'm Penny. I'm engaged to Brad."

Penny waved a massive diamond ring in her face. While Grace normally took the opportunity to introduce herself and her wedding-planning business to newly engaged people, Penny was rushing forward.

"Derek talks about you nonstop. You should have heard him last Thursday. You know all about Brad's annual cookout."

Grace did not. Then again, she didn't know who Brad was, either.

"Derek is just so excited about your relationship."

"Uh…" Grace found that odd considering this was only their fourth date. The other three had hardly been groundbreaking.

Once again, she felt that neon warning sign blinking away when the chatty woman continued.

"Oh, and have an amazing time in Turks and Caicos! I gave Derek some tips and hot spots. You know that's where Brad proposed."

Nope, she sure didn't. But how could she when she hadn't been aware she was going on vacation with her fake boyfriend.

She decided it was beyond time to offer Derek a piece of her mind. His delusions needed to be set straight. They weren't dating. She wasn't his girlfriend. And there was no way she would ever consider going on vacation with him—let alone go out with him again.

Grace could feel herself getting worked up. She should have never come to this party with Derek tonight.

She heard him laughing loudly and saw a fresh drink in his hand. *Great. Guess I'll be Ubering back home.*

Although, that was the least of her problems. She could have been at home, catching up on work or binging that new romcom series she had in her Netflix queue. Heck, she could have been watching glue dry and had more fun.

Well, she wasn't helpless. She could walk out of here at any time.

Mind made up, Grace put her plate on the table, turned… and ran into a solid wall of muscle.

"Ow," she squeaked.

"Sorry, I didn't see…"

The deep baritone voice caused goose bumps to pop up all over her arms. Grace inhaled sharply—she knew exactly whom that delicious voice belonged to. She looked up to find the one person she actually despised.

"Xander," she groaned.

The surprise quickly faded from his face and his eyebrows drew together. "Grace."

What was with the universe tonight? Was there any other way this night could suck?

"What are you doing here?" she asked, suspicion in her voice.

She didn't know what it was about Alexander Ryan, but the man brought out the absolute worst in her.

A frown marred what some people would call an incredibly handsome face. Xander was the best friend of Jack, Emerson's fiancé. They'd met a few times now and each time only further solidified the fact that they had nothing in common.

Actually, there was one thing they shared. An intense dislike for each other.

Too bad. Because if he wasn't so annoying, she might find him attractive. After all, he had classic movie-star looks that certainly turned heads everywhere he went. He was tall and fit, with broad shoulders, hair so thick and dark a woman—well, not her, but some woman!—might love to run her fingers through it and the most mesmerizing blue-green eyes that stood out even more because of the dark lashes that surrounded them.

She had no idea why, but the two of them had been at odds since the moment they'd met. Maybe it was because their professions were polar opposites. Xander was a divorce attorney. She helped couples start their lives together and he helped them end them. Maybe it was the fact that he'd made quick work of dismissing wedding planning the first time they met. Maybe it was his utter self-confidence, which she normally would find appealing in other men, but with Xander it just came off as arrogant.

Or maybe it was that the air became riddled with electricity whenever they were in the same room together. And she didn't have the faintest idea what to do about that.

"Work thing," Xander said, answering her question.

God, he smelled amazing. It was then that Grace realized how close they were standing. And her hand was on his chest. She removed it as if she'd placed it on burning coals, which made Xander grin. A slow and completely knowing grin.

"You look…good," he said slowly. "Really good." His eyes narrowed as he glanced around the room. "Too good for this party."

Was that a compliment or an insult? She never knew with him.

Looked like she'd found one more way to be miserable at this hot mess of a party.

Chapter Two

Xander couldn't wait for this party to be over, and he'd only been here for five minutes. He was an attorney, not a socialite. Yet somehow, attending these events was becoming as common as waltzing into the courtroom.

Not that Xander didn't like a good party. But tonight's soiree was definitely not his idea of a fun time. In fact, he'd been racking his brain and still couldn't remember exactly whose party this was, or what occasion they were celebrating. All he knew was that his boss had "strongly encouraged" him to attend. He'd much rather be at the office finishing up some overdue work and then head to his best friend's bar for a beer and to watch the Nationals game.

Instead, he was at someone's wife's party celebrating... something or other. And he knew exactly how it was going to go. He would make insanely boring small talk with his boss and other coworkers. He would laugh at their spouses' lame jokes. And he would pretend he was having a great time while he perused a buffet of fancy food that would taste exactly like the last buffet at the last party.

He didn't remember any classes in law school that prepared him for this side of law. Schmoozing 101.

The cherry on top of this disappointing cake was running into Grace Harris. Wedding planner, eternal optimist and organizer of unnecessarily extravagant parties to celebrate unions that probably wouldn't last five years.

Grace was best friends and roommates with Emerson

Dewitt, the fiancée of his best friend, Jack Wright. Xander adored Emerson. She was fun and sweet and charming and good-natured. Even though he wasn't a big fan of marriage, if Jack insisted on getting hitched, Emerson was the best woman for it.

But Grace Harris was the complete opposite of the likable Emerson. He didn't know what it was, but Grace had long ago made it known that she wasn't a fan of his.

The feeling was mutual.

It hadn't happened often, but every time they were in the same room together, he could practically feel his blood pressure rising. Something about her brought out the worst in him.

Maybe it was the way she saw everything in life as some kind of movie moment, with a picture-perfect happy ending just around the corner. Plus, there was the fact that she turned up her prim little nose at his chosen profession. Just because she couldn't fathom one of *her* perfect wedding couples splitting up, she was down on the concept of divorce.

Well, she might not like divorce attorneys but that didn't mean people didn't need them.

Still, he couldn't deny that she was beautiful. Truly take-your-breath-away gorgeous. With her long legs and perfect skin and a river of thick dark hair that cascaded down her back, she seemed truly unaware of how exquisite she was. Like tonight. She definitely looked stunning in a cherry-red dress and high heels.

Not that her looks mattered. Her beauty did nothing to offset the fact that they had nothing in common.

Standing in front of him, she forgot about the plate of food in her hand and placed her other hand on her hip. He knew she meant to look annoyed or even nonchalant. Instead, the gesture only further defined her hourglass curves.

"As great as this little chat has been—" Grace gestured

to her plate, which contained one carrot and three pieces of shrimp "—I have people to mingle with."

"Have fun with that. I'm sure you'll find some scintillating conversations at this shindig."

Grace rolled her eyes. "Is there *anything* you enjoy?"

He enjoyed verbally sparring with her because she could always hold her own. Her confidence and refusal to back down was appealing. Plus, her green eyes sparkled with every jab.

Eyes sparkling? What the hell was he thinking? He shook his head and swept his arm for her to walk past him.

"I enjoy a great many things, Grace Harris. Maybe one day you'll find out."

She stepped closer to him. So close that her floral scent teased him. He didn't know if it was her shampoo or perfume or lotion. Not that it mattered one bit. Grace smelled absolutely delectable.

"Oh, I think I know plenty about you now, Xander Ryan."

He didn't back down. He leaned into her. "Astound me."

"You're way too arrogant," she said. "You think wedding planners and weddings are a joke." She took a breath. "If you weren't Jack's best friend and if Emerson wasn't the most important person in my life, I wouldn't even waste my precious time talking to you now."

He pinned her with his best seductive stare and lowered his voice. "But you *are* talking to me now."

She gulped. "Not for long." She broke eye contact and shoved past him.

He couldn't help but laugh. "Oh, Grace," he called.

She stopped and glanced over her shoulder.

"Great running into you."

Again, she rolled her eyes. "Goodbye, Xander."

With that, she continued through the dining room and disappeared around the corner. Xander couldn't help but watch her retreating form, which was just as gorgeous from the back as from the front.

To be honest, he was a little sorry they'd gotten off on the wrong foot. Not that he would admit this to anyone else, but when he'd first seen her, he'd had a visceral reaction like never before, to any woman he'd ever met. It had been as if she'd punched him in the gut. It wasn't just her beauty that had called out to him. It was something else, something indefinable.

Then she'd opened her mouth.

Maybe he shouldn't have made that joke about her planning unions that would inevitably end up in his office. Yeah…that hadn't gone over so well. That was probably when she'd decided that he was an unreasonable, unfeeling person. Well, the thought was mutual. Grace was—

"Xander, welcome."

He turned to see Carl, his colleague at the firm, and had to stifle the urge to yell "aha."

"Hey, Carl. Thanks for the invite."

"No problem. Happy to have you at the housewarming."

Housewarming—double aha. It was all coming back now.

"Great place, man," Xander offered.

"Thanks. Make sure you tell Maggie that. She's been stressing about this party for weeks."

"Everything looks amazing."

Carl swirled his drink. "You need help planning a wedding?"

"Huh?" Xander asked, confusion in his voice.

Carl chuckled. "Saw you talking to Grace Harris. Didn't realize you knew her."

"Friend of a friend," he offered. "You know her?"

"A little. I've run into her a couple times. She's here with Derek Whittaker."

Oh, come on! Xander couldn't stop his eyebrows from

raising. Derek wasn't one of his favorite people. In fact, he thought the guy was a total jerk. "Seriously? What the hell is she doing here with *him*?"

"Not sure what's going on there to be honest. Derek claims they're dating, but if they are, it's a really new thing."

At that moment, Xander spotted Grace and Derek in the next room. Seemed like Derek only had eyes for Grace. Xander couldn't blame the guy, but still. Yuck. Derek was such an egotistical ass. Someone who took locker-room talk to a whole new level by boasting about his conquests in a little too much detail.

What did Grace see in the guy? Maybe Derek was putting on some kind of facade with her. Maybe he should just go over there and let her know—

"Do you need to get that?" Carl asked.

Huh? What? He realized his cell was ringing. "Uh…" Xander stared down at his mother's name. Which was the lesser of two evils? This party or talking to his mother?

Since his night was already a bust, he decided to go for it.

"I do need to take this, sorry," he said to Carl and quickly made his way outside to the long front porch, which was covered with flowerpots.

"Xander, darling, I can't believe I'm actually hearing your voice. I was just telling my stylist the other day that I was sure my handsome yet extremely aloof son was a myth."

He choked back a groan. "It hasn't been that long. I saw you last month." He switched the phone to his other ear and clamped down on the annoyance that had been growing since he'd stepped into this party.

Eloise Ryan elicited a delicate cough, which was her signature way of saying "bull." "That was two months ago and in any case it's quite shameful to not see you more often when you live less than ten miles from us. You should be over here all the time doing your laundry and scavenging for food."

He ran a hand through his hair. "You do realize I'm not a nineteen-year-old college student, right? I'm capable of doing my own laundry, I have a cleaning person and I actually can cook a couple meals."

Ignoring his comment, Eloise continued. "I'd love for you to come to dinner soon. There's someone I'd like you to meet. Someone special. Someone special to me, that is."

If Xander had been a dog, this was when the fur on the back of his neck would stand at full attention. He'd been down this road with his mom before. Come to think of it, he'd been down it with his father, as well.

He took a deep breath and braced himself. "Who is he?"

"His name is Gareth. He's a musician."

Xander paced away from the gray house with tasteful white trim as he spotted some of his coworkers making their way toward it. That was all he needed. People to learn about how dysfunctional his parents were.

"A musician, really?"

"Well," his mom replied in a singsong voice, "he teaches guitar lessons when he's not working."

At least this one works, he thought bitterly.

"He's a barista," Eloise said this with the amount of a pride one might reserve for a brain surgeon.

"He works at Starbucks?" Xander said through gritted teeth.

"No, he does not work at Starbucks. He works at a local and very exclusive coffeehouse in North Arlington, smartypants. No need to be snobby about it."

Xander ran a hand through his hair again, and then silently cursed himself for messing it up. "How old is Gareth?"

"A robust and mature twenty-four."

Now Xander let out another curse, and this time it was not silent.

"Xander Michael Ryan, watch your language."

"Are you seriously trying to discipline me? You're dating a twenty-four-year-old. Does Dad know?"

"Who knows? He's been spending so much time up in Sag Harbor with his little trollop that I doubt he would care."

And so it went.

Xander's parents had been married for thirty-two years. He'd come along eight months into their marriage. Clearly he'd been the reason they'd gotten hitched. Still, he often wondered if they'd ever loved each other. Had they ever been faithful? As long as he could remember, their relationship had always been contentious. Fighting and cheating and accusations and denials.

He wished he could be truly surprised to hear his mom's latest news but sadly, he was all too used to it. If it wasn't his mom bragging about a new boyfriend, it was his dad gallivanting with someone half his age. Then his mom would retaliate by buying expensive jewelry while his dad would try to one-up her with an exotic trip.

Nothing shocked Xander.

The only question he did have was why had they never divorced. The psychologist he'd been forced to see during adolescence would surely draw a comparison between his confusion over his parents and his chosen profession as a divorce attorney.

"Listen, Mom, I have to run. I'm at a work event."

"You're taking your father's side, aren't you?"

He stifled a groan. "No, I'm not taking anyone's side. But I do have to go."

They said their goodbyes, and Xander actually felt grateful as he ascended the stairs and reentered the party. He was immediately met by Carl's wife, Maggie, who just had to give him a tour of their new house. Along the way he was cornered by his boss and drawn into an insanely dull conversation. Could this night get any worse?

As his boss talked shop with one of his other colleagues, Xander couldn't stop himself from scanning the party, searching for something. Not something. Someone. Someone named Grace. He cursed himself silently. Why was he looking for her? What was this pull between them? It didn't make any sense. She'd made known her feelings for him.

And yet, when he spotted her talking to that jerk Derek, he actually smiled. He could stare at her all day. He was fascinated by the way she carried herself. Her looks made her seem delicate, but she definitely had a pretty strong dose of confidence about her, too.

But as he watched, something caught his eye. Derek was latching on to Grace's arm and pulling her around the wall into a very dark and secluded corner. Xander craned his neck. Even from his vantage point, he could see that Derek's grip was too hard. Grace's smile faltered and her eyes registered anger. Anger and something worse. Fear.

Xander ignored everything around him. Instead, he placed his empty glass on a nearby tray and crossed the room in several fast strides.

It all happened so quickly he didn't have time to register anything. Not the fact that he'd just blown off his boss. Not that he'd been completely rude. Not even that he was interrupting something that was none of his business.

All he knew as he watched Derek's grip tighten around her arm was that Grace might need help.

"Derek, let go," she said.

"You listen to me," Derek said between clenched teeth. His eyes had darkened. Neither of them noticed Xander standing there.

There was still a chance to back out, still a chance to mind his own business. But seeing the expression on Grace's face, he knew he couldn't do that.

In the end, it didn't matter—because Grace brought her knee up to Derek's groin and then quickly and deftly twisted out of his grasp. She twisted his wrist behind his back in some kind of complicated-looking hold.

Before Xander could swoop in and save her, she'd saved herself.

And despite their mutual disdain of each other, he'd never been more attracted to her.

Chapter Three

Nothing like breaking out your self-defense skills at a cocktail party, Grace thought sarcastically.

Thank goodness Emerson had talked her into that self-defense course. And the occasional follow-up class. Grace didn't even want to think how this situation would have ended otherwise. She clamped down on the shiver that threatened to crawl up her spine. While she was holding strong on the outside, on the inside, Derek had really scared her.

She'd informed him that he had no right to call her his girlfriend. That this would be their last date. And that she didn't appreciate his getting sloshed five minutes into a party.

That's when any semblance of charm had vanished from him and been replaced by anger and outrage.

You have this under control, she reminded herself. As she tried to catch her breath, she slowly realized that Xander was standing by her side.

"Xander," she growled. "What are you doing?"

He was frowning. "What do you mean what am I doing?" He flicked his eyes down to where she had Derek's wrist in a tight grasp. "What are *you* doing?"

"I'm on a date." *Duh.*

A slow grin spread over his handsome face. "How's it going?"

Her lips twitched. She couldn't help it. "I've been on better."

Derek winced in pain. "Let go of me, you little bitch."

Xander stepped forward and leaned down to get in Derek's face. "Excuse me—what did you call her?"

Without missing a beat, Xander gently took Grace's hand and untangled her fingers from Derek's wrist. At the same time, he used his free arm to bend the creep's arm behind him, far enough to cause just enough pain to get the guy's attention. "She's not your property. And it seems she doesn't want to be, either. So if you ever put your hands on her again, I'm pretty sure she'll do far worse than put you in a basic self-defense hold."

Derek glanced at Grace, who leaned closer and whispered, "I'll use my Taser on you."

The jerk looked like he was about to say something, but she grabbed the purse she'd dropped on the floor and left both men behind. All she wanted to do was get out of there as quickly as possible, go home and get out of this dress. *I mean, I wore Spanx for this?*

But Xander quickly caught up to her right before she could exit the living room.

"You handled that really smoothly," he said, amusement and something else in his voice. Surprise, maybe?

"You think?"

"What I think is that it was impressive. Damn impressive."

Aware that quite a few sets of eyes had turned in her direction and the whispers were beginning, she decided to throw all her attention at Xander. She whirled back to face him. "I've been dating since I was fifteen years old. Do you honestly think this was the first time I've had to deal with some creep? I really didn't need your help, you know." Although, if she were being honest with herself, deep down...she was grateful. Grateful she hadn't had to deal with Derek's brutishness alone.

Even if it had to be Xander, of all people, who'd helped her!

"Well, I… I'm sorry. I just hated to see you being treated that way." His jaw worked, as if he couldn't figure out what to say. "How many creeps?"

She pretended to look at a watch she wasn't wearing. "How much time do you have?"

The party hosts, Carl and Maggie, rushed to her side. "Grace, are you okay? We heard something happened with Derek."

"I'm okay," she said, trying to reassure them.

"You may want to check on Derek, though," Xander added, tucking his tongue into his cheek.

Maggie looked back and forth between the two of them. "Oh, wait, what? What happened?"

Carl was shaking his head. "I knew I shouldn't have invited him. It's just, his boss and our boss," he said gesturing to Xander, "are tight. They all golf together."

"It's okay," Grace said.

Suddenly, all the energy drained from Grace's body. She was exhausted. But she didn't want to be rude, so she said her goodbyes as fast as she could, if a bit robotically.

"I'm so sorry to have caused any kind of scene. I truly am fine, but I'm ready to head home. I've got an early day tomorrow. Congratulations on the new home. It really is beautiful."

Then she made a quick getaway toward the front porch. Once outside, she breathed in the fresh night air deeply, as if she'd been stuck in some kind of hole for the last couple of hours. In a way, she felt as though she had been. But things with Derek were over and she was fine. Just fine.

She sensed Xander before he spoke. His deep voice washed over her like some kind of security blanket. She wanted to feel his arms around her, wanted to hold on tight and forget about this whole horrible evening.

"Grace, are you okay?" he asked. Worry laced that sexy baritone.

She inhaled deeply and then plastered the same smile she used with unruly brides on her face. She turned around to face Xander. "Of course—I'm fine. I just want to get out of here."

Uncertainty filled his eyes. "How are you planning on doing that? How did you get here?"

"Derek drove. But I actually don't live far from here. I'm going to walk."

"Walk? Why don't you take an Uber or Lyft, at least?"

"I think I can make it on my own, Xander," she said with a confidence she knew was false, as she hugged her purse closer to her.

"After what I witnessed tonight, I'm sure you can. But to be honest, I'd feel a lot better if you weren't out on the streets all by yourself." He stared out into the inky black darkness of the night. "If you insist on walking, why don't you at least let me accompany you?"

Was he implying that she was some damsel in distress who needed saving? Sure, she'd been a little nervous there for a second, but she was completely safe now. If she was honest with herself, she longed to find that one perfect person who would always be by her side, to be her knight in shining armor—hell, she'd built a career out of doing that for others. But deep down, well…she knew it wasn't realistic to have a handsome rescuer at your disposal, to swoop in and save you whenever you got into trouble. And she definitely didn't want to cast Xander, of all people, in the role of prince. Besides, she was more than capable of taking care of herself.

She'd certainly done it long enough.

Then why are you shaking? a little voice whispered in the back of her mind.

"Look, Xander, I appreciate the offer, but I said I was fine. I think I can manage walking a couple of blocks."

And yet, once again, her mad faded. After all, Xander

was trying to do something nice for her. If it had been anyone else, she would have gladly accepted the offer. So why
didn't she want Xander to walk her home?

Because you don't want to be alone with him. Really, she
was afraid of what she would do *if* she was alone with him.

"Please, go back to the party," she said with little hope
he actually would.

Xander turned back toward the house. He gazed at the
large picture window of the living room, where people were
swirling their martinis and comparing the square footage of
their houses. "You want me to go back in *there*?"

"That's what I said."

He gestured between the two of them. "Were we at the
same party? And I use the term *party* loosely."

Unable to help it, she smiled.

"Come on." He nodded toward the street. "Let me walk
you home. I'll even let you insult me and my job on the way."

"Hmm, tempting." She gave one more glance at the party,
where she saw Carl talking to Derek. She shivered.

You're fine. You handled it.

Her quick pep talk didn't work. Suddenly, her mind was
going through every possible scenario.

"Hey, what's that?" Xander placed a hand lightly on her arm.

She shifted until she was right under the porch light,
where she could already see a bruise forming on her arm
from that idiot's hand.

"Does it hurt?" he asked.

"It, um, it…"

With that, the last bits of adrenaline left her. Without
warning, without a moment to stop herself, she collapsed
into Xander's arms.

Xander would have been less shocked if Grace had told
everyone at the party that they were best friends.

Truth was, he shouldn't be surprised that Grace was in his arms, holding on tightly. She'd had quite the night. Plus, during their discussion, he'd spotted her shivering.

Still, she'd been so confident, even while handling Derek's attempted abuse. In every interaction he'd ever had with her, Grace had always been completely poised. For once, it was kind of nice to see that armor disappear, though he wished it was for a different reason.

He heard her take a deep shuddering breath and rubbed his hands up and down her back.

"It's okay, Grace. You don't have to worry about him anymore."

After a long moment, she finally straightened. He watched as she pulled herself together, putting on that armor once again. She smoothed a hand over her hair and took a deep breath.

"Thanks, and sorry," she said.

"Sorry? What for?"

A flush crept across her cheeks. "For having to deal with me just now. When I, uh…"

"Had a perfectly natural human moment?" he offered.

As expected, her flush disappeared and she narrowed her eyes. "I just needed a second to gather myself."

"Whatever you say." He grinned, and she made a low sound that actually resembled a growl. "But I'm still walking you home."

It looked like she was going to fight him on it. But then she glanced back at the house and finally nodded in agreement. They descended the stairs of the porch and turned left onto the sidewalk.

"So," she began, "I don't get it. I was at that party on a date. I barely knew those people. But it seems like you do. Is this the type of event you go to often?"

He groaned. "Unfortunately, I do more often than I would like. It's a work thing."

"Your boss requires you to?"

"Let's say he strongly suggests it."

"Ah. One of the perks of working for myself," she said.

They fell into silence for a moment, the only sound the *click-clack* of her heels on the sidewalk.

It was a beautiful night for the first day of October. There was a full moon overhead, lighting the way. The weather was still warm, but a refreshing breeze was blowing through the trees, which were just on the cusp of changing colors.

Xander realized this was the first time he'd ever been completely alone with Grace. Not that they'd spent all that much time together to begin with. But usually Jack and Emerson were around, or they were surrounded by customers at The Wright Drink, Jack's bustling bar in Old Town. "Speaking of being your own boss, how's the wedding business going?"

She sighed.

"What? I'm trying to be nice here."

"You had an attitude when you asked that."

"No, I didn't," he protested.

"There was a tone."

"A tone? Come on."

"I already know how you feel about my profession, Xander. You made it crystal clear the first time we met."

"It goes both ways. You've made it evident that you hate my job."

"You're a divorce attorney. You see the end of marriages every day. What is there to like?"

He shrugged. "There's more to it than that."

"Oh, really? Astound me."

"People come to me when they're ready for a change in

their life. It's not always fighting and yelling. Sometimes a breakup is a healthy thing."

"Oh, please."

"Not everything can be rainbows and lace and tiered cakes," he said.

She threw her arms in the air. "Some of those tiered cakes are really fantastic."

"What's your favorite?" he asked out of the blue. His impromptu question made her halt briefly.

"You'd think it was gross," she answered.

"Try me."

"Carrot cake. I really love it."

Interesting. "That's my favorite, too."

"My grandmother used to make it for me all the time. Her recipe is to die for. Speaking of," she said as her phone started playing "When You Wish Upon a Star." "Excuse me." She held her phone to her ear. "Grammy, hi, is everything okay? It's late... What?... Oh, sorry about that. I had to rush from work to this party."

As she spoke to her grandmother, they continued walking. Xander tried to give her some space by taking in their surroundings. The streets had definitely emptied since he'd arrived at the party, but there were still some stragglers out and about. Some were returning from work, others were coming or going to a night out. There was a softball field about a block away and he could hear hooting and hollering right before the crack of a bat and the roar of a crowd.

When he turned back to Grace, she'd ended the call and was putting her phone in her purse. "I'm sorry about that. I talk to my Grammy almost every day and she was worried when she didn't hear from me today."

"That's nice you talk so much to your grandmother. I'm sure your parents appreciate the effort."

She glanced down at the ground, suddenly very interested

in the red brick sidewalk. She had such expressive eyes and right now they were emitting a clear sadness. He wanted to know what had made her feel that way.

Instead, he decided to change the subject. He realized he knew very little about Grace Harris. Other than that she got under his skin like no else ever had.

But suddenly, he really, really wanted to know more.

"What made you go into wedding planning?"

"I've always loved weddings. I even did the Disney internship program back when I was learning the business."

"So you like the planning aspect?"

"I like everything about weddings. My grandmother used to read me all of these wonderful fairy tales. They always ended with a marriage. A perfect happily-ever-after. I guess I just wanted to help others make that happen."

"You seem close with your grandmother."

"She and my grandfather raised me."

He wondered where her parents had been in this scenario.

They continued to walk along the streets of Old Town, which grew brighter and busier as they reached the town center. Xander couldn't help but take it all in. He'd grown up not far from here, in a very large house with acres of lush lawns and gardens. Unfortunately, those lawns and gardens were showpieces and not for playing. That's one of the reasons he'd loved visiting Old Town. The entire area always seemed alive to him. As a kid, he couldn't get enough of the excitement. He could run around the marina and look at the ships docked there. A man would sit on the corner and play his saxophone as people went in and out of the different shops. Street artists would display their work. And at Christmas, there were lights strung across King Street that seemed to go on forever, lighting up the sky.

"I love Old Town at this time of year," Grace said, as if reading his mind.

"I was just thinking the same thing."

She laughed, and he realized he liked the sound of it. It had an almost bell-like quality.

"It feels like there's always something new here," she said.

"Yeah," he agreed. "It definitely keeps you on your toes. But at the same time, I love the old feel of this area."

"Exactly," she exclaimed. "Take this block. Who knows? Maybe George Washington walked down this same street. I know he used to stop here on his way to Mount Vernon."

"It's cool to think about. I love that old-time feel. It's stable."

Stability was not something that Xander had had in his youth. His family was anything but stable. Chaos ran that household more than any one person. Maybe that's why he very rarely made the short trek to the very prestigious mansion where his parents still resided.

"Have you been to that bakery on Princess Street? You know, the one with the amazing biscotti."

"One of my favorite places on earth." His mouth watered just thinking about it.

"The cannoli?" she asked, wiggling her eyebrows and making him smile.

"Ah-mazing."

It had been a couple blocks without any arguments breaking out between the two of them. It was kind of nice, Xander thought. When she wasn't driving him out of his mind, Grace Harris was actually kind of cool to be around.

"Sorry about your date tonight." Xander wasn't sure why he said the words. But he felt like someone should apologize to her. Especially since he knew Derek wouldn't.

She shrugged. "In a way it's my own fault."

"How is it your fault that the jerk grabbed your arm and tried to get rough with you?" His fingers curled into fists as he remembered it.

"No, not that part. Derek is a jerk. But I shouldn't have gone out with him tonight."

"Why did you then?"

"I guess I just wanted to give it one more chance, see if there were any sparks. That's my bad habit. I would have much rather been at home catching up on Netflix."

"I know the feeling. I also like a good night at home. Bum out on the couch. Order some pizza. Or go to a baseball game. What about you?"

"To be honest, I've been working so hard lately I don't even know how to relax anymore."

"What made you start your own business rather than joining an established firm?" He realized he was actually interested.

"I've been working since I was a teenager. For all different kinds of people. The last couple of years, I've been gaining contacts and puffing up my résumé. I decided to make the leap from employee to boss."

"Any regrets?"

"Occasionally." She laughed.

There was that sound again. Something about it had him sucking in a breath.

"My favorite part of being a business owner, though, is that it's all mine." She did a dramatic dancer-turn thing, her hair flying behind her head.

He glanced down at her feet. She was wearing tall strappy high heels. He had no idea how women stood on those in general. But the fact that they were walking over uneven and very old bricks, and she'd just done one hell of a turn, was even more impressive.

"Are your feet okay?"

"Are you kidding? These shoes are fabulous. Any pain associated with them is totally and completely worth it."

As if the universe was ready to disagree with her, she suddenly stumbled as they were turning the corner. She wobbled on her feet for one second, two seconds, and then she was falling. He reached out his arms and grabbed her just before her knees hit the hard sidewalk below.

As soon as his arms went around her, her scent engulfed him. She smelled of orange blossoms. And how in the hell he knew what orange blossoms smelled like was beyond him. Only he knew that it was an amazing scent and he would never eat another orange without thinking about her.

Her arms circled around his neck and he automatically pulled her to him, bringing their bodies even closer together than they'd been earlier.

She had the most intense eyes. They were a beautiful emerald color, and he knew that if he stared long enough he would become completely lost.

"Xander," she uttered, her voice breathy.

"Grace," he replied.

He didn't know what else to say. His eyes flicked down to take in her lips. Her full, very pouty, very enticing lips. Her tongue slipped out at that moment to wet them. He had to clamp down on a shudder. Was it his imagination or had she moved her head closer to his?

The breeze picked up and her hair floated around her head. Somewhere in the distance a dog was barking. And he could hear the usual sounds of nightlife, people talking and laughing as they headed out to a local bar.

Neither of them moved. They stood there on the corner staring into each other's eyes under the full moon.

He realized he wanted to kiss her. He wanted that more than he wanted air to breathe. He began to tilt his head toward her. Her eyelids fluttered, then closed.

All of a sudden, the intrusive sound of a loud horn honking startled both of them. Grace jumped back.

"What the…?"

"Grace," he began, but had no idea how to finish the sentence.

"Were you going to…? I mean were you about to…?"

He ran a hand through his hair. "I—I don't know. I think we were going to…"

She put even more space between them. Somehow, he felt a chill. That didn't make sense. It wasn't even cold out.

"We were going to do nothing," she said adamantly. "*That* can't happen between us."

"Nothing happened, Grace. Don't overreact."

"I'm not overreacting. You almost kissed me."

It was true. He had. "I didn't almost kiss you." He had to save face. "You were right there with me. It was a joint effort."

She held her small purse out in front of her like a shield. Although the only thing the tiny clutch could protect her from was a gnat.

"You know what, Xander? We had a nice walk home. Let's leave it at that. My house is right down the street. I'm fine from here."

He watched her retreating form as she headed down the street. Xander stood there for a long time. Long after Grace ran up the steps to her town house, let herself in and closed the door.

What had just happened between them? He didn't even like Grace Harris. And as far as he knew, she sure as heck didn't like him, either.

Yet something had happened on the streets of Old Town. Just like Grace had pointed out earlier, something was always changing in Old Town.

Too bad change wasn't always a good thing.

Chapter Four

Change was a good thing. Well, mostly. Usually. In most situations.

Grace scrunched up her nose as she thought about all the things that had been changing in her life lately. Her business was taking off and she was acquiring more clients than ever. That was a good thing. Emerson had met the love of her life and was getting married. A definite plus.

Although…they wouldn't be roommates for much longer. Unless Jack was okay with his wife living with another woman. Not likely.

And maybe their social life had been altered a bit, too. They used to spend their free nights roaming Old Town, popping into fun, eclectic shops, or stopping at one of their favorite bars for a glass of wine.

Now, things were different. She saw less of Emerson, who was splitting her free time between Grace and her fiancé. That's why she knew tonight was important.

They were on their way to Jack's house for dinner. Grace loved Jack. He was funny and smart. Most important, he loved her best friend more than life itself. So Grace couldn't complain about being the third wheel. She was happy to be there for Em.

"It's nice of Jack to spend his night off cooking us dinner."

Emerson made a left turn onto Jack's street. "Don't be too impressed. I'm fairly certain he ordered food in. But I think he's going to try and pass it off as homemade. Or he'll default to the grill."

"I'll take it either way. I'm starved."

It had been another long day. She'd spent hours negotiating a hotel contract with an employee who was not in a giving mood. Grace hoped she never had to coordinate a wedding in that particular location again.

Emerson pulled her car into Jack's driveway. They walked to the front door and Em whipped out her key to let them into the house. Grace smiled as she watched her friend so at ease in her new phase of life.

At least she had a best friend who included her often, even though she had a fiancé. Grace knew plenty of women who turned their backs on their friends when they found "the one." Heaven knew she'd seen her share of Bridezillas who alienated most of their friends before they could pick a color for their wedding party.

"What?" Emerson asked.

Grace gave her a swift hug. "Nothing. Just happy you invited me tonight. I'm glad that the three of us can…" She let her words trail off as something caught her eye on the street. A sleek black Lexus was parked outside Jack's house.

No. Freaking. Way.

"Emerson…" Grace had to fight hard not to grind her teeth.

Emerson held her hands up in front of her. "Before you say anything—"

"Like, why is Xander Ryan's car parked here?" She crossed her arms over her chest and began tapping one foot.

"Well, see, the thing is, he's kind of joining us for dinner."

"Kind of? Or is he *definitely* joining us for dinner?" Grace practically growled the words.

"Definitely joining us?" Emerson said hesitantly, her face an example of contriteness if Grace had ever seen one.

"Emm-m-m-m," Grace moaned. A thought occurred and Grace grimaced. "Please tell me that you and Jack are not trying to set us up."

Emerson snorted. "Absolutely not. We've seen the two of you together. Although, physically, I think you'd make a hot couple. But my ears would have to stop ringing from the constant fighting."

"It's not constant...and what do you mean we'd make a hot couple?"

Emerson laughed and shook her head. "Listen, Gracie, you're my best friend. And Xander is Jack's best friend. You guys have to start getting along. You're going to be in each other's lives from now on."

Suddenly, Grace's appetite disappeared. Emerson was right. She was marrying Jack and if Grace wanted to keep having nights like these with her best friend, she was going to have to learn to put up with Xander, too.

She attempted to run a hand through her hair until she remembered she'd thrown it up into a messy bun. And she hadn't touched up her makeup since this morning. Plus, she was wearing loose-fitting boyfriend jeans and an old royal blue top that she'd owned forever and a day. She'd definitely looked better.

Dammit. Why in the world was she even caring about her appearance? She glanced back at the Lexus. She didn't want to answer that.

"Come on, Gracie. Do it for me. Ple-e-e-ease."

"Fine, I'll have dinner with the evil one." She quickly ran her index fingers under her eyes, hopefully ridding herself of any errant eyeliner and mascara. She wished she had her makeup bag.

Emerson chuckled. "He's not evil, Gracie. Just give him a chance. He's a really nice guy. Trust me."

She did trust Emerson. But as far as Xander was concerned, she'd have to get some examples of him being a good guy first. Walking her home one time hardly constituted Man of the Year. Especially when he'd tried to kiss her.

It was days later and she still wasn't sure what irked her more—the fact that Jack had tried to kiss her, or her disappointment that he hadn't.

They pushed open the door, crossed the threshold, and were immediately engulfed in a flurry of fluffy exuberance. Jack's dog, Cosmo, was so excited to see them that he couldn't seem to wag his tail fast enough. His entire little twenty-five-pound body was shaking back and forth. How could anyone stay in a bad mood when they were greeted with this?

"Hello, handsome boy," Emerson said in a high-pitched voice which seemed to set Cosmo over the moon. She scratched and rubbed him as he attempted to lick her anywhere he could reach.

Then it was Grace's turn to shower Cosmo with affection. "What a good boy. Who's a fluffy puppy," Grace said in her own version of a doggy-voice.

Cosmo sat and held his paw up.

"Oh my goodness, you can shake. What a good dog. What a smart doggy."

Emerson snorted. "Oh yeah, he's smart all right. He knows he gets a treat if he does that."

Emerson dropped her purse onto the console table by the door and grabbed a treat out of a jar next to it. Then she led Grace through the house, as Cosmo happily marched alongside them. Grace had been to Jack's a handful of times. It used to belong to his father, before he passed away, and it was definitely a bachelor pad done up in dark colors. Although, now that she glanced around, she could see Emerson's hand. Colorful throw blankets and pillows were in the family room and she noticed some of Em's favorite artwork hanging on the walls. There was a lamp in the corner that used to sit next to the chaise in Emerson's office. And in the living room, she spotted a pair of Em's flip-flops peeking out from under the couch and her sweater tossed over a chair.

She could hear the men's voices coming from the kitchen. Sighing internally, she vowed to give Xander a fair shot and actively work to change her impression of him.

"I couldn't be happier to see a marriage end. Their breakup was a long time coming," Xander said as he leaned back against the counter, a beer bottle dangling from his fingers.

Grace gritted her teeth. Then again, maybe first impressions were right for a reason.

They entered the kitchen and Jack's face lit up as he took in his fiancée. Cosmo danced around, clearly thrilled that something new was happening. Then he made a beeline for his water dish.

"There's my bride-to-be," Jack said, oblivious to Grace's boiling temper. He scooped up Emerson into his arms.

"I like the sound of that," Emerson said and kissed him.

"Where's my kiss?" Xander asked.

Jack's arms tightened around Emerson. "Get your own."

Emerson laughed and squirmed out of Jack's arms to hug Xander. Then she gave Grace a pointed look that clearly suggested she should play nice.

Did she not just hear Xander dissing marriage?

She smiled. "Hi, Jack." She sighed. "Xander."

"Grace, great to see you again. And so soon." He was all confidence and ease. He must have come straight from the office because he was still wearing a suit. Although, he'd removed his jacket and she noticed a baby blue tie hanging over one of the chairs in the kitchen. The sleeves of his dress shirt were rolled up, revealing strong, muscular arms. Arms

that looked like they could wrap around her tightly and securely, protecting her from the evils of the world.

Stop it! She needed a drink. "Twice in one week. Am I
lucky or what?"

"Yeah, or what," Xander replied, sarcasm dripping from
his voice.

"Drink?" Jack asked, quickly holding up a bottle of wine.

"Yes," Grace and Xander said at the same time.

Jack laughed and uncorked the wine, then poured a glass
before handing it to Grace, who took a long swallow to steel
her nerves. Xander, too, seemed to accept another beer from
his friend rather eagerly.

"What's on the menu, babe?" Emerson asked.

"I thought I would grill."

Grace exchanged a glance with Emerson and they both
started giggling.

"I think we missed something," Xander said.

"Better to simply nod and smile," Jack said in a stage
whisper.

While Emerson and Jack talked about the food situation,
Grace couldn't keep her eyes off Xander. And wasn't that
just annoying? Why did the man have to be so attractive?
Couldn't he have scales or rampant acne or something? No,
he just had to possess one of the most handsome faces she'd
ever seen. He could pass for a movie star. Instead, he was
an arrogant jerk.

"I'm going to fire up the grill," Jack announced. "Em, I
know you were out there last weekend. Did you move the
grill tools?"

"Yep, I was rearranging."

"Uh-oh, there she goes, Jack. Your independence is dwin-
dling away." Xander poked Emerson in the side and she
poked him right back.

"Shut up. I had to rearrange some stuff so we have room for the lounge chairs."

Jack turned from the refrigerator, burger patties in hand. "See...wait, what? I don't have lounge chairs."

"You will on Thursday." Emerson gave him another kiss. "That patio space is awesome, but you weren't utilizing it."

Jack laughed as he and Emerson headed out the sliding glass door to the patio in question, Cosmo happily following in their wake.

Xander called after them, "It all starts with some lounge chairs."

And then they were alone in the kitchen. Grace decided to look at everything but Xander. She took in the counters that Jack had recently replaced with a light gray granite. She noticed the cabinets that Emerson wanted to paint white. She even looked down at the worn-in pair of Sperrys she was wearing on her feet.

"So," Xander said.

"So," she countered with an eyebrow quirk for good measure.

Then, silence. They both stared at each other, then she rolled her eyes. Finally, he cleared his throat as if to speak. She could tell he was choosing his words carefully. "I happen to really like Emerson."

She crossed her hands over her chest.

"Seriously," he said. "She's awesome. And I was only teasing them."

"Hmm." Grace supposed she could take his word for it.

Xander leaned back against the counter and took a long swig of his beer. Grace's gaze was drawn to his lips. Those smooth lips that had almost been on hers the other night...

"Moving on," he finally said, cutting off *that* train of thought. "How was your day, dear? How's the wedding biz?"

Grace mirrored his stance by leaning up against the opposite counter. "Quite busy, actually."

She talked about a recent bridesmaid brunch she'd put
together on the fly, as well as an upcoming bridal shower
and two different bachelorette parties. Then she regaled him
with the hotel contract woes she'd experienced today, and
threw in a couple of nightmare stories of her dealings with
florists for good measure.

Finally, Grace finished her wedding overload. She had
to bite her lip from laughing at Xander's blank expression.

"Well," he said. "That's a lot for one day in a couple's life.
I mean, I've been to plenty of weddings, but I never really
thought about what went on behind the scenes. You really
take on a lot of responsibility."

"Some couples want to make sure everything is perfect,"
she said with a shrug.

He nodded his head. "I guess. But it still seems like a
waste of money."

She growled under her breath. "It's a special day. Think
about your own wedding."

He let out a mirthless laugh. "Never going to happen."

"What do you mean? You're never getting married?"

"Nope. I don't believe in marriage. At all."

The look on Grace's face was priceless.

He would have laughed. But Xander had a feeling if he
did, Grace wouldn't take too kindly to it. Telling this particular wedding planner that he didn't believe in marriage
was probably akin to telling a cartographer that he didn't
think the earth was round.

Yes, he wanted to get under her skin, but he happened to
be telling the truth. After his experience with his parents, not
to mention what he saw every single day at work, there was

o way he could be all rah-rah about the idea of weddings
nd commitment. Because he didn't believe in them at all.

Frankly, he never should've started this conversation. Jack
adn't mentioned Grace would be coming to dinner until he'd
lready arrived and popped open a beer. Smart man. Once
hey were comfortably catching up on the latest Nationals
win in the kitchen, there was no way he could make an ex-
use to get out of the evening. And it definitely hadn't taken
ong for the usual disagreements between him and Grace to
urface. Xander considered himself a fairly patient man, yet
when this raven-haired beauty came around, any semblance
f patience flew out the window.

Even with the shocked expression on her face, she was
beautiful, especially with her thick, dark hair piled on top
f her head. He'd love to get his hands in it and mess it up
ven more. Watch it fall around her heart-shaped face be-
ore he kissed her...

Her mouth opened and then closed as she seemed to strug-
le for words. "You really don't believe in marriage?"

Jack walked into the kitchen, heard Grace's question,
ooked between the two of them, grabbed another beer and
uickly backed out.

Xander shook his head. "No."

"No marriages?"

"Nope."

"I'm not just asking about you personally. I get that mar-
iage is a personal choice. By all means, feel free to not want
o get married."

"Thanks," he said dryly.

"But you don't believe in marriage at all? Like, between
ny two people?"

"That's what I said."

"But...*why*?"

Xander had the impression that he could have said he

threw kittens over cliffs and she would have reacted les
harshly. If she only knew what he'd grown up with. What h
continued to see transpire between his parents—two peopl
whose marriage was the foundation for some of the wors
fights on the planet.

"It's hardly a shocking thing, Grace. A lot of people don'
believe in marriage."

"Oh, yes, I see that every day in my line of work. That'
why I have a waiting list to plan those big, fancy parties tha
you think cost too much money."

"They do cost way too much. Come on, it's one singl
day."

She shook her head and ignored his comment. "Wha
about children?"

He shrugged. "I don't know if kids are for me. But I don'
have anything against children. Besides, you don't need
piece of paper to have children."

"What about commitment?" she persisted. "Showing th
person you love that they can trust you?"

"Again, you don't need that little piece of paper to sho
you're committed. If you even choose to be 'committed.'
He used air quotes when he said the word *committed*.

Her eyes narrowed and she pointed a finger at him. "Wha
does that mean?"

"You can say some words in front of your friends in
church or a hotel ballroom or under a chuppah or wherever
Doesn't mean squat. That's what *I see* every day in *my* job.'

"Not everyone gets divorced."

"Half of married couples split up."

"Half of married couples stay together," she countered
stepping close to him. They were nose-to-nose. "Do you hav
any idea how much love I see on a daily basis?"

He had to stifle a groan. She was beyond delusional

Love? You see wedding dresses and china patterns and dollar signs."

Her mouth dropped open and an indignant huff escaped. "You know nothing about my job. I happen to see couples who want to celebrate their love with the people in their lives." She returned to the other side of the kitchen, picked up her wineglass and took a long drink.

"Oh, please," he snorted. "Just this morning, I met with a couple who had one of the biggest, grandest, most extravagant weddings of all time. You know when they got married? Three years ago."

Grace narrowed her eyes. "Is that the marriage I overheard you talking about? The one you were so thrilled had ended?"

Xander felt his face fall. He would have cast his gaze to the floor, only there was no way he was letting Grace win this round. She was glaring darts at him, but she had no idea what she was talking about. There was a very important reason why he was happy to assist with this particular divorce.

"No," he said slowly. "What I saw today was the end of one of the worst unions I've ever witnessed."

He'd known Jess since college. She'd dated his roommate. She had always been a fun, outgoing and kind person. The relationship with his roommate hadn't worked out, but Jess had stayed in touch, even after she got married to someone else. She'd always been a bright light in his world.

Unfortunately, Xander had no idea that while she was smiling on the outside, her world had been falling apart.

Xander ran a hand through his hair. "Today, I finalized a divorce for an old friend. Her scumbag of a husband had been abusing her, both physically and verbally."

Grace gasped.

"She'd felt trapped, alone," Xander said.

"That's awful." She bit her lip. "I'm sorry. I guess... I ca
see why you were so happy it ended."

Progress, he thought. "I'm not a monster, Grace. I don
believe in marriage, but that doesn't mean I get some kin
of perverse joy out of seeing people's happiness crushe
when a union ends."

She put her wineglass on the counter. He thought she wa
going to walk to him, but in the end, she stayed where sh
was. She did meet his eyes though.

"I'm glad to hear that. I guess it's the optimistic part (
me that wishes everyone could be happy all the time."

Xander actually loved that aspect of her. Sometimes, h
wished he could be more positive in life. Only, he'd seen to
much, witnessed too many unhappy endings.

"Unfortunately, life isn't a fairy tale, Grace. The worl
has evolved."

"You might not believe it, but I do understand that." Sh
offered a small, sheepish smile. "I guess I just hate the ide
that someone might never plan to find your soul mate an
fall in love. That you'll never know what it feels like."

She raised her arm in emphasis, and Xander's eyes wer
drawn there. He searched, but didn't see any of the bruis
from the other night.

"Now that we've talked about my unwillingness to set
tle down, I wanted to find out how you're feeling after th
other night."

Confusion crossed her face. "The other night? You mean
when we ran into each other?"

"Yeah."

"When you almost kissed—"

"When Derek was a total jerk to you." Xander pointed hi
beer bottle at her arm. "I see the bruise has faded."

"Ah." Her cheeks reddened. "*That* part of the other night.

"Well, yeah. I don't know him well, but what I have heard of Derek hasn't been all that complimentary."

What he didn't tell her was that their almost kiss had shaken him up more than he wanted to admit. Even now, he had to actively work to keep the desire to press his lips to hers from surfacing again.

"Has he contacted you since the party?" Xander asked, pushing the unbidden need to the back of his mind.

She shook her head. "Nah. I don't expect him to."

"Let me know if you do hear from him."

Her eyes widened. "Why?"

"Because I don't want him bothering you."

"Are you trying to protect me, Xander Ryan?"

Was he? Xander wasn't sure. All he knew was that seeing Derek grab Grace had set something off inside him.

"I think you proved the other night that you are perfectly capable of protecting yourself."

She grinned. "Thank you for saying that."

"You're welcome."

Silence engulfed the kitchen for a few moments. Something had just shifted between them. Xander could feel it as clearly as he felt the cold bottle of beer in his hand.

"Are we getting along right now?" Grace asked.

"We might be."

"Shocking," she said, her eyes sparkling.

"It is shocking," he agreed. "Who would have thought that we could stand in Jack's kitchen together and have a civil conversation."

Grace raised her glass. "How about a toast to getting along for five whole minutes."

"I'll drink to that."

He closed the gap between them, his gaze shooting down to Grace's enticing lips. He could see her chest rising and falling as he tapped his beer bottle to her wineglass.

Xander wasn't sure how they came to this point. Maybe—just maybe—they'd learned something about each other tonight. All he did know—and he knew for damn sure—was that just like the night he'd walked her home, he wanted to kiss her more than he wanted air to breathe.

The door opened and the aroma of charred beef and cheddar cheese wafted over to them. Cosmo let out a little *yip* right before Emerson poked her head in. They sprang apart, guiltily. "Hm, I don't see any blood or guts," she said. "Is it possible you two are getting along?"

"We even toasted each other," Grace said.

"The temperature did drop pretty drastically outside," Emerson said.

"Really?" Grace asked.

Emerson rolled her eyes. "Oh yeah, when hell froze over."

"Clever," Xander said.

"Thank you. In any case, the food is ready. Want to come out here and eat? Cosmo is dying for one of us to drop something."

"I got your back, Cosmo," Xander said.

Slowly, Xander made his way onto the patio. Grace was facing the other way and Emerson was whispering something to her.

"Are we one big, happy family yet?" Jack asked wryly. He swiveled and cocked his head at his fiancée and Grace. Then raised an eyebrow in question at Xander.

Xander shrugged. He may not have the answers to life's biggest questions, but there was one thing he knew for sure. Things had just gotten interesting between him and Grace.

Chapter Five

Grace hated fidgeting when she was with a client. And to-day's client was no ordinary bride. It was Emerson.

She wanted everything to be perfect for her best friend. Even if she had to work twenty-four hours a day from now until the wedding, she would make sure that every table looked perfect, each flower petal was pristine and all *i*'s were dotted on the invitations even if she had to write them out in her own hand.

If only she could concentrate.

She'd been having issues all week. Unfortunately, she knew the cause. *Xander Ryan.* She blew out a long, frus-trated whoosh of air.

"You okay over there?"

She offered Emerson a smile. "Sorry. Yes, I'm fine. Where were we?"

"We were right in the middle of squashing my most re-cent wedding-induced panic attack."

"Right." Notebook poised on her lap, Grace nodded at her best friend. "Okay, let's review the choices that you've made already. I'm telling you, you're ahead of the game."

"Venue, check." A big smile blossomed on Emerson's face. "I still can't believe we got that space. It's my dream wedding site."

"A spring wedding in a vineyard," Grace said dreamily. "It's going to be amazing."

Emerson scrunched up her nose. "You don't think the

timing is weird? I know most people do the whole autumn-in-a-vineyard thing."

Grace squeezed her hand. "The timing didn't work ou unless you wanted to wait another couple of months."

"No way," Emerson said. "I'm way too excited to become Mrs. Wright."

Both women laughed, as they did every time Emerson' new surname came up. After all, who couldn't help grin-ning at the thought of marrying the real Mr. Wright? "That' what I thought. Spring wedding it is. The cherry blossoms and dogwoods will be in bloom. It's going to look beautiful."

Grace continued down her checklist. "You've picked you dress. Which the groom has already seen," she added as she narrowed her eyes at Emerson.

"I'm sure he doesn't remember that. And, anyway, it' not like he's seen me all done up and ready to walk down the aisle."

"Fine, fine. I'll let it go for now. But you have to promise not to break any other cardinal prewedding rules."

"Hate to break it to you, Gracie, but Jack and I have al-ready done it."

Grace stuck out her tongue. "How about you commit to not spending the night before the wedding together?"

"I'll consider it."

"Let's see. The save-the-date cards are ready to be mailed." Grace scrolled down the page in her notebook "You've already picked out the invitations. We've narrowed i down to two caterers. Jack is taking care of the honeymoon."

"We have to pick out your maid-of-honor dress," Emer-son said excitedly. "My mom got in this really cute line o bridesmaids' dresses last week at her shop. We should ge over there and take a look."

As Emerson began leafing through a bridal magazine and dog-earing pages with different dresses she liked, Grace' mind began to wander again. To her dismay, it found its way right back to Xander.

She was still processing the two times she'd seen him recently. How she'd been so upset at *not* being kissed by him after that awful party!

Then there was the other night at Jack's house. They'd started off at odds, but in the end, something changed.

Hearing about his client had affected her. Not to mention his concern over her after the party. Not even the hosts had called or emailed to make sure she was okay.

Xander was right. He wasn't a monster. Far from it. He was actually turning out to be…kind of a nice guy.

She felt so confused. Did she like Xander or not? Did she want to kiss him or not?

"I almost kissed Xander," Grace blurted out.

Emerson stared at her for a long moment before blinking once, twice. Then she coughed delicately and closed the bridal magazine. "I was going to bring up the idea of tea-length bridesmaid dresses but let's talk about your news instead."

Grace dropped her head into her hands and groaned.

"I assume we're talking about the one and only Xander Ryan, your nemesis here?"

Grace acknowledged this with a long groan. Was he still her nemesis? "I don't even want to talk about it."

"Uh-uh, you have to spill now. You can't drop a bombshell on me like that and just clam up. Let's start with where this almost kiss happened. Was it the other night at Jack's?"

Grace sat up straight. "Actually, I saw him at that horrible party I went to with Derek earlier this week."

Emerson held up a hand. "Excuse me, that was several days ago. Why didn't you tell me this earlier?"

"I was in shock, I think. I don't know what happened."

"Take a deep breath. Then start with how you got to the

point where you almost kissed him and end with why you didn't."

So Grace did. She spilled every detail she could remember. When she finished, Emerson just sat there.

"Em, say something."

Emerson ran a hand through her curly hair. "It's a lot to take in. I'm processing." She sighed. "I really wish I could have seen you take that creep down."

"It was pretty amazing. But, back to the issue at hand. What about Xander?" Grace asked impatiently, fidgeting in her chair.

"What about him?"

Was Emerson serious right now?

"He walked you home, which I give him high points for. You guys finally started getting along and then you tripped, he caught you and there was an epic romance moment."

"An almost moment because nothing actually happened."

Emerson studied her for a long time. Grace actually began squirming in her chair.

"You sound disappointed that nothing happened."

Grace's mouth dropped open and Emerson laughed. "Stop laughing at me. You're my best friend and you're supposed to be supportive."

"I am. I just don't get what the problem is. Xander is a great guy. I know a ton of women who would kill to go out with him. He's stable. He has a great job."

Grace grumbled at that.

"He's successful. He's really funny when you get to know him. He has great taste in best friends." Emerson got the gooey face she usually did when talking about her fiancé. "And, he's hot."

"He really is," she said without thinking.

Emerson's eyebrows went up.

"Well, I'm not blind," Grace said defensively. "He's incredibly attractive."

"I'm glad to hear that." Emerson avoided eye contact. "Because Jack is going to ask him to be his best man."

Grace shrugged. "I figured as much."

"So you're okay walking down the aisle with him?"

"What am I? Five? Of course I'm okay."

Emerson took a big breath. "Then you also won't mind planning a couples' shower with him?" She popped up out of her chair. "Want some coffee?"

Grace's head started spinning. "Wait, what did you say?"

Emerson paused and slowly turned back around. "Jack and I decided that instead of having a separate bridal shower and bachelor party that we'd like to have a couples' shower with all of our friends and family in one place."

"O-ka-a-a-y," Grace said slowly. "That's a good idea. Very modern. I like it."

"And…we'd kind of like for the two of you to plan it together." Emerson bit her lip and scrunched her nose.

The gesture would have been endearing if Grace hadn't gotten the sudden urge to throw up. "Both professional-wedding-planner Grace and best-friend Grace are offended."

"Gracie, don't be like that."

"Come on, Em. I can handle planning a shower all on my own, thank you very much. I don't need Xander in the mix, getting in my way and messing up my flow."

"Listen, this was Jack's idea. He's not having a bachelor party and he thought it would be nice for Xander to have something to do besides just standing next to him on the big day. Plus, Xander knows all of Jack's friends."

Grace narrowed her eyes and crossed her arms over her chest. "I'm going to ask you this question for a second time. Are you and Jack trying to play matchmaker? Be honest, Emerson Rose."

"No, we are not. Trust me," she said with emphatic eyes. "Although, you did almost kiss the other night."

Grace stuck her nose in the air. "I regret telling you that now."

"No, you don't." Emerson crossed back to her, grabbed her hand and pulled her to her feet. "I know this isn't ideal for you, but please try. For me? I promise he'll be at his best." She put on her most winning smile.

Grace blew out a puff of air. "Fine. I'll plan a shower with Xander."

Emerson was right—this was not going to be her favorite part of planning the wedding. In fact, spending more time with Xander was sure to have her reconsidering her entire profession.

"You want me to do *what*?"

Jack had to be kidding him. What did he know about throwing a wedding shower?

Xander stared at his best friend and attempted to display his most pained face. Jack appeared unmoved.

"Seriously, Jack."

Jack was working behind the bar at The Wright Drink, the bar he'd inherited from his father. Even though the bar was located in the heart of Old Town, the place had fallen on hard times during Jack's father's illness and become a less-than-desirable hangout spot. But once Emerson came along, she'd helped Jack turn the business around. Now, it was bustling every night of the week. Jack hosted trivia nights, ladies' nights out, sporting events and even a board-game challenge. Plus, Emerson booked plenty of special events, like parties and receptions.

Xander enjoyed coming here. There was a large square-shaped bar in the middle of the room, plenty of high and low tables, a stage and dance floor for karaoke and great framed photos of Alexandria along the walls.

"I am being serious," Jack said. He poured a beer from the tap and slid it over to Xander's waiting hand.

"Why can't you just have a bachelor party like every other man on the planet?"

Jack flipped a rag over his shoulder. "Because I don't want a bachelor party. Besides, once Em explained what a joint shower could be like, I thought it sounded fun. Plus, her mom was pushing for an engagement party and Emerson didn't want one. Too fussy for her, and frankly, for me, too. So this was a decent compromise."

Xander took a good, long swallow of his favorite beer. Too bad it did nothing to calm his nerves. "I don't even know where to start in planning something like this. Do I have to find a venue?"

Jack shook his head. "We want to have it here."

"Okay, but what about everything else? Do I have to do invitations or is this an e-vite situation? And who do I invite? How do I know what kind of decorations to use? Do you need decorations for this thing?"

Jack held his hands out in front of him. "Whoa, slow down."

"Order up."

Jack turned to grab the plate of chicken fingers and sweet-potato fries the waiter had placed on the bar. "Your food's ready." He snatched a rolled napkin with silverware and made his way out from behind the bar. "Oscar, you got this?" His bartender nodded.

Jack gestured for Xander to follow him to one of the tables. Xander took his beer and sat across from his friend. He dove into the chicken fingers.

As he ate, he began to reiterate why he was not going to be a good party planner. "I'm happy to be your best man

but hanging up streamers and blowing up balloons isn't ▮
thing."

Jack snorted. "Streamers? Balloons? This isn't a party
a bunch of five-year-olds. Anyway, I thought you might h▮
this type of reaction," Jack said, snagging a fry. "That's w
Emerson and I are bringing in some help for you."

Okay, this was something he could get behind. He
Someone who planned parties. Someone who especia
knew how to plan wedding-type parties. He froze, his h▮
pausing in midair with a sweet-potato fry in his fingers.

Oh, crap.

"Wait a minute…" he began.

"You just said you didn't know what you were doing

"Don't tell me," Xander said, a pleading note enter▮
his voice.

"She's the maid of honor."

"Stop." Xander threw down his fry. "Not her."

"Grace is a professional wedding planner."

She was also the star of his recent dreams. Ever since ▮
walked her home after the party, he hadn't been able to ▮
her out of his mind.

She'd looked amazing in that killer red dress with ▮
sexy-as-hell heels. Her long hair was begging for him to ▮
his fingers through. And those legs… All he could imag▮
was them wrapped around him.

Then there was the fact that she'd been able to hold ▮
▮n with Derek. Grace Harris was anything but vulnera▮
And damn if that didn't turn him on. Which was exactly
he shouldn't plan this party with her.

Xander noticed the door open and Emerson waltz▮
with Cosmo at her side. She beamed at Jack and then le▮
down and undid Cosmo's leash. The perpetually happy ▮
bounced right over to them while Emerson stopped to ▮
hi to some people at a table near the entrance. Cosmo s▮

on his hind legs, leaning on Xander's thigh. His little brown nose was twitching as he took in the scent of food.

"You're lucky you're so cute." He broke off a small piece of his fry and gave it to the dog. Cosmo devoured the fry in one gulp and then again turned expectant eyes on Xander.

"Dude, I just gave you something. Jack, you need to teach this mutt to—"

He broke off when he noticed his friend wasn't paying the slightest bit of attention to him or his dog. Instead, he was staring at Emerson. Xander wouldn't have been surprised if hearts had poured out of his eyes.

Jack had found a life partner. Someone who would stay by his side forever. Xander couldn't help but think about his parents, married for over thirty years and no sign of true emotional connection between them. No evidence—other than him, anyway—that they'd ever really cared about each other. Togetherness wasn't always a good thing.

There was always the option of divorce. He wasn't sure why his parents had never pursued it, but if something went off the rails between Jack and Em, there was an escape clause. What would the happily-ever-after-believing Grace say if she knew he was considering her best friend and divorce at the same time.

"I can't work with her," he said abruptly to Jack, who snapped to attention after making moony eyes at Emerson.

"Why not?"

"Because—because..." he stammered like a petulant child. Jack raised an eyebrow. "Because I don't like her."

"Name one thing you don't like about her." There was a challenging gleam in Jack's eye.

"Just one?"

"Come on."

"Get out," Xander said and took a big bite of his chicken finger to buy himself time.

"I'm serious. Name one thing about Grace that rubs you the wrong way."

The room suddenly felt hot. Xander refrained from loosening his tie.

Jack pointed at him. "You can't do it."

"Give me a minute."

"I'll give you twenty. But I don't think that will help."

Realizing Jack wasn't going to let this go, Xander struggled to come up with a reason why Grace drove him nuts. Besides the fact that she just did.

"She's so…"

"Yes?"

"She's too perfect. What's with the optimism? How can someone be that happy all the time? It's not natural."

"Too perfect? Are you kidding me? You're really stretching now."

Cosmo batted his paw against Xander's leg. "Don't you feed this dog?"

Jack beamed. "He enjoys chicken tenders."

"And fries, and all other food in the world apparently." He slipped another piece of fry to Cosmo who gobbled it right up.

"Back to Grace."

Xander shook his head.

Jack offered a smirk. "You force my hand."

Xander narrowed his eyes. "Meaning?"

"Time to call in the big guns." Jack turned toward the bar, where Emerson was now getting a drink from Oscar. "Hey, babe, can you come over here for a sec?"

Xander leveled a hard stare at his friend. "That's low, man. You know I can't resist her."

He thought about spending hours with Grace planning this party. In any other situation, he would go for it. If he was attracted to a woman, he'd simply ask her out. With Grace, it was different. Xander knew what he wanted out of life. Or, more accurately, what he didn't want. His life path would never mesh with Grace.

Emerson made her way to their table. She set down her glass of Scotch and kissed Jack. Then she took a seat between the two of them. "What's going on?"

"Xander doesn't want to plan our couples' shower."

Emerson made her pretty eyes go wide and batted her lashes. "You don't want to help us out? You, the best man. In our special time?"

"No, see, that's not what this is about. Stop looking at me like that," he said to her. "Seriously, you're killing me."

Jack laughed. "Seems like Xander here is afraid to work with Grace."

Emerson nodded knowingly. "She is pretty scary."

"I don't know what's more frightening, all that pink she wears or those tiny purses she carries around. I wouldn't want to plan a party with her, either."

Xander stifled a laugh. "Stop making fun of me. I'm serious. I can't do it with her."

Jack and Emerson paused, mischief dancing in both their eyes.

"They have pills for that," Jack said.

Xander threw a fry at him. "Shut up."

"How about you do it for me?" Emerson said, suddenly turning serious. "Listen, I'm worried about Grace. I've thrown this wedding at her last-minute and given her practically zero time to plan it. If I was anyone else, she would have turned me down. She has so many other brides to handle. And my sister, well, she can't help out at the moment."

He groaned. "Come on, Emerson…" But he realized she meant it—for once, it did sound as though Grace was overwhelmed. Especially after she explained how much goes into one wedding the other night. Not only does she put together all the details for a wedding, but she also does showers and bachelorette parties and brunches and more. And really, how hard could it be to plan a couples' shower? "Fine, fine. You win. I'll help plan the party."

"Only if you want to," Emerson said, making Jack chuckle.

"You play dirty," Xander said to his friends, then downed the rest of his drink. He was going to need the fortification if he was about to work side by side with Grace.

Then again, he thought...what could happen?

Chapter Six

"Is this a good time?"

A few days later, Grace paused outside Jack's bar with her hand poised on the door handle. Sophie Miller, one of her younger brides, had just called out of the blue. Never a good sign. Neither was the anxiety Grace detected in Sophie's voice.

"It's always a good time to talk to you," Grace said, trying to add as much enthusiasm as she could to her voice.

"I'm so sorry to call without warning or anything."

Grace wasn't sorry. In fact, she was downright giddy about it. She wasn't a procrastinator by nature, but she definitely appreciated the delay today.

She stepped to the side of the door to allow two women to enter the bar. Glancing in the window, she couldn't miss Xander sitting at the corner of the bar.

It had been more than a week since she'd seen him. Although, she'd been thinking about him plenty. Not long after she learned of Emerson and Jack's desire for a couples' shower, Xander had texted her. He'd asked her to meet him at the bar to start talking about the shower. She'd suggested meeting at her office—her turf—but Xander insisted they'd be more comfortable at Jack's bar. To Grace's mind, it was completely unprofessional. Still, she made exceptions for her clients all the time.

But Xander wasn't a client.

He was a man that she was growing more and more attracted to.

Well, he could wait a little longer. She had a bride to talk to.

"You never have to apologize, Sophie. That's what I'm here for. Now, what's going on?"

"I think I'm making a mistake." This statement was followed by the distinct sound of sobs.

Grace took a deep breath. She'd dealt with plenty of cold feet. There was usually something bigger going on. Even though Sophie was only twenty-four, she'd been nothing but cool and collected in their dealings so far.

"Oh, Sophie, what would make you say something like that? You and Adam are perfect for each other. I knew it from the first time I saw you together."

Grace meant every word. She'd worked with plenty of brides and she'd never seen a groom look at his fiancée the way Adam did. A wave of jealousy washed over her. She could only wish and hope that someday she would find a man who would gaze at her in the same way. Like she was the only woman on the planet.

Grace pivoted toward the window. Xander was watching her from the bar, wearing an expression that she couldn't decipher. But his gaze was intense, and if she wasn't mistaken, she saw a tic in his jaw. She didn't want to acknowledge the way her pulse had picked up. Instead, she gestured to her cell phone and held up a finger so he would know she needed a minute. Then she promptly turned her back and returned to her conversation with Sophie.

Ten minutes later, she had a happy bride again. As she suspected, Sophie wasn't nervous about marrying Adam. Rather, she was anxious about moving to New York City right after the wedding and starting a brand-new life in a new city without any friends or contacts. Grace threw out a couple ideas to help her with the adjustment and by the end of the conversation, Sophie was laughing again and talking excitedly about her upcoming wedding-dress shopping.

Grace made her way toward the bar and joined Xander, making sure to leave a seat between them. She made a big show of pulling out of her large tote the various catalogs, magazines and other material she thought would be helpful in planning a shower.

"Thanks for finally joining me," Xander said in lieu of a hello.

"Sorry for keeping you waiting, but I got a business call on my way into the bar."

Xander's eyebrows went up. "Did I just get an apology?"

Grace offered him her most winning smile. "Even princesses make mistakes."

Jack sidled up to them then. "Hey, Grace, how are you?"

"Great," she said. "Look at this place. You're pretty packed for a random Wednesday."

Jack grinned. "I'd love to take credit, but it was all Emerson. Just wait until Saturday, when we have our Oktoberfest extravaganza. Are you going to stop by?"

"Of course. I wouldn't miss it."

"Great. What can I get you to drink?"

"A glass of that house red I like, please."

Jack reached for a wineglass. He jutted his chin in Xander's direction. "Need a refill?"

"Nah, I'm good. I just want to get to planning this super-fun party."

Grace didn't get it. The last time they'd been together they'd gotten along. Maybe not at first, but eventually. She didn't really want to plan the shower with him, but she was hopeful they would at least get along. Instead, she heard the sarcasm in his voice. Heck, the people playing darts in the corner could probably hear it. Grace decided to take advantage.

"If you'd rather not plan the shower, I'm perfectly willing to do it all by myself." She crossed her fingers under the bar, hoping he'd take the bait.

Xander eyed her suspiciously, but after a blatant don't-even-think-about-it look from Jack, he backed down.

"After all, this is my job. And I'm getting paid to do this," she added.

A wrinkle formed on Xander's forehead. "Hey, that's right. I'm not getting paid."

Jack poured Grace's wine and then punched Xander in the arm. "Have you ever paid for a drink here? Not to mention all the food I give you."

Xander raised his glass in toast to his friend. "Touché."

"That's what I thought. I'll just leave you to it, then."

Jack moved down the bar, taking orders and starting tabs. Grace took a fortifying sip of wine and then faced Xander.

"So," Xander said. "Where do we start?"

She flipped open her notebook. "I've already talked to Emerson. She gave me a bunch of dates that will work."

She showed Xander the list and the two of them consulted with their own planners and schedules. Ten minutes later they had a date. Progress.

"We know they want to have the party here," she said. Grace had been in this bar plenty of times, but she still took a moment to look around the space and visualize possible ideas.

"Awesome," Xander said. "So we can use the food they already serve here. Chicken fingers, burgers, poppers..." Xander trailed off as she sighed loudly. "What's wrong with french fries and wings?"

"Nothing, when you're watching the game," she said.

"I don't get it," he said, frowning. "They want to have the